Transoceanic Blackface

performance works

SERIES EDITORS
Patrick Anderson and
Nicholas Ridout

This series publishes books in theater and performance studies, focused in particular on the material conditions in which performance acts are staged, and to which performance itself might contribute. We define "performance" in the broadest sense, including traditional theatrical productions and performance art, but also cultural ritual, political demonstration, social practice, and other forms of interpersonal, social, and political interaction that may fruitfully be understood in terms of performance.

Transocean Blackface

Empire, Race, Performance

✦

Kellen Hoxworth

NORTHWESTERN UNIVERSITY PRESS
EVANSTON, ILLINOIS

Northwestern University Press
www.nupress.northwestern.edu

Printed in the United States of America

10 9 8 7 6 5 4 3 2 1

Library of Congress Cataloging-in-Publication Data

Names: Hoxworth, Kellen, author.
Title: Transoceanic blackface : empire, race, performance / Kellen Hoxworth.
Other titles: Performance works.
Description: Evanston : Northwestern University Press, 2024. | Series: Performance works | Includes index.
Identifiers: LCCN 2023054222 | ISBN 9780810147072 (paperback) | ISBN 9780810147089 (cloth) | ISBN 9780810147096 (ebook)
Subjects: LCSH: Blackface minstrel shows—English-speaking countries—History. | Blackface entertainers—English-speaking countries—History. | Race in the theater—History.
Classification: LCC PN1969.B43 H69 2024 | DDC 791.12—dc23/eng/20231127
LC record available at https://lccn.loc.gov/2023054222

CONTENTS

ILLUSTRATIONS

A NOTE ON TERMINOLOGY

Throughout this book, I capitalize *Black* to refer to people of African descent both on the continent and across the diaspora. The capitalization of *Black* traces the shared structures and practices that subjected disparate peoples to the imperial discourses of "blackness" as well as the intentional embrace of this term as a shared mode of identification across transnational sites. Its use occasionally modifies "American" or "African"—as in *Black American* or *Black African*—to denote specific geographies and social formations. When quoting from others who do not capitalize the term, I have left it as found in the original.

Terminology referring to other racial or ethnic categories is also capitalized throughout: *Asian*, *Indigenous*, and so on. *Asian* refers to people from across the Asian continent, including "East Asian" and "South Asian" people. Where appropriate, I also capitalize *Cape Colored* in accordance with common practice in South Africa to refer to the non-white and non-Black people who have occupied the middle position in the nation's tripartite racial classification system since the colonial era. However, I do not capitalize *brown* as it refers to a capacious and indefinite set of discourses that—until recently—did not constitute a shared mode of identification and that still does not conform to a singular coherent identity across its usage. I also do not capitalize *white* as the use of the capital W has been widely adopted by white supremacists and their organizations. Suffice it to say that this book intends a thorough historicization and critique of white supremacy across its transnational formations.

Paradoxically, because this book assembles an expansive archive and critique of the many-headed hydra of white supremacy, it reproduces racist language as it is found in archival materials. In particular, the derogatory term commonly known in the United States as the "N-word" recurs throughout the archives that constitute the basis for this project and therefore in material quoted herein. I have chosen to reprint the term exactly as it appears for two reasons. First, it was an occasional practice of the historical period in question to redact parts of the term (e.g., *n----r*), and similar redactions sometimes appear in relation to other derogatory language (e.g., *H-tt-nt-ts*). As much of this language is local and potentially unfamiliar beyond its specific discursive communities, such redactions risk confusion. Moreover, it is impossible to conduct similar redactions without misleading readers as to the widespread, explicitly derogatory usage of such language and thereby to whitewash the discursive violence of blackface or minstrelsy rather than to account for it.

Second, I view this project as a work of remembering transnational histories that have been willfully forgotten, omitted, and obscured. Though readers may be unsurprised to find racist terminology in archival documents pertaining to minstrelsy and the derogation of Black Americans, it is remarkable the extent to which the "N-word" was deployed transnationally as a means of denigrating disparate colonized subjects and subalterns. Though it is a term that repeats incessantly—and that reproduces discursive violence in each repetition—the violence performed by this term is not the same in each usage as it has been mobilized against numerous peoples across multiple contexts. This term traces an assemblage of unfamiliar, secreted histories of transnational, imperial racialization that endure in the present. Can such entangled racial histories—specifically, those not widely known or narrated—be remembered without reproducing discursive violence? The critical problem here relates to our inability (and our consequent failure) to escape from that which we have not yet understood as our history. We cannot pursue lines of flight from grammars of violence unless we recognize the endurance of past structures as formative of our present. This book intends to trace these histories, their afterlives, and their ongoing violence in the hope that such knowledge might afford us new conditions of possibility.

Nevertheless, I insist that there is no need to give voice to this language, and I would encourage anyone reading or assigning material from this book to students to adopt a class policy that discourages any further enunciation of derogatory language that appears in these pages. Koritha Mitchell has devised a "Class Covenant" that is helpful in structuring ground rules for class discussions on this material; I recommend anyone teaching from this book to consult this resource.[1]

Transoceanic Blackface

Introduction

✦

Furnishing the Empire

In July 1881, the Parsee Victoria Theatrical Company performed "a new comic pantomime" in Singapore during a tour of Southeast Asia.[1] The touring troupe consisted of Parsi performers who specialized in a syncretic form of theater that originated among Parsi communities in Mumbai (Bombay), India. Competing with rival touring Parsi theater troupes, the Parsee Victoria Theatrical Company drew on their extensive repertoire to attract audiences.[2] They therefore chose to entertain their Singaporean audience with several short selections from popular plays, concluding with a lighthearted afterpiece titled *The Quack Doctor*. A newspaper review of the evening's entertainments celebrated the comic finale, making special mention of the performers' "Chinese costume" and their "capital imitation of a Chinese burlesque."[3] Likely inspired by the significant Chinese population in Singapore, the Parsee Victoria Theatrical Company's production presented its audiences with a racial spectacle: South Asian performers in Chinese costume and caricature. The Parsee Victoria Theatrical Company's staging of *The Quack Doctor* thus exemplified their theatrical savvy in localizing popular material to suit their audiences' particular tastes and desires.

Yet, *The Quack Doctor* was a curious choice. The script of *The Quack Doctor* does not include any Chinese characters or references to China whatsoever; rather, it was originally written as a blackface burlesque. First produced in 1851 and later published in a collection of blackface minstrel "Darkey Plays," *The Quack Doctor* staged a travesty of Black actor Ira Aldridge and *The Black Doctor*, an 1847 melodramatic interracial romance that he performed regularly throughout Britain.[4] *The Quack Doctor* followed the standard template of blackface burlesque. It transposed sober, serious, "high" cultural material from the legitimate stage and brought it into the "low" frame of blackface minstrelsy. Such burlesques implicitly scripted the blackening of cultural material as a mode of comic abasement and abjection. They also explicitly derogated prominent representatives and representations of blackness by figuring them as objects of ridicule. Written within this dramaturgical frame, *The Quack*

Doctor derided Aldridge's prominence on the British and European stage and mocked his political advocacy for Black equality and the abolition of slavery. Thus, *The Quack Doctor* burlesqued Aldridge and his theatrical and political enterprises through the abject inversion of one of his famous heroic roles. Why, then, would the Parsee Victoria Theatrical Company have elected to stage this particular comic afterpiece from the blackface minstrel repertoire?

Though it is uncertain whether any member of the Parsee Victoria Theatrical Company was aware of the origin of *The Quack Doctor* as a racist lampoon of Aldridge, Parsi theater makers were well acquainted with the performance repertoires of blackface minstrelsy. Parsi troupes frequently drew from Anglophone theatrical repertoires by staging Shakespeare, melodrama, and farce in English and in South Asian–language translations. Blackface minstrelsy was a centerpiece in the Anglophone imperial theatrical repertoire, and prominent Parsi troupes regularly incorporated minstrel songs and sketches into their theatrical and musical productions.[5] Parsi theater makers even fashioned their own bespoke minstrel material, as when Parsi theater impresario Kuvarjī Nājar wrote a new minstrel song titled "Ratae Madame Is My Name" as a burlesque parody of "The Parsi Girl of the Period."[6] As Parsi theater makers were keen to localize the widely circulating scripts of blackface minstrelsy, it is likely that the choice to stage *The Quack Doctor* in Singapore as a yellowface spectacle was no mere coincidence.[7] That the British colonial newspaper the *Straits Times Overland Journal* singled out the sketch for favorable mention evinces this mock "Chinese" enactment's success in entertaining the white British subjects in the audience. It is therefore likely that the Parsee Victoria Theatrical Company chose to stage *The Quack Doctor* as a "capital imitation of a *Chinese* burlesque" specifically to appeal to their white imperial audience, particularly considering that the sketch targeted for comic ridicule the Singaporean Chinese who constituted a majority (roughly 60 percent) of Singapore's total population.[8] By adapting a blackface sketch into a yellowface act, the Parsee Victoria Theatrical Company touched on and assuaged their white audience's imperial anxieties about feeling outnumbered and threatened by the non-white subjects and subalterns in their midst. Their racial masquerade also aligned the Parsi troupe with whiteness by tacitly enfolding Parsis into racial discourses of Aryanism.[9] Thus, the Parsi theatrical enactment of a "new comic pantomime in Chinese costume" demonstrates how the repertoires of blackface minstrelsy afforded flexible dramaturgies for managing the racial anxieties of empire: they provided scripts and scenarios for an extensive array of racialized performances that animated racial discourses across vast distances and disparate contexts.[10]

Transoceanic Blackface maps the wide and prolific circulations of racialized performance throughout the Anglophone empire and the ways in which blackface (and) minstrelsy enfolded incommensurate imperial subjects and subalterns into colonial racial discourses.[11] For more than a century, the Anglophone empire—encompassing the British Empire, the United States, and their respective imperial projects—was awash in blackface, minstrelsy, and related forms of racialized performance. This book traces multiple entangled imperial histories of racialized performance from the mid-eighteenth century through the early twentieth century, thereby demonstrating that blackface (and) minstrelsy were never bound to any single nation or its particular racial formations. Rather, blackface, minstrelsy, and related forms of racialized performance (e.g., yellowface, brownface, etc.) mediated racial thinking and feeling throughout the Anglophone empire. The constant transoceanic circulation of racialized performance practices and cultural materials linked performance cultures throughout the United States, Britain, and the British colonies in southern Africa, South Asia, Australia, Aotearoa New Zealand, and the Caribbean.[12] Across these disparate sites, performers and audiences engaged the Anglophone imperial performance repertoire in a material practice of making and remaking race. Anglophone theater makers produced shows that animated popular ideas and feelings, thereby forging new social relations around transoceanic blackface and its imperial performance economies of racial "common sense."[13] Transoceanic blackface lent materiality to everyday racial affects through embodied performances of popular racial scenarios. The circulations of racialized performance throughout the long eighteenth and nineteenth centuries played a formative role in shaping imperial "structures of feeling" and the racial orders of the Anglophone world.[14]

This introduction offers a brief overview of blackface minstrelsy and scholarship on the form before outlining three primary coordinates of this book: the transoceanic Anglophone empire that made the world "global"; race as an affective complex of "common sense" that functioned as a centerpiece in the "furniture of empire"; and performance as a mode of "furnishing forth" the imperial common sense of racial thinking and feeling. To this end, I recuperate what Ann Laura Stoler terms "decoupled, severed histories" of racialized performance, particularly those heretofore imagined to be distinctively national or regional performance forms.[15] By tracing the interrelations among ostensibly disparate histories of racialized performance, I map a global assemblage of performances now known as blackface (or) minstrelsy that I term *transoceanic blackface*. Therefore, this term necessarily refers to an expansive body of racialized performance that exceeds "blackface minstrelsy." I use it both to trace what Tavia Nyong'o identifies as a "complex performance genealogy that gets the inadequate modern shorthand 'blackface minstrelsy'" and to contest the presumptive origins and historical narratives surrounding blackface minstrelsy and its relationships with other forms of racialized performance.[16]

This project does not map a singular genealogy of performance. Rather, it traces an assemblage of intertwined and overlapping genealogies of racialized performance, charting imbrications among blackface minstrelsy, its antecedent forms, and its many offshoots such as yellowface and brownface that entangle to form what Lisa Lowe terms "linked, but not identical genealogies" within a shared imperial performance culture.[17] As an assemblage of intertwined racial repertoires, transoceanic blackface performance was integral to the multidirectional, global circulations of imperial popular culture and to the concomitant formation of imperial structures of racial feeling. Therefore, it is necessary to reevaluate blackface beyond the ubiquitous framework of the "nation" and to interpret its racial politics beyond the boundaries of any singular national politics, particularly those of the United States.

Transoceanic Blackface

Blackface minstrelsy most frequently refers to the spectacular form of nineteenth-century entertainment known as the minstrel show. Histories of blackface minstrelsy usually situate the origin of the minstrel show in the early 1840s in the urban North of the United States, where the Virginia Minstrels and the Original Christy Minstrels fashioned the minstrel show as an evening-length ensemble performance form with a regular, repeatable dramaturgy. The minstrel show followed a three-part format: first, a choral performance in which the minstrels sat in a semicircle and alternated comic and sentimental songs with comedic repartee; second, an "olio" featuring individual specialty acts, short skits, stump speeches, and instrumental music; third, a spectacular finale consisting of either a plantation dance breakdown or a burlesque of a popular play or opera. The minstrel show's flexible dramaturgy mediated numerous enactments of Black abjection while also facilitating other forms of derogatory racialized performance such as yellowface, wherein minstrels swapped burnt cork for yellow face paint or Orientalist costuming to stage abject figurations of Asian subjects. Across its several acts, the minstrel show mobilized racial masquerade to stage disparate figures of racial difference as abjectly absurd and bound to comic failure.

Yet, the minstrel show was not fashioned spontaneously out of tattered cloth and burnt cork. Several historians have traced antecedent and precedent forms of racialized performance in the popular solo practitioners of "early blackface minstrelsy" who populated the US American stage in the 1820s and 1830s. Through this historical frame, blackface minstrelsy has long been narrated as a performative articulation of US American national and racial politics. Indeed, in Michael Rogin's view, minstrelsy is a "distinctively American cultural form."[18] Rogin's assertion aptly summarizes an extensive critical genealogy that harks back to Brander Matthews's 1915 celebratory historiography of minstrelsy, in which Matthews proclaimed that "negro-minstrelsy is the one [theatrical entertainment] which is absolutely native to [the United] States and which could not have come into existence anywhere else in the civilized world."[19] Matthews was deeply invested in a broader project of legitimating US American culture and its study, and his scholarly appropriation of blackface minstrelsy as a uniquely US American performance form was integral to this nationalistic endeavor.[20] It is therefore unsurprising that blackface minstrelsy has remained a mainstay of scholarship in the field of American studies, with conflicting strains of minstrel scholarship reinterpreting the significance and function of the "national" form.

Indeed, much minstrel scholarship emerged in the wake of the US civil rights movement and the end of de jure racial segregation in the United States, with minstrelsy serving as a refracting lens through which competing histories of US American racial politics have been interpreted. One thread of scholarship advanced by Robert C. Toll, Jean H. Baker, Alexander Saxton, David R. Roediger, and Eric Lott situates blackface minstrelsy's origins among the working-class popular culture of the antebellum US urban North during the consolidation of Jacksonian racial and class politics.[21] In this line of analysis, blackface minstrelsy manifests what Lott terms the "social unconscious" of US American racism.[22] This school of blackface historiography has analyzed the centrality of minstrelsy in the racial formation of whiteness and in the political formation of white supremacy in the antebellum United States. By contrast, a separate thread of scholarship has argued that minstrelsy was the product of intercultural creolization, echoing Matthews's interpretation of minstrelsy as emerging from cultural exchanges among enslaved Africans and European immigrants.[23] In this vein, Dale Cockrell, W. T. Lhamon Jr., and Christopher J. Smith have interpreted blackface minstrelsy as a hybridized cultural form reflective of what Cockrell views as an "urban, brotherhood-based, American" popular culture and which Lhamon identifies as a "mudsill mutuality" constituted by emergent, lumpen, interracial politics.[24] This line of analysis views minstrelsy as occasioning the subversion of racism and classism rather than their reification, frequently conflating racism tout court with the specific structures and practices of Jim Crow segregation. In this schema, any intercultural contact or exchange among Black and white Americans contravenes racial segregation. Put simply, this "creolization thesis" envisions blackface as a site of interracial contact and, therefore, of the possibility of anti-racist politics. This framing of blackface as politically subversive undertheorizes racism as limited to racial segregation and imagines anti-racism to be accomplished through the mere presence of interracial contact and cultural exchange; it also overstates the potential of individual performances to effect material changes to racial formations.

Yet, despite its facile apprehension of racism and its idealist theorizations of performance, the "creolization thesis" shares with the "social unconscious" thesis a common foundation in Matthews's unquestioned assertion that blackface minstrelsy is a distinctively US American performance form that is a direct reflection of US American politics. Though much ink has been spilled in the debates regarding the meanings and functions of blackface minstrelsy, these debates have amounted to little more than rehashes of arguments over the essence and origins of US national and racial politics. Suffice it to say that the vast majority of blackface minstrel scholarship has remained faithful to Matthews's nationalist project that imagines minstrelsy, its politics, and its cultural meanings to be uniquely US American.

Fortunately, recent scholarship on the global traffics of blackface minstrelsy has charted alternative modes of analysis by mapping the form's prolific transnationalization. This body of work gives the lie to the US American exceptionalism that previously dominated the study of blackface minstrelsy. Foundational texts such as Catherine M. Cole's *Ghana's Concert Party Theatre* and Jill Lane's *Blackface Cuba* have demonstrated the limitations of US American frameworks in apprehending the social meanings and political significances of blackface in distinct colonial and postcolonial contexts.[25] In a different vein, Robert Nowatzki has offered a compelling analysis of nineteenth-century blackface minstrelsy as tightly imbricated with abolitionism and antiabolitionism throughout the nineteenth-century Anglophone circum-Atlantic.[26] Additionally, Richard Waterhouse's study of minstrelsy in Australia, Matthew Wittmann's survey of minstrelsy's traffics through the "Pacific circuit," and Chinua Thelwell's study of the "export" of US American minstrelsy to South Africa collectively trace the material routes of a transoceanic performance form that was not limited to the United States nor its particular racial politics.[27] *Transoceanic Blackface* builds on and remains deeply indebted to this body of transnational scholarship on blackface (and) minstrelsy.

However, in this book, I demonstrate that blackface minstrelsy was not crafted in the bounded national context of the United States and then shipped elsewhere. Rather, blackface functioned as a core element in the transoceanic performance culture of the Anglophone empire since prior to the American Revolution. Transoceanic blackface emerged from the relays between eighteenth-century London and its colonies in North America and the Caribbean, and it remained central to the repertoires of Anglophone popular culture well into the twentieth century. The earliest forms of transoceanic blackface circulated throughout and beyond the circum-Atlantic through the networks of popular visual, print, and performance culture. As blackface formalized into the distinct performance form of minstrelsy, amateur performers staged solo blackface enactments and ensemble minstrel shows throughout the United States and the British

Empire. Professional minstrel troupes later capitalized on the form's transoceanic popularity by trafficking the minstrel show throughout the Anglophone world. Minstrelsy's imperial audiences were also itinerant. These audiences consisted of white settlers, merchants, and travelers who carried with them minstrelsy's material cultures and embodied performance repertoires. Across these several lines of transmission throughout the Anglophone empire, transoceanic blackface mobilized affective and material investments from global performers and audiences to reproduce its racial repertoires in local contexts.

Whether staged in imperial metropoles or on colonial frontiers, transoceanic blackface constituted a popular, everyday mode of performance that involved all classes of white imperial society. The white, male, working-class environment in which minstrelsy flourished throughout the United States during the Jacksonian era (ca. 1820s–1830s) was not the only—nor the primary—basis for its transoceanic popularity, which drew together "high" and "low" performance cultures of the Anglophone empire. Transoceanic traffics of racialized performance fostered cross-class affiliations within local white communities. Imperial circuits of blackface performance linked urban, white, working-class performance cultures that US American audiences forged through blackface minstrelsy to US American and British imperial middle classes, as well as to state officials and royalty. Figureheads for disparate political ideologies—Tories, Whigs (British and US American), Federalists, Anti-Federalists, Democrats, Republicans—patronized minstrel performances. Their regular attendance signals the capacity of transoceanic blackface to encompass the complex and contradictory political ideologies of the Anglophone empire, which were bound together through the imperial subjugation of Black, brown, Asian, and Indigenous subjects and subalterns. Minstrelsy's broad, transoceanic appeal among white imperial audiences—and beyond the urban, working-class theaters of the US American North—evinces the popularity of blackface performance across classes. Indeed, though blackface minstrelsy constituted an unquestionably *popular* form of performance, it was also a distinctly *imperial* form of popular performance culture.

Minstrelsy was a cross-class, state-sponsored entertainment that circulated throughout the deeply intertwined cultural networks that braided together the United States and the British Empire through shared performance repertoires. Perhaps most famously, on March 27, 1854, US commodore Mathew Perry's crew staged a blackface minstrel show aboard the USS *Powhatan* while it was docked in Tokyo Bay as part of the US American mission to "open" Japan to global trade.[28] Staged within a complex array of enactments of US American imperial power, Perry's diplomatic use of blackface minstrelsy signals the performance's tacit purpose: global Anglophone supremacy—military, economic, and racial. Similar state performances of blackface were ubiquitous throughout the

United States, Britain, and their respective colonial empires. As early as 1841, former US president Martin Van Buren attended a blackface performance by Joel Sweeney at New York's Bowery Theatre.[29] In 1844, the Ethiopian Serenaders staged a commissioned performance of blackface minstrelsy for sitting US president John Tyler.[30] As blackface minstrelsy grew in popularity, it became a standard entertainment for ensuing US American presidents, including James K. Polk, Millard Fillmore, Franklin Pierce, and Abraham Lincoln.[31] Polk not only attended minstrel shows but also celebrated individual minstrel performers, as when he gave Fred Buckley a diamond ring at a command blackface performance at the White House. Notably, this performance was a bipartisan affair, for it was also attended by Polk's political rival in the 1844 US presidential election, Henry Clay, who was reportedly "much pleased" by Buckley's blackface act.[32] Beyond this command performance, Polk also lent state support and legitimacy to Gilbert Pell's Ethiopian Serenaders' first British tour in 1846 by writing letters of recommendation to the British public.[33] These numerous instances of state-sponsored blackface demonstrate that social and political investments in blackface minstrelsy were hardly unconscious.

Nor were such state performances limited to the United States and its imperial ambit. State sponsorship was also integral to what Zine Magubane terms "the precocious transnationalization of minstrelsy" throughout the nineteenth-century Anglophone empire.[34] Across the Atlantic, Queen Victoria and her royal family were also frequent patrons of state performances of blackface: Pell's Ethiopian Serenaders performed at Gloucester House on February 24, 1846, and the Wilson and Montague Minstrels performed at Balmoral Castle on October 23, 1868.[35] Royal legitimation animated a performance economy that circulated through the capillaries of empire to reach colonial frontiers, tracing the expansive breadth of transoceanic blackface circuits. News of state-sanctioned performances encircled the globe: when the Wilson and Montague Minstrels performed at Balmoral, a newspaper in the Eastern Cape Colony of southern Africa reprinted London press accounts in full, concurrent with the southern African tour of another blackface troupe featuring star performer Washington Norton.[36] While such advertisements traded on the approbation of the imperial state to promote blackface troupes, they also encouraged colonial dignitaries to patronize blackface performances so as to trade on its transoceanic popularity. Colonial governors, magistrates, ministers, viceroys, and royal family members regularly attended blackface minstrel performances in the British colonies throughout the empire.[37]

Touring blackface troupes played on these mechanisms of imperial legitimation in their advertisements. On February 10, 1872, a troupe of "Christy's Minstrels" organized by Washington Norton promoted their first appearance in Kingston, Jamaica, by advertising their previous audiences with royal and political dignitaries:

> These celebrated *Artistes* from 472 Broadway, New York, and the Great St. James's Hall, Piccadilly, London, who have had the honor of appearing before all the Crowned Heads of Europe, inclusive of: Her Most Gracious Majesty Queen Victoria. H.R.H. The Late Prince Consort. Their Royal Highnesses the Prince & Princess of Wales. H.R.H. The Duke of Edinburgh. Their Imperial Majesties of the Emperor and Empress of the French. His Majesty the King of the Belgians.—As also—The Emperor and Empress of the Brazils. The Count d'Eu and the Princess Regent of Brazil. President Lincoln. President Grant. Sir John Young, late Governor of Sydney (Australia). Sir Charles Darling, late Governor of Melbourne. The Governor General of Canada. Sir P. Woodhouse, late Governor of Capetown, Cape of Good Hope. Sir Dominic Daly, Governor of South Australia. The President of the Argentine Republics. The President of the Republic of Chili. The President of the Republic of Peru. Etc., Etc.; will give their first Grand Fashionable Entertainment in this City on Tuesday evening, the 13th February 1872, at the Theatre Royal. [*sic*][38]

In a demonstration of the political efficacy of state performances in binding together the Anglophone empire, the governor of Jamaica, Sir John Peter Grant, responded to the Christy's Minstrels' advertisements by attending the troupe's second performance in Kingston the following week.[39] The presence of prominent imperial figures at minstrel shows in the United States and Britain, and across their colonial empires, frequently served as testimonials to the global, cross-class appeal of blackface troupes throughout their transoceanic tours. Royalty and colonial dignitaries ratified the respectability of affective investments in blackface performance while the mass popularity of the performances in turn fashioned the events as opportunities for figureheads of the imperial state to align themselves with minstrelsy's popular culture.

Though state-supported minstrelsy was ubiquitous throughout the Anglophone empire, it did not unilaterally manufacture colonial consent to white supremacist racial thinking. Rather, transoceanic blackface and its racial discourses suffused everyday life throughout the Anglophone empire. As early as the mid-eighteenth century, blackface songs, scripts, and visual materials circulated widely across Britain and its colonies in North America and the Caribbean. Forging a dense, interrelated repertoire, these theatrical and paratheatrical materials promulgated antiblack tropes that satirized Black emancipation, freedom, and equality. Though performances of transoceanic blackface were staged in colonial theaters across the Anglophone empire, they were not limited to formal performances or official theaters. The theatrical materials of transoceanic blackface circulated throughout public and private spaces, spectacular enactments, and closet dramas. Its performance cultures constituted material sites in which processes of imperial subjection and subjectification were both rehearsed and enacted. Across its wide circulations, transoceanic blackface animated popular impressions of racial being and belonging. Its repertoires of racial tropes structured feelings and precognitive apprehensions that cohered to produce material and political effects. Thus transoceanic blackface animated what Sara Ahmed terms "affective economies," wherein its extensive racial repertoires "mediate[d] the relationship between the psychic and the social, between the individual and the collective," thereby solidifying racial thinking and feeling as central to the imperial order.[40] Within the affective economies of transoceanic blackface and its performance cultures, white subjects were bound together through shared investments in the subjection of the empire's non-white others. Enslaved and colonized peoples were excluded from or abjected within dominant structures of feeling and belief. Minstrelsy's affective performance economies were intimately intertwined with imperial projects that managed the public and private lifeworlds of the Anglophone empire through processes of racialization, gendering, and sexual management. Transoceanic blackface, its racial repertoires, and its cultural materials transmitted colonial common sense well beyond the bounds of the theater proper, animating commonsense impressions about the biopolitical orders of empire. In other words, the repertoires of blackface minstrelsy were formative of racial epistemologies, white supremacist sentiments, and imperial sensibilities.

Empire

From June 1864 to July 1865, a "Lady"—a cross-gendered pseudonym for Sir John Robinson, who in 1893 would become the first premier of Natal—published a series of letters in the South African *Cape Monthly Magazine*.[41] Each letter described the author's experiences of the Cape's sister colony of Natal. During an inland trip to Maritzburg on December 5, 1864, Robinson recounted his first impressions of African Christian converts, or "Mission Kafirs," by remarking, "I could not but be reminded of *Uncle Tom's Cabin* by what I saw, and when a fat, good-humoured old body handed us some home-made sweet cake, Aunt Chloe stood before me."[42] Twelve years after the publication of Harriet Beecher Stowe's landmark 1852 abolitionist novel, Robinson troped on *Uncle Tom's Cabin* to translate for his Cape Town readers his encounter with an unfamiliar colonized subject. Reimagining a scene of colonial contact through a domestic scenario of slave sentimentality from *Uncle Tom's Cabin*, Robinson identified a Christian Tswana woman as a dehumanized "fat good-humoured old body" that he associated with "Aunt Chloe," the dutiful wife of Uncle Tom.[43] In the wake of transatlantic "Uncle Tom mania,"

Robinson's citation presumed that Stowe's romantic racialist depiction of a plantation in the American South offered an apt racial lens for interpreting the colonial frontiers of the British Empire.[44] Through this citation of a scene from US American literature, Robinson's account demonstrated that Britain's southern African colony of Natal and its principal Indian Ocean port city of eThekwini (Durban) not only were bound strategically to British imperial economic interests in Australia, China, and India but also were tied intimately to the cultural repertoires of the circum-Atlantic world. Robinson's anonymous travel writings situated southern Africa as a relay point between two oceanic systems central to the imperial circuits of the Anglophone empire. The Tswana "Aunt Chloe" appears at the juncture between the circum-Atlantic plantation economy—forged by the first British Empire and the United States—and the emergent second British Empire centered on the Indian and Pacific Ocean worlds.

The circuits connecting these oceanic systems were integral in forging the global Anglophone empire. The Anglophone circum-Atlantic world and its "oceanic interculture" were at the center of early capitalism, the transatlantic slave trade, and their systems of routinized racial violence and subjugation.[45] Yet, following the British defeat in the War for American Independence in 1783, Britain reoriented its imperial imaginaries and material investments beyond the Atlantic. As Eric Williams observes in *Capitalism & Slavery*, "When the American colonies won their independence[,] [t]he center of gravity in the British Empire shifted from the Caribbean Sea to the Indian Ocean, from the West Indies to India."[46] South Africa—and specifically, Cape Town—has historically appeared at the center of the transoceanic conjuncture between these two phases of Britain's centuries-long imperial project, as Cape Town linked the circum-Atlantic to the Indian Ocean and Pacific worlds through the global circulation of peoples, capital, material, affect, and ideology.

Two foundational texts on political economy situate the emergence of global capitalism at the transoceanic conjuncture at the Cape. Adam Smith's *An Inquiry into the Nature and Causes of the Wealth of Nations* (1776) points to the significance of the "discovery" of this oceanic passage and its effects: "The discovery of America and that of a passage to the East Indies by the Cape of Good Hope, are the two greatest and most important events recorded in the history of mankind."[47] His Eurocentric celebration of these "discoveries" as beneficial to "mankind" notwithstanding, Smith observed that the European encounter with the Americas and the subsequent development of transatlantic trade networks were not the sole forces animating the modern world. Transoceanic navigation between the Atlantic and Indian Ocean basins was integral to the formation of a global system of trade. Attesting to the significance of transoceanic trade, seventy years after the publication of *The Wealth of Nations*, Karl Marx and Friedrich Engels's *Communist Manifesto* returned to Smith's primal scene: "The discovery of America, the rounding of the Cape, opened up fresh ground for the rising bourgeoisie."[48] In 1848, the year of European revolutions, Marx and Engels asserted the inherent globality of nineteenth-century economic and political crises. By highlighting the connections among the Americas, Africa, and the Indian and Pacific Oceans, Marx and Engels provided a lens for considering the bourgeois investment in capitalism not merely as a revolutionary force that toppled feudalism in Europe but rather as a process of imperial world-making by which the rising bourgeoisie transferred its erstwhile role as an underclass onto enslaved and colonized peoples. As Marx and Engels knew, colonial projects were often the direct result of—and a primary arena for—European capitalist extraction and imperial rivalry.[49] Thus, Asia, Africa, the Americas, and Europe were intimately linked together through the Cape in the formation of the capitalist world-system.[50]

The entanglements of capitalist expansion and imperialism at the Cape signal the intimacy with which the modern capitalist world-system was bound up with empire.[51] After the British claimed the Cape Colony following a series of battles with the Dutch in the early nineteenth century, it served as a critical port in its transoceanic, imperial trade network. With their capture of Cape Town, Britain secured a vital resupply for Atlantic ships bound for Asia and the antipodes. British control of the Cape passage cleared the way for the proliferation of imperial projects throughout the Indian Ocean world and the antipodes, including sugar plantations in Natal and Mauritius to buttress Caribbean production; settler colonies in Australia to house convicts who prior to 1783 would have been transported to plantations in the former American colonies; and other colonial enterprises in Australia, Hong Kong, South Asia, southern Africa, and Aotearoa New Zealand. This second British Empire centered on India as the "jewel in the crown," replacing the triangular geometry of the transatlantic system with an expansive polygonal network that bound together a global world-system.

Though the British Empire shifted its center, it did not disentangle itself from the enduring transoceanic systems of the circum-Atlantic world. Beginning in the eighteenth century, Britain, its global empire, and the nascent United States of America constituted an Anglophone empire sustained by transoceanic imperial circuits that proved to be remarkably durable. In Giovanni Arrighi's analysis, the *longue durée* of capital accumulation developed globally through transoceanic circuits dominated by a succession of empires.[52] Beginning in 1750, London reigned for 175 years as the preeminent global financial center and naval power. Throughout the eighteenth and nineteenth centuries, the British Empire governed the economy of the capitalist world-system through its colonial-imperial networks, transoceanic circulations, and financial investments. The twentieth-century successor to Britain's transoceanic, global dominance was its former colonial empire in the Americas: the United States. Therefore, this epochal transition was characterized not so much by disruption as by continuity, with the financial center of the world-system moving from one Anglophone circum-Atlantic metropole (London) to another (New York). Though after 1783 they were never reunited as a single juridical body or state, Britain, the United States, and their respective imperial projects remained deeply interdependent. The year 1750 therefore marks the beginning of an ongoing, centuries-long period in which the Anglophone empire dominated the global capitalist systems of finance, trade, expropriation, and exploitation.

These two successive Anglophone imperial projects were knitted together not only through economic interests but also through centuries of tightly interwoven cultural traffics. The Anglophone empire comprised an imperial network of ports, way stations, entrepôts, colonial hubs, and metropolises connected via transoceanic circuits. Beyond the circum-Atlantic, the Anglophone empire linked colonies and metropoles, financial centers and imperial frontiers. Colonies across the Indian and Pacific Oceans—in Australia, Aotearoa New Zealand, South Africa, and South and Southeast Asia—burgeoned with new port cities emerging as key nodes within the imperial circuit. The British and US American empires also established significant military and commercial presences in several Chinese ports and Japanese harbors. These imperial nodes were linked to the already established Anglophone ports of the circum-Atlantic in the United States, Britain, and the Caribbean. While these far-flung harbors mediated the circulation of enslaved, indentured, and working-class labor, precious metals and gems, and the commodity crops that provided the material basis for the capitalist world-system, they also served as way stations for the global traffics of cultural material and performance that intimately bound together the empire through a shared performance culture. The Anglophone empire was constituted by the multidirectional circulation of persons, things, capital, and performance, which forged a distinct transoceanic interculture animated by global capitalism, colonialism, and imperial structures of feeling.

The theatrical itineraries traced in this book are testament to the material intimacies of empire. Scripts, popular imagery, and songs were trafficked throughout and beyond the eighteenth- and nineteenth-century circum-Atlantic, circulating the performance cultures of early blackface minstrelsy to the farthest reaches of the Anglophone empire. By the mid-nineteenth century, professional blackface minstrel troupes embarked on transoceanic tours that bound together British colonies with the performance economies of Britain and the United States. Minstrelsy's theatrical repertoires suffused the empire, providing performers and audiences with burlesque blackface and brownface renditions of Shakespeare and a proliferation of racialized enactments in yellowface, brownface, and drag. Imperial material networks of performance furnished British colonies and

British and US American metropoles with discourses and repertoires of racialized performance that mediated affective economies of race. These transoceanic performance repertoires were regularly adapted to animate—and to police—local racial dynamics.

Race

On April 19, 1847, amid a wave of British mania for blackface minstrelsy incited by the 1846 transatlantic tour of Gilbert Pell's Ethiopian Serenaders, a playlet titled *The Buffalo Girls; or, Female Ethiopian Serenaders* opened at the Surrey Theatre in London.[53] The musical comedy featured a plot set on a New Orleans plantation in which enslaved Black women are conscripted into a minstrel troupe. Their minstrel performance on the plantation inspires the white slave master to a paradigmatic act of nineteenth-century racial magnanimity: he frees the female serenaders so that they may exhibit their minstrel talents via a transatlantic tour to Britain. This plot is striking in its investment in a self-congratulatory nationalist contrast between the putative racial benevolence of post-abolition Britain and the unenlightened slave societies of the southern United States. Yet, this comic sentimental slave plot opens with the following scene directions that confuse the play's contrasting framing of the United States and imperial Britain:

> *Act 1. Sc 1. An extensive Sugar Cane Plantation in ~~Jamaica~~ New Orleans. The Trees—Orange—Lemon &c. RH. The Planter's House, with Verandah. LH. A range of Negro Huts. The whole scene glowing with a tropical Sun. When the Curtain rises a number of Slaves, Male & Female, are working among the Sugar Canes.*[54]

In the British Library manuscript of *The Buffalo Girls*, the post-abolition British colony of Jamaica appears under erasure, replaced by the primary nineteenth-century slave market of the US American plantation South, New Orleans. The attempted erasure of Jamaica marks the perennial displacement of the British Empire's enduring transoceanic investments in spectacles of Black enslavement. Moreover, the juxtaposition of "*~~Jamaica~~*" and "*New Orleans*" as interchangeable sites of slave subjection underscores the tight imbrications between British imperial and US American racial orders.

The Anglophone empire's enduring investments in racial subjection reappear as traces marked by their simultaneous disavowal. The erasure of Jamaica as the original setting for the minstrelsy of *The Buffalo Girls* redoubles the historical erasure of the Caribbean in minstrelsy's origin narratives, which insistently forget the formative role of John Moody and Lewis Hallam Jr. in fashioning early blackface dialect and caricature from their travels through Jamaica (more on this in chapters 1 and 2). Nevertheless, the manuscript's evocation of a sugarcane plantation—whether in Jamaica or New Orleans—indexes minstrelsy's recourse to fantasies of the plantation that were central to its performance repertoires throughout the United States, Britain, and the colonial world. To wit, in 1840, four years after US American blackface minstrel Thomas Dartmouth Rice introduced "Jump Jim Crow" to London stages, one of several proliferating penny-press versions of the popular blackface song included a verse in which Jim Crow—who hailed from the frontier territories of the Ohio River valley and occupied an ambiguous, liminal relationship to freedom and slavery—announced his unsurpassed capabilities in the plantation activities of "hoeing of de sugar, or picking cotton."[55] Three years later, when the Virginia Minstrels became the first blackface troupe to tour the British Isles, they advertised their "Grand Ethiopian concerts" as featuring songs taken directly "from among the sable inhabitants of the Southern States in America, the subject of each ascribing the manner in which the slaves celebrate their holidays, which commence at the gathering-in of the sugar and cotton crops."[56] Across these ubiquitous transoceanic stagings of the affect-laden site that Stephen C. Foster sentimentally called "de old plantation," the racialized labor of harvesting sugar and cotton indelibly linked racialized bodies to figurations of docile and compliant labor within the transnational capitalist economies that subtended the Anglophone empire.[57]

Blackface minstrelsy staged its fantasies of the plantation as central to its racialized performance economies. The plantation functioned as a capacious site for enacting the intimacies of empire—interracial habitation, labor, sexuality, and violence—through spectacular scenarios of Black enslavement. As Douglas A. Jones has observed, blackface minstrelsy functioned as an "aesthetic surrogate" of the plantation.[58] Minstrelsy's scenarios mediated romantic racialist imaginings of harmonious plantations and attendant fantasies of enslaved and colonized Black, brown, and Asian laborers. The frequency with which US American and British performers and audiences returned to plantation scenarios underscores the extent to which the plantation provided Anglophone popular culture with a capacious model for the imagination of white racial domination and for the spectacularization of racial subjection. The enduring presence of the plantation on the theatrical stages of the "democratic" United States and imperial Britain alike gives credence to Édouard Glissant's assertion that "socially, the Plantation is not the product of a politics but the emanation of a fantasy."[59] The plantation fantasy reappeared on Anglophone stages across disparate geographies and historical conjunctures as a singular site for the coherence of complex and contradictory racial projects unaffixed to any particular social or political ideology or to any single historical period. The insistent return to the plantation scene as a transoceanic, transhistorical fantasy signals that the Anglophone empire's racial economies were not a secondary effect of the capitalist world-system but rather were constitutive of it.[60] Saturated with spectacle, sentiment, and sorrow, the plantation fantasy provided a capacious site for circulations of affect and reimaginations of asymmetrical relations of imperial racism. Across its reappearances, the minstrel plantation served as a fantastical arena in the carnivalesque racial play of blackface performance that consistently concluded with the reification of white supremacist domination and subordination.

Minstrelsy's plantation fantasies animated everyday racial thinking across both public and private life, in metropolitan centers and along colonial frontiers. Yet, the plantation was not the only "imaginative geography" of popular racial discourse—discourses of Orientalism, stereotypes of Indigenous savagery, and scientific racism populated minstrelsy's imperial imaginary.[61] These racial discourses were imbricated with popular performances, which enlivened the racial fantasies and imaginative geographies of the Anglophone empire. The prolific popularity of transoceanic blackface overlapped with the coalescence of white supremacist racial discourses in the sciences during the late eighteenth and nineteenth centuries.

Transoceanic blackface and its global circulations of manifold racial scenarios functioned as key mechanisms by which race, in the terms of W. E. B. Du Bois, "worked itself through the warp and woof of our daily thought with a thoroughness that few realize."[62] Du Bois's account of race as woven into "daily thought" signals how racial thinking was, in Antonio Gramsci's terms, "common sense"—an ambiguous and contradictory "spontaneous philosophy of the multitude . . . which has to be made ideologically coherent."[63] Whereas Du Bois's analysis offers a compelling assessment of the intimacies of racial thought and practice in the United States, everyday racial thinking and its privileging of whiteness was hardly limited to a single nation within the capitalist world-system. White supremacy was integral to the intimate lifeworlds of the Anglophone empire, and race was an ideological and affective centerpiece. Catherine Hall has elaborated on Gramsci's concept to intervene critically in British history by demonstrating the centrality of racial discourse to Anglophone imperial life, noting that race was "part of instinctive common sense" across the British Empire both at home and abroad.[64] In response to critiques of her project that minimized the racism of nineteenth-century British culture, Hall revised her central claim: "Racial thinking was part of the furniture of nineteenth-century society."[65] In this revision, Hall mobilized the idiom "part of the furniture" to highlight the everydayness of racial thinking and feeling, particularly its tacit presence even when not explicitly articulated. Yet, her use of the metaphor of furniture for "common sense" signals another register. Conceptualizing race as "common sense" attends to its affective and ideological valences—what Raymond Williams would call its "structures of feeling." By contrast, the metaphorical language of "furniture" situates race not only as a fluid "social experience in *solution*"—one mediated by the bodies and minds of imperial subjects and subalterns—but also as obdurate material that has sedimented into enduring structures and formations.[66] Approaching race as "part of the furniture" invites consideration of the ways in which race flexibly yet materially structured the social and political life of empire. As "part of the furniture" of the Anglophone empire, racial thinking was simultaneously structural and intimate, material and affective. It shaped seemingly spontaneous discourses, ideologies, and popular beliefs into enduring cultural material, formations, and practices.

The racial furniture of empire supported and comforted some orientations, identities, subjectivities, and positions—but not others. Imperial racial formations and practices were organized around tacit and explicit beliefs in the superiority of whiteness. As Laura Doyle notes, across the Anglophone empire, discourses of liberty and freedom functioned as "a race myth" in which "to be white [was] to be fit for freedom, and the white man's burden [was] to lead others by forging the institutions and modeling the subjectivities required to practice proper freedom."[67] In this way, race subtended discourses of freedom and unfreedom: it delimited the property of freedom to white people while confining both enslaved and nominally free non-white peoples within the shifting terrain of de jure and de facto white supremacist rule. Under the imperial dominion of freedom, colonial common sense enfolded colonized and enslaved persons into racial orders that secured what Edward Said identifies as the "flexible *positional* superiority" of white imperial subjects.[68] This is to say that the Anglophone imperial furniture of race was not always arranged in the same manner, upholstered with the same cloth, or decorated in the same colors. It was regularly fashioned, refashioned, and refurbished to satisfy the imperial needs of particular subjects—namely, to support and comfort white subjects of the empire and those who identified with or aligned themselves with whiteness. The asymmetrical social relations of Anglophone imperial culture propped up whiteness through the uneven distribution of affect and affectability, sentiment and sensibility.[69] Fabricated in support of the emergent European bourgeoisie, the racialized political discourses of liberalism oriented imperial subjects and subalterns around the unmarked yet intimate familiarity of whiteness.[70] At the same time, the racial furniture of empire positioned non-white subjects and subalterns as inherently *unfree*. Even when enslaved subjects were emancipated or when colonized subjects were granted nominal liberties and rights, they were necessarily debarred from the enjoyment of freedom that defined imperial white subjectivity and subjecthood.[71] Across disparate geographies, the imperial discourses of racial liberalism figured Black, brown, Indigenous, and

Asian peoples of the Anglophone empire as racially abject—that is, such disparate peoples were figured as unfree subjects of empire whose transnational presence shored up the borders of whiteness and the coherence of the white subject.[72]

Throughout this book, I trace how blackface minstrelsy's performances of race functioned affectively, ideologically, and materially—as imperial common sense and as part of the furniture of Anglophone empire. In doing so, I aim both to encompass the global breadth of white supremacist racial thinking and to loosen the enduring essentialisms accorded to color as a definite signifier of race—for instance, where blackness signals exclusively Black diasporic histories of enslavement.[73] Transoceanic racial formations were deeply structured by chattel slavery and its discourses, yet they also exceeded such formations and discourses as the Anglophone empire shifted its center from the circum-Atlantic to the Indian Ocean world. As Jenny Sharpe observes, Anglophone imperial racial discourses were capacious and mutable as they "sanctioned *both* the management of free slaves *and* the expansion of Empire."[74] Though minstrelsy's plantation fantasy originally cohered around Black subjugation in scenarios of chattel slavery in the British West Indies and the US American South, its fantastic animation of racial common sense readily enfolded disparate colonized peoples within its symbolic and affective economies. Minstrelsy's characters were fungible. They were readily replaced by abject figurations of the unfree subjects of the expanding British and US American empires—such as the "coolies" and "Chinamen" who were trafficked globally following the abolition of the slave trade and Aboriginal Australians who were subjected to genocidal projects of empire.

Transoceanic blackface circulated densely intertwined imperial discourses of race, nation, gender, and sexuality. Twenty-first-century identity politics typically imagine identitarian categories to be static, separable, and stable formations.[75] By contrast to this prevailing framework, it is crucial to remember, as Tavia Nyong'o observes, that "race was mobilized in [the nineteenth century] as itself a mutable and even volatile category."[76] Nyong'o here refers to how nineteenth-century racial discourses mediated anxieties surrounding gender and sexuality as a dense transfer point of power, moral respectability, and bodily purity.[77] Moreover, the tendency to focus on the nation as a container for race obscures the ways in which racial biopolitics were central to the intimate and public animation of the "microphysics of colonial rule" and "the affective grid of colonial politics" throughout the Anglophone empire and across national boundaries.[78] Minstrelsy's racial discourses mediated such intimate anxieties globally, and they served as key devices in the management of imperial populations. Indeed, white imperial subjects' fascination with interracial sexual contact in *Othello* (see chapter 4) and the proliferation of forms of antiblack and Orientalist drag throughout the Anglophone empire (see chapter 5) extravagantly demonstrated the imperial entanglements among popular discourses of race, gender, and sexuality. Mapping the discursive terrain of transoceanic blackface reveals the dense imbrications among the promulgation of racial thinking, the performativity of gender, the policing of sexuality, and the performance cultures of the Anglophone empire. Put differently, the performance economies of transoceanic blackface were integral to the popularization of conceptions of race as an essential property of (national) subjectivity, gender as a domain separable from race, and sexuality as a moral issue. As a dense transfer point of power among these discourses, race functioned as a mutable assemblage that was regularly adapted, reworked, and reimagined in new colonial-imperial contexts. As this book demonstrates, race coalesced as a biopolitical device of empire—a capacious means for maintaining the material and affective economies of the Anglophone empire. Nowhere were the intimate imperial entanglements of materiality, affect, and race more evident than in the empire's transoceanic economies of performance.

Performance

In the early 1840s, dance-hall impresario E. P. Christy founded a minstrel troupe in Buffalo, New York. At this major port city situated on the confluence of the Erie Canal and the Great Lakes and near the border between the United States and British Canada, Christy's troupe quickly established itself as a preeminent blackface performance ensemble. By 1847, the Original Christy Minstrels (also known as Christy's Minstrels) had relocated to New York City, where they advertised their regular performances on Broadway with a series of vignettes from their repertoire. One of these illustrations featured a minstrel burlesque of Shakespearean tragedy, in which Christy's Minstrels enacted a comic iteration of famous characters, speeches, and scenarios from *Hamlet* (see fig. 1).

Though this vignette ostensibly advertised Christy's troupe and their "original" blackface performances, Christy's Minstrels were not the inventors of blackface burlesque or of minstrel burlesques of *Hamlet*. Indeed, the image cited several prior performances, most centrally British comedian Charles Mathews's infamous imitation of a Black performer at William A. Brown's African Theatre in New York City. In a racist mockery of one of the African Theatre's performers (likely James Hewlett), Mathews enacted a travesty version of Hamlet's soliloquy: "To be or not to be? That is the question; whether it is nobler in *de* mind to suffer, tak' up arms against a sea of trouble, and by *opossum* end 'em."[79] Mathews's blackface burlesque of Brown's African Theatre was based on a fictive performance that never occurred.[80] Nevertheless, the wide circulation of Mathews's anti-black joke was integral to the popularization of the early blackface song

Fig. 1. Detail from "Scenes from the Original Christy Minstrels at Mechanics Hall, 472 Broadway, N.Y. in 1847." Courtesy of the Harry Ransom Center, University of Texas at Austin.

"Opossum up a Gum-Tree" and the frequent recourse to opossum jokes in the transoceanic blackface repertoire. Thus, the Christy Minstrels image advertised their performances not only by visualizing their blackface Shakespearean burlesques but also by citing Mathews's famous contribution to the minstrel repertoire. By posing Hamlet in contemplation not of the deceased jester Yorick but rather of the skull of an opossum, the Christy Minstrels advertisement compressed into an indelible image the relays between performances of blackface burlesque, mockeries of Black and brown people, and minstrel self-referentiality. It condensed a genealogy of blackface performance into a crystalline visual joke immediately recognizable to a knowing audience. Through this condensation of numerous citations, the advertisement epitomizes how blackface minstrelsy drew on extant repertoires to develop "original" performance material. In turn, such novel minstrel material circulated widely and prompted new performances.

The Christy Minstrels advertisement demonstrates that blackface minstrelsy was a densely intertextual and citational practice. It exemplifies how transoceanic blackface supplied disparate Anglophone audiences with intertheatrical repertoires that insistently referenced other performances, cultural artifacts, and topical events. "Intertheatricality," for Jacky Bratton, refers to "the mesh of connections between all kinds of theatre texts, and between texts and their users."[81] Rather than focusing on individual, singular performers and performances, Bratton's method of intertheatrical analysis focuses on the interconnections between embodied performers, audiences, and expansive bodies of textual and visual material. Approaching historical performances intertheatrically requires that we attend to both archival documents and the historical embodiment of theatrical repertoires that endured across generations through active re-citation and reanimation. In this vein, Tracy C. Davis defines repertoires as "wider system[s] of transmission involving recognisability among audiences who make sense of performance."[82] Theatrical repertoires were shared systems that situated individual performances within grids of intelligibility and structures of feeling. Attending to the intertheatricality of blackface performance allows us to map the *how* of performance history: how performance networks were formed, how performance repertoires furnished performers with theatrical material, and how such repertoires shaped popular culture. By apprehending the material circulations of transoceanic blackface as constitutive of a complex intertheatrical repertoire, we can better understand the ways in which scripts, paratheatrical texts, visual culture, music, and embodied performance coalesced to animate the performance cultures of the Anglophone empire.

Unremarked on yet intimately familiar, minstrelsy's performance repertoires were part of the imperial furniture that white subjects relied on for ideological coherence and affective security. Performance was integral to the fashioning of race throughout the Anglophone empire, and the intertheatrical repertoires of transoceanic blackface constituted a critical arena for the animation of imperial racial common sense. Diana Taylor has analyzed how performances function as "vital acts of transfer" through which epistemologies of colonial common sense circulate and cohere in repertoires and scenarios.[83] Following in this line of thinking, I am interested in how the repertoires and scenarios of transoceanic blackface circulated broadly throughout the Anglophone empire, animating performance cultures across national boundaries and beyond schemas of lineal genealogical transmission and replacement.[84] In this approach, the archive does not signify a passive collection of materials disinvested from embodied performance. Quite the opposite: the archive itself functions as a trace of widely performed repertoires as well as of scripts that have prompted disparate performances.

Engaging with these archives of racialized performance facilitates a reapprehension of the material repertoires of imperial performance, their multiple circulations, and their lines of influence. The archive assembled in this book recuperates the intertheatrical repertoires of transoceanic blackface by bringing together archival material scattered throughout the Anglophone empire—across Australia, Aotearoa New Zealand, Britain, Canada, India, Jamaica, South Africa, and the United States. In doing so, it retraces the circuitous, transoceanic itineraries of minstrel performers and blackface materials, demonstrating that blackface traffics were multidirectional, with performers, songs, scripts, and other stage materials crossing juridical boundaries and geographical borders. For instance, one of the earliest blackface minstrel troupes to form in the antebellum United States was the Buckley family, themselves British transplants who immigrated to the United States in 1839 prior to forming the Congo Melodists in 1843.[85] During numerous transoceanic tours, the Buckley family returned several times to perform in the British Isles. In Britain, along with other popular blackface minstrel ensembles, the Buckleys inspired countless British blackface performers and companies who further wove blackface minstrelsy into the warp and woof of nineteenth-century Anglophone popular culture.

Indeed, blackface performance remained immensely popular in both the United States and the British Empire throughout the nineteenth century. In 1847, the London periodical *Punch* remarked on the ubiquity of blackface minstrelsy in Britain, noting how "universal [was] the taste for these dingy melodists."[86] A quarter century later, Reverend Hugh Reginald Haweis observed that blackface minstrels "furnish one of the most remarkable and original elements of [British] street music."[87] Haweis celebrated with transparent nationalistic pride that "original" blackface songs arrived "[f]rom St. James's Hall, and not from 'Old Virginny'" and that "from that new source of negro pathos and humor[,] numbers of songs and choruses continue to flow, some of them good imitations, and many of them retaining the characteristic form of the negro melody."[88] Importantly, Haweis claimed blackface not as a US American export but rather as an "original" source of British popular culture—a local performance form that "retain[ed] the characteristic form" of minstrelsy's racial repertoires despite its status as "imitation." For Haweis, the geographic distance between minstrelsy's putative US American site of "origin" and its enjoyment by the British public mattered little. Throughout the Anglophone empire—in Britain, its global empire, and the United States alike—transoceanic blackface "furnish[ed]" popular culture with intertheatrical repertoires.

The conjuncture of minstrelsy's repertoires as a means of "furnish[ing]" the empire and of race as "part of the furniture" of empire underscores the integral role of performance in animating imperial popular culture. Moreover, it invites reconsideration of a well-worn debate about the meaning of *performance*. The English word "performance," according to Victor Turner, derives from the "Old French *parfournir*, literally 'to furnish completely or thoroughly.'"[89] In *Cities of the Dead*, Joseph Roach cites Turner's etymology to theorize performance as a completed action or a thing done. Yet, in his theorization of circum-Atlantic performance, Roach subtly reconceives of performance as a means "to furnish forth": "to bring forth, to make manifest, and to transmit" cultural memory.[90] Into Turner's definition, Roach interpolates the phrase "to furnish forth"—an evocative phrase that does not appear in Turner's text. Instead, Roach's definition of "performance" as "to furnish forth" likely derives from an unacknowledged reference to William Shakespeare's *Hamlet*: "The funeral baked meats / Did coldly *furnish forth* the marriage tables."[91]

Roach's definition of performance as a "furnishing forth" thus smuggled the key word "forth" into Turner's *parfournir* in a subtle revision of the grounds of performance.[92] Countering the then-prevalent idealist strain in performance theory with an investment in the materiality of history, Roach's redefinition of performance as "to furnish forth" insisted on the material manifestation of embodied performance. Roach's emphasis on embodiment, in turn, countered the positivism then prevalent in theater history that delimited what was considered valid material evidence to textual documentation. Indeed, Roach's theoretical keywords of performance all hinge on conceptualizing performance as a material, embodied practice. "Kinesthetic imagination . . . inhabits the realm of the virtual," but manifests in gestures, bodily movements, and social enactments as performing bodies materialize affect and affect material bodies.[93] Similarly, his theorization of "effigy" as a verb central to performance emphasizes the ways in which physical effigies make manifest that which is absent by "body[ing] something forth."[94] I posit that Roach interpolated the adverb "forth" into his definition because it marks a critical moment in the actualization of performance—where the invisible becomes visible and the ostensibly absent becomes manifestly present. Yet, there is another latent meaning that is also key to Roach's theorization of performance as a cultural process. The adverb "forth" bears a temporal valence indicating immediate, continuous, or future action, as in *forthwith*, *henceforth*, or *from this day forth*. Bearing temporality in mind, Roach's definition of performance as "to furnish forth" indicates a material embodiment that fulfills a present action and also endures into the future as performance material, whether in the archive or the repertoire. "Forth" marks the macabre materiality at the center of performance, through which the dead and departed ("the funeral baked meats") remain an enduring presence that constitutes the conditions of possibility for future performances ("the marriage tables"). If performance is understood as furnishing forth, then it carries a double valence. First, performance makes manifest latent discourses, scripts, kinesthetic imaginations, and affective economies. Second, performance materializes into archives and repertoires by sedimenting as imagery, writing, sound, and corporeal memory that endures both as cultural material and as potential prompts for future enactments, borrowings, and adaptations.

What possibilities of performance were manifest materially in the repertoires of transoceanic blackface? Attending to the popular circulation of blackface burlesques of *Hamlet* discloses the extent to which the citational network of performance theory has not engaged significantly with the broad circulations and global popularity of blackface minstrelsy, preferring instead to theorize performance on the "universal" model of Shakespeare and especially of *Hamlet*.[95] Though Roach's immensely useful theorization of circum-Atlantic performance analyzes blackface performance alongside Shakespearean drama, he posits them as separate performance genealogies with little overlap aside from dramatic stagings of *Othello*.[96] Here, Roach follows a deeply entrenched pattern in performance studies, which not only has privileged *Hamlet* above other Shakespearean works but also has disregarded the marked differences among the First and Second Quarto and the First Folio versions of *Hamlet* in its universalizing theorizations.[97] More to the point, performance studies has also refrained from considering popular circulations of Shakespeare's play on the minstrel stage. Framed as an exceptional site of US American politics in the early nineteenth century, blackface minstrelsy has been imagined as a discrete historical performance form delimited to a specific national geography—unlike, for instance, the transhistorical and transnational endurance of Shakespeare's *Hamlet*.

One result of this lack of attention to blackface minstrelsy as a critical site for theorizing performance has been the effective whitewashing of "performance" as a universal category of analysis. Performance is often understood as a key mechanism in the social construction of race, while race need not be understood as integral to theorizations of performance. My return to Roach's conceptualization of performance as a "furnish[ing] forth" expands on his theorization of circum-Atlantic performance to trace not only how transoceanic blackface furnished forth the racial discourses of the Anglophone empire but also how imperial formations of race furnished forth enduring racialized conceptualizations of performance.[98] Who can perform? Whose actions matter as performance? Which performances are written into history and through what discourses? Transoceanic blackface functioned as a centerpiece in the popular performance economies of the Anglophone empire and in its enduring imperial racial formations. It constituted a capacious repertoire through which the racialized discourses of liberal subjectivity and subjecthood were rehearsed. Its ubiquitous popularity worked to delimit the popular conceptualization of freedom and agency to white subjects while abjecting non-white subjects and subalterns as racial liberalism's unfree, dependent others. In other words, Haweis's claim that minstrelsy "furnish[ed]" Britain with "elements" of its national repertoire was more perceptive than he knew—it underscored how blackface, minstrelsy, and related forms of racialized performance not only furnished the Anglophone empire with an expansive intertheatrical repertoire but also furnished forth enduring racial formations.

Furnishing the Empire, Furnishing Forth Racial Subjects

Blackface performance was the paradigmatic theatrical form that habituated Anglophone audiences and performers to imperial apparatuses of racial thinking, feeling, and doing. The audiences of transoceanic blackface consisted primarily of white imperial subjects, and its repertoires furnished these audiences with racial scripts of white supremacy that affirmed white subjects' place at the top of imperial racial hierarchies. At the same time, transoceanic blackface also conscripted non-white subjects and subalterns into its racial repertoires.[99] Yet, the vast majority of colonized subjects and subalterns who engaged with racialized performances did not leave material traces of their experiences. There remain few enduring accounts of their experiences or impressions. When such traces appear, they linger silently, barely perceptible in the margins of the archive. Scant writings therefore must stand in for the numerous Black, brown, Asian, and Indigenous audiences of minstrelsy in the Anglophone colonial world. Most of these accounts were authored by white Anglophone writers—a dynamic that demands careful critical attention so as to avoid reducing enslaved or colonized subjects and subalterns "to conditions of domination or romanticizing them as pure forces of resistance."[100] Relinquishing such romanticized and essentialist modes of interpretation facilitates granular analysis of how transoceanic blackface and its attendant racial discourses structured and constrained the presence of non-white subjects and subalterns in imperial life as well as how it conscripted them into the entanglements of imperial racial orders well beyond the minstrel stage.

The colonial archive documents the presence of colonized audiences at minstrel shows through narrated scenes of subaltern enjoyment that are anxiously, if only occasionally, repeated. In colonial South Africa, for instance, non-white domestic workers regularly attended the theater while performing caretaking labor for the white children of their employers. They constituted a significant part of the audience at special matinee blackface minstrel shows staged specifically for the empire's children.[101] Reportage in colonial newspapers celebrated such spectacles of interracial audiences, as evident in the words of one white colonial reporter for Cape

Town's *Standard & Mail* describing the audience at an 1872 performance of the Harvey-Dougherty-Leslie-Braham Minstrels:

> Crowds of pretty children, with half anxious and half merry-looking nurses of every shade of colour from European white to African ebony, filled the hall, and the shouts of shrill laughter from the little ones, their sparkling eyes and joyous clapping of hands, were fitted to thaw the heart of the most inveterate old bachelor that ever abominated children; while the broad grins of their sable attendants showing the double rows of ivories, which a Duchess might envy, and combining the most comical expressions of laughter and wonderment, formed a picture worth studying.[102]

Far from a transparent transcript of subaltern enjoyment, this passage models the ambiguities and ambivalences of colonial reports on colonized audiences. First and foremost, the provisional presence of domestic workers in the audience of a children's matinee depended on their social equivalence with the empire's white children rather than their full inclusion in Anglophone imperial performance culture: the "nurses of every shade of colour" here appear akin to the children in their charge. Moreover, this passage presents a hyperbolic figuration of a scene of interracial harmony. The author's observation of "half anxious and half merry-looking" domestic workers both signals their possible experience of something other than merriment (e.g., anxiety) and indicates the author's reliance on the external appearance ("merry-*looking*") as a definitive sign of their experience. By the end of this passage, the author resolves its ambivalences by fashioning a scene in which racialized subjects express their approbation of minstrel spectacle, in which "the broad grins of [the children's] sable attendants" mimetically double the grotesque smiles of blackface minstrels. Crucially, the reporter elides the possible displeasure signified by the domestic workers' "half anxious" appearance in favor of what Hartman terms the "simulated contentment" and "simulated jollity" of scenes of racial subjection.[103] If the domestic workers did not invest themselves in the affective economies of the transoceanic blackface, such dissent was muted in colonial discourses that inscribed spectatorial pleasure as the normative audience response.

Nevertheless, such ambivalently celebratory passages also raise the possibility that non-white audiences *did* find pleasure in minstrelsy, and that they did not necessarily resist or oppose its spectacles of racial burlesque. How might we understand the possibility of "sable" South African domestic workers experiencing "laughter and wonderment" at a colonial minstrel show? One possibility is presented by bell hooks, who recounts her childhood encounter with the Black female character Sapphire from the television version of *Amos 'n' Andy*. hooks describes how she identified not *with* but *against* the Black female character Sapphire: "*She was not us.* We laughed with the black men, with the white people. We laughed at this black woman who was not us."[104] Despite her personal counteridentification against Sapphire, hooks also notes that adult Black women often embraced Sapphire as an embodiment of "that angry part of themselves white folks and black men could not even begin to understand."[105] Might the colonial domestic workers have counteridentified against the mammies of the blackface minstrel stage? Perhaps. Or might they have "disidentified" with the minstrel caricatures, to borrow José Esteban Muñoz's term, by selectively and subversively identifying with figures of blackface abjection so as to work through the parts of themselves that eluded dominant figurations of minoritarian and subaltern life under imperial rule?[106] However the empire's racialized subjects and subalterns thought or felt about minstrelsy, their responses are not transparent and they remain shrouded in opacity.

Throughout this book, I want to hold open the possibility that colonized subjects and subalterns experienced transoceanic blackface in similarly unpredictable and counterintuitive ways that cannot be reduced to binaries of mystification and resistance. Instead, I posit that performances of blackface and minstrelsy furnished forth the intricate operations of racial subjection by shaping the very terms of racialized subjecthood and identification. I attend to such scenes of subjection to recount how popular performance subjected colonized and enslaved peoples into the racial formations of empire. The repertoires of transoceanic blackface enfolded minoritarian subjects and subalterns into colonial orders by conditioning the possibilities of racial legibility and agency while also delimiting and proscribing transparent articulations of resistance. At the same time, I trace how blackface, minstrelsy, and related forms of racialized performance conscripted audiences into imperial racial subjectivities, furnished white imperial subjects with their felt sense of superiority, and consolidated the racial orders of empire. Transoceanic blackface was prolific in its furnishing forth of imperial racial discourses and colonial common sense. It was both theatrical and performative, both material and affective, both furniture and a means of furnishing forth, both a subjunctive performance and a constitutive enactment of knowledges, habituated behaviors, and orientations.

This book demonstrates how the racial repertoires of empire were forged through Anglophone performance circuits that spanned the globe. Though racial formations have long been bound up with nationalist projects in the United States of America and across the British Empire, the entangled routes and repertoires of the Anglophone empire belie attempts to frame race and racialized performance as discrete national products or projects. The transnational Anglophone empire that coalesced through two centuries of British and US American economic domination was premised on mutually reinforcing racial projects and shared repertoires of racialized performance. Transoceanic blackface was a simultaneously global and local practice that animated the intimate interrelations between racial thinking and the affective matrixes of the Anglophone empire. It forged racialized subjectivities through performance by conscripting enslaved and colonized subalterns into colonial discourse and onto imperial stages. In other words, blackface and related forms of racialized performance furnished forth the racial scripts and repertoires of the modern world. These performances enlivened global discourses and practices of white supremacy, antiblackness, structural violence, and racial capitalism that endure to this day. This book is therefore a history of our global present, one that seeks out the transoceanic roots and routes of our forgotten past so that we might reckon with the lasting entanglements of empire, race, and performance.

Chapter 1

✦

Eddies in the Anglophone Imperial Stream

In September 1764, John Adams wrote to his future wife, Abigail, of an anonymous "Gentleman" performer that he encountered somewhere in colonial British America. He asked:

> Do you wonder, my Dear, why that Gentleman does not succeed in Business, when his whole study and Attention has so manifestly been engaged in the nobler Arts of smutt, Double Entendre, and Mimickry of Dutchmen and Negroes? I have heard that Imitators, tho they imitate well, Master Pieces in elegant and valuable Arts, are a servile Cattle. And that Mimicks are the lowest Species of Imitators, and I should think that Mimicks of Dutchmen and Negroes were the most sordid of Mimicks.[1]

Adams does not specify the occasion of his encounter with this "Gentleman" performer, nor does he indicate that there was anything unusual about the performance. Indeed, rather than express surprise at what he terms a "sordid" form of theatrical mimicry, Adams refers to "Mimicks of Dutchmen and Negroes" as a commonplace that, though distasteful to Adams's aesthetic sensibilities, was familiar enough for Adams to have formed a critical opinion. Instead, the "Gentleman" performer serves as an occasion for Adams's disapproval and disdain, his antitheatrical prejudices, his classed respectability politics, and his attempt to contain what was evidently an already popular performance form. Therefore his 1764 letter offers a trace of the "origins" of blackface performance within the everyday repertoires of the transatlantic British Empire a full sixty years prior to the oft-cited "origins" of blackface in the urban North of the 1820s United States.

Despite prevailing associations of blackface minstrelsy as a "distinctively American cultural form" forged in the furnaces of Jacksonian politics, histories of blackface minstrelsy have long cited the earliest appearances of US American racial impersonation in the prerevolutionary period of British colonialism.[2] As Lynne Fauley Emery has noted, "Even before the

Revolutionary War, [US] Americans were being entertained by impersonations of Negroes, and particularly of Negro dancing."[3] Attesting to this claim, S. Foster Damon cites the "first evidence of the impersonation of a native black" in the Americas as "a negro dance in character" by Mr. Tea in New York City on April 14, 1767.[4] Yet, even when scholars such as Emery and Damon have carefully excavated traces of blackface performance in the early American colonies, they usually situate these performances explicitly as stray antecedents of a determinately US American cultural form of racial impersonation. These narratives exemplify Eric Lott's claim that "all positions on the origins and makeup of blackface minstrelsy implicitly or explicitly rely on a theory of the racial politics of American culture."[5] Posited as genealogical forebears of blackface minstrelsy, such performances appear as isolated examples of blackface in colonial America. By contrast, John Adams's account suggests that blackface performers were so ubiquitous as to form a distinct class of "Mimicks" common enough to warrant censure and disdain. Viewed in context with other "Mimicks of Dutchmen and Negroes," Mr. Tea's "negro dance in character" appears not so much as an origin point for US American blackface as a nodal point within an extensive Anglophone imperial performance network. To whom were Adams's "Mimicks of Dutchmen and Negroes" and Mr. Tea's "negro dance in character" connected? From whence did performers in this network derive their theatrical materials and conventions?

In this chapter, I chart the traffics of blackface performance throughout the circum-Atlantic Anglophone empire from the mid-eighteenth through the early nineteenth century. By contrast to national framings of minstrelsy's beginnings, this chapter traces blackface's emergence through the relays and relations of a transoceanic performance culture that bound together the eighteenth-century transatlantic British Empire, including and exceeding the colonies that would become the United States of America. In this chapter, I follow Walter Benjamin's comments regarding origins: "The term origin is not intended to describe the process by which the existent came into being, but rather to describe that which emerges from the process of becoming and disappearance. Origin is an eddy in the stream of becoming."[6] Instead of locating a singular, determinant "origin" of blackface minstrelsy as the birth of a national cultural form from a singular source, I seek blackface's beginnings in the eddies of the transoceanic Anglophone empire's processes of becoming. Moreover, departing from discrete analyses of blackface performance modes (e.g., theater, dance, music, popular culture), I highlight the transmedial, intertheatrical, and transnational relays between multiple modes of Anglophone performance culture. Throughout the middle to late eighteenth century, transoceanic circulations of blackface interwove performance genealogies of comic opera, comedic theater, popular dance, comic songs, print minstrelsy—or *scriptive blackface*—and closet dramas. Cultural flows between these variegated strains of popular Anglophone culture culminated in waves of transmedial blackface in the early nineteenth-century transatlantic. I analyze blackface as a capacious genre for manifold theatrical and paratheatrical racial enactments, each an eddy that furnished new performance material. These several flows converged in the proliferation of tropes that abjected blackness in the colonial racial orders of the Anglophone empire. Throughout its prolific circulations across the Anglophone empire, blackface animated racial common sense which consolidated around tropes of blackness as inherently servile, as a burlesqued performance of whiteness, and as beyond the pale of white brotherhood.

The Spectacular Sights and Sounds of Early Anglophone Blackface

On February 16, 1825, a month after departing from Gravesend, England, the ship *Lady Campbell* crossed the equator en route to Kolkata, India. Somewhere south of the equator near the coast of West Africa, sailors marked the passage with a "crossing the line" ceremony, a ritual for European sailors entering the Southern Hemisphere for the first time. Such novices, referred to as "children passengers" or "pollywogs," were inducted into the seasoned shipboard fraternity by a sailor costumed as the Roman sea-god Neptune. As pollywog cadet Robert Ramsay recounted in his diary, their induction involved a series of trials, including Neptune blackfacing the initiates, shaving their faces with a dull razor, and generally abusing and abjecting the blackened sailors with rough treatment.[7] Ramsay repeatedly noted the ritual's insistent braiding of violence and blackness:

> After getting a brush from ear to ear with black paint . . . I was next lifted up and set on a board, my chin shaved with rather an inferior kind of Windsor soap (attempts were made to shove the brush into my mouth) and then tumbled head over heels amongst some water; the vessel containing the water being rather shallow, my head came in contact with the deck . . . . most of our visage[s] had a blackish tinge, from Neptune's paint-brush, but especially that of Mr. Moore, who was as black as a chimney-sweep, not even excepting his hair and clothes.[8]

In a symbolic *rite de passage*, the novice white sailors were separated from their identities at home by being blackened and abused in order to make them fit for the unfamiliar and potentially dangerous seas on the southern, "inverted" world below the equator.[9] Here, blackface abjection manifests in a specifically racialized modality—that of *denigration*, which, as Nicole R. Fleetwood reminds us, is linked etymologically to Latinate roots that entangle abjection with blackening (de-*nigra*-tion).[10] The rite marked a transition from the white world of the Global North into the darker, mysterious oceanic realm of the Anglophone empire by turning white sailors black.

Blackface soon reappeared on the *Lady Campbell* in theatrical guise. On February 17, 1825, sailors posted playbills advertising a shipboard performance of James Townley's *High Life below Stairs* (1759) at the "Theatre Royal Lady Campbell." Townley's farce centers on the bad behavior of servants toward a West Indian plantation owner. The play's servants adopt the titles of their masters and ladies, and they adorn themselves with the styles of the upper classes; in turn, they are mocked for aspiring above their station. After the play's shipboard performance on February 22, Ramsay recorded in his diary that the sailors in the audience "were highly amused," especially by Mr. Clayhills's rendition of Kingston, the comical Black servant character, noting that Clayhills "acted the drunken blackey very well."[11] Derived from British actor John Moody's imitation of West Indian patois, Kingston is the earliest known Black comic servant character in the Anglophone repertoire.[12] Through the blackface figure of Kingston, *High Life below Stairs* forged popular racial common sense by inscribing blackness within a vertical hierarchy wherein Black servants occupied the lowest and most abject position.

Performed in blackface throughout the transoceanic Anglophone world, Kingston was a floating signifier for both colonial racial subjection in Jamaica and racialized domestic servitude in English homes. The character of Kingston charts the translocation of the colonial plantation economy of West Indian chattel slavery to the domestic geography of the English country house and its vertical hierarchies of "high" and "low." Kingston's translocation traces an affective economy of race, in which colonial geographies and colonized persons were folded into the imaginary of Anglophone empire in the form of racialized characters. Occupying the lowest rank below the white gentry and the white servant class, the Black servant became legible as "uppity" insofar as he aspired to the "high life" above stairs beyond his station as the lowest of the below-stairs servants. Far from excluding Black people from Anglophone popular culture, *High Life below Stairs* insisted on the inclusion of racialized subjects within the intimate lifeworlds of empire so long as racialized laborers were put in their place. Aboard the *Lady Campbell*, itself organized around rigid shipboard racial hierarchies of labor between white sailors and non-white lascars, the white sailors' enjoyment of the comical "drunken blackey" marked the confluence of multiple streams of colonial common sense through the racializing performances of the Anglophone empire.

Before and after its staging aboard the *Lady Campbell*, Townley's *High Life below Stairs* circulated throughout the Anglophone empire wherein it established a transoceanic imaginary of blackness and disseminated classed and racialized structures of feeling and belief globally. Popular in London and on the British provincial theater circuit, *High Life below Stairs* received 146 productions in London by the end of 1776, and 106 additional productions at the Drury Lane, Haymarket, and Covent Garden theaters by 1800.[13] Townley's farce was also frequently produced in the British American colonies, as the farce was restaged at least eighty-one times throughout the British American colonies and the United States from 1767 to 1852.[14] Its earliest known staging in colonial America occurred on January 26, 1767, at the Southwark Theatre in Philadelphia courtesy of David Douglass and Lewis Hallam Jr.'s combined American Company, which made *High Life below Stairs* a central comic piece in their repertoire.[15] The farce was also staged throughout the British Empire. It was performed across South Asia, including its earliest known production in Kolkata on December 22, 1781, a second staging in Kolkata on April 4, 1786, and another at the governor's gardens in Chennai on August 11, 1788.[16] Across the Indian Ocean, it received its earliest known performance in southern Africa at the military garrison African Theatre in Cape Town on October 10, 1807.[17] Through these promiscuous circulations and frequent reproductions, *High Life below Stairs* emerged as a formative—and performative—scenario of blackface abjection, which embedded a deep strain of racializing humor within transoceanic Anglophone popular culture. Noting the enduring popularity of *High Life below Stairs* on New York's antebellum stage, theater historian George C. D. Odell quipped, "If I told the reader how many times this antiquated farce was performed during 1852–53, [they] would not believe me."[18]

Indeed, Townley's *High Life below Stairs* attained such extensive transatlantic popularity that "High Life below Stairs" became an Anglophone catchphrase that indexed intersecting anxieties about eighteenth-century formations of race, class, and sexuality as well as the threat of status inversions to turn the world upside down.[19] Townley's farce produced racial and class humor by upending the Anglophone social order through scenarios in which the servant class subverted expectations of their complacent obedience, only to restore comic harmony through a reification of classed and racialized social hierarchies. For instance, in a scene of physical humor, the West Indian plantation owner Lovel disguises himself as a servant to surreptitiously observe the behavior of his below-stairs staff. Lovel finds the white Coachman and the Black servant Kingston both drunk. In response, Lovel physically abuses them, slapping Coachman in the face and pulling Kingston by the nose.[20] Such physical comedy choreographs the might and right of the white gentleman Lovel as a representative restorer of Anglophone social hierarchies.

While these comic scenarios acted out a social formation clearly structured along class lines, racial hierarchies interlaced with class to animate the intimate sexual anxieties at the center of the domestic scene. Theatrical enactments of *High Life below Stairs* circulated an emergent trope of the Anglophone racial order in which, per Jan Nederveen Pieterse, "the little black servant serves as a code to denote illicit sexual relations."[21] Such anxieties structured the racial choreographies of intimate space such that Black maids were publicly separated from white gentlemen and Black male servants from both white ladies and white ladies' maids. To wit, *High Life below Stairs* introduces the Black female servant, Cloe, as the source of miscegenatory desire. Upon seeing Lovel still disguised as a white servant, she immediately begins to seduce him by proclaiming her affection and physically touching him on his chin.[22] The play tropes on stereotypes of Black women as sexually available and eager partners to white men while literally touching on miscegenatory anxieties by placing a Black woman and a white man in a theatrical scenario of sexualized contact. Despite this dalliance with interracial sexual contact, Townley restores the Anglophone racial order in an ensuing scene, wherein the white servant Philip happily proclaims, "The two Devils [Kingston and Cloe] dance together."[23] During the dance, "Kingston kisses Cloe *heartily*," prompting Sir Harry to proclaim, "See how the Devils kiss."[24] The servants dance together segregated by race in a comic restoration of the racial-sexual order. Within the empire, the concluding scene promises, everyone will play their part, stay in their place, and pair with racially appropriate sexual partners.

Despite the comic restoration of racial hierarchies in *High Life below Stairs*, Anglophone figurations of Black servants as potential sexual threats to the dominion of white men and to the virtue of white women reappeared throughout British imperial theatrical and popular culture. This trope was epitomized in Isaac Bickerstaffe and Charles Dibdin's exceedingly successful comic opera *The Padlock* (1768), which David Garrick staged a remarkable fifty-four times in its premiere 1768–1769 season at the Drury Lane and 369 times by 1800.[25] *The Padlock* quickly entered the transatlantic repertoire, receiving its first staging in New York on May 29, 1769, and in Philadelphia on November 16, 1769, in addition to at least eighty additional theatrical productions throughout the mainland British American colonies and the United States between 1769 and 1840—on average more than one production per year for over seventy years.[26] *The Padlock* also traveled throughout the British Empire, including its earliest known performance in Jamaica at Montego Bay on March 19, 1777, its first recorded staging in Kolkata on December 3, 1781, as well as its inaugural production in the Cape Colony of South Africa on May 27, 1815.[27] After its sensational debut at the Theatre Royal, Drury Lane in 1768, *The Padlock* transmitted the comic blackface character Mungo throughout the British Empire and the United States, where it became a common term for Black peoples of all statuses and ranks.[28] As Monica L. Miller observes, Dibdin's performance as Mungo had an "electrifying effect" on his audiences, and it popularized an early version of the "black dandy" character through the character's extravagant costuming and caricatured West Indian dialect.[29] Subsequent versions significantly expanded the comic opera's musical and dance interludes, which further highlighted the blackface figure's audience appeal through extended scenes of comic abjection.[30] White Anglophone audiences on either side of the Atlantic and in British colonies north and south of the equator became enamored of the capacious comic possibilities of blackness animated by what a 1773 commentator termed "the facetious distresses of that jetty varlet Mungo."[31]

Itself an oft-cited "origin" of blackface minstrelsy, the character of Mungo drew directly from the racial repertoires outlined in *High Life below Stairs*. Like Kingston, Mungo embodied tropes of Black drunkenness, impudence, and sexual promiscuity—often simultaneously, as in Mungo's inebriated attempt to seduce the white lady's maid Ursula.[32] Beyond these figural similarities with Kingston, Bickerstaffe and Dibdin's scripting of Mungo's blackface abjection relied on the putative firsthand knowledge of Black dialect provided by actor John Moody, who according to Dibdin "had been in the West-Indies, and knew, of course, the dialect of the negroes."[33] Yet, Dibdin's assertion that Moody presented quasi-ethnological knowledge of Caribbean articulations of Black speech omitted mention of Moody's remarkable theatrical success as the originator of the Kingston role in Townley's *High Life below Stairs*. Was it Moody's putative firsthand knowledge of "the dialect of the negroes" or his prior success in farcical blackface performances that authenticated Mungo as a representative Black figure on the Anglophone stage? It was likely a combination of both, as Moody necessarily performed his claim to ethnological knowledge onstage, braiding together his appeal to racial realism with his farcical embodiment of a comic blackface figure. Moody's travels to Jamaica were followed by those of American colonial actor Lewis Hallam Jr., who also imbued his "original" American colonial performances of Mungo with an aura of authenticity derived from his ostensible close study of Black captives in the Caribbean.[34] Kingston—as colonial site and blackface caricature—functioned as a durable sign of "authentic" Black abjection throughout the transatlantic British imperium, subtending the drunken servant characters in both *High Life below Stairs* and *The Padlock*. Such claims to authenticity framed the comic figuration of Black suffering and drunken Black lust for white women as manifestations of racial realism rather than as well-worn comic tropes drawn from literary, visual, and theatrical repertoires.

High Life below Stairs and *The Padlock* staged tropes of Black abjection that whorled throughout intertheatrical Anglophone circum-Atlantic culture. Blackface circulated well beyond the stage, animating a prolific cottage industry of blackface visual materials, songs, and scripts. Print imagery both informed and cited theatrical practice, which staged the blackface figures of eighteenth-century farces and comic operas in the visual languages of popular comic imagery. As David Dabydeen has aptly summarized, following the representational schemas laid out by William Hogarth, Anglophone visual artists and printmakers turned eighteenth-century London "*visually* black" insofar as it was "swamped" by comic prints of abject Black figures.[35] Though the prices of such prints ensured that they were sold primarily to the upper and upper-middle classes, the display windows of eighteenth- and early nineteenth-century print shops constituted "free galler[ies] for the poor."[36] At print shops, quasi-theatrical scenes of public spectatorship centered around "caricatures sold as single-sheet prints, hung on the walls of taverns and coffee houses, and displayed in the windows of urban print shops and thus available to viewing by a public that extended beyond a learned elite."[37] Such public scenes blurred the boundaries between theatrical enactments and print imagery, which were already cross-pollinated through copious citations, borrowings, and outright acts of plagiarism.

For instance, in a 1772 William Humphrey lithographic print, *High Life below Stairs, or Mungo, Addressing My Ladys Maid* (fig. 2), a Black servant embraces a white British maid, wrapping his arm around her chest as the pair gaze into each other's eyes. The print satirizes the primal scene of interracial amalgamation. Citing Hogarth's *Four Times of Day—Noon* (1738) and its figuration of a Black man fondling a white woman's breast on a public London street as a scene of "savagery," Humphrey's lithograph makes interracial sexual contact a domestic concern.[38] Framing the print, the title refers to the two comedic figurations of Black servitude in both *High Life below Stairs* and *The Padlock*. Anticipating Laurence Hutton's description of the act 2 plot of *The Padlock* in which "Mungo got drunk . . . and was very profane throughout," a moral is inscribed at the bottom of the image: "For Wine inspires us, and fires us with Courage, Love, and Joy, &c."[39] Humphrey's satirical image positions the two entwined servants not as devoted lovers who have transcended the bounds of race but rather as having jointly tumbled down into the abasement of drunken ardor "below stairs." Another Black servant sits nearby with a hunting horn pressed to his lips, comically poised to interrupt the seduction. The anticipated interruption promises the viewer that the scene of interracial desire will not be consummated. The scene will conclude as comedies do: with the social, sexual, and racial order restored. The humor circulated through this print reproduces a theatrical scene of domestic interracial sexual contact that haunts both *High Life below Stairs* and *The Padlock*, while framing the scene with distancing devices and commentary that emphasize the presumptive incongruity of interracial affection. As the titular inversions of *high* life *below* stairs suggest, these Black servant characters exercise a tightly circumscribed sexual agency, one bounded by the artist's insistence on the restoration of the racial order and the spectator's investments in viewing such interracial sexual scenarios as comic rather than tragic.[40]

Fig. 2. William Humphrey, *High Life below Stairs, or Mungo, Addressing my Ladys Maid* (1772). Courtesy of the Yale Center for British Art. https://collections.britishart.yale.edu/catalog/tms:22660.

In the wake of the circum-Atlantic popularity of the blackface inversions staged in *High Life below Stairs* and *The Padlock*, a transmedial proliferation of playscripts, imagery, songs, and performances circulated core scenarios of blackface abjection.[41] To this intertheatrical complex of visual and theatrical citation, Charles Dibdin offered a novel musical score. In his solo performances, Dibdin introduced several popular blackface comic songs. Well before Stephen C. Foster transformed the plantation South into a fantastical scene of romantic racialism, Dibdin scored blackness to the sound of the banjo. In "The Negro and His Banjer" (from *The Wags, or The Camp of Pleasure* [1790]), Dibdin sang in the voice of a complacent "Negro" on the plantation of a white ("buckra") enslaver.[42] In a similar vein, in his "Negro Duet" titled "The Sun Go Down" (from *The Round Robin* [1811]), Dibdin prefigured a core minstrel scenario of Black enjoyment in spite of the extremities of slave subjection, and introduced a carefree, singing-and-dancing blackface character named "uncle Tom":

> *1st Negro.* The sun go down, the world take breath,
> The lazy monkey rest him;
> Poor working neger tir'd to death,
> And so him dance to rest him;
> Lilly yam, and Lilly sing,—
> He frisk and know no sorrow,
> Wid banjer merry as one king,
> To drive away to-morrow.
> *Both.* Chingering! chingering! next world come.
> Overseer no jerk ye;
> Meet tipsy quashy uncle Tom,
> No more to workee workee.
> *2nd Negro.* To-morrow come, the sunshine shoot,
> Poor neger can't endure him,
> He blister all from head to foot,
> And so the cart-whip cure him.
> Night come again—he frisk, he prance,—
> What signify him fretting?
> The banjer sound, the neger dance,
> And pain him soon forgetting.
>
> *Both.* Chingering, chingering, &c.[43]

Here, Dibdin animated a core minstrel scenario of Black singing and dancing despite the ravages of enslavement. The song scripted a sonic metacommentary that promised the "forgetting" of slavery's brutalities by fashioning enslavement as a scene of transitory suffering culminating in minstrelesque enjoyment.

As further demonstrated in his "Negro Philosophy" (from *General Election* [1796]), Dibdin's blackface songs insisted on Black resignation to enduring the abuse of white enslavers:

> Chingaring, Chingaring, never mind,
> No use to fret about it;
> Buckra yam, yam, but negrokind
> Forced to go widout it:

Nothing to do but lie down flat,
While overseer he jerk ye;
No peace, no sleep, no yam, get fat,
And after worky, worky.[44]

In the ensuing stanza, the singer, Cudgo, narrates a scenario of the slave master raping Cudgo's wife, Quashy, that concludes, "Chingaring, chingaring, never mind, / What done can't be prevented. / Buckra, well a negrokind, / Wear horns and be contented." Neither Dibdin nor his blackface character Cudgo expresses any concern for Quashy: this narrated rape is framed as the "contented" cuckolding of Cudgo rather than as the traumatic sexual violation of an enslaved Black woman. As in his wider blackface oeuvre, Dibdin narrated scenes of Black subjection as comical anecdotes in which Black captives enjoy their individual and collective suffering with song and good humor.

The recurrence of such figurations across several songs traces Dibdin's instrumentalization of blackness, whereby Dibdin refuses to imagine the interiority of his enslaved Black figures. Instead, the chorus of "chingering" repeats a nonsense phrase of Black speech that doubles as an approximation of the sound of a banjo. Blurring the distinction between the articulation of the Black voice and that of an inanimate instrument, Dibdin sonically inscribed the instrumentalization of blackness. Like his figuration of Mungo, Dibdin's songs gave voice to the suffering of Black captives but only insofar as such pain was mediated as comic music, framed as humorous, temporal, evanescent, and "soon forgetting." Numerous subsequent comic songwriters and playwrights would remember and re-cite the comic potentiality of Black suffering as early blackface songs circulated throughout the eddies of the transoceanic Anglophone empire. For instance, Dibdin's "Negro Philosophy" was advertised for sale in Philadelphia in December 1797 and in New York in January 1798, and its earliest known public performance in New York occurred on August 16, 1806.[45] Circulated in print and restaged throughout the British American colonies, Dibdin's music laid the groundwork for the sonic repertoires of minstrelsy.

Meanwhile, theatrical scripts adapted tropes of complacent, carefree Black servitude into the Anglophone repertoire, as in Isaac Jackman's *The Divorce: A Farce* (1781), William Macready's *The Irishman in London, or The Happy African* (1793), Prince Hoare's *The Prize; or, 2, 3, 5, 8* (1793), and Frederick Reynolds's *Laugh When You Can* (1798). While these plays staged Black servants in ambivalent relation to abolitionism, they insisted on the servility and abasement of blackness in toto. This is to say that early Anglophone blackface did not fall neatly into a pro- and antislavery binary, but rather figured unfree Black characters within a proliferating array of antiblack articulations of Anglophone racial discourses. For instance, Jackman's *The Divorce: A Farce* (1781) premiered in London prior to the conclusion of the War for American Independence and prior to the coalescence of the British nationalist abolition movement. Jackman's farce articulates a markedly abject figuration of Black servitude in the caricatured figure of Sambo, who expresses ambitions for class ascendance ("Yes, Massa, I should like to be a Man of Fashion of all tings"), miscegenatory desires ("Yes, Massa—me want to marry a pretty white woman"), and their fantastical imbrication in his attempt to purchase a white wife for ten guineas.[46] In response to Sambo's attempts to enter the white world, the white lawyer Qui Tam instructs his white associate, Timothy, to restore racial order by returning Sambo to his "downstairs" position among the servants.[47] Potentially staged as a scene of slapstick violence with Sambo comically tumbling back below stairs, *The Divorce* scripted a recurrent scenario in which blackness was subjected to physical violence for white amusement. In a scene of "the disciplinary vengeance of farce," to borrow Hartman's phrase, the play returned the "uppity" Sambo below stairs, where the Anglophone imperial racial order insisted that he belonged.[48]

By contrast, Macready's *The Irishman in London; or, The Happy African* proscribes any physical antiblack violence, instead sublimating antiblackness into epistemic violence wherein its central Black character elects to remain in perpetual servitude. Ostensibly abolitionist in orientation, Macready's comedy features a scene-stealing, dialect-speaking Black maidservant, Cubba, who exemplifies the ambiguous ontological status of Black servants within abolitionist theater. Cubba professes devotion to her white mistress, attesting, "Missa be every ting to poor Cubba."[49] Moreover, Cubba braids together two central tropes of eighteenth-century British abolitionism. First, she claims royal African parentage to assert her nobility and her role as a model, servile Black subject. Second, she disparages acts of Black resistance as a futile activity justly punished by "whip and chain," contrasting insurrectionary acts with her complacent contentedness: "Why every body no be happy like me?"[50] These discursive inscriptions of nominally free Black subjects as servile and docile resonated with white Anglophone audiences and were taken up in subsequent productions.

For example, Hoare's *The Prize* introduces the Black servant figure Juba, who insists on working for his master, Hartwell, for "no money" due to his master's impoverishment.[51] Emphasizing his sentimental investment in his master, Juba sings a song of his undying fidelity, "Poor Black Boy":

> You good to me, dat keepy here;
> No, Massa! dat you never fear;
> Long time destroy:
> You know death kill, but leave one part,
> He never kill de loving heart
> Of poor black boy![52]

Ensuring that the audience understood the sentimentality of the scene, Hartwell responds, "This kind creature's gratitude for the freedom I procured for him is without bounds."[53] Far from celebrating Black freedom, the play instead revels in the restoration of the imperial racial order: freed from slavery in a fantastic scenario of white benevolence, Juba voluntarily commits his future labor to Hartwell for free. Reynolds's *Laugh When You Can* repeats this figuration with its character of Sambo—an emancipated Black servant who "feels [he] couldn't exist without" his master Delville.[54] In a scene redolent with the ontological confusion endemic to abolitionist fantasies of emancipation, Sambo asserts that he is still Delville's "slave," prompting the ensuing exchange:

> DELVILLE: No—not my slave—I gave you liberty.
> SAMBO: You did, sir; and that made me your slave.—Gratitude has bound me faster to you than all the chains of Africa![55]

These several plays retrace a prevalent trope of British abolitionism that performs what David Brion Davis terms "a leap of psychological imperialism . . . by picturing emancipation as a conversion to voluntary servitude."[56] In these scenarios of emancipation as enduring subjection, abolition literarily reproduces slavery by another name. Nevertheless, enslavement continually irrupts throughout these scenes, voiced by Black servants who choose to remain "slaves" to white masters.

Given their articulations of emancipation as perpetual subjection, it is unsurprising that these plays and their intertheatrical media (songs, prints, etc.) were as popular on the early US American stage as they were in London. *The Prize* was performed repeatedly in New York and throughout the country, including stagings in southern frontier theaters in Mississippi (1814) and Kentucky (1811 and 1815).[57] Meanwhile, the song "Poor Black Boy" was a favorite of the early US American stage as evidenced by five printings between 1794 and 1796.[58] Similarly, *The Irishman in London* and *Laugh When You Can* were two of the most popular plays on the antebellum US American stage, receiving over one hundred productions each in the period from 1751 to 1843.[59] None were as impactful on the formations of early blackface as Jackman's *The Divorce*, which was staged by Lewis Hallam Jr.'s itinerant company in Charleston (1787), New York (1791), Dumfries, Virginia (1796), and Boston (1797).[60]

The Divorce introduced Sambo to transoceanic Anglophone racial discourse, where the name came to symbolize the ambivalent status of the carefree, comic, singing-and-dancing Black servant. For instance, the early US American play *Triumphs of Love* (1795) by John Murdock featured a freed Black man named Sambo who, in Heather Nathans's apt phrasing, "celebrates his liberty by getting drunk."[61] *The Triumphs of Love*, like the emergent abolitionist theater in Britain, staged white US American fears of Black freedom, as in the white character George's expectation that "our friend Sambo will make a bad use of his liberty."[62] Sambo soon fulfills this prediction in his drunken and dissolute embodiment of freedom, which confirmed for white US Americans that free Black people would require education to attain equality. Like Kingston in *High Life below Stairs* and Mungo in *The Padlock*, Murdock's Sambo enacts Black liberty not as sober rationality but rather as intoxicated libertinism. Like the Black servant characters in contemporaneous British-authored plays, Sambo embodies Black emancipation as enduring subjection. This is to say, Sambo's freedom appears as an external gift rather than an inherent right—a property he is unable to properly possess without continued tutelage from his erstwhile masters.

Such early Anglophone blackface characters became entangled with the sonic figuration of blackness as a nonsensical banjo refrain that scripted blackness as a state of perpetual enjoyment. For instance, in Lazarus Beach's *Jonathan Postfree; or, The Honest Yankee* (1807), the Black servant Cesar echoes "Poor Black Boy" and Dibdin's blackface songs:

> O sing chink-a-chink chink-a-chink;
> O sing chink-a-chink cheery;
> Let the poor negro be joy, be dance,
> And never poor negro be weary.[63]

Re-citing Dibdin's "chingering" choruses, such US American songs furnished forth a transoceanic repertoire of Black embodiments, speech, and sonics. Moreover, the intertheatrical citations of Black contentment with slavery and servitude provided the Anglophone empire with a web of racial discourses that delimited the imagined possibilities of Black freedom across the circum-Atlantic.

This intertheatrical repertoire of transoceanic blackface demonstrates that the ruses of emancipation and abolition were not peculiar racial formations within a US American national context but rather were deeply embedded in the popular culture of the Anglophone empire. As Robert Nowatzki observes, "Blackface was not an American import to Britain, but a trope that in its repeated crossings of the ocean formed the Blackface Atlantic."[64] While US American playwrights began staging variations within this repertoire in the late eighteenth century, they drew from well-rehearsed precedents that circulated globally. Moreover, the transmedial relays of intertheatrical Anglophone materials supplied early US American playwrights with alternative strains of cultural production. Specifically, during the colonial and early national period, US American dramatic writers had limited opportunities to stage plays or to elaborate embodied variations on Anglophone blackface. Instead, they authored closet dramas, paratheatrical writings, comic almanacs, and proliferating visual materials through which they forged a paratheatrical network of what I term *scriptive blackface*.

Scriptive Blackface

One of the most fecund strains of early blackface aggregated offstage in a transmedial complex of print and performance cultures. This complex of scriptive blackface inscribed popular impressions of blackness through discursive tropes of racialized speech and character that prompted racial imaginations, transmitted racial beliefs, and provided scripts for private and public theatricals. In parallel to the spectacular embodiments of Anglophone theatrical blackface, manifold artifacts of scriptive blackface circulated early blackface burlesque not as public transcripts of legitimate performance but rather as what James C. Scott calls "hidden transcript[s] of the powerful."[65] Recent studies have retraced the transatlantic circulations of early nineteenth-century blackface while overlooking the capacious archives of eighteenth-century blackface print and performance cultures in large part because these transcripts have remained concealed by simplified schemas of national theatrical development and celebratory narratives of national and transnational abolitionist projects. The hidden transcripts of scriptive blackface reveal the inadequacy of such schematic frames to histories of blackface performance, prompting us instead to attend to the transoceanic citational networks of eighteenth-century minstrelsy and the relays of performance scenarios between private and public spheres.

A critical node in the networks of eighteenth-century scriptive blackface is the 1767 play *The Disappointment*, written under the pseudonym of Andrew Barton.[66] Though it was intended for performance at Philadelphia's Southwark Theatre by Douglass and Hallam's American Company, the play was deemed "unfit for the Stage"—too scandalous for public performance—because it "contain[ed] personal reflections" of actual Philadelphians and commentary on contemporary events.[67] Nevertheless, the play was not considered unfit for publication. Scripts of the unperformed play were advertised for purchase in the *Pennsylvania Chronicle* and remained in circulation for decades following its abortive premiere.[68] Thus *The Disappointment* was published contemporaneously with the earliest known American colonial "Negro dance in character" by "Mr. Tea" in New York in April 1767 and circulated in print throughout the British North American colonies two years prior to the colonial premiere of *The Padlock* and Lewis Hallam Jr.'s famous enactment of the blackface servant role of Mungo.[69] *The Disappointment* therefore traces an alternative performance genealogy mediated not only by embodied enactments but also by the circulating corpus of scriptive blackface.

The lack of any public, embodied performance of *The Disappointment* or of any documentation thereof has presented a historiographical challenge to analyses of the play, especially regarding the racial character of Raccoon. In the playscript for *The Disappointment*, Raccoon is not explicitly racialized but instead receives the sole descriptor of "an old debauchee."[70] As the play was not staged, there is no performance evidence or critical commentary indicating that the role was intended to be acted in blackface. Theater historian Hugh F. Rankin made an early claim that Raccoon's "thick dialect" fashioned a blackface prototype for the "stock minstrel formula" of the nineteenth-century stage, noting that the character also exhibited stereotypical blackface behaviors, including "vanity, greed, cowardice, and a fear of spirits and ghosts."[71] David Mays, Carolyn Rabson, and William Torbert Leonard have since contested Rankin's interpretation of Raccoon's blackness, asserting that he was intended to be an ethnic caricature either of a Frenchman or of Swedish or Pennsylvania Dutch members of the colonial militia.[72] Yet, these critics fail to address Raccoon's inscription within common blackface tropes, motifs, and discursive figurations, instead delimiting their considerations of Raccoon's blackness with reference to dialect and skin color. Perhaps most importantly, none of the extant accounts of *The Disappointment* discuss Raccoon's articulation of protominstrel discourses of Black Christianity, which situate the play in an emerging network of scriptive blackface.

Raccoon positions himself within extant discourses on blackness by articulating a dense biblical allusion. Threading together two emergent motifs on Black Christianity, Raccoon promises to lavish his paramour, the white prostitute Moll Placket, by "dress[ing] her off as fine as de Queen of Sheba, when she come to see broder Solomon."[73] As early as the twelfth century, Christian iconography figured the Queen of Sheba as an unambiguously Black Ethiopian.[74] By promising to spend his newfound wealth in dressing Moll "as fine as de Queen of Sheba," Raccoon tropes on an implicit joke that his affective and economic investment in her vestments would not make her "fine" but would rather denigrate her—presumably remaking her racial status to accord with his own. Moreover, Raccoon's invocation of "broder Solomon" suggests an early inscription of one of the most persistent tropes of scriptive blackface: the figuration of white, Christian brotherhood as aurally and visually different from Black "broder"-hood. The appellation of "broder Solomon"—rather than *King* Solomon—indexes the biblical Solomon's African ancestry and his concomitant eighteenth-century racialization as Black. Moreover, the mispronunciation of "brother" displaces Solomon from the status of biblical royalty to a figure whose entrée into white Christian brotherhood remained in doubt. Was Solomon a true *brother*, or a Black "broder" who could not articulate his place within the human family? These parodic citations of Black Christianity underscore the racial travesty implicit in Raccoon's aspiration to wealth, status, and marriage to a white woman. Indeed, the play's tropes of racial mockery are condensed in Raccoon's expectant claim that a newfound fortune "will make [him] cut de proper figure in life, and appear in the world wid the proper impo'tance."[75] The loaded malapropism (avant la lettre) of "impo'tance" prefigured countless minstrel jokes that would invert socially ambitious and sexually desirous Black men into impotent fools, while situating the play's titular disappointment on Raccoon's betrayal by his would-be white wife and his failure to attain a fortune due to his excessive credulity.[76] Taken together with a white character's reference to Raccoon's "black mout' [mouth]," it is plausible that Raccoon was scripted as—or, at the very least, was understood by readers to be—a parody of a presumptuously aspirational Black male figure who needed to be comically restored to his properly impotent place.[77]

Though this assemblage of evidence indicates the plausibility of Raccoon's blackness, it cannot definitively establish Raccoon's racial identity. Nevertheless, this evidence presented eighteenth-century readers of the closet drama with a series of textual clues through which they interpreted the character and imagined his race. As the play was not performed by embodied, costumed actors, readers necessarily relied on their interpretive capacities to envisage the play's characters. At least some of these readers imagined Raccoon to be not only an "old debauchee" but also racially Black. In other words, despite never being staged, and even if it did not intentionally script Raccoon as a blackface figure, *The Disappointment* furnished forth a scriptive model for several other inscriptions of blackface character. Robert Munford's closet drama *The Candidates* (1770; published 1798) includes a comic Black servant character, Ralpho, who shares Raccoon's desire to "cut de proper figure in life." Ralpho declares in another malapropic articulation of broken speech, "When I'm dressed out like a gentleman, the girls, I'm a thinking, will find me desistible."[78] Ralpho was succeeded by the anonymous closet drama *The Trial of Atticus, before Justice Beau, for a Rape* (1771), which includes the brief appearance of the comic dialect-speaking blackface figure Caesar, whom the judge dismisses as a "black impudent villain."[79] Samuel Low's closet drama *The Politician Out-Witted* (1788) similarly features the dialect-speaking Black character Cuffy, who would later reappear to voice one of the earliest examples of a blackface stump speech in Hugh Henry Brackenridge's early US American novel, *Modern Chivalry* (1792).[80] The anonymous closet drama *Occurrences of the Times* (the script of which was advertised for sale in Boston, 1789) features yet another misspeaking Black "Debauchee," whom a white female character calls a "black son of satan."[81] With its explicit citation of *The Disappointment*'s "old debauchee," *Occurrences of the Times* traces the enduring circulation of scriptive blackface over thirty years, from prerevolutionary Philadelphia to Boston following the election of President George Washington.[82]

Despite (or because of) its status as an unintentional closet drama, *The Disappointment* prompts consideration of how racial performativity works not only through theatrical enactments of racial impersonation but also through the opaque, hidden performance of reading racial scripts. As Catherine Burroughs notes, closet drama "does not so much fly in the face of theatricality as encourage[] alternative ways of thinking about the embodied stage and the staging of the body."[83] These early articulations of scriptive blackface signal not a conservative retreat from theatrical publicity but rather a thriving oral performance culture mediated by print—a domestic network of readers who spoke scandalous Black speech in private theatricals.[84] Indeed, in May 1767, William Paterson, a student at the College of New Jersey, wrote a letter about "hearing [*The Disappointment*] read" at a private college and asked a Philadelphian friend for more information about the play.[85] In response, Paterson's friend, John MacPherson Jr., responded that *The Disappointment* "was very well rec'd [received] by the people here, who found no fault in it."[86] Similarly, in his 1811 memoir, Alexander Graydon referred to the play as "a very popular drama, though never brought to the stage."[87] Paterson's and MacPherson's letters and Graydon's memoir indicate a seeming paradox: *The Disappointment* was a *popular* colonial American play that never received a full public performance yet nevertheless furnished forth multiple private performances of scriptive blackface. These archival documents demonstrate that theatrical popularity was not necessarily indexed to public theatrical productions but rather to the circulation and reading of theatrical print materials. They thereby trace the ubiquitous hidden transcripts that extended the performance arena of blackface well beyond the public sphere through countless engagements with racial closet dramas.

This paratheatrical performance genealogy cannot offer a positivist accounting of early blackface performances. Instead, it maps how the articulation of scripted racialized speech imbricated with tropes and scriptive references to blackness to prompt readers' interpretations and private, amateur performances of "Black" speech. In the performance economies of scriptive blackface, semipublic reading engaged both the archive and the repertoire as it entailed both textual interpretation and performative articulation in speech.[88] Scriptive blackface manifests the textual trace of an intertheatrical mode of performance—a white, imperial Anglophone orature. Drawing from Pio Zirimu, Austin Bukenya, and Mĩcere Gĩthae Mũgo, Ngũgĩ wa Thiong'o theorizes "orature" as a transmedial mode of performance culture that "transcends the narrow binaries of the written and the oral that condition so much of anthropological and literary thought today. It suggests a transcendence over both the purely oral, the purely literary, and the purely performed."[89] As generically impure artifacts of Anglophone imperial orature, items of scriptive blackface circulated both as textual matter and as promptbooks for private and semipublic enactments.

Scriptive blackface performatively articulated the oral and aural texture of race in the circum-Atlantic imperium, forging what Houston A. Baker Jr. defines as a "mis-hearing" of blackness that framed Black subjects as "*mis-speakers* bereft of humanity."[90] Amid a period of theatrical conservativism in the late-colonial and early US American national period, these playscripts mediated practices of imagining, articulating, and hearing blackface speech in everyday eighteenth-century Anglophone popular culture. Scriptive blackface constituted what Mĩcere terms "reactionary orature," a form of popular performance culture mobilized to reify the racial common sense of the Anglophone empire.[91] Across its broad circulations, scriptive blackface prompted imperial performances that laid the groundwork for the popular practice of blackface minstrelsy as it is more commonly understood in the early nineteenth century. Within the context of Puritanical antitheatrical prejudice that delimited popular theatrical practice in the mainland British American colonies, Jeffrey H. Richards asserts that "the closet and satiric dramatists of the eighteenth century paved the way for those who would have real theaters to write for."[92] As public colonial American theater culture developed, scriptive blackface provided Anglophone playwrights, amateur performers, songwriters, journalists, and other writers and artists with an archived repertoire from which to draw novel articulations of blackface speech.

One such early US American dramatist was John Murdock, whose theatrical output exemplified the transmediality of Anglophone imperial orature. As we have seen, Murdock drew from colonial and early US American articulations of scriptive blackface to adapt the British figure Sambo to the Philadelphia stage in *Triumphs of Love*. Murdock's sequel to this play, *The Politicians; or, A State of Things* (1798), attempted to capitalize on the popularity of Sambo. However, *The Politicians* unwittingly repeated a paratheatrical scenario inaugurated by *The Disappointment* when the Chestnut Street Theatre refused to stage *The Politicians* due to its commentary on contemporary political controversies.[93] As an unintended racial closet drama, *The Politicians* reintroduced Sambo as an articulator of scriptive blackface. Readers encountered—and likely voiced—Sambo alongside three new Black servant characters: Pompey, Caesar, and Cato. In one of the play's central comic scenes, the four blackface figures engage in a debate on US American politics in the aftermath of Jay's Treaty, with each Black servant imitating the respective political positions of their prominent, white "massas." The argument culminates in Cato's advice to his fellow Black citizens that they avoid politics altogether:

> neber quarrel bout politic, it bring much trouble, what you do wid such tings? it seem to me, Negro head got quite wrong now-a-day,

> you must all be gemmem, must dress in fashion, talk high slow, must have cue and-wool powder, dat foolish, only make your face look more black, howeber, let me advise you no quarrel bout politic.[94]

As Alan W. C. Green observes, this scene animated a scenario in which "none of [the Black servant characters] knows anything more than the opinions of their respective masters, reflecting the widely-held belief that Negroes were purely imitative and had no genuine critical ability."[95] When staged in private readings, *The Politicians* scripted vertiginous voicings and mishearings of Black speech, with white readers acting out imagined Black impersonations of upper-class white discourse.

Though it is difficult to trace the circulations of a theatrical corpus that was intentionally hidden from public view, faint echoes of these private theatricals offer suggestive traces of likely transmissions. For instance, on August 3, 1821, New York sheriff, playwright, and journalist Mordecai M. Noah published in the *National Advocate* a description of Black social gatherings at William A. Brown's African Grove ice cream garden. This passage bears striking similarities to Murdock's *The Politicians*. As part of his broader denigration of Brown's theatrical and political endeavors and of free Black life in New York writ large, Noah's account concludes that Black Americans were uninterested in the political machinations that subtended their freedom. According to Noah, they "care[d] for no political rights; happy in being permitted to dress fashionable, walk the streets, visit African Grove, and talk scandal."[96] Framing Black Americans as inherently imitative of upper-class white people, his account describes a scene of four "black dandies and dandizettes" conversing in their box in the theater audience. With their conversation touching on contemporary political events in the Mediterranean as well as national electoral politics, Noah scripts a burlesque scenario in which free Black Americans "run the rounds of fashion; ape their masters and mistresses in every thing; talk of projected matches; reherse [*sic*] the news of the kitchen, and the follies of the day."[97] As Elizabeth Maddock Dillon observes, this piece of "journalism" exemplifies how Noah deployed scriptive blackface "to de-authorize blacks as eligible for full political and cultural citizenship."[98] Noah's "journalistic" scriptive blackface was effective white supremacist propaganda. It galvanized the popular denigration of Black theatrical and political projects and entrained white audiences to mishear Black speech, especially the speech voiced by Black actors at Brown's theaters. For this reason, Noah's inscriptions of Black stereotype in print culture have been framed as foundational to the emergence of blackface minstrelsy—most notably, Samuel A. Hay hails Noah as the "father of blackface minstrelsy."[99]

Yet, as we have seen, Noah was hardly the first practitioner of scriptive blackface. Rather, he drew from multiple hidden transcripts to fashion his burlesque of Black Americans as inarticulate, unfashionable, and imitative figures of scorn. As a journalist, Noah was well familiar with the articulations of scriptive blackface that were "ubiquitous in the almanacs and the newspapers of the 1790s."[100] Moreover, as a playwright, Noah may have possessed a copy of Murdock's *The Politicians* or, at the very least, committed its comic scenario of Sambo, Caesar, Cato, and Pompey's political debate to memory. Murdock's script offered Noah a model for how to script Black speech as an inherently failed imitation of white speech—an inarticulate articulation that promulgated the argument that free Blacks were not fit for full citizenship insofar as they could not participate properly in political discourse. Thus, Noah's scene of four Black "dandies and dandizettes" at the African Grove was not so much a faithful account of Black life in New York as it was a paratheatrical staging of abject blackness—one designed to animate popular anxieties about Black freedom and political agency during a period of emancipation. Far from inventing blackface minstrelsy in 1820s New York, Noah's account of the African Grove drew from a well-established discursive practice and an extant theatrical script of racial closet drama to animate a novel comic scene of Black abjection. In other words, Noah's journalistic minstrelsy was one of many eddies in the stream of scriptive blackface. Indeed, Noah's publications circulated throughout the circum-Atlantic world contemporaneous with William Moncrieff's *Tom and Jerry; or, Life in London* (1821) and the popular visual impressions of Black life fashioned by George Cruikshank, David Claypoole Johnston, and Edward Williams Clay, numerous anonymously fashioned "Bobalition" broadsides, and countless comic annuals that incessantly reproduced images and jokes on the theme of antiblackness.

Figural Economies of Blackface

Eighteenth-century British imperial visual artists drew from and contributed to theatrical figurations of blackness. The intertheatrical relays between visual print culture and the theatrical stage scripted emergent figural economies of blackface.[101] From Hogarth's Black figures to satirical prints troping on *High Life below Stairs*, eighteenth-century Anglophone visual culture was suffused with images and scriptive imaginings of Black peoples. Though the British quickly reimagined their national racial politics as benevolently abolitionist following the 1807 abolition of the slave trade, the anxieties animated by the specter of Black freedom lingered. British subjects began to imagine themselves as racially beneficent (especially when measured against the slaveholding United States), despite the British Empire's enduring investments in colonial slavery and in the racial supremacy of white Anglophone subjects. Notwithstanding ostensible national differences on the subject of racial politics, the racial imaginaries of the British Empire and the nascent United States remained densely intertwined through the constant circulation of visual and scriptive blackface.

Figurations of Black abjection carried over from eighteenth-century British culture into postrevolutionary US American visual culture. Mediating the Anglophone empire's uneasy racial affect in the protracted period of emancipation, popular imagery insistently figured Black subjects as a constant, anxiety-inducing presence in the imperial racial order. Anglophone visual culture mediated and defused such anxieties by circulating popular impressions of Black abjection. These antiblack tropes circulated comic renderings of Black subjects that subjected Black figures to racist scorn. In the United States, this phenomenon was most evident in "Bobalition" broadsides, an array of cheap print images that satirized Black political mobilizations and agitations such as Emancipation Day parades. In these parades, Black Americans took public space as the grounds for performative embodiments and enunciations of Black freedom and equality.[102] In response, white subjects staged public actions and voiced performative speech acts that attempted to displace Black people from the public commons. At times, such violent white acts were literal, physical confrontations: theater manager Sol Smith recounted fondly his memories of joining with other "Republican boys" in Boston to "chase all the niggers off the Common, as was usually done on occasions of gatherings."[103] Smith's violent confrontations with nominally free Black citizens typify the social function of charivari and racial riots in the antebellum period: to assert the public as a strictly white domain and to deny Black claims to freedom and equality.[104] Through such contestations of public space, free Black people claimed their rights to civic belonging and equality where they were met by violent counterclaims to enforce the imperial whiteness of the public "Common[s]."[105]

Physical confrontations and violence between white citizen-subjects and free Black people were novel racial enactments that arose at the historical conjuncture of Black emancipation in the US American North. In the eighteenth century, prior to emancipation, Black captives throughout the US North annually staged Negro Election Days and Pinkster celebrations as ephemeral, carnivalesque inversions of the prevailing racial order that, paradoxically, were integral to the maintenance of the northern system of slavery.[106] By contrast, after the passage of gradual emancipation acts across northern states that promised Black subjects the possibilities of freedom, equality, and citizenship, white US Americans mobilized to enforce postemancipation racial orders that increasingly delimited public enactments of Black freedom and performative assertions of Black equality. Emancipation confronted white subjects with what they found to be an uncomfortable and threatening reality: Black people could—and did—claim equal status and rights previously enshrined as white properties. When Black people mobilized to celebrate abolition, northern whites drew from the repertoires of scriptive blackface to mock articulations of Black freedom in cheaply printed "Bobalition" broadsides.

As the term "Bobalition" indexes and articulates, the broadsides circulated the core tropes of scriptive blackface—namely, the mishearing of Black speech. Following the precedents of Raccoon's "impo'tance" (in *The Disappointment*) and Ralpho's "desistible" disposition (in *The Candidates*), the Bobalition broadsides staged Black claims to importance, desirability, and political freedom as abject failures. In the words of Jean Baker, the Bobalition broadsides figured processions asserting Black political agency instead as evidence of "a feckless black population unable to pronounce even the words of freedom."[107] In keeping with previous articulations of scriptive blackface, the Bobalition broadsides were visual materials designed to be read aloud.[108] The broadsides were complex texts that included multiple modes of discursive impressions of blackness, encompassing crude wood-block images of Black figures, mock toasts articulated in broken English, and protominstrel songs in the form of parodic love ballads. While the images staged theatrical scenes of Black "freedom"—either as ostensibly comical parade scenes or as stereotypical impressions of Black freedom as drunken dissolution—the print material offered white readers scripts to be read or sung aloud. For instance, the 1827 broadside "GRAND JUBELUM!!! Order 12f Annebersary ob Affricum BOBALITION" includes two protominstrel songs in the right-hand column.[109] The first, a mock love ballad to "Phillesee Queen," bears striking similarities to later popular blackface ballads such as "Lucy Long." The second is a parody of abolitionist songs recounting Black enslavement akin to *The Prize*'s "Poor Black Boy." Bobalition broadsides furnished white readers in private homes and public houses with theatrical scripts for both comic and mock-sentimental modes of blackface minstrelsy. Such readers frequently became performers, articulating scriptive blackface as blackface speech and song.

Through such private and semipublic performances, the Bobalition broadsides impressed performers and auditors alike with a synesthetic sense of Black abjection. Structured as mock oratory, the broadsides usually took epistolary form addressed to a Black recipient identified as "broder," "sisser," or a similar mocking honorific. Bobalition broadsides responded to the rhetorical questions inscribed in abolitionist popular culture—"Am I Not a Man and a Brother?" and "Am I Not a Woman and a Sister?"—with resounding negations insofar as the titles "broder" and "sisser" articulate blackness as sonically beyond the realm of the human family. According to this racial grammar, Black people could not claim their place as brethren because they were instead figured as "bredren." By terming this mode of address a "racial grammar," I am interpreting

Bobalition broadsides within what Hortense Spillers calls "a class of symbolic paradigms that 1) inscribe 'ethnicity' as a scene of negation and 2) confirm the human body as a metonymic figure for an entire repertoire of human and social arrangements."[110] As sonic scenes of negation, the Bobalition broadsides troped on theatrical and scriptive scenarios that negated Black freedom, entrenching an aural repertoire of racial abjection in which liberation, equality, and humanity ("brotherhood") resounded as exclusively white properties.

Like the racial closet dramas on which they drew, the broadsides staged these scenes of negation through a double performative. As texts, they iterated racial constructs, repeating and circulating discourses that accreted into a common-sense impression of blackness as the negative imagination and sounding of whiteness. As scripts, they invited readers to enunciate and enact such linguistic and visual scenarios. Whereas racial closet dramas and theatrical blackface embodiments on the Anglophone stage figured Black freedom as an ambivalent discourse, Douglas A. Jones notes that the Bobalition broadsides advanced a singular and determinate racial politics that was "emphatically oppositional" to Black freedom.[111] No longer would scriptive blackface circulate absurd scenarios in which nominally free Black figures volunteer to remain "slaves" to their erstwhile masters. Instead, Bobalition broadsides figured Black claims to freedom and equality as ontological impossibilities. White readers embodied their positive freedom and their racial brotherhood in contradistinction to what Saidiya Hartman terms the "travestied liberation" of their avowedly unequal and insistently unfree Black "bredren."[112]

Though they were published primarily in Boston, the Bobalition broadsides circulated widely, reanimating scriptive enactments of Black abjection on both sides of the Atlantic. Quickly reproduced in comic periodicals and plagiarized in the popular press, the broadsides transmitted their racial grammars to other northern cities, as well as to southern US American and transatlantic markets where they animated anxieties about the specter of Black freedom. For instance, as early as 1819, the *Country Almanack, for 1820—Calculated for North and South Carolina* published a series of Bobalition toasts "Drank, in Commemoration of the Abolition of Slavery, by the African Society" in typical scriptive blackface that bore strong resemblance to an 1819 Bobalition broadside from Boston.[113] Though similar in form, the *Almanack*'s toasts were not copied directly from the 1819 Boston Bobalition broadside. Instead, they either were copies from an earlier, now-lost broadside or were novel elaborations on the 1819 broadside's model. Regardless of whether the Carolinian Bobalition toasts were originals, adaptations, or outright copies, they demonstrated the cross-regional investments in scriptive forms of Black abjection at the advent of early blackface minstrelsy as well as the ease with which such material traveled.

The scriptive blackface of Bobalition circulated broadly and influenced popular journalism. In 1823, Mordecai Noah's *National Advocate* published a mock advertisement for a "GRAND CONCERT OF DE BOB-LINK SOCIETY":

> De public is spectfully formed dat a *new* gumpany of *Africans* habe commenced *noying* de *pop-lace* at de above place. De *ladies* and *gemmen* of dis *korps* are ferior to *none* in point of *low langage*, and de *vulgar talons* of some of the latter are *first rate*.[114]

Noah's mock advertisement relied on his readers' familiarity with the Bobalition broadsides, using them as a discursive reference for yet another racist parody of the theatrical projects of William A. Brown. In making this connection between Black Emancipation Day parades and Black theatricality, Noah linked Brown's attempts to forge a Black theatrical public with broader Black political advocacy, thereby revealing anxieties about the political potential of Black theater. Like the Bobalition broadsides, the *National Advocate* scripted a mishearing of Black claims to humanity ("*gemmen*"). However, Noah situated his parody not along a Boston parade route but instead in the public sphere of New York's Five Points district at "*Cross and Orange streets*," which the author alleges was infamous for scenes of Black dissolution—"riots, dram drinking, and an assemblage of blacks, who herd in large squads, 'making night hideous' by their quarrelling and intemperance."[115] In this riotous and "hideous" scene, Noah translated the broadsides' visual impressions of Black liberty qua libertinism into a theatrical scenario that imagines Black freedom as a threat to the social order. Moreover, the *National Advocate*'s mock playbill spelled out Noah's antiabolitionist stance, suggesting that "[o]ur federal president makers, who are for liberating the slaves of the south, had better pay a visit to these haunts of freemen" so that the Federalists might reconsider their abolitionism. Through his translation of the broadsides' racial grammar to newspaper journalism, Noah amplified the sonic potential of scriptive blackface, playing a leading role in the formation of a print-based public sphere around the figural body of Black abjection.

One avid reader of Noah's publications was British theatrical impresario and comic actor Charles Mathews, whose *Trip to America* (1824) drew from Noah's scriptive blackface and Bobalition broadsides. Robert C. Toll famously cited Mathews as "the first certain example of a white man borrowing Negro material for a blackfaced act."[116] Following Samuel Hay, several scholars have traced how Noah's scriptive blackface functioned as source material for Mathews's mockery of Black actor James Hewlett in *A Trip to America* (1824).[117] Most centrally, Mathews's infamous characterization of a "Negro Tragedian" derived from Noah's racist accounts of Brown's theater rather than from Mathews's own amateur performance ethnography.[118] In addition to cribbing from Noah's journalism, Mathews transcribed a mock Black love ballad, "Love is like de pepper-corn," from an 1822 Bobalition broadside.[119] Indeed, Mathews likely encountered both Noah's journalism and Bobalition broadsides prior to his famous "trip to America" via print reproductions, such as the transcriptions of Noah's account of the African Theatre published in the *London Literary Gazette* or in British traveler William Faux's account of his 1819–1823 trip to America in which he described a firsthand encounter with Bobalition.[120] In his entry for February 4, 1819, Faux wrote,

> At a recent anniversary in Boston of Free Blacks, met to celebrate the abolition, or as they term it the *Boblition* [*sic*] of the slave-trade; the chairman rose after dinner, and said, "Gemmen, I be Massa Peter Guss, and give you this toast, That President Madison be no more like General Washington than puté finger in the fire, and haul it out again!" great applause. And another toast was, "Mr. Wilberforce be the blacky-man's friend, and may he never want polish to his boots."[121]

Faux does not quote from any extant broadside from 1819 but instead adapts the emergent US American racial grammar of scriptive blackface to a British antiabolitionist readership, invoking not only the standard mocking references to US American presidents but also to leading British abolitionist William Wilberforce. The similarity between Faux's and Mathews's transcriptions of Bobalition to British contexts was apparent enough to contemporary readers that *Blackwood's Edinburgh Magazine* compared Mathews's *Trip to America* unfavorably to Faux's item of scriptive blackface.[122] The broad circulation of scriptive blackface—and not any primal scene of Mathews's contact with and appropriation of Black performance material—was central to the formation of circum-Atlantic repertoires of racialized performance.

Dethroning Noah and Mathews as founding fathers of blackface invites a reappraisal of British imperial racial formations in the interval between the 1807 abolition of the slave trade and the 1833 Emancipation Act. Recent studies of British blackface emphasize the national differences between British and US American perspectives on slavery, interpreting Mathews's personal politics through the lens of national identity and figuring him as more invested in the comic potential to be mined from (British) class distinctions than from (US American) racial hierarchies.[123] These interpretations posit class and race as distinct and separable, notwithstanding that eighteenth-century theatrical and visual culture had already densely entangled class hierarchies with Anglophone racial orders. The "low" of the below stairs and of urban slums were symbolized by their proximity to and intimate contact with blackness. In Pierce Egan's picaresque novel *Life in London* (1821) and in the stage version adapted by William Thomas Moncrieff (*Tom and Jerry; or, Life in London* [1821]), white upper-class figures spend their leisure time slumming amid scenes of lower-class "high life" at the All Max club. Stage versions of *Life in London* featured scenes of Black dancing by the blackface figure "African Sal," while the print version included George Cruikshank's color lithograph of the "Lowest 'Life in London'" that fixated on interracial dancing and sexual contact at the All Max.[124] Though Peter Reed views such scenes as harboring "unruly" political potential, such slumming repeats (with little difference) the eighteenth-century theatrical scenarios of "high life below stairs" wherein white masters temporarily enter the "low," interracial world of the servant class to comically reinstall class and racial orders.[125] As with Townley's farce fifty years prior, *Life in London* indexed the "low" of low class to scenes of racial confusion in which lower-class white people were denigrated—that is, blackened—through their intimate contact with Black people.

Within the citational networks of scriptive blackface, Anglophone audiences and readers often found humor in class and racial abjection alike, while theatrical and visual materials transmitted white bourgeois scripts of class and racial respectability premised on the denial of Black equality. Two years prior to making his print of the "Lowest 'Life in London,'" Cruikshank illustrated an apocalyptic vision of postemancipation British society in *The New Union Club, Being a Representation of What Took Place, at a Celebrated Dinner, Given by a Celebrated—Society* (1819) (see fig. 3).

Theatrically depicting a gathering of the abolitionist African Society, Cruikshank's *The New Union Club* imagines Black emancipation as a scenario of interracial chaos and disorder. In this comic print, leading white British abolitionists such as Zachary Macaulay engage in interracial sexual contact with Black women while Black radical abolitionist Robert Wedderburn appears on the same visual plane as Black street entertainer Billy Waters. Other prominent Black British figures such as boxer Tom Molineaux populate the background, while the entire back wall of the scene is littered with imagery of abolitionists and famous Black individuals such as "The Apotheosis of William Wilberforce," a portrait of the king of Haiti, and a mostly obscured image of Sara Baartman.[126] Cruikshank thereby collapses any distinction between Black individuals and disparate Black and African peoples, figuring them as an unruly mass defined by licentious sexuality, dissolute drunkenness, and violent physicality. Moreover, Cruikshank reproduces abolitionist images to juxtapose them with his scene of riotous Black freedom, tacitly figuring his antiblack, antiabolitionist illustration as a more "realistic" projection of postemancipation society. Epitomizing Anglophone anxieties that an interracial social order would inexorably lead to interracial sex, the left-hand side of the image features a Black man and a white woman holding their infant child, who is

Fig. 3. George Cruikshank, *The New Union Club* (1819). Courtesy of the Lewis Walpole Library, Yale University. https://collections.library.yale.edu/catalog/16034920.

figured as visually half Black and half white. Cruikshank's antiabolitionist impressions manifested a comparatively more refined antiblack imaginary than the Bobalition broadsides—one that braided antiblack representations of Black freedom with tropes of class inversion and interracial sexuality. Nevertheless, for Cruikshank and his Anglophone audiences, emancipation threatened the stability of the racialized and classed system that permitted slumming in the "high life below stairs" by transforming all of British society into the "low."

US Americans quickly incorporated Cruikshank's visual repertoires of Black abjection into their antiblack imaginaries. Philadelphian visual artist Edward Williams Clay embarked on a European tour from 1825 to 1828, during which he encountered Cruikshank's illustrations of *Life in London* in the window of a London printseller.[127] Upon his return to Philadelphia, Clay fashioned his popular series of prints, *Life in Philadelphia* (1828–1830), which featured popular images of Black abjection that drew from visual repertoires on both sides of the Atlantic. Clay's ninth plate in the series, "*How you like de new fashion shirt . . . ?*" (1830), encapsulates the confluence of different streams of scriptive blackface (see fig. 4).

Clay's image figures a theatrical encounter between two Black figures adorned in high-class fashion, while framing the visual representation of Black abjection with quasi-theatrical dialogue in scriptive blackface.[128] Drawing from a technique elaborated in Bobalition broadsides, Clay

Fig. 4. Edward Williams Clay, *Life in Philadelphia: "How you like de new fashion shirt? . . ."* (1830), plate 9. Courtesy of the Library Company of Philadelphia. https://digital.librarycompany.org/islandora/object/Islandora%3A60208.

reverses the typical left-to-right scripting of visual dialogue by beginning the imagined conversation on the right-hand side and thereby framing the scene within an inverted world.[129] The Black dandy asks his partner, "How you like de new fashion shirt, Miss Florinda?" She responds, "I tink dey mighty elegum—I see you on New Year Day when you carry de colour in de Abolition 'siety—You look just like Pluto de God of War!" While the visual image exaggerates their dress, the characters mispronounce words and confuse their references to Greek mythology. The complimentary association of the Black dandy with "Pluto de God of War" contains several densely entangled jokes. First, it posits the Abolition Society as threatening by associating its parades with warlike processions. Second, it confuses the Greek god of war, Mars, with the god of the underworld, Pluto. Taken together, these confusions posit the Black dandy as both a militant threat and a figure of an inverted world, the convergence of which embodies the possibility of a Black uprising. Clay's image comically defuses such anxious potentialities, framing Black attempts at fashion, speech, freedom, equality, and class status as all equally ludicrous.

Clay's impressions of Black abjection quickly recirculated to Britain, where they were reprinted and adapted to British contexts. Several of his prints were republished in London in Thomas Hood's *New Comic Annual for 1831* along with a short narrative linking together the visual scenes under the heading "Life in Philadelphia" (see fig. 5).[130] The London publication repurposed the third plate of Clay's series as the frontispiece for its narrative of scriptive blackface. The selection of this image signals how, throughout the Atlantic world, Anglophone readers were intimately familiar with the core tropes and citational references of scriptive blackface. For example, Hood's *New Comic Annual* repeated (with minor variation) dialogue from Clay's image: "'Is Miss Dinah at home?'—'Yes, Sir, but she petickly ingaged in washing *de dishes*.'—'Ah! I am sorry I can't hab de honour to pay my *devours* to her—give her my card.'" As standard to the "Life in Philadelphia" series, the characters' broken speech features familiar mispronunciations that comically invert Black enactments of classed respectability: the linguistic substitution of "devours" for "devoirs" links Black classed articulations of Black courtship to well-rehearsed tropes of African cannibalism and insatiable sexual desire.[131] Once again, the visual repertoires of the Anglophone empire staged Black embodiments of "high" culture as comic proof of their indelibly "low" status.

The visual economy of Clay's image also symbolically tropes on "high life below stairs." In both the Clay and Hood versions, a Black male dandy adorned with a top hat, fancy overcoat, and walking stick addresses a Black servant-woman. The dandy stands at street level as he stoops to conquer the affections of the servant-woman, who emerges from a cellar. The image stages a comic scenario that undermines the dandy's aspirational performance to the decorum of high society while also situating Black life as literally below stairs (given Miss Dinah's role as a washing woman who inhabits the below stairs of a home, presumably that of her white master).[132] The narrative text accompanying the Hood image impressed this point on readers, asserting that a free Black man could only "ape his master in the upper story."[133] For a circum-Atlantic readership of white

147

LIFE IN PHILADELPHIA.

"Is Miss Dinah at home?"—"Yes, Sir, but she petickly ingaged in washing *de dishes*."—"Ah! I am sorry I can't hab de honour to pay my *devours* to her—give her my card."

L 2

Fig. 5. "Life in Philadelphia," from *The New Comic Annual for 1831*, ed. Thomas Hood (London: Hurst, Chance, and Co., 1830), 147. Courtesy of HathiTrust.

Anglophone subjects anxious about the prospect of Black emancipation, the proliferation of abject figurations of blackness affirmed white supremacy as natural and inevitable. The image traces the continuities between pre- and postemancipation racial structures throughout the Atlantic world, wherein an "uppity" Black male dandy unwittingly abases himself in his simultaneous aspiration toward white fashions and his courtship of a Black woman who still occupies the position of the erstwhile slave quarters "below stairs."

The transoceanic circulation of Clay's images familiarized circum-Atlantic Anglophone audiences with the racial grammars and figural economies that would subtend the performance repertoires of blackface minstrelsy. Indeed, Clay's images directly inspired blackface minstrel productions. In 1833, Thomas Dartmouth Rice, the originator of "Jump Jim Crow," incorporated into his performance repertory a piece titled *Life in Philadelphia; or, How Do They Go On.*[134] More broadly, the "early" blackface minstrel repertoire of the 1820s–1830s furnished a concatenation of performance material derived from the preceding seventy years. Several solo performers attained immense fame in the theater and the circus by popularizing blackface songs and comic routines.[135] These early blackface singers and clowns elaborated new songs by recombining tropes and characters from the blackface repertoire—most notably, George Washington Dixon's "Long Tail Blue" (1827), "Coal Black Rose" (1829), and "Zip Coon" (1834); and Rice's "Jump Jim Crow" (1830) and his proliferation of variations, songs, and skits.

Simultaneously, several now-forgotten performers specialized in the rapidly expanding repertoire of blackface music. For instance, on December 25, 1835, "Mr. Leicester, The celebrated EXTRAVAGANZA SINGER" performed at New York's Franklin Theatre, featuring several popular blackface songs such as "The Racoon Hunt, or Sitting on a Rail" [sic] and "Ching A Ring Ching."[136] Published in 1833, the latter song was sung in the character of Sambo, and was also known as "Ching-A-Ring-Chaw" or "Sambo's 'Dress to He' Bred'ren."[137] Though it has received little critical attention, "Sambo's Address" encapsulates the enduring appeal and familiarity of decades of blackface practice in a single song that narrates a parodic fantasy of Black emigration to Haiti:

> Broder let us leabe, Bucra lan for Hettee.
> Dar you be receive Gran as LaFayette;
> Make a mity show, wen we lan from steamship
> I be like Munro, You like Louis Philip,
> Chinger ringer, ring ching, ching
> Ho ah, ding ah ding kum darkee,
> Chinger ringer, ring ching chaw,
> Ho ah ding kum darkee.[138]

A parody of Black Christian appeals to African colonization projects that promised to relocate free Black people outside the national boundaries of the United States, the song takes the form of a mock sermon redolent of the scriptive blackface speeches and toasts of Bobalition broadsides and their addresses to Black "bredren."[139] It also tropes on the burlesqued image of Black dandies and dandizettes as misfiring imitators of white respectability, concluding with the hope that in Haiti free Black people might find themselves equal to prominent white figures such as US president James Monroe, French king Louis Philippe I, General George Washington, and the Marquis de Lafayette.[140] The song posited that free Black people and prominent white figures were laughably incommensurate, thereby framing the abolitionist discourse of colonization as ludicrous insofar as it imagined Black people could attain the trappings of white civilization anywhere. Simultaneously, the song did not oppose or denigrate African (or Haitian) colonization. Rather, it tacitly supported the antiblack discourse that underwrote abolitionist colonization projects and their promises to remove Black people from the United States. The song's blackface burlesque was broad. It emphasized the humor to be found in Black abjection, returning to Charles Dibdin's evocation of ostensibly harmonious Black enslavement as an onomatopoeic nonsense chorus of the banjo's strum: "chingaring." Sung on stages and in music halls, in parlors and in pubs, such voicings of Black abjection codified the synesthetic sonics of blackness throughout the circum-Atlantic Anglophone world. Like the extensive repertoire of early blackface minstrelsy, "Sambo's Address" braided together numerous streams of scriptive blackface—of banjos, Bobalition, and "bredren"—synthesizing them into a form of popular culture that quickly washed over the Anglophone world. It is to the ensuing waves of blackface minstrelsy that we now turn.

Chapter 2

✦

Jim Crow Puts a Girdle Round about the Earth

In 1845, US American writer James Kennard Jr. published a sardonic paean to blackface minstrelsy, hailing the nascent performance form as the "National Opera" of the United States. Kennard's tone of mock grandiloquence parodied the "prerequisites of national poetry" codified by emerging bourgeois nationalist discourses on art and literature—the impossible purities of origin and identity "necessary to make the poet national."[1] Contrasting the "cosmopolitan" identity of respectable, white society with the purportedly provincial identities of Black peoples, Kennard acerbically pronounced "the Jim Crows, the Zip Cooons [*sic*], and the Dandy Jims . . . our ONLY TRULY NATIONAL POETS."[2] Kennard attributed the status of US American national genius to blackface minstrel characters who functioned as stand-ins for the absent presence of Black people in circum-Atlantic popular culture. In minstrel fashion, Kennard conflated blackness with blackface, juxtaposing minstrelsy's ersatz "Black" with the national "white." With mordant irony, he celebrated the popularity of blackface minstrelsy to scorn the paucity of white bourgeois US American national culture. Kennard's essay therefore offers a condensation of blackface's ubiquitous presence in nineteenth-century US American life and its simultaneous function as both object and modality of cultural critique.

Yet, Kennard's parodic argument for the "national" stature of blackface minstrelsy took a surprisingly transnational form:

> How transcendent, then, must be the genius of the authors of our negro operas! Are not snatches of their songs in every body's mouth, from John O'Groat's to Land's End, and from Labrador to Mexico? Three hundred and fifty times a day, (we took the pains to count, once,) we have been amused and instructed with "Zip Coon," "Jim Crow," and the tale of a "Fat Raccoon, a-sittin on a rail." Let Webster tell of the tap of Britain's drum, that encircles the world! Compared with the time occupied by Great Britain in bringing this to pass, "Jim Crow" has put a girdle round about the earth in forty minutes.[3]

Kennard's references to historical blackface minstrel traffics map forgotten genealogies of performance. Charting an itinerary from the northernmost point of Scotland to the southwesterly tip of England and from northeastern Canada to Mexico, Kennard asserts as self-evident the circulation of minstrel repertoires throughout and beyond the circum-Atlantic Anglophone empire. Moreover, Kennard's comparison of the expanse of Britain's global empire to the transoceanic popularity of "Jim Crow" traces the forgotten entanglements of Anglophone imperialism and blackface performance. Indeed, Kennard's declaration that "'Jim Crow' has put a girdle round about the earth" was more accurate than he might have imagined. Amateur and professional early nineteenth-century blackface minstrel performers charted transoceanic routes that encircled the globe, expanding on the circum-Atlantic transmissions of eighteenth-century blackface theatrical scripts, closet dramas, music, performance, and visual culture. Drawing from the extensive repertoires of blackface, manifold performers, playwrights, and songwriters forged a transoceanic Anglophone popular culture from minstrel materials.

The citational networks of transoceanic blackface performances mediated racial thinking and practice common throughout the early and mid-nineteenth-century Anglophone world. Returning to these networks reveals the intimate imbrications among ostensibly disparate regional, national, and colonial discourses on race. As several studies of blackface minstrelsy have illuminated, the blackface figure "Jim Crow" symptomatized the equivocations, contradictions, and unresolved ambivalences that underpinned racial governmentality in the US American North and South alike: its racializing performances animated popular white supremacist investments in managing, containing, and delimiting Black freedom.[4] In the United States, perhaps no racial formation is as well known as Jim Crow, nor does another term so readily evoke the assemblage of juridical systems and everyday practices that structure white supremacy, particularly in the US American South. In his landmark analysis of the Jim Crow system, C. Vann Woodward traces the early history of de jure racial segregation—enshrined by *Plessy v. Ferguson* (1896)—to de facto practices of separate and unequal development in the antebellum South that limited the political rights and social lives of "free, or quasi-free" Black subjects who "shared many of the deprivations of the [enslaved]."[5] These ambivalently "free, or quasi-free" subjects were, in Woodward's analysis, "[d]enied full rights and privileges of citizens, deprived of equality in the courts, and restricted in their freedom of assembly and freedom of movement."[6] However, these conditions of Black unfreedom were not delimited to the US American South but also governed Black life in the antebellum US American North, where Black emancipation was greeted with white supremacist discrimination, violence, and the proslavery propaganda of the minstrel stage.

Although recent analyses of blackface minstrelsy and its racial politics perceptively diagnose the lineaments of US American racial formations and their entanglements with popular performance, such research has been, in Catherine M. Cole's terms, "nationalistically myopic."[7] Across these studies, "Jim Crow" (as popular performance) and Jim Crow politics (as racial formation) appear as national figurations axiomatically bound to the United States. Even recent transnational studies that address British performances of early blackface minstrelsy have presumed that "Jim Crow" functioned as an exemplar of US American racial politics, and that its political significance was necessarily different within British contexts.[8] The nationalistic myopia of blackface minstrel scholarship has limited considerations of how performance cultures forged transnational political and racial formations beyond the Anglo-American cultural traffics of the circum–North Atlantic.[9]

This chapter traces the transmissions of "Jim Crow" throughout the nineteenth-century Anglophone empire. This performance genealogy refuses the premise of a uniquely US American origin of blackface. Instead, it traces the entanglements among transnational transmissions of early blackface and the Anglophone imperial racial formations of the 1830s and '40s. Rather than positing the nation as a container for racial performance and politics, I map the intimate connections between US American and British national politics and the imperial contexts of transoceanic Anglophone politics, particularly between the 1807 Act for the Abolition of the Slave Trade and the emancipation of enslaved peoples of the British Empire in 1838. Early blackface minstrelsy inundated Anglophone popular culture not only in metropoles of the circum–North Atlantic but also throughout colonial worlds in Australia, Canada, South Asia, Jamaica, and southern Africa. Although the blackface figure "Jim Crow" appeared in variable guises throughout its travels, it transmitted enduring discursive structures that underpinned globalizing logics of Anglophone white supremacy, as well as imperial political and racial formations densely imbricated with the unfreedom of the Jim Crow South. Rather than limit my focus to one exemplary colonial site, I map the transoceanic circulation of "Jim Crow" across multiple nineteenth-century British imperial locations to consider how blackface minstrelsy furnished white imperial audiences across the globe with the capacious yet durable racial discourses of liberalism.

Performances of "Jump Jim Crow" toured circum-Atlantic metropoles and transoceanic colonial ports, furnishing the Anglophone empire with racial scripts and scenarios that were premised on liberalism's paradoxes of Black emancipation. Throughout the Anglophone empire, white performers and audiences animated "Jim Crow" as an abject Black figure. Moreover, "Jim Crow" provided white Anglophone colonists with racial scripts adapted to local contexts, as epitomized by the early South African playlet *Kaatje Kekkelbek; or, Life among the Hottentots* (1838).

Transoceanic blackface thus forged popular conceptions of global politics centered on the figure of the exemplary Anglophone national-imperial citizen-subject: a white, free, rights-bearing individual whose political inclusion was secured through the exclusion of unfree racialized figures such as the enslaved and colonized peoples of the Anglophone empire.[10] In other words, transoceanic performance networks of early blackface minstrelsy were tightly imbricated with imperial discourses of liberalism, race, and freedom, all of which were constitutive of global formations of power.

Transoceanic traffics of early blackface minstrelsy densely entangled the racial repertoires centered on the early blackface figure "Jim Crow," the US American racial formation of Jim Crow, and Anglophone imperial formations. Analyzing these overlapping racial discourses and practices facilitates consideration of these interwoven histories of racialization on a global scale. Expanding on the transoceanic performance genealogy of early blackface performance traced in the previous chapter, this chapter demonstrates how the global itineraries of "Jim Crow" challenge the presumption that imperial centers were the "origins" of representations of colonized subjects by demonstrating how such discourses emerged through the material traffics, relays, and relations that bound together the Anglophone imperial world. As exemplified by early blackface circulation across the United States, Britain, and the colonial world, transoceanic blackface encircled the globe, consolidating racial discourses in the colonies as it did in circum–North Atlantic metropoles. Not merely exported by northern metropoles and imported by Anglophone colonists, blackface minstrelsy staged the dynamic, multidirectional relays of imperialism and its racial discourses.[11] Waves of blackface washed over the Anglophone empire throughout the Global North and South. Unbounded by national borders, transoceanic blackface liberally staged the enduring figural economies of race that coalesced into global relations of imperial racism in the mode of "Jim Crow" minstrelsy.

The Jim Crow Circum–North Atlantic

US American performer Thomas Dartmouth ("Daddy") Rice premiered his signature minstrel act, "Jump Jim Crow," in Louisville, Kentucky, on May 21, 1830.[12] Citing from and elaborating on the expanding repertoires of blackface theater and early blackface minstrelsy, Rice forged his signature song and character. Regularly revised and adapted, "Jump Jim Crow" followed a general verse form:

> Come listen all you galls and boys,
> I'm just from Tuckyhoe;
> I'm going to sing a leetle song,

Fig. 6. Edward Williams Clay, "Mr. T. Rice as the Original Jim Crow" (ca. 1830). Courtesy of the Harry Ransom Center, University of Texas at Austin.

> My name's Jim Crow.
> Weel about, and turn about, and do jis so;
> Eb'ry time I weel about, I jump Jim Crow.[13]

In 1832, after two years of perfecting his racist song and dance in theaters along the major port cities of the Ohio River, Rice attained immense popularity throughout the United States, touring the major cities of the Atlantic Seaboard and the US American South and West, while also circulating "Jump Jim Crow" through the song sheet-music market (see fig. 6). For six years he performed his signature act incessantly, including stops in Boston,

Baltimore, Cincinnati, New Orleans, New York, Pittsburgh, Philadelphia, and Washington, DC.[14]

Throughout Rice's tours, "Jump Jim Crow" maintained its popularity, in no small part due to its fungibility. Like other blackface songs of the early minstrel period, "Jump Jim Crow" was densely intertextual. It was open to revision and improvisation, and sung by numerous performers, all of whom participated in a popular culture premised on racial denigration performed by and among white men. Indeed, early blackface minstrelsy was a competitive ground for individual white male solo performers—George Washington Dixon, Thomas Blakeley, John Washington Smith, Joel Sweeney, Mr. Hall, Mr. Leicester, Mr. Foster, and Rice himself, among others—whose mutual support and petty rivalries constituted a core element in the popular and commercial appeals of minstrelsy's burgeoning culture industry.[15] To distinguish himself among this crowded field and to provoke audience interest, Rice produced countless versions of his signature song that recombined elements from the extant repertoires of blackface, entangling snatches of other popular blackface songs (e.g., "Ching a Ring Chaw"), embodiments drawn from the blackface theatrical stage, and irreverent commentary on contemporary US American racial politics.[16] Far from offering audiences what W. T. Lhamon Jr. terms "slippery and multisignificant" performances harboring insurgent and subversive potential, Rice's "Jim Crow" variations capitalized on white Anglophone audiences' familiarity with extant blackface practices and their investments in extravagant performances of racial denigration.[17]

The success of Rice's "Jim Crow" hinged on the proliferation of other blackface figures—the minstrel doubles that both preceded him and shared the blackface stage. Perhaps the most infamous doubles of "Jim Crow" were the apocryphal Black Americans that Rice purportedly imitated in his signature song. In Robert Nevin's specious historiography of minstrelsy's beginnings, the genesis of "Jump Jim Crow" receives two tellings. First, Nevin introduces a mythical encounter in the streets of Cincinnati between Rice and a "negro stage-driver" who sang the "Jim Crow" refrain.[18] Then Nevin offers a minstrel scene on the banks of the Monongahela River in Pittsburgh, wherein Rice meets "Cuff," a poor Black freeman who lends Rice his clothing so that Rice may perform "Jump Jim Crow" in costume for the first time. The account concludes with a minstrel joke denigrating "Cuff," who runs onstage in a state of undress to reclaim his clothing, unwittingly becoming the butt of the joke.[19] Nevin's twinned "authentic" sources for Rice's song have yet another double. In actor and theater manager Noah Miller Ludlow's diary, Rice learns the song from "a very black, clumsy negro [who] used to clean and rub down horses" in a stable yard near the Louisville Theatre.[20] The setting of these doubly doubled minstrel sources slips from Cincinnati to Pittsburgh to Louisville—and crosses the Mason-Dixon Line from free to slave states. As a result, these various figurations furnish forth a character with an ambiguous relationship with freedom: "Jim Crow" might be "free, or quasi-free," or still enslaved. Thus, these sources furnish a dizzying assemblage of possible origins—and onto-political statuses—for Rice's signature character.

Rather than dismiss these "Jim Crow" doubles as the "dubious" artifacts of minstrel "legend," it is more generative to consider why Rice proliferated so many avatars.[21] The origin narratives of "Jump Jim Crow" do not typically refer to the Black sources of Rice's song, costuming, or corporeal performance as "originals." Most tellings do not even grant the Black figures names, with the figures appearing instead as raw material that Rice shapes into his "original" act through his signature genius. Exemplifying Rice's incessant production of doubles and the slipperiness of his "originality," a painted theatrical poster currently held by the Harry Ransom Center at the University of Texas advertises Rice's "Jim Crow" alongside a miniature double (see fig. 7).

In the poster, a tall, blackface figure standing center stage holds an upturned sack, below which a smaller blackface figure in identical dress strikes the famous "Jim Crow" pose. The caption to the image reads, in the patter of the "Jump Jim Crow" song: "LADIES AND GEM'MN I'LL HAVE YOU ALL TO KNOW / I HAVE A LITTLE NIGGER HERE TO JUMP JIM CROW." This uncanny doubling of Jim Crow presents a scene strikingly similar to the scenario recounted in Joseph Jefferson's memoir, in which Jefferson, as a child performer, was "blacked up and dressed as a complete miniature likeness of the original"—which is to say, in imitation of Rice's "Jim Crow."[22] Jefferson then recalls a scene in which Rice carried him onstage in a sack and sang a variation on the "Jim Crow" opening stanza—"O Ladies and Gentlemen, I'd have you for to know / That I've got a little darky here that jumps Jim Crow"—before emptying Jefferson out of the sack so that the pair could perform a double "Jim Crow" act.[23] This spectacular scene of minstrel reproduction demonstrates Rice's propensity for proliferating doubles. Rice's double act of blackface mimesis positioned him as the "original" Jim Crow, displacing the several Black figures that circulated as the authentic source(s) of his signature song in a spectacle of uncanny reproduction. It symptomatizes how his retinue of Black "originals" were, like Jefferson, all blackface figures propping up his claims to artistic originality. Here, the several narratives of Rice's originality illustrate Rebecca Schneider's observation that doubles function by belatedly "having *made* the first (at least by making the first first, making the origin original)."[24] By claiming to be minstrelsy's "Daddy," Rice reveled in the patriarchal presumptions of claims to "origins," and of being "author, father, First."[25]

Positing Rice as the singular paternal source of blackface minstrelsy, these multiple origin narratives of "Jim Crow" insistently forget Rice's theatrical training and his intimate familiarity with the repertoires of early minstrel blackface. When Rice first staged "Jim Crow" while touring with

Fig. 7. Advertising poster of Mr. "Jim Crow" (undated). Courtesy of the Harry Ransom Center, University of Texas at Austin.

Samuel Drake's theater company, he specialized in eighteenth-century British blackface roles such as Mungo from *The Padlock* (1768) and Sambo from *Laugh When You Can* (1798).[26] Elaborating on these blackface precedents, Rice forged "Jim Crow" as a popular blackface surrogate to Mungo and Sambo. Moreover, in his claims to perform "authentic" Black material on the Anglophone stage, Rice surrogated the white actors John Moody and Lewis Hallam Jr., both of whom claimed firsthand knowledge of Black life in Jamaica as epistemic grounds for their eighteenth-century blackface performances. As discussed in chapter 1, Moody originated the role of Kingston in James Townley's *High Life below Stairs* (1759), the earliest known comic blackface servant role on the British stage. Beyond this foundational role, Moody also helped to write the blackface dialogue for Mungo in Charles Dibdin and Isaac Bickerstaffe's *The Padlock*. In Dibdin's 1803 memoir, the playwright claimed that the role of Mungo "would never have been written as it is but for Moody's suggestions, who had been in the West-Indies, and knew, of course, the dialect of the negroes."[27] Dibdin's account furnished a foundational script for claiming blackface authenticity on the basis of "ethnographic realism."[28] It is therefore unsurprising that William Dunlap's 1832 history of the US American theater, published contemporaneously with Rice's phenomenal popularity, attributed the success of Hallam's eighteenth-century colonial performances in the role of Mungo to the "truth derived from the study of the Negro slave character"—a "truth" presumably attained during his travels throughout the British colonies on the mainland and in the Caribbean.[29] Dunlap's praise for Hallam repeated Dibdin's claim to ethnographic realism, replacing Moody with Hallam in a nationalistic counterclaim of US American (rather than British colonial) blackface originality. Taken together, Dibdin's and Dunlap's narratives posit blackface as a transoceanic "colonial product": its "authenticity" was bound to imperial knowledge of enslaved peoples, and its theatrical repertoires and racial discourses made such racializing knowledges intimately familiar to performers and audiences throughout the Anglophone imperium.[30] Rice was able to sell "Jump Jim Crow" as an "original" to be imitated and reproduced only by remembering multiple specious sources for "Jump Jim Crow" and by forgetting its citations of enduringly popular eighteenth-century blackface repertoires and "Daddy" Rice's many blackface forebears.[31]

Paradoxically, Rice's sensational and singular popularity depended on the ubiquity of blackface throughout the Anglophone empire. In the wake of the transatlantic circulations of Kingston, Mungo, and Sambo, Rice's "Jump Jim Crow" reanimated and recombined extant blackface scripts and antiblack tropes amid heated Anglophone debates on abolitionism. In June 1836, Rice traveled to London, where he premiered his signature blackface song and dance to packed houses at the Adelphi and Surrey Theatres.[32] Soon thereafter London magazines and newspapers reprinted more minstrel doubles in the form of bespoke variations on "Jump Jim Crow," including mock biographies such as *The Origin of Jim Crow: Being an Authentic Account of the Life and Adventures of That Comic American Nigger* (1837).[33] As a US American newspaper noted of Rice's popularity in England,

> Jim Crow is now sung in every nook and alley of the kingdom, from the aristocratic drawing room of his Grace of Devonshire down to the hovels of the unwashed dustmen of Maiden-lane—for whom, by the bye, the song does not seem altogether unsuited; in fact, we may say that a Jim Crow mania has seized on all classes of the community.[34]

Rice's song quickly entered the British repertoire, with British performers such as John Dunn and J. A. Cave regularly adapting "Jim Crow," while Rice himself acted in a proliferation of "Jim Crow" comic plays, burlesques, and extravaganzas.[35] "Jim Crow" saturated British culture, permeating the everyday lifeworld of London and producing a "Jim Crow mania" twenty years prior to the "Uncle Tom mania" of the 1850s.[36] Whereas the later Uncle Tom mania traced transnational circulations of abolitionism and antiabolitionism, the circum–North Atlantic Jim Crow mania of the 1830s was more univocal in its antiblack and antiabolitionist politics.

In London, Rice performed in a proliferation of comic plays and burlesques that centered on the escapades of "Jim Crow." There, as in the United States and in keeping with his eighteenth-century Anglophone blackface forebears, "Jim Crow" staged complex enactments of antiabolitionism and antiblackness in densely ironic racial spectacles. For instance, in *Flight to America* (1836), a blackface extravaganza that directly cited Charles Mathews's popular blackface enactments in *Trip to America* (1824), Rice's "Jim Crow" was introduced by a chorus of Black female characters singing a minstrelized version of the "Finale to Obi" from John Fawcett's *Obi; or, Three-Finger'd Jack* (1800):

> Fifth July Fifth July!
> Eb'ry color'd soul be gay
> Banish Care Banish Care
> Strike de bango dance and play
> Freedom reigns o'er the plains
> Bobolition for de nigger
> Beat big drum, tambourine thrum
> On dis happy day
> Fifth July, etc.[37]

Immediately following this "Grand Procession of Niggers," Jim Crow rode onstage on a white horse to deliver a speech:

> Gemmen, I's 'puted to dress you on dis occasion. I wish de task had fall'n into better hands, but though oder gemmen speak more abler, no gemman could feel more deeper. You, de enlighten'd gemmen, whom I dress, know dis is de day of our Bobolition. Well, gemmen, I make no long rigmarole furder dan to say, the gemmen I 'tend 'pon hab gone out for de day. And I hab trown open his room for a Ball![38]

Rice's theatrical spectacle braids together numerous antiabolitionist blackface jokes. Though Lhamon asserts that Jim Crow's oratory constituted "an abolitionist speech" with antislavery significance, in *Flight to America*, Jim Crow never spoke the word "abolition."[39] Rather than celebrating emancipation, Jim Crow mispronounced "abolition" as "Bobolition" in reference to Bobalition broadsides. Moreover, *Flight to America*'s "Fifth July" chorus parodied New York's Emancipation Day parades, which were held annually on July 5 following the state's abolition of slavery in 1827, with Black parade marshal Samuel Hardenburgh leading the march on a white horse.[40] Last, in parodically citing the "Finale to Obi," Rice burlesqued *Obi*'s threatening scenario of Black insurgency by reciting the "Finale" as a blackface song in the banjo-laden minstrel mode of plantation docility.[41] The density of Rice's intertheatrical troping on antiblack discourses attests to the legibility of "Jim Crow" as a durable symbol of racial denigration as it crossed national boundaries and was adapted to new circum–North Atlantic contexts. Together, these entangled strains of blackface burlesque staged a mockery of Black freedom in London.

The transoceanic circulation of "Jim Crow" demonstrates that early blackface minstrelsy's enactments of racial subjection were not distinctively US American, for they functioned as articulations of broader Anglophone theatrical repertoires and colonial discourses about racial freedom. In the wake of the 1833 Act for the Abolition of Slavery throughout the British Empire, Rice's antiabolitionist blackface spectacle offered the predominantly antiblack, proslavery, white Anglophone public a figure that affirmed their social power and feelings of racial superiority through performances of Black abjection.[42] Through his antiabolitionist performances, Rice fulfilled the propagandistic hopes of proslavery US American audiences, such as those published by the editor of the *New Orleans Rambler* prior to Rice's London debut in 1836: "We hope Rice will do something towards opening John Bull's eyes on this subject, and convincing him, by giving a genuine specimen of the 'nigger,' that, even supposing black slavery an evil, the notion of any thing [*sic*] like immediate emancipation to such an informed race, should not be entertained for a single moment."[43] This correspondent imagined Rice's theatrical tour as a nationalist mission in the service of antiabolitionism, in which Rice's "Jim Crow" would serve as a "genuine specimen" of abject blackness to be presented to the British public.

Upon his return to the United States in 1837, Rice proclaimed to an enthusiastic white crowd in Baltimore that his antiabolitionist evangelism was a success. He announced that the British "were under the impression that negroes were naturally equal to the whites, and their degraded condition was consequent entirely upon our 'institutions;' but I effectually proved that negroes are essentially an inferior species of the human family, and they ought to remain slaves."[44] In this speech, Rice traded on the national chauvinism of his US American audience to promote his blackface performance as an efficacious antiabolitionist instrument, which he used to enlighten the benighted British throngs regarding the "negro character [of] the southern plantations."[45] It is hardly likely, however, that his performance transformed his British audience's sensibilities, not because his British audiences failed to become antiabolitionist but rather because they already were immersed in transoceanic blackface performance culture. Rice's British variations neither muted his antiabolitionism nor challenged extant Anglophone racial discourses by making blackness respectable. His London "Jim Crow" productions aimed to translate his antiabolitionist and antiblack politics to appeal to British audiences who were familiar with a slightly different, but substantively shared, Anglophone intertheatrical repertoire of blackface figures and discourses.

Rice's tours throughout the antebellum United States made "Jim Crow" into a ribald commentator on national political controversies such as nullification. In London, Rice fashioned new, Africanized "Jim Crow" doubles with an eye to antiabolitionist and antiblack tropes already in British circulation. In several of his London "Jim Crow" plays, including *Flight to America*, *The Foreign Prince*, *Mr. Midshipman Easy*, and *Yankee Notes for English Circulation*, "Jim Crow" claimed to have been born an African prince prior to his enslavement in the United States.[46] *The Foreign Prince*, for instance, called his claims to noble birth into question: he was fashioned as a "foreign Prince," an "African Prince," a "sable and sentimental Prince," and a "Black Prince" who was markedly not regal because he spoke "African English."[47] Moreover, Jim Crow braided his claim to royalty with discourses of racial amalgamation—that is, interracial sexuality—when he announced his intent to "captivate English lad[ies]."[48] Jim Crow's aspirations to seduce English women were underscored by the ironic disjunctures between Britain and his unnamed tropical homeland:

> Oh! Ladies, if you were to wander in my lubly country—not like dis London, bere you am run ober ten times a day by dose omnibusters, dere am de beautiful walks wid de lion and de tigers and de hippopotamus frisking before you. So I be come to lay all my beasts—serpents and crocodiles, at your lubly feet.[49]

Echoing Jim Crow's illustrative description of African animality, J. Fairburn's London print also indexed "Jim Crow" to the discourses of "Monkeyism" and animacy hierarchies that linked Black Africans to apes, a linkage recently inscribed in the popular Anglophone imaginary by Thomas Landseer's *Monkey-ana, or, Men in Miniature* (1827) (see fig. 8). The Fairburn print visually manifested minstrel humor that framed Jim Crow as an abject misfit: this "African prince" was a clownish, ape-like buffoon, made a mockery by the discordance among his claims to royal status

Fig. 8. "Mr. T. Rice as Jim Crow" (London: J. Fairburn, ca. 1836). Courtesy of the Harry Ransom Center, University of Texas at Austin.

through oral and sartorial self-fashioning, his insistently misheard speech, and his tatterdemalion appearance.[50]

Across this intertheatrical repertoire of blackface songs, performances, and visual material, "Jim Crow" appeared either as an African whose quasi-animalistic status abased the rank of a "prince," or as a royal pretender whose specious claims to princely status undercut similar claims by abolitionists and Africans. Specifically, Rice's royal "Jim Crow" variations parodied the titular character of Aphra Behn's popular novel *Oroonoko; or, The Royal Slave* (1688), which was adapted for the British stage by Thomas Southerne (1695). Rice's London adaptations of "Jim Crow" also targeted the figure of the "African prince" made famous by *The Royal African* (1749), the biography of William Ansah Sessarakoo, a Fante noble from the Gold Coast (present-day Ghana) who was "Barbadosed" and sold into slavery before the recognition of his royal status led to his emancipation. Additionally, only five years prior to Rice's arrival in London, Thomas Pringle, the secretary of the Anti-Slavery Society, published *The History of Mary Prince, a West Indian Slave* (1831), making this sentimental African "Prince" a prime target for antiabolitionist parody. Rice's British adaptations covered expansive antiabolitionist ground, with the figurative backdrop of "Jim Crow" shifting from the plantations of Kentucky to the circum-Atlantic imperial coastlines of Britain, the Caribbean, and the Gold Coast. As Rice's performances targeted not only Black Americans but also African and West Indian Black imperial subjects, his "Jim Crow" doubles reveal both the fungibility of "Jim Crow" and the expansive imaginative terrain of Rice's antiabolitionist racial project throughout the Anglophone empire. The transoceanic career of "Jim Crow" demonstrates that blackface minstrelsy's enactments of racial subjection were not distinctively US American but rather functioned as novel articulations of broader theatrical repertoires and colonial discourses about race.

The Imperial Repertoires of Jim Crow

"Jim Crow" was a staple of imperial theaters, through which it circulated and reproduced Black abjection across national borders, colonial boundaries, and oceanic expanses. As early as 1831, a troupe of three US American blackface minstrels toured to Ontario, Canada, "to sing several comic Negro Songs, among others the celebrated JIM CROW."[51] By July 20, 1840, blackface performance was common enough in Toronto that Black Canadians petitioned the mayor "to forbid in future the performance" of minstrel material that "turn[s] into ridicule and hold[s] up to contempt the coloured population, cause[s] them much heart-burning and lead[s] occasionally to violence."[52] In 1842, Black Canadians specifically cited "comic Songs known by the Name of Jim Crow and Aunt Dinah" as the source of "base ridicule."[53] The following year, petitioners asserted, "certain acts, and songs, such as Jim Crow and what they call other Negro Characters, performed by [minstrels have] heretofore been productive of many broils and suits between the white and colord [*sic*] inhabitants of this city."[54] These petitions were advanced by nominally free Black subjects of the British Empire who collectively embodied the vexed ambivalences of freedom and unfreedom amid the shifting political geographies of the global Anglophone empire. Many Black Torontonians likely had migrated to Canada in hopes of escaping racial subjugation in the "south" (that is, the United States). Yet, their protests echoed contemporaneous Black American protests of the popularity of scriptive blackface, which Black

American abolitionist minister Hosea Easton denounced as "cuts and placards descriptive of the negroe's deformity . . . with corresponding broken lingo" that promulgated antiblackness.[55] Therefore, rather than escaping antiblackness by following the North Star, Black Canadians found white Canadian colonists to be much like white US Americans: all too accommodating of blackface performance but not of free Black people.[56] Although Black Torontonians voiced their protests as equal subjects of the empire, their appeals were ignored due to the inequities of imperial racial politics. Toronto's antiminstrel petitions offer a rare transcript of how Black and non-white colonial subjects experienced the popular practice of blackface and its attendant forms of racist violence in the wake of "Jim Crow." Taken together, the complaints of Black Canadians and the nonresponse of the colonial state signal how early blackface minstrelsy did not so much adapt to extant racial formations as extend the domain of the Anglophone empire through rearticulations of white supremacist power over "free, or quasi-free" colonial subjects.[57]

Performances of "Jim Crow" attained immense popularity across all classes of white Anglophone society throughout its transoceanic circulations, with amateur performers regularly restaging "Jim Crow" and its doubles in disparate colonial sites. In January 1838, following Rice's immensely successful London performances, "Jim Crow, '[w]ho came from ole Kentucky a long time ago,'" made an appearance in Hobart Town, Tasmania, when the song and dance was staged as an entr'acte.[58] "Jim Crow" also remained in Australian circulation through stagings of Rice's extravaganzas, as in an 1839 Sydney production of *Flight to America*.[59]

Though it was the first circum-Atlantic blackface act to circulate to the antipodes, "Jim Crow" was not the first blackface character on the Australian stage. Both David Burn's *The Bushrangers* (written in Australia but first staged in Edinburgh in 1829) and Henry Melville's *The Bushrangers; or, Norwood Vale* (premiered in Hobart Town in 1834) mobilized extant transoceanic Anglophone blackface practices to enact white supremacist figurations of Aboriginal Australians.[60] For instance, Burn's play features the character of Tom as the "Chief of the Blacks" and his wife Sal, who is likely named after "African Sal" in *Tom and Jerry; or, Life in London* (1821).[61] This pair's dialogue draws directly from the repertoire of scriptive blackface, as when Tom addresses the white colonist Jemmy as "Matta [Master]," calling him a "merry goot, fine man."[62] Tom asks Jemmy for bread, tea, and tobacco, to which Jemmy responds by calling him "a black dandy," tracing the transoceanic circulation of that figure of Black denigration. After receiving charity from the white colonists, Tom, Sally, and the rest of the "Blacks"—that is, Aboriginal Australians—stage a "Corobbora" [corroborree], or "*a rude dance in which they go spinning round and round and throwing their arms about in an extravagant manner and singing.*" This scene anticipates the "breakdown" dances that would conclude blackface minstrel shows, figuring Aboriginal Australians as comically minstrelized colonial dependents. The comedy ends abruptly following the corroboree when Jemmy responds to Tom's additional request for rum by shooting and killing Tom "and one or two" other Aboriginals. Burn's play stages the propinquity between the Anglophone empire's fantasies of subalterns' enjoyment of their subjugation and its desire for spectacles of racial domination and genocidal violence. Melville's *The Bushrangers*, by contrast, condenses its figuration of Aboriginal people in the singular figure of the "Native," Murrahwa. In Murrahwa's first appearance, Melville repeats Burn's scenario of Aboriginal blackface when he "*sings and dances the corroberee*" in exchange for tobacco. Soon thereafter, the play offers a novel figuration of Aboriginal Australians as sympathetic. Murrahwa complains about the titular bushrangers (i.e., outlaws) who "rob, steal, kill, murder" and claims that "black native love white man, till [the bushrangers] murder wife, piccaniny."[63] Following this complaint, Murrahwa allies with the play's white protagonists to defeat the bushrangers in a confrontation that culminates in Murrahwa's violent revenge on the bushrangers for their murder of his family. Though Melville's play contrasts with Burn's by fostering sympathy for Aboriginal people, it situates Murrahwa as a stereotypical Black noble savage who evokes white colonial pity insofar as he remains reliant on and allied with the "good" white colonists. In a fittingly ambivalent conclusion, the play ends abruptly after Murrahwa attains his vengeance, leaving unstaged the uncertain future awaiting Murrahwa and other Aboriginals living among the white colonists of Norwood Vale.

In addition to these local adaptations of eighteenth-century Anglophone blackface, in 1837, Australian theater makers staged Maurice Dowling's British blackface burlesque *Othello Travestie* (1834), which featured an Othello translocated and abased from his status as a noble Moor to the abject, ambivalently "free" status of a "formerly . . . independent Nigger, from the Island of Hayti" (more on this in chapter 4).[64] The Australian popular press also circulated scenarios of scriptive blackface: written comic scenes emphasizing minstrelized Black dialect that could function as scripts for private and amateur performance. For instance, in March 1837, the *Sydney Herald* published a protominstrel courtroom scene of "The fair Lady and the Dark Man; or Madame versus Nigger," with the latter figure explicitly compared to "the vulgo-immortalized 'Jim Crow'" who sings a British minstrel song, "Nigger man, nigger man, / Alway do him best he can, / Ring a ting a tare oh."[65] These several articulations of Australian blackface, and their insistent recourse to the denigration of unfree racial subjects through the term "nigger," trace how the racial figuration of the empire's enslaved and colonized subjects was, in Australia as in the circum–North Atlantic, scripted by the tropes and scenarios of early blackface minstrelsy.

In March 1838, a few months after "Jim Crow" arrived in Australia, a piece called a "*fac simile* of the London *Jem Crow*" took the stage in Kolkata, India, where it was popularly received.[66] Kolkata, which in 1745 was legally segregated into a "White Town" of British colonists and a "Black Town" of colonized South Asian subjects, presents another compelling case for the capaciousness of Anglophone imperial figurations of blackness as encompassing any and all unfree, racialized subjects of empire.[67] A reviewer of the earliest known performance of "Jim Crow" in South Asia commented on its ubiquitous popularity throughout the empire:

> The tunes which now vex the ear of the great metropolis, are "Sweet Jenny Jones" and Jim Crow; these are sung, whistled, and played by ambulatory professors and amateurs . . . . Nearly all the very little children, whether of those classes who play in the gutters, or who walk the pavement attended by nursery maids, amuse themselves by singing and jumping Jim Crow.[68]

Further attesting to popular colonial enthusiasm for blackface theatricality, a local white Kolkata performer took "Jim Crow" as his stage name when performing in Richard Brinsley Peake's *Hundred-Pound Note* (1828) in the role of "Billy Black."[69] The unknown amateur British performer used "Jim Crow" as a mask of his everyday identity, performing for several weeks under the pseudonym. This act, however minor, traces the extension of a shared circum–North Atlantic Anglophone performance culture to the Indian Ocean world. "Billy Black" was scripted as a blackface role, and Rice frequently played the role of "Billy Black" and performed "Billy Black's Bundle of Conundrums" as an entr'acte alongside "Jim Crow," anticipating the centrality of "conundrums" to the minstrel stage.[70] A "Jim Crow" entr'acte accompanied the Kolkata performance of *The Hundred-Pound Note*, with a reviewer praising "Billy Black's ludicrous 'conundiedrums'" before declaring that "Jim Crow was, as usual, capital, and the *grand morceau* of the night."[71] In Kolkata the pseudonymous "Jim Crow" surrogated Rice as "Billy Black," while simultaneously performing Rice's blackface repertoire far beyond Rice's own stage circulations and transatlantic itineraries. Whether Anglophone colonial audiences in South Asia understood "Billy Black" or "Jim Crow" as representative of Black Americans remains unclear. Nevertheless, the enthusiastic uptake of early blackface minstrelsy within this colonial scene traces how minstrelsy's racial discourses of blackness suffused popular theatrical repertoires and racial imaginations throughout the Anglophone empire.

Two years later, in October 1840, colonial Jamaican theater audiences, comprising predominantly white landowners in the period immediately following emancipation, were introduced to "Jim Crow" in an amateur production of *Jim Crow in London; or, The Creole Ball.*[72] This title traces the promiscuous circulation of early blackface scripts, for it could refer to either of two popular blackface burlesques: either *Jim Crow; or, The Creole Ball* (1836), written in London by T. P. Taylor to capitalize on Rice's sensational popularity, or William Moncrieff's *Jim Crow in England* (1837), which was "written for the purpose of displaying the peculiar talent of Rice in the delineation of the Southern American Nigger."[73] As Taylor's script was a major success and was published in 1839 in "a collection of the most approved and popular dramas," it is more likely that Jamaica's colonial amateurs staged his version than Moncrieff's. Taylor's *Jim Crow* centers on Jim Crow and Sambo as rivals for the affections of "Lubly Rosa" and features a variation of "Jump Jim Crow" as a showstopper, making the amateur troupe's staging of the play the earliest known performance of "Jump Jim Crow" in the Caribbean.[74] Rice's signature song was evidently as popular in Kingston as in London—in 1841, several solo performers staged variations of "Jump Jim Crow," and an itinerant actor named Mr. Lawson gave four encores of his rendition.[75] In November 1842, the Royal Victoria Theatre in Kingston staged several evenings of minstrel songs as well as *The Virginny Mummy; or, The Liquor of Life*—a version of Rice's *The Virginia Mummy* (1835).[76] The popularity of these several "Jim Crow" variations signals the investments of postemancipation Jamaica's white colonial performers and audiences in the Anglophone imperial racial discourses of transoceanic blackface.

In South Africa, "Jim Crow" appeared by 1842, where the song leaped the bounds of the Anglophone public when the Cape Town paper *De Verzamelaar* published a translated version of the chorus in Cape Dutch (proto-Afrikaans):

> Draai maar rond, en krui maar rond,
> En doe juist zoo,
> En elken tyd, krui ik maar rond,
> Ik spring Jim Crow!
>
> A heah, heah, whooh.[77]

In January 1846, at an amateur performance in Pietermaritzburg, soldiers in the Forty-Fifth British Regiment staged "Jim Crow" as an entr'acte. They then staged "The Popular Dance of 'Jim Crow'" at least twice more that year.[78] In these performances, white British soldiers and colonists from all corners of the Anglophone empire took pleasure in the "excellent effect" produced by Jim Crow's abject figuration of blackness.[79] Jim Crow was popular throughout the British colonies in southern Africa: as historian Jan Bouws recounts, "In 1846, [Cape Town journalist] Sam Sly, in a satirical ballad to a famous singer, advised her to sing 'Jim Crow' before she departed from the stage, 'for,' he wrote, 'it is a song which we can recommend if circulation is your only aim.'"[80] Indeed, the song circulated widely throughout southern Africa as, that same year, early South African playwright Charles Étienne Boniface published a closet drama in the Natal Colony that set a new song to the "Air: de Jim Crow."[81] Two years later, on November 10, 1848, in Cape Town, W. F. H. Parker incorporated the "Character of Jim Crow" who "dance[d] a Jig and s[a]ng a Comic Song" into his retinue of "automaton figures."[82] In August 1852, an amateur performance of minstrel songs included "Old Jim Crow" alongside several standards from the blackface repertoire.[83] Jim Crow and his proliferating doubles danced from the US American borderlands along the Ohio River valley to the South African frontier by way of metropolitan London, stopping off in colonial India, Jamaica, and Australia, while forging a transoceanic Anglophone performance empire through its circulations.

Throughout these promiscuous traffics, scanty documentation accounts for how white Anglophone colonists and non-white colonized peoples engaged with the racial significances of early blackface performance. The strongest evidence arises from the sheer ubiquity and enduring popularity of blackface with the predominantly white theater audiences of the British Empire. Although Rice himself performed "Jim Crow" at Toronto's Lyceum in March 1855, he never toured the British colonies in Africa, Asia, or the antipodes.[84] Nevertheless, once "Jim Crow" arrived in the colonies, he never left. As James Kennard Jr. noted, by 1845 "'Jim Crow' ha[d] put a girdle round about the earth."

Kaatje Kekkelbek; or Jim Crow among the Khoekhoe

Throughout the nineteenth century, blackface repertoires remained in circulation in the Anglophone empire in several different articulations of colonial minstrelsy. As the popular face of Black unfreedom, "Jim Crow" and his doubles furnished Anglophone performers and audiences with a capacious repertoire of racial scripts, which were taken up and adapted to new contexts. These multiple avatars of "Jim Crow" signal how intimately blackface affected popular imaginations of race in the wake of British discourses of emancipation.

Kaatje Kekkelbek; or, Life among the Hottentots constitutes a nodal point in the transoceanic relays of blackface performance culture. This short playlet took the form of a short song and dance that premiered at the Graham's Town Theatre in the Cape Colony on November 7, 1838.[85] Written by white colonist Andrew Geddes Bain, *Kaatje Kekkelbek* was performed by an unknown white male actor in racial drag. In the opening lines of the "Characteristic Comic Song," Kaatje introduces herself while playing a mouth harp and singing doggerel to the tune of "Calder Fair" in an amalgam of English and Cape Dutch (proto-Afrikaans):

My name is Kaatje Kekkelbek,	My name is Kaatje Kekkelbek,
I come from Katrivier,	I come from Kat River,
Daar is van water geen gebreek,	Where there is no lack of water,
But scarce of wine and beer.	But scarce of wine and beer.
Myn A B C at Ph'lipes school,	My ABC's at [Rev. John] Philip's school,
I learnt a kleine beetje,	I learnt a little bit,
But left it just as great a fool	But left it just as great a fool
As gekke Tante Meitje.[86]	As crazy Aunt Meitje.

The playlet presents a Khoekhoe woman, Kaatje, who lives in the settlement at Kat River, which was created in 1829 as a colonial buffer zone between the white settlers at the frontier of the Cape Colony and the amaXhosa who lived beyond the colonial border. Through a monologue rife with minstrel braggadocio, Kaatje describes her escapades in the communities in and around the Kat River Settlement.[87]

Staged in the immediate wake of the requisite four-year apprenticeship period for emancipated slaves that followed Britain's 1833 Act for the Abolition of Slavery and the Cape Colony's 1834 Vagrancy Ordinance—the latter enacted to contain and control the population of newly emancipated subjects—*Kaatje Kekkelbek* gave figural form to imperial anxieties about the place of nominally free colonized subjects in the expanding British Empire.[88] Performed in 1838, the year that full freedom was nominally extended to the formerly enslaved subjects of the empire, *Kaatje Kekkelbek* theatricalized emancipation as an ambivalent process. In the playlet's staging of imperial racial liberalism, emancipation required enduring structures of colonial unfreedom: the panoply of discursive and legal frameworks that subjected the Khoekhoe and other African peoples to limited rights, consigned them to circumscribed areas, and limited their capacity to own land. Kaatje embodied this zone of unfreedom as a contradictory amalgam of racial stereotypes that limned the political and affective divides between savagery and civilization, slavery and freedom. The racial scripts of early blackface minstrelsy proved fungible enough to draw multiple racialized colonial populations into the imperial terrain of the circum-Atlantic fold.[89]

Analyzing *Kaatje Kekkelbek* as a citational and intertheatrical performance entangled with transoceanic networks of blackface minstrelsy illuminates how British colonists troped on Anglophone discourses on abolitionism and antiabolitionism. Parodically referencing Sara Baartman's ethnographic display in London as well as acerbically lampooning Mary Prince's 1833 slave narrative, *Kaatje Kekkelbek* mocks Black and Khoekhoe freedom in song, dance, and racial drag.[90] Not only a local, colonial South African articulation of early blackface minstrel performance, *Kaatje Kekkelbek* is also structurally a minstrel song. It is set to a popular British song ("Calder Fair") and features multiple verses in which she brags about putting her liberty to criminal use.

The resonances between *Kaatje Kekkelbek* and "Jim Crow" extend beyond formal similarities and shared dramaturgical strategies, for Kaatje sings in a voice eerily reminiscent of "Jim Crow." In one of the numerous penny-press chapbook adaptations of "Jim Crow" that circulated in London amid "Jim Crow mania" following Rice's initial British tour, the printer James Hodson published a version of the popular minstrel song titled "The Original Song of Jump Jim Crow," which features the following verse:

> Me lib amang de niggers,
> Dey larn me for to sing,
> And sometimes dance a lilly
> When centipede him sting.
> At nigger-school dey larn me
> For spell de A, B, Cs;
> Den for kiss de gals I larn'd,
> Among de orange-trees.[91]

This verse exemplifies the British adaptations of "Jim Crow" in its transformation of Black pain into blackface dancing, its antiabolitionist burlesque of Black education, and its translocation of "Jim Crow" to a tropical setting among abundant orange groves. These adaptations not only attended to British anxieties about Black freedom but also situated "Jim Crow" in the British colonies.

The secondhand *Origin of Jim Crow* allowed the titular figure to travel to the Cape Colony both figuratively and, likely, materially in the form of a script. Comparing the Hodson version of "Jim Crow" to *Kaatje Kekkelbek*, a set of citations of shared antiabolitionist tropes becomes apparent. In the second verse of *Kaatje Kekkelbek*, the titular character proclaims, "But a b, *ab*, and i n, *ine*, / I dagt met uncle Plaatje." Although the nonsensical string of syllables is likely a playful reference to the song's author (Bain), this line also tropes on a prevalent antiabolitionist motif that accused abolitionist ministers of indoctrinating their parishioners through alphabet lessons that "A B stands for abolition."[92] The song makes the target of this accusation unambiguous in the first verse when Kaatje sings, "Mijn A. B. C. at Ph'lips school, / I learnt a kleine beetje." Naming South African emancipationist Reverend John Philip as the instructor of Kaatje's ABC's, *Kaatje Kekkelbek* frames the titular character as Philip's unwitting puppet who parrots his propaganda of misguided reform. Moreover, Kaatje, like "Jim Crow," attends a "nigger-school" (Reverend Philip's colonial missionary school) to learn her ABC's, only to fail in her attempt to enter into educated and civilized white English subjecthood by remaining an ignorant "fool." This citation demonstrates that *Kaatje Kekkelbek* was also a localized version of "Jim Crow"—an adaptation of early blackface to the context of the Cape Colony's unfree Khoekhoe population. The playlet thus makes a mockery of Kaatje's desires for freedom and equality and, by extension, of the rights of the empire's racialized subjects. As with the circum–North Atlantic performances of "Jim Crow," *Kaatje* staged a complex articulation of antiabolitionist politics—a voicing of abolitionist aspirations by a racialized figure in order to mock the freedom dreams of enslaved and colonized peoples.

In tracing these intertheatrical citations across *Kaatje Kekkelbek* and "Jim Crow," I do not suggest that *Kaatje* is a mere copy of a US American or British original. Like Rice's "Jim Crow," *Kaatje* was an amalgam of blackface scripts, tropes, discourses, and performance practices that were popular throughout the Anglophone empire. In addition to the playlet's likely citations of "Jim Crow," *Kaatje* also drew from racial scripts familiar to white South African colonists. For instance, the full title of Bain's work—*Kaatje Kekkelbek; or, Life among the Hottentots*—cited a popular trope of Anglophone visual and musical culture used to represent the British Empire's relatively new colonial enterprise in southern Africa. In 1819, in anticipation of a new British colonial settlement in the Cape Colony, George Cruikshank published a political cartoon titled *All Among the Hottentots Capering Ashore!! The Blessings of Emigration to the Cape of (Forlorn) Good Hope; i.e., to Be Half Roasted by the Sun & Devoured by the Natives!!*[93] Cruikshank's image ironically figured the encounter between white British settlers and African "Hottentots" as an apocalyptic scenario in which predatory animals and "native" Africans conspire to consume the newly arriving white colonists, thereby framing the African continent as anathema to British civilization. Charles Dibdin the younger reanimated this trope in his popular song "The Sailor-Boy Capering Ashore" (ca. 1834), which narrated the tale of an imperial British sailor temporarily abandoned in southern Africa who finds himself "All among the Hottentots, A capering ashore."[94] In addition to these pieces of visual and sonic Anglophone blackface, *Kaatje Kekkelbek* also drew from antecedent local Dutch forms of racialized caricature. Namely, Cape dramatist Charles Étienne Boniface's *De Burger Edelman* (1825)—a Dutch-language adaptation of Molière's *Le Bourgeois Gentilhomme*—featured a female servant named Kaatje. Additionally, his closet drama *De Nieuwe Ridderorde of de Temperantisten* (1832) included several comically drunken, credulous, and belligerent Khoekhoe caricatures who speak a mangled form of Dutch.[95] Along with the song's explicit references to Sara Baartman, Bain's citations of popular figurations of Khoekhoe people and early blackface minstrelsy mark the overlapping waves of Anglophone and Dutch racial caricature as they coalesced in the spectacular figure of Kaatje Kekkelbek.

More than a proslavery parody, *Kaatje* incorporated scraps of "Jim Crow" and Anglophone (and Cape Dutch) popular culture much as Rice interwove popular Anglophone blackface songs into his many versions of "Jim Crow." In each case, blackface functioned to manage white Anglophone anxieties about the freedom of non-white imperial subjects and subalterns by extending white supremacist imperial projects to new terrains. Kaatje drew from circum-Atlantic blackface source material that explicitly satirized abolition as "bobalition" and that framed Black and colonial freedom as at best a provisional possession, particularly when situated on the imperial frontier. Performed by a white male actor masked as a female Khoekhoe character in an embodiment of antiabolitionist blackface, *Kaatje Kekkelbek* staged the intimacies between the theatrical discourses and embodied practices of imperial racial projects in the antebellum United States, imperial Britain, and colonial South Africa. Taken together as distinct yet interrelated nodes within blackface minstrelsy's transoceanic relays between the circum–North Atlantic and South Africa, "Jim Crow" and *Kaatje* outline the centrality of early blackface and its intertheatrical repertoires of racial unfreedom in the making of transoceanic Anglophone empire.[96]

Coda: Jim Crow and the "Freed Slave"

A final artifact of colonial South African culture signals the density of entanglements between Anglophone discourses on antiabolitionism and figurations of racial unfreedom in the wake of the 1833 Abolition Act. In 1840, two years after the manumission of the formerly enslaved persons of the Cape Colony, Frederick Timpson I'Ons fashioned an archetype of *The Freed Slave* (see fig. 9). This image has become iconic in the memorialization of Cape slavery, appearing across South African history textbooks and academic volumes, as well as on the walls of the Iziko Slave Lodge in Cape Town.[97] This ubiquitous image, however, is hardly a transparent celebration of freedom, as it participates in a complex representational economy premised on citations of early blackface that bound scenes of racial subjection to processes of liberal subjectification and subjugation.

Troping on the widely circulating intertheatrical repertoires of early blackface minstrelsy and anticipating similar discursive formations in the postbellum US American South, the representation of *The Freed Slave*'s freedom relies on marking his erstwhile enslavement: a chain hanging from his wrist, a copy of the Abolition Act clenched in his hand, and threadbare shoes that signal the tenuousness of his newfound liberty. Most centrally, he dances his freedom, rocking to the side, arms raised above his head,

Fig. 9. Frederick Timpson I'Ons, *The Freed Slave* (1840). Courtesy of the National Library of South Africa, Cape Town Campus.

in a corporeal expression of enjoyment that chafes against his bedraggled appearance. In this gestural embodiment, *The Freed Slave* uncannily mirrors the early blackface minstrel figure of "Jim Along Josey" (see fig. 10)—another "Jim Crow" double—that first appeared in a racist drama by Edward Harper, *The Free Nigger of New York* (1838), wherein "Jim" bragged that his sole "ambition" was to "show de science of his heels" by dancing on a shingle.[98] Tellingly, I'Ons's supposedly celebratory image likely borrowed its title from the derogatory title of Harper's play, which Harper toured through London and the English provinces in 1840.[99] Even if I'Ons did not directly cite "Jim Along Josey," both I'Ons's *Freed Slave* and Harper's *The Free Nigger of New York* dance their freedom in markedly similar expressions of ambivalent emancipation that signal the precariousness of racial liberation throughout the Anglophone empire.

Fig. 10. George Endicott, "Jim Along Josey" (New York: Firth & Hall, 1838). Courtesy of the Miriam and Ira D. Wallach Division of Art, Prints and Photographs: Picture Collection, New York Public Library, New York City. https://digitalcollections.nypl.org/items/510d47e3-33de-a3d9-e040-e00a18064a99.

These transmissions of Anglophone popular performance invite a reconsideration of the scope and directionality of circum-Atlantic traffics. The discursive imbrications among multiple articulations of blackface performance trace the multidirectional circulations, relays, and relations that forged intimately intertwined performance cultures and racial regimes throughout the Anglophone empire. Here, I am interested in how blackface minstrelsy's ubiquitous figurations of racial liberation have structured transnational racial discourses of freedom. The *Freed Slave* animates the constellation of unfreedom traced by the transoceanic articulations of early blackface minstrelsy, signaling how the minstrel figuration of Black abjection operated as a central racial device of Anglophone empire and its discourses of racial liberalism.[100] The articulation of *Kaatje Kekkelbek* and *The Freed Slave* at the borderlands of the Cape Colony on the British imperial frontier eerily evokes the "origin" of "Jim Crow" at the US American borderlands along the Ohio River, insistently reinscribing the ambivalent boundary between slavery and freedom through the blackface repertoire. Together, these performances embodied the impossibilities of freedom under Anglophone imperialism, tracing the ways that the sense-making apparatuses of imperial racial thinking ordered the world according to liberal and colonial discourses constitutive of the Anglophone empire.

Chapter 3

✦

Ensemble Blackface Minstrelsy Belts the World

In February 1843, the Virginia Minstrels staged a musical performance in New York City, thereby debuting the earliest recorded ensemble blackface minstrel concert. Following this inaugural performance, they quickly embarked on a tour of the British Isles. Their transatlantic tour launched a wave of ensemble minstrelsy that rippled across the Anglophone empire. As with antecedent waves of solo blackface performance, imperial discourses of antiblackness and the reactionary politics of antiabolitionism were integral to the formation of ensemble minstrelsy. Throughout its transoceanic itineraries, ensemble blackface minstrelsy furnished a proliferation of racialized performances that encircled the globe with white supremacist spectacle.

This chapter maps global circulations of ensemble blackface minstrelsy and its imperial racial repertoires. Earlier waves of blackface featured solo acts and theatrical extravaganzas. By contrast, blackface minstrelsy popularized the ensemble format of the minstrel show and its concomitant dramaturgies. The transatlantic tour of the Virginia Minstrels established a pattern for subsequent blackface troupes. A successful troupe embarked on a transnational tour. In the wake of their performances, new troupes formed to capitalize on the increased popularity of blackface minstrelsy. The initial troupe inevitably dissolved, and its constituent members would then form yet more troupes. The formation of new blackface minstrel ensembles across the empire facilitated local adaptations of minstrelsy. In this way, blackface minstrelsy constituted a distinctly transoceanic performance culture, with professionals touring transnationally, amateur troupes enacting local imitations of the leading professionals, and new professional troupes forming throughout the Anglophone empire. Ensemble blackface minstrelsy was simultaneously a global and local phenomenon, one that was produced through the transoceanic circulation of blackface performers, scripts, and material cultures.

As with blackface solo acts, scriptive blackface, and blackface visual culture, transoceanic networks of ensemble minstrelsy were not instantaneously forged through imperial ideology or discourse. In metropolitan centers and colonies alike, imperial performers and audiences fashioned minstrelsy's material and performance cultures through iterative, ad hoc processes that in turn created translocal theatrical networks, repertoires, and circuits. These performance networks formed through overlapping and frequently synchronous, amplifying waves that traversed oceanic expanses and washed across imperial shores. Crucially, there were not isolated national performance cultures that developed and exported ensemble blackface minstrelsy. The ensemble form emerged from the commonplace ubiquity of Anglophone blackface performance, and it constituted a central device in the dissemination of imperial racial thinking. Despite the ad hoc quality of global networks of ensemble blackface minstrelsy, its performance economies furnished forth enduring racial formations of imperial white supremacy. Most centrally, minstrelsy delimited opportunities for Black performers while it conscripted the empire's racialized subjects and subalterns into minstrelsy's figural economies of blackface denigration. In this chapter, I trace the tours and itineraries of ensemble blackface troupes to map how transoceanically touring blackface minstrels furnished forth minstrelsy's racial repertoires as an integral part of the Anglophone empire and its colonial common sense.

Abolitionist Minstrels and the "Origins" of Ensemble Blackface Minstrelsy

On December 30, 1842, US American abolitionist Nathaniel P. Rogers published in the *Liberator* a performance review of the Hutchinson Family Singers that professed, "Perhaps I am partial to the Hutchinsons, for they are abolitionists."[1] The Hutchinsons modeled their ensemble singing on the Rainer Family Singers, a troupe of "Tyrolese Minstrels" from the Alpine region who toured Britain, Europe, and the United States throughout the late 1820s and 1830s. Beginning in February 1842, the Hutchinson family traveled throughout the northeastern United States, performing their distinctive brand of religiously devout and respectably middle-class white minstrelsy.[2] Adapting the recently popularized close harmonies of European folk singing to the imaginative geography of New England, the Hutchinsons were also known as the "New-Hampshire Minstrels," the "New England Minstrels," and the "minstrels from the Granite State."[3] The Hutchinsons emphasized their geographic origins, fashioning their signature song, "The Old Granite State," which incorporated regularly revised verses alongside a standard chorus announcing, "We're a band of brothers" from "the mountains of the old Granite State!"[4] Though the chorus was seemingly anodyne in its emphasis on familial sentimentality, the Hutchinsons were avowedly political and participated actively in the abolitionist movement. In early January 1843, they attended William

Lloyd Garrison's abolitionist meeting in their hometown of Milford, New Hampshire. Later that month, they performed at a Massachusetts Anti-Slavery Society gathering at Boston's Faneuil Hall.[5] The Hutchinsons previously had not concealed their abolitionist politics; nevertheless, their performance at a major antislavery convention placed their abolitionism on the national stage. At the Boston meeting, the Hutchinsons sang "The Negro's Lament" and an improvised, explicitly abolitionist version of "The Old Granite State," about which Rogers declared, "Slavery would have died of that music and the response of the multitude."[6] Later versions of "The Old Granite State" proclaimed the Hutchinsons' abolitionism proudly: "We're the friends of emancipation."[7]

A week after the Hutchinsons' performance for the Massachusetts Anti-Slavery Society, on February 6, 1843, the *New York Herald* announced the first ensemble blackface minstrel show:

> First Night of the novel, grotesque, original and surpassingly melodious Ethiopian band, entitled the VIRGINIA MINSTRELS. Being an exclusively musical entertainment, combining the banjo, violin, bone castanets, and tambourine; and entirely exempt from the vulgarities and other objectionable features, which have hitherto characterized negro extravaganzas.[8]

Four formerly solo blackface performers—Dan Emmett, Billy Whitlock, Dick Pelham, and Frank Brower—joined together to form the Virginia Minstrels troupe. Though they had performed together in various combinations prior to February 1843, and though Emmett had advertised himself as an "Ethiopian Minstrel" a few months prior, the advertisement for the Virginia Minstrels was the first to associate blackface with the ensemble form of "minstrelsy" popularized by the Rainers and the Hutchinsons.[9] It remains unclear whether the Virginia Minstrels intended their name and their performance as a direct parody of the Hutchinson Family Singers. Nevertheless, the consonance between the "New-Hampshire Minstrels" and the "Virginia Minstrels" is suggestive, particularly considering blackface performers' propensity to parody abolitionism. In any case, the antagonism between the Hutchinsons and early blackface minstrel troupes was obvious: as Brian Roberts notes, "The Hutchinsons have been referred to as the period's 'anti-minstrels.'"[10] However, this formulation succumbs to the ruses of blackface hagiography that insistently claimed originality and authenticity for blackface performers. By contrast to this aggrandizing framework, it is important to recall that the Hutchinsons performed as "minstrels" *prior* to the advent of ensemble blackface minstrelsy. In opposition to the Hutchinsons and their abolitionist minstrelsy, blackface minstrels invented themselves as "anti-minstrels"—or, in the discomfiting joke that identified blackface performers as burlesque negations of white minstrelsy throughout the Anglophone empire: "nigger minstrels."[11] In other words, "blackface minstrelsy" began as an antiblack joke, and it was an exceedingly popular one.

Blackface performers soon realized the potential of "minstrel" ensemble singing as yet another means of antiabolitionist and antiblack burlesque. Following their successful New York debut, the Virginia Minstrels toured to Boston and Worcester, Massachusetts. Troping on the Rainers' and Hutchinsons' use of minstrelsy as a vehicle for ethnic and regional white particularism, the Virginia Minstrels billed their performance as "truly delineating" the cultural practices of "the Virginia Colored Race"—"all their Merry Meetings, such as the gathering in of the Cotton and Sugar Crops, Corn Huskings, Slave Weddings and Junketings"—while also offering a "masterly and chaste" concert for respectable audiences.[12] Here, the Virginia Minstrels played on the perceived incongruity between the "chaste" songs of the Hutchinsons and the performances of "Southern Slaves"—an incongruity palpable in the punning advertisement of the Minstrels' "masterly" performance of "slave" culture. Throughout their performances, the Virginia Minstrels effected a complex parody of the "Granite State Minstrels" and their abolitionist politics by driving a wedge between their enactments of sentimental white respectability and popular conceptions of blackness. Simultaneously, the Virginia Minstrels traded on the language of bourgeois propriety in their approximation of the Hutchinsons to legitimate their "extravaganzas" to white middle-class audiences, all while denigrating blackness as beyond the bounds of classed respectability.

The Virginia Minstrels' strategy was a marked success throughout their tours of the major US American cities along the Atlantic Seaboard. By the end of April 1843, the troupe departed the United States for a tour of Britain and Ireland, which lasted until July 1844.[13] The duration of their transatlantic tour signals the significant British investment in minstrelsy from its earliest beginnings. Advertisements for their London performances at the Adelphi Theatre invited audiences to "enjoy a hearty laugh at the extraordinary grimaces of the Black Minstrels," while their tour of the provinces drew praise for "their personation of the real down south (not south down) negroes, with their dancing, singing, and banjo playing, prov[ing] highly attractive."[14] Almost as soon as it was invented, ensemble blackface minstrelsy became a transoceanic phenomenon popular throughout the Anglophone empire.

Meanwhile, within a month of the Virginia Minstrels' debut, P. T. Barnum's American Museum in New York City featured a performance of "Ethiopean melodies and dances" by the "Kentucky Minstrels" in an apparent imitation of the Virginia Minstrels' new burlesque on minstrelsy.[15] Several other early blackface minstrel troupes followed in the wake of the Virginia Minstrels, repeating the central joke of blackface minstrelsy by naming themselves the African Serenaders, Alabama Minstrels, Christy Minstrels, Columbia Minstrels, Congo Minstrels, Ethiopian Minstrels, Ethiopian Serenaders, Missouri Minstrels, New Orleans Serenaders, New York Minstrels, Sable Harmonists, San Francisco Minstrels, Southern Minstrels, and Virginia Serenaders, among many others.[16] Through the sheer ubiquity of such ensembles, "minstrelsy" was denigrated—that is, blackened—such that it became synonymous with blackface performance.

Throughout its transoceanic circulations, ensemble blackface minstrelsy troped on and elaborated the repertoires of early blackface, particularly its insistent ideological opposition to abolitionism, Black freedom, and Black equality. As such, the "minstrelsy" of the Hutchinson Family Singers remained a frequent target for blackface minstrel burlesque. For instance, the *Turner's Comic Almanac for 1848* published in New York and Philadelphia featured a paratheatrical image of scriptive blackface in which two Black Americans attend a Hutchinson concert (see fig. 11). Two grotesquely exaggerated blackface caricatures—Missy Phillis and Sambo—comment on the "bobbolition song" of the Hutchinson family before Phillis expresses her desire to "larn dem tunes and join de singers [her]self."[17] Sambo cautions Phillis against her plan, warning her that she "is too 'spectable to 'tand up dar and sing song for odder people." Phillis replies with an alternative plan: she will marry "dat white gemman dat advertises for a wife" in the local paper. The scenario concludes with Sambo expressing his outrage that Phillis would betray him for a white man. Referring to a racial panic surrounding the Hutchinsons' abolitionist insistence on allowing interracial audiences at their concerts, the print traces the racial and sexual anxieties undergirding blackface burlesque and its investments in opposing any form of racial amalgamation.[18] Staging Sambo and Phillis as comically out-of-place arrivistes, this scriptive blackface scene posits the immediate slippage from a racially integrated audience to an imagined racially integrated performance to an imagined interracial marriage of Phillis with a "white gemman." The print thus frames the Hutchinsons' abolitionist minstrelsy as the first step toward miscegenation and ensuing racial confusions.

The Hutchinsons later actualized antiabolitionist fears when they inspired the Luca Family Singers, a Black abolitionist troupe who performed at the Anti-Slavery Society convention in May 1850. Led by John W. Luca, the Luca family shared the stage with the Hutchinsons for a series of abolitionist concerts in Ohio in 1859.[19] Blackface minstrel performers responded to the threat posed by such interracial abolitionist performance by insistently parodying the Hutchinsons and burlesquing their egalitarian refrain "We're a Band of Brothers" as a blackface paean to essentialized racial difference.[20] The Christy's Minstrels made such burlesques of the Hutchinsons a mainstay of their concerts, performing "We're A Band of Brothers! A Burlesque on the Hutchinson Family" throughout the British

him to sleep.

THE HUTCHINSON FAMILY.

"Wot you tink Missy Phillis; dat consart am berry good music?" "Berry well, Sambo. Dat white gal got moss as good eddication as me. I tink de superlatives ob her voice am berry obnoxious." "Ah, dat am de truff. Bekase dey gib de bobbolition song dat am de reason dat de music sound so doloriferous dis ebening." "I tell you wot, Sambo, I tink I larn dem tunes and join de singers myself. Den I gib dem de rail colored sound wen I sing de same." "Phew! Missy Phillis—you aint in arnest 'bout dat—wot you want to 'spose yourself for to go 'round wid singers arter dat fashion? Young lady, like you, is too 'spectable to 'tand up dar and sing song for odder people." "Praps you is right, Sambo. Praps I better marry dat white gemman dat advertises for a wife in de Tribune. Missus tinks dat I better hab de white gemman." "Wot dat you say, Missy Phillis! You tink you stoop to hab a white man, wen dis darkey hab been payin' 'tention to you for six monfs. You is de most onsconciable colored female dat I ebber seen sense Dorcas Gumbo died."

Fig. 11. "The Hutchinson Family," *Turner's Comic Almanac for 1848* (Philadelphia and New York: Turner & Fisher, 1847), 32. Courtesy of the American Antiquarian Society.

Isles.[21] The piece remained in the Christy's Minstrels' repertoire during their transoceanic imperial tours of the 1860s, prompting amateur and professional blackface troupes in Cape Town, Mumbai, and across Australia's goldfields to reprise the antiabolitionist burlesque.[22] Through its wide circulations, the repertoire of transoceanic blackface was adamant in its opposition to the Hutchinsons and their brand of righteously abolitionist and respectably middle-class white sentimentality. Founded on antiabolitionism and invested in racial subjection, blackface minstrelsy entrenched antiblack proslavery politics as central to discourses of Anglophone imperial popular culture.

An Amateur Empire of Blackface

The 1843 British tour of the Virginia Minstrels cast a wide wake. Following the troupe's successes in the British Isles, local performers and amateurs throughout the Anglophone empire assembled their own blackface minstrel shows. One leading producer of colonial blackface minstrelsy was Australian theater impresario George Coppin, the proverbial "father of the Australian theatre" who departed England for the antipodes in late 1842, prior to the formation of the Virginia Minstrels and their inaugural transatlantic tour.[23] A mere six months after his arrival in Sydney in March 1843, Coppin began staging blackface performances, including appearances "as the Old Kentucky Nigger, . . . screech[ing] 'Sich a Getting Up Stairs,' and 'Jim Along Josey.'"[24] By June 1844, Coppin reproduced the model of the Virginia Minstrels and offered Australian audiences an evening-length bill comprising blackface minstrel songs, dances, and sketches. Coppin's earliest evening of blackface entertainment highlighted several solo songs—such as "Zip Coon" and "Jim Along Josey"—but only featured one ensemble "glee" and three duets including "Chingaringcomechaw." Nevertheless, the advertisement announced the central appeal of the minstrel show's ensemble model of blackface performance, presenting white Anglophone audiences with "More Niggers!"[25] Coppin's minstrel shows offer insight into how colonial blackface reproduced metropolitan stage practices locally. Coppin's playbill had little in common with the formal structure of the early programs of the Virginia Minstrels and their full-chorus renditions of blackface songs. Nevertheless, Coppin assembled an evening of blackface minstrelsy that approximated the form of the minstrel show while investing in its extravagant stagings of Black abjection.

Simultaneously, Coppin's minstrelsy fashioned novel, colonial tropes of blackface denigration such as his ethnographic figurations of Black characters like "Jim Brown," who was advertised as "not a white nigger, or a copper coloured nigger but a regular beautifully polished Day and Martin, just arrived in the colony from Long Island, in a high state of preservation."[26] Coppin framed his show through a persistent trope of colonial stagings of blackface, promising his audiences that Australian blackface was an authentic import directly from New York. As Coppin and his fellow colonial actors staged their own minstrel shows for eager audiences, this framing obscured Australian colonial investments in embodying and spectating on blackface denigration—a local economy of enjoyment that exceeded the conceptual frame of import-export. Instead, Coppin's entertainment saloon constituted a parallel development to E. P. Christy's evenings of blackface entertainments at his theater-saloon in Buffalo, New York (ca. 1843).[27] The antipodal variations on the blackface minstrel show signal that its enduring appeal relied on its formal flexibility, a characteristic that facilitated its adaptation across disparate contexts. White Anglophone audiences in the US American North and throughout the British Empire were similarly invested in performances of Black denigration, especially when presented as "authentic" and "original" representations of blackness.

Coppin was hardly the only British colonist to seize on minstrelsy's transoceanic popularity and to stage a local colonial production of ensemble blackface. Contemporaneous to Coppin's blackface saloons, an anonymously authored localized Australian adaptation of W. T. Moncrieff's *Life in London* (1821) appeared as an unintended closet drama resulting from a canceled premiere. *Life in Sydney; or, The Ran Dan Club* (1843) adapted yet another Anglophone blackface script to the colonies, reimagining "African Sal" as "New Zealand Sal," a minstrelized Māori dancer who appeared alongside "Jim Brown, a blackface entertainer."[28] The inclusion of a comic Māori figure alongside a "Jim Brown" minstrel character signals both the enduring capaciousness of transoceanic blackface to encompass disparate colonial subjects of the Anglophone empire and the fluidity between ethnographic and burlesque figurations of the empire's racialized subjects. Meanwhile, in the Cape Colony of southern Africa, the earliest known articulations of transoceanic blackface echoed those in the US American and British minstrel repertoires. Alongside "Jump Jim Crow," minstrel songs circulated in the streets of Cape Town. For instance, Cape journalist Sam Sly reports having "heard one general *song*, or universal favorite, sung in the open air by the *Mobility*, since [he had] been in the Cape": the minstrel song "Miss Lucy Long."[29] Sly's reportage traces the ubiquitous popularity of early blackface songs among the British colonial "Mobility"—that is, the "mob," or the "low" counterpart to the "high" nobility—well prior to the arrival of professional blackface troupes. In both colonial Sydney and Cape Town, amateur theatricals and everyday performances of blackface song and dance constituted the initial vectors for the transmission of blackface popular culture throughout the Anglophone empire.

After the earliest waves of solo transoceanic blackface performance in the 1830s and 1840s during which "Jim Crow mania" girdled the globe, an amateur troupe staged the earliest known ensemble performance of blackface minstrelsy in southern Africa at the Hope Street Theatre in Cape Town on September 15, 1848. After the English Amateur Company's production of *The Country Squire, or, Two Days at the Hall*, the "Ethiopian Serenaders" sang a series of blackface minstrel standbys, including "Buffalo Gals," "The Boatman Dance," "Old Joe," and "Walk Jaw Bone."[30]

Though the local reviewer bemoaned the "low" character of the performance, he also observed that the songs resonated with the local audience: "not a face was rigid, but every countenance relaxed and puckered up with the loud burst of laughter."[31] Attesting to the popularity of ensemble blackface minstrelsy at the Cape, an encore performance followed on September 21, featuring the new songs "The Dandy Broadway Swell" and "My Skiff Is on the Shore," as well as repeat performances on October 3 and October 6, 1848, and January 3, 1849.[32] The identities of this colonial troupe of Ethiopian Serenaders are difficult to trace, as amateur blackface performers in the colonies frequently performed anonymously or under pseudonyms. Nevertheless, it is likely that the Cape Colony's band of Ethiopian Serenaders were amateur colonists invested in staging the latest hits from the transoceanic blackface repertoire.

The colonial troupe of "Ethiopian Serenaders" who introduced ensemble blackface minstrelsy to the Cape Colony modeled themselves directly on the US American troupe of Ethiopian Serenaders led by Gilbert Pell, whose two years of successful performances in London (1846–1848) inaugurated a new style of ensemble minstrelsy.[33] By contrast to the Virginia Minstrels' caricature of "authentic" plantation life, Pell's Ethiopian Serenaders dispensed with minstrel burlesques and extravaganzas and instead performed musical concerts and dances while adorned in "dandy costume, *à la Jullien*—that is, waistcoated and wristbanded, turned up in the most approved D'Orsay fashion."[34] Though their sartorial styling staged blackness in the guise of bourgeois respectability, audiences understood this as yet another blackface joke on the perceived incongruity between their "grotesque" appearance "painted jet black, with ruddy lips, and large mouths" and their performance of "the compositions of the great European masters."[35]

British audiences celebrated the novel blackface burlesques of Pell's Ethiopian Serenaders amid an intensifying British backlash against both the abolition of slavery and the prospect of racial equality. In 1849, Thomas Carlyle anonymously published his essay "Occasional Discourse on the Nigger Question," in which he troped on blackface minstrelsy's fantasies of plantation docility and harmony. Specifically, Carlyle posited that the postemancipation prosperity of imperial white British subjects was inversely related to the well-being of "Negroes": "The Negroes are all very happy and doing well . . . . West-Indian Whites, it is admitted, are far enough from happy; West-Indian Colonies not unlike sinking wholly into ruin: at home too, the British Whites are rather badly off."[36] This framing reduplicated the racial discourses of proslavery imagery that contrasted minstrelsy's figuration of "Slavery as It Exists in America"—that is, as happy, dancing, and contented enslaved people existing in communal harmony—with "Slavery as It Exists in England"—that is, as "wage slavery" or "white slavery" in which working-class white British subjects

Fig. 12. *Slavery As It Exists in America. Slavery As It Exists in England* (Boston: J. Haven, 1850). Courtesy of the Library of Congress. https://www.loc.gov/pictures/resource/cph.3a05113/.

suffer from impoverishment, exploitation, and neglect (see fig. 12).[37] By contrast to such nationalistic comparisons, Carlyle envisioned a racist fantasy in which "the Negroes" were unvaryingly "happy and doing well" at the expense of both "West-Indian Whites" and "British Whites," all of whom were uniformly exploited. In response to Carlyle's racist diatribe, John Stuart Mill published a rebuttal that critiqued Carlyle's "picture of negro inactivity, copied from the wildest prophecies of the slavery party before emancipation."[38] Though Mill's complaint perceptively identified Carlyle's citation of proslavery materials in circulation throughout the 1820s and 1830s, he failed to connect Carlyle's proslavery vision of the racially harmonious plantation to the transoceanic popularity of blackface minstrelsy throughout the Anglophone empire following emancipation. Carlyle's racist imagination of natural Black servitude was unquestionably drawn from blackface characters and scenarios of the minstrel stage, including those popularized by the Ethiopian Serenaders.[39]

Indeed, the London performances of the Ethiopian Serenaders were a grand success, and they inspired several imitators. As a midcentury amateur British blackface performer recounted, the Ethiopian Serenaders "made a deal of money . . . . After them sprang up the 'Lantum Serenaders' and the 'Ohio Serenaders,' the 'South Carolina Serenaders,' the 'Kentucky Minstrels,' and many other schools of them; but Pell's gang was at the top of the tree."[40] Commenting on this proliferation of blackface troupes, the comic magazine *Punch* mocked the "glut of Ethiopians" on the London stage, suggesting that the appearance of "the New Orleans Ethiopians" would likely inspire the formation of a surfeit of local British blackface troupes: "the Brentford Bohemians, the Chelsea Cherokees, or the Mary-le-bone Mulattos" along with "the Kensington Coolies" and "the Houndsditch Half-Castes."[41] In a different vein, *Punch* published a mocking paean to a Māori woman titled "To the Squaw Quareeshee" that was replete with an image of a blackface minstrel wooing the titular figure on bended knee.[42] Across these several parodies of blackface minstrelsy, *Punch*'s satires signal the extent of minstrelsy's popularity and offer insight as to how British audiences interpreted and adapted blackface to British imperial racial imaginaries that abjected not only Black Americans but also the unfree Black, brown, and Indigenous subjects of the Anglophone empire. Pell's Ethiopian Serenaders affirmed white supremacy as imperial common sense by mediating renewed investments in the enjoyment of spectacles of racial abjection.

Indeed, the circulation of blackface minstrelsy throughout the British Empire popularized imperial racial discourses not only in London and the United States but also in British colonies wherein blackface was fitted to anxieties relating to the ambiguously "free" status of the empire's colonized and racialized subjects. For instance, the performances of Pell's Ethiopian Serenaders in London transmitted minstrelsy's antiblack repertoires broadly throughout the Anglophone empire, a process exemplified by the amateur Ethiopian Serenaders concerts in Cape Town. A key vector for the transmission of Pell's Ethiopian Serenaders' articulation of blackface minstrelsy took the form of a songbook featuring "52 of the most Popular" blackface melodies "performed by the Serenaders, and other Nigger Melodists."[43] This collection included several of the songs performed at the Cape colonial Ethiopian Serenaders' concerts, and it was likely used by the colonial amateurs who mounted their own minstrel shows. As in London, the print transmission of minstrel materials allowed white Anglophone subjects to become intimately familiar with blackface minstrelsy. Amateurs could adorn themselves in burnt cork and sing from a minstrel songbook onstage while families and their guests could harmonize to minstrel melodies at home. Through print circulation, in Cape Town as in London, amateur minstrelsy became a common element of imperial popular culture.

Despite their instantiation of ensemble blackface minstrelsy as a performance form in South Africa, the troupe of Cape colonial Ethiopian Serenaders proved unable to sustain their popularity.[44] Nevertheless, several other colonial minstrel performances soon followed in South Africa. In 1850, an English actor named John Russell staged four performances in Makhanda (Grahamstown) that featured a troupe of "Celebrated Ethiopian Serenaders, [who . . .] perform[ed] some of the more popular Nigger Melodies."[45] A playbill from August 21, 1852, at the Drury Lane Theatre in Cape Town, advertised a minstrel show that included the most popular songs from the early minstrel repertoire, including "The Boatman's Dance," "Old Ned," "Jim Crow," "Blue-Tailed Fly."[46] Other white colonial amateur troupes across southern Africa continued to stage minstrel shows throughout the 1850s and early 1860s. In 1857, the Graham's Town Amateur Theatre hosted yet another troupe of "Ethiopian Serenaders" as an entr'acte performance.[47] In 1858, Mr. Gough advertised a "newly-formed band of Ethiopian serenaders" at his Cape Town theater.[48] When Prince Alfred toured the Cape in 1860, a grand fete and fair held in his honor featured a troupe of "Ethiopian Serenaders" who presented "Choice Negro Ballads." These serenaders "were loudly applauded by an immense concourse of people who surrounded the platform upon which they performed the whole time the fair was open."[49] In March 1861, the Theatre Royal, Cape Town, featured a performance by D'Urban's Ethiopian Minstrels.[50] By the end of the year, blackface minstrel songs were familiar enough to Cape colonists that they were sung in the open air as part of a Christmas Eve ritual. As prominent Cape denizen John Rose recounted in his diaries, "A party of serenaders of whom I was one, discoursed some very fair music (C[hristy] Minstrel's songs) under the windows of their friends."[51] In eThekwini, Mr. Haygarth staged an Ethiopian Serenaders performance in January 1858.[52] Mr. Galt (St. George) also mounted a local colonial amateur minstrel show in eThekwini—first in 1863 and again in 1867.[53] Along with Coppin's blackface saloon performances, these several enactments signal that by the 1860s, amateur blackface minstrelsy was commonplace in colonial Australian and South African popular culture, well prior to the arrival of transoceanically touring professional minstrel troupes.

Professional Minstrelsy

The earliest known professional minstrel troupe to perform in the British colonies was the Congo Minstrels. In March 1846, contemporaneous to Pell's Ethiopian Serenaders' performances in London, the Congo Minstrels performed in Falmouth, Jamaica, tracing a forgotten blackface minstrel touring circuit through the Caribbean and Latin America.[54] Just two months later, in May 1846, the earliest known professional blackface minstrel ensemble to perform in Australia took the stage at the Launceston Theatre Royal Olympic in Tasmania. Performing with Professor Risley's acrobatic troupe, the Sable Minstrels were advertised as a recent arrival from the United States: "From the New York Theatre, [they] will electrify the audience by singing some of their most popular Negro Melodies, accompanied with their native music."[55] Simultaneous to the British tour of Pell's Ethiopian Serenaders, several blackface minstrel troupes traversed the Americas and the antipodes. A mere three years after the formation of the Virginia Minstrels, blackface companies charted itineraries to the farthest reaches of the Anglophone empire.

Though archives of these tours are scattershot, it is evident that professional blackface companies increased the popularity of amateur and local stagings of blackface minstrelsy throughout the Anglophone empire. For instance, a year after the Sable Minstrels' tour to Australia, a troupe of amateur Ethiopian Serenaders performed at Sydney's Royal Victoria Theatre in September 1847.[56] A year later, in August 1848, another troupe of Ethiopian Serenaders assembled a playbill at the Albert Theatre in Hobart featuring "the American Melodies which were received in London with the most enthusiastic applause."[57] The following year, a troupe billed as the "Four Ethiopian Serenaders" performed in Melbourne, performing many of the same songs as were sung in Cape Town in late 1848, including "Dance the Boatman" and "Dance the Buffalo Gals."[58] Contemporaneous to the earliest known South African amateur Ethiopian Serenaders, these troupes explicitly cited and reperformed the popular songs and pieces from London.

Amid this wave of amateur performances, in March 1850, a second professional minstrel troupe landed in Australia. The Blythe Waterland Serenaders announced that they had "arrived from England, and [would] give their popular and fashionable Ethiopian Concerts in Sydney."[59] Local audiences welcomed the troupe, and a leading Sydney newspaper proclaimed them "the first [company] that has brought the peculiarities of the 'Nigger,' in a contracted way, before the Sydney public."[60] The Blythe Waterland Serenaders capitalized on local familiarity with blackface minstrelsy by promoting their talent and refinement as a professional troupe. They performed for months in Sydney and the surrounding colonial towns before the troupe split into two rival factions: Waterland and Reading's

Serenaders, and Howard's Serenaders.[61] Howard's troupe proved to be more successful and enduring, touring as far afield as Aotearoa New Zealand in 1852. Though it was preceded by several amateur minstrel shows, this troupe became the first of many professional ensembles to incorporate Aotearoa New Zealand into the transoceanic circuit of minstrelsy.[62] Meanwhile, the Waterland and Reading troupe disbanded.[63] The dissolution of this blackface troupe paradoxically proliferated more minstrelsy, as J. W. Reading partnered with Australian colonist and amateur blackface performer John Hydes to form Hydes and Reading's Serenaders.[64] This was an early instance in an enduring pattern wherein professional troupes disbanded only to form new companies consisting of both professional minstrels and also local amateur performers from the colonies.

In 1851, the New York Serenaders became the next major professional blackface minstrel troupe to tour Australia. The company formed in New York City before touring to California amid the gold rush. They departed the goldfields in 1849, toured to Honolulu in early 1850, then returned to California before sailing to Tasmania in early 1851.[65] This troupe advertised themselves as a successful band of globe-trotting singers, emphasizing the transoceanic scope of their tours across "Mexico, the cities of South America, California, the islands of the Pacific, and Van Diemen's Land, and en route to the East Indies, the continent of Europe, and Great Britain."[66] The troupe arrived amid the discovery of the Australian goldfields and altered their itinerary to capitalize on the newfound wealth of the colony. As in California, minstrelsy became the popular performance repertoire of—and the soundtrack to—the masculine, homosocial world of Australian mining towns. Nevertheless, the New York Serenaders did not appeal exclusively to a white working-class audience. They also appealed to middle-class audiences by publishing a songbook of their "Ethiopian Melodies" designed for use in the parlors of respectable homes.[67] As in the United States and Britain, blackface minstrelsy proliferated numerous discourses and cultural materials that animated classed identities and divergent positions on slavery. However, the form drew together white audiences from different classes and ideological positions through its antiblack and white supremacist racial repertoires.

Attesting to the broad appeal of the New York Serenaders, the troupe found eager audiences throughout the Indian subcontinent when they mounted the first professional tour of South Asia from 1852 to 1853. This iteration of the troupe slightly altered its established cast of performers by adding J. W. Reading (formerly of the Blythe Waterland Serenaders). Advertising their show as an "Entertainment" representing the "True American Negro Character," the New York Serenaders staged the core repertory of mid-nineteenth-century blackface minstrelsy, including "Dandy Broadway Swell," "Buffalo Gals," and the plantation breakdown "Niggers from the South."[68] There were relatively fewer amateur performances of blackface minstrelsy in South Asia than in other colonial sites, likely due to its smaller permanent white colonial population. Nevertheless, professional ensemble minstrelsy was an immediate hit with the white colonial audiences of Kolkata and Mumbai. A local reviewer of this inaugural performance in January 1852 reported an eager audience who sought

> to have a hearty laugh at their sable brethren across the waters—the American Negroes—the rude "images of God cut in ebony." It was expected that a humorous picture of the black gentry's imperfect imitations of white-faced civilizations would afford a delightful treat to people snugly triple folded in a comfortable sense of their own immeasurable superiority, natural and conventional.[69]

This frank description aptly summarized the colonial audience's psychic and affective investments in blackface minstrelsy. It also explicitly acknowledged that the appeal of the form derived from its affordance of racist comforts—the feeling of "immeasurable superiority" furnished by minstrelsy's racial repertoires. This review's avowed embrace of ensemble minstrelsy as a tool of white supremacy strongly suggests that the audiences who enjoyed the New York Serenaders' performances in Kolkata were primarily white and cross-class: they included the masses of "white-faced civilization" as well as "some of the élite of Calcutta Society," most notably "the Most Noble Governor General and Lady Dalhousie."[70] I have been unable to identify any evidence indicating that non-white colonized subjects attended these early ensemble minstrel shows, nor have I encountered material that definitively discounts this possibility. The questions of whether South Asian members of the "élite" attended and whether they enjoyed these spectacles of blackface abjection or counteridentified against the performance's explicit white supremacy must remain unanswered, as they are occluded by the absences of the colonial archive. It is nevertheless undeniable that all classes of white British residents of Kolkata patronized the Serenaders' minstrel concerts, enjoying the comforts afforded by minstrelsy's white supremacist spectacle.

Following their successes in Kolkata, the New York Serenaders toured the subcontinent, including several stops at Sri Lanka and Mumbai.[71] The troupe found similar popularity in Mumbai during a six-month series of concerts beginning in July 1852, with a review of their debut Mumbai performance recounting that "the humourous delineation of negro character and the drollery of the conundrums and 'leetle anecdotes,' kept the audience in a roar of laughter."[72] The troupe returned to Kolkata in January 1853 and performed there through March 1853 before returning to Australia.[73] The New York Serenaders initially planned to conclude their tour of India in mid-February 1853; however, they extended their stay in Kolkata nearly a month after "receiv[ing] by Overland Mail, a collection of New Songs," which provided them with enough fresh material to stage additional "Ethiopian Musical Soirees."[74] The extension of the Serenaders' tour traces how minstrelsy's print archives and performance repertoires reinforced one another to furnish forth the global hegemony of transoceanic blackface across the Anglophone empire. Moreover, in 1853 US American author Bayard Taylor visited Delhi, where he encountered a "Hindoo minstrel" who regaled him not only with "Indian airs" but also with the latest blackface minstrel songs: "Old Dan Tucker," "Oh, Susannah," and "Buffalo Gals," among "other choice Ethiopian melodies"—all of which were drawn from the repertoire of the New York Serenaders and from the proliferation of blackface minstrel songbooks circulating throughout the subcontinent.[75] Cementing the popularity of minstrelsy in the subcontinent, a reconstituted version of the New York Serenaders returned once more to Kolkata in May 1855, performing in the city for two months before departing for Malaysia and Singapore.[76] Following the departure of the New York Serenaders, amateur minstrelsy continued to draw crowds in South Asia, particularly through the military performances of the H.M. 86th Regiment Ethiopian Serenaders.[77]

Though the New York Serenaders were the only professional troupe to tour the Indian subcontinent during the 1850s, many more journeyed to Australia. The next major professional troupe to tour the Pacific circuit was Rainer's Original Ethiopian Serenaders, who arrived in Australia in late 1852. Claiming speciously to be "the first to harmonise Nigger Melodies, and originators of the present popular style of Ethiopian Entertainments," Rainer's troupe promoted themselves as a global success that had been patronized by "Her Majesty Queen Victoria, Her Royal Consort Prince Albert, and the Court" as well as by "the President and heads of departments of the United States."[78] Following the precedent of other touring blackface ensembles, Rainer's Serenaders explicitly targeted a cross-class Anglophone white audience—a respectable audience who could find comfort in the legitimation promised by patronage from heads of state, and a lower-class crowd who could enjoy the "popular style" of minstrelsy. The troupe arrived at the beginning of the Australian gold rush, and they found great success throughout the Australian colonies. Though they popularized many sentimental songs with antislavery valences, the troupe did not promote racial equity or any critical reflections among Australian audiences. Their popular renditions of "Uncle Tom's Farewell" trafficked in minstrelsy's economy of enjoyment, which allowed Australian colonists to condemn the brutality of US American slavery, to mourn the sentimental death of Uncle Tom, and to avoid any reckoning with the racial dominion of the British Empire or its genocidal violence against Aboriginal Australians.[79] After the troupe dissolved in September 1855, several of the core members of Rainer's troupe continued performing in the antipodes and other colonial sites for decades, while others returned to the circum–North Atlantic circuit.[80]

In October 1855, yet another professional minstrel troupe arrived in Australia, introducing themselves as "the world wide celebrated Backus's Minstrels, from the New York and California Theatres."[81] As with the New York Serenaders and Rainer's troupe, Backus's company advertised the global scope of their tours "through the principal cities of the United States, Mexico, South America, and the Sandwich Islands."[82] Soon after the troupe's arrival, T. P. Brower and J. M. Foans (both formerly of Rainer's Serenaders) joined the Backus Minstrels for a special production of T. D. Rice's *Oh, Hush! Or, The Virginny Cupids*.[83] The troupe found immediate success in Sydney before touring to Melbourne, where they performed at Coppin's Olympic Theatre.[84] While in Melbourne, Neil Bryant—also formerly of Rainer's Serenaders and brother to company member Jerry Bryant—joined the ensemble.[85] Charles Backus, the troupe's leader, was a popular "Tambourine" (or "Tambo") who was well versed in the repertoires of blackface minstrelsy. A review of the debut performance of the Backus Minstrels in Melbourne traces the racial investments of their Australian audiences:

> Everybody will return from the theatre with aching sides, and a sort of misty impression upon their minds of having spent a good many hours (brief and pleasant hours) upon a plantation in South Carolina, among the happiest, merriest, and most musical assemblage of Uncle Toms that ever congregated together.[86]

The description of blackface minstrel figures as "Uncle Toms" signals the transformation effected by the minstrel burlesque of the sentimental abolitionist figure. No longer an abolitionist symbol of Black humanity, on the transoceanic minstrel stage "Uncle Tom" signified yet another denigrated and abject blackface archetype in the mode of Mungo, Sambo, and Jim Crow. Backus further expanded on this extensive minstrel repertoire in his comic songs and skits such as a burlesque of Othello's oration to the Venetian Senate and "his personation of a Chinaman."[87] The Backus Minstrels were the earliest known troupe to incorporate yellowface into their minstrel shows (more on this in chapter 5). They thereby adapted the form to the racial politics of the Pacific circuit and instantiated a novel mode of racialized performance that would endure long after the dissolution of Backus's company. Several members of the troupe departed Australia following their final performance of the tour in April 1856, while others remained to form new ensembles.[88]

By August 1856, a troupe of veteran professional minstrels from Rainer's Serenaders and the Backus Minstrels joined together to form a new company of "Ethiopian Serenaders" in which veteran performers T. P. Brower,

W. A. Porter, and D. F. Boley were joined by a young amateur named Dave Carson.[89] Other troupes continued to tour through the Pacific circuit, such as the Empire Minstrels starring Harry Leslie.[90] Several other ensembles formed from the dispersed members of professional troupes while countless minstrel shows were staged throughout mining towns on the colonial frontier. For instance, in November 1857, two veterans of the Backus Minstrels (D. F. Boley and Otto Burbank) joined with US American minstrel performer G. W. Demerest in Sydney to form the (inaccurately named) San Francisco Minstrels, and within a month, Dave Carson also joined this company.[91] From 1857 through 1861, this iteration of the San Francisco Minstrels toured throughout Australia's cities and mining encampments, regularly incorporating popular minstrel performers into their lineup.[92]

In October 1861, Carson led a reconstituted version of the San Francisco Minstrels on a five-year tour of the Indian subcontinent.[93] Their initial overland tour brought them through northern India along the Ganges—Varanasi, Prayagraj, Lucknow, Kanpur, Agra, Meerut, Delhi, Ambala, Ludhiana, Anarkali, Lahore, Kashmir, and Shimla—before returning to Kolkata. A second tour followed a sea route between Mumbai and Kolkata with stops at Chennai and Goa.[94] The troupe toured throughout the subcontinent until 1866, with Kolkata as their primary base of operations. During their five-year tour of South Asia, the San Francisco Minstrels' repertoire featured many popular minstrel pieces, including a burlesque of the Hutchinson Singers, "Quartet by the Unhappy Family, the Band of Brothers."[95] In their tours, the San Francisco Minstrels circulated throughout the subcontinent not only individual songs and skits but also the generic form of the ensemble blackface minstrel show.

Carson established himself as a leading theater impresario of South Asia until his death in 1896. During his career, he assembled numerous minstrel troupes that toured through present-day India, Pakistan, Sri Lanka, Myanmar, Malaysia, Singapore, China, and Japan.[96] Carson's successful relocation to South Asia signaled the transoceanic portability of the regional model of blackface minstrel touring in which various professional troupes competed for hegemony over local touring circuits. Once established on the subcontinent, Carson continued to draw new performers from the Pacific circuit as well as from London and the United States. He regularly updated his repertoire with both popular routines from the circum-Atlantic circuit and local brownface caricatures and skits elaborated on Backus's yellowface model (more on this in chapter 5). Meanwhile, the successes of the San Francisco Minstrels inspired the formation of local amateur blackface companies throughout the subcontinent. As a newspaper correspondent noted, "Carson, I may remark, occupies [in India], in a limited degree, a similar position to what George Coppin filled in Australia in years gone by."[97] Like Coppin before him in Australia, Carson invested his minstrel profits into several theatrical ventures, founding the Anglophone theater of the subcontinent on the grounds of blackface minstrelsy.

Contemporaneous to Carson's extended tour of South Asia, a separate troupe of San Francisco Minstrels staged a concurrent tour to Aotearoa New Zealand in 1861–1862. Starring George Chittendon, Walter Howson, O. P. Ritchie, J. J. Burgess, Harry Leslie, and J. R. Taylor, these San Francisco Minstrels followed a flood of Australian colonists who flocked to the neighboring colony upon the discovery of gold near Dunedin.[98] Several additional amateur and professional troupes soon followed, profiting from the new wealth that aggregated in mining towns throughout the empire.

By 1861, nearly the entirety of the transoceanic Anglophone empire was inundated by amateur and professional blackface performances. Regularly adapted to local conventions, transoceanic blackface was invariably an explicitly and transparently white supremacist form that traded on proslavery and antiblack racial discourses. For instance, Richard Waterhouse notes how transnational tours of blackface troupes led increasingly to the comic minstrelization of Aboriginal Australians.[99] Though some performers such as Charles Backus and Dave Carson fashioned Asian yellowface and brownface caricatures drawing from the blackface repertoire, blackness consistently provided Anglophone audiences with a theatrical screen on which imperial white subjects projected their feelings of "immeasurable superiority" as natural and conventional.[100] With the racial furniture of minstrelsy's empire firmly in place, a leading minstrel troupe embarked on a global tour of the British Empire, knitting together several local and regional circuits.

The Transoceanic Tours of the Christy's Minstrels; or, The Silver Belt Jig

In August 1857, a troupe of Christy's Minstrels headed by J. W. Raynor arrived in London and staged the first performances of their transatlantic tour.[101] This was a splinter group of the troupe that was founded by E. P. Christy in Buffalo, New York, in the early 1840s and that attained prominence on Broadway in 1847. Though Raynor's company featured neither E. P. Christy nor George Harrington (aka "George N. Christy"), this transatlantic tour and the troupe's ensuing global tour were so popular that "Christy Minstrels" became a common term for blackface minstrel performers throughout the British Empire.[102] Several troupes ultimately performed under the title of "Christy's Minstrels," all of which shared a common format for an evening of blackface performance: part 1 featured a concert of popular comic and sentimental blackface songs; part 2 presented an olio, or a "musical and terpsichorean mélange"; part 3 staged scenarios of "Plantation Life in the Sunny South"; and the evening concluded with an operatic or Shakespearean burlesque. In August 1862, after five successful years in Britain, several members of Raynor's troupe under the leadership of Anthony Nish embarked on a transoceanic tour of the British colonies in southern Africa and the antipodes. Nish's company included internationally famous minstrels such as Joe Brown, Washington Norton, James Melvyn, Charles Steele, Thomas Rainford, and Charles Stewart.[103] Between 1862 and 1866, several troupes—many formed by members of Raynor's initial troupe—developed an imperial circuit of minstrel performance that bound together the Anglophone empire of the Indian Ocean world in a shared performance culture of transoceanic blackface.

As in the United States and London, Nish's Christy's Minstrel concerts in the colonies also frequently featured their signature "Hutchinson Family Burlesque" decades after the formation of ensemble blackface minstrelsy as an antiblack riposte to the abolitionist and teetotaling family singers. Because these mockeries of the Hutchinson Family Singers risked alienating audiences who were unfamiliar with the particularities of US American antiabolitionism and minstrelsy's dense proslavery parodies, Nish's troupe routinely published explanatory notes on their playbills and in advance press in local colonial newspapers. For instance, prior to their first performance in Cape Town, the *Cape Monitor* ran an extended preview that highlighted the troupe's

> inimitable burlesque of that Puritanical "Band of Brothers"—the Hutchinson Family—who some years since visited London, became the guests of the aristocracy,—the Duke [and] Duchess of Sutherland among their number—and from their extreme solemnity of style excited the ridicule of some portion of the public.[104]

This passage offered an affective script to potential audience members, explaining not only the significance of the Christy's parody of the Hutchinsons but also the political matrix through which to understand the minstrels' mockery. A reader of this passage could identify the target of blackface scorn as "Puritanical" figures whose "extreme solemnity" was risible to "some portion of the public"—presumably those who were not members of the British aristocracy. Thus, far from making blackface respectable, the Christy's advertised their performances as mockeries of bourgeois respectability and reform. Simultaneously, this same item of advance press noted the attendance of "Governor and Mrs. Wodehouse, and other notables" at the Cape Town premiere of the Christy's Minstrels, indicating the troupe's ambivalent and equivocal embrace of bourgeois politics. Their minstrel shows derided white bourgeois reformers and middle-class morality while promoting their popularity with bourgeois and aristocratic white audiences, all while making racist "fun" out of blackness that appealed to cross-class white Anglophone audiences. As the *Cape Argus* summarized at the end of the Christy's tour to Cape Town, "Even at the Cape, where the Nigger character is so well understood, the caricatures of these performers created a perfect furore."[105]

Nish's Christy's Minstrels derived their popularity in large part through their stagings of widely circulating antiblack and proslavery songs and sketches from the blackface repertoire. Yet, the Christy's transoceanic tours also offered unique specialty acts that were remarkably popular throughout the colonial world. Their blackface competition dancing was particularly effective at eliciting the affective and material investments of white imperial audiences in blackface minstrelsy and its racial scripts. In particular, Joe Brown's signature dance, the "Silver Belt Jig," encapsulated the complex affective dramaturgy of blackface minstrel performance, weaving together the valorization of white masculinity through spectacles of competition, the erasure of Black performers and their contributions to blackface repertoires, and collective imperial investments in blackface minstrelsy's popular cultures.

Advance press for the Christy's in Cape Town singled out Brown's "remarkable jig dance" as a special attraction, noting that it "ha[d] everywhere created quite a *furore*."[106] After their opening performance, the *Cape Monitor* enthusiastically reported, "Mr. Brown's Silver Belt Jig is impossible to describe. All we can state is, that it is an excessively clever thing, and should be seen by every one fond of wholesome exercise, of skilful [*sic*] and graceful dramas."[107] The *Cape Chronicle* reported that his "Silver Belt Jig" presented audiences with "one of the most intricate and difficult specimens of step-dancing that [they] ever remember[ed] witnessing."[108] Such reviews echoed and amplified Brown's own self-promotional strategy. Beginning with the Christy's Minstrels' initial British tour, Brown billed himself as a "champion dancer" and performed while wearing a silver belt that he claimed to have won in a dance competition with Dick Sliter in Chicago in 1856.[109] Prior to his match dance against Brown, Sliter's dancing was recognized by "the citizens of Cincinnati" at a "public presentation of a CHAMPION BELT" that featured "the word 'Champion' engraved thereon in silver letters."[110] Ostensibly, the match dance between Sliter and Brown was a competition for ownership of this silver belt and the claim of "champion dancer."

The competition between Sliter and Brown enacted the dramaturgy of blackface minstrelsy's challenge (or "trial") dances, which furnished a central formal structure for blackface dancing in the early nineteenth century as a means of establishing white mastery over Black performance. Yet, Brown's claim to have defeated Sliter in a trial dance and to have won his signature silver belt was a misrepresentation of events—or rather, it was a case of commonplace minstrel puffery. Initial reports of the match dance between Sliter and Brown announced Sliter as the winner. Soon thereafter, Brown enlisted several prominent blackface minstrels to announce that the competition had produced no clear winner and that the match should be considered a draw.[111] Though Brown did not win his contest with Sliter, he nevertheless claimed victory in advertisements for later performances. By September 1857, adorned with a signature silver belt commemorating his ersatz championship, Brown performed a "Silver Belt Jig" to rapturous audiences throughout Britain.[112] Playbills advertised Brown's performances with the African Opera Troupe in Hull, England, in 1859, highlighting Brown's "American Silver Prize Jig . . . As danced by him upwards of 800 Times in London, at the St. James Theatre; Polygraphic Hall, St. James Hall; &c., and by Special Command by the 'EMPEROR and EMPRESS of the FRENCH.'"[113] Soon after news of Brown's performances in Britain reached the United States, the popular press noted that he had "arrogated to himself the title of 'champion dancer of the world,'" with a rival blackface dancer named Mickey Warren decrying Brown's claims and challenging Brown to a new match dance.[114] Brown did not respond to Warren's challenge, nor was it necessary for him to do so in order for the dramaturgy of the "challenge dance" to function. Across this back-and-forth of claim and counterclaim, Brown and Warren's rivalry schematizes how blackface minstrel performers played out "challenges" as promotional strategies of white masculine bravado, often founded on ersatz claims to supremacy manifest as material ornamentation.

The "Silver Belt Jig" furnished forth material proof of individual claims to white supremacy through the alchemical work of the performance's titular prop. The performance genealogy of the "Silver Belt Jig" traces a complex interanimation of racialized performance and racist erasure. The prizes awarded to champion dancers were integral to the dramaturgy of trial dances insofar as they materialized the audience's valuation of the winning dancer. Challenge dances staged what Arjun Appadurai terms "tournament[s] of value"—competitions that imbue objects with additional meaning and value through ritual exchange.[115] W. T. Lhamon Jr. traces a genealogy of blackface dance extending to an informal practice of Black dancers in New York City's Five Points neighborhood in 1820 who competed for the prize of eels awarded by spectating white butchers.[116] As blackface dance formalized within the minstrel show, other material awards supplanted eels as tokens of terpsichorean preeminence, while white blackface dancers displaced Catherine Market's Black performers by excluding them from the minstrel stage.

Initially staged as stand-alone events between solo performers prior to the emergence of ensemble minstrelsy, challenge dances quickly became staples of the ensemble minstrel show. As William J. Mahar summarizes, "These dances were typical examples of the male competitiveness theme symbolized as a mock duel beginning with a challenge, proceeding to a contest showing off the dancer's skills, and ending with the audiences' acclamations of the champion."[117] They functioned as interactive spectacle in which the audience collectively identified and celebrated an individual winner. Challenge dances were soon folded into the dramaturgy of the minstrel show when they were transformed into minstrel skits performed during the "olio" sections of an evening's performance, as exemplified by the Bryant's Minstrels' 1857 *The Challenge Dance*. In this sketch, two white blackface minstrels perform as a "Hibernerian darkey" and "an Ethiopian exquisite" in a competition for a "silver cup."[118] This minstrel scenario demonstrates how, even in scripted form, trial dances rehearsed "tournaments of value" in which two white minstrels—one embodying the stage Irish figure and the other a blackface caricature—performed blackface dance in pursuit of a silver prize. In this vein, Brown's "Silver Belt Jig" reanimated this scripted scenario explicitly designed to score the audience's approbation through the spectacle of his celebrated silver belt.

Challenge dances brought minstrel figurations of "Black dance" to the Anglophone imperium in the form of blackface spectacle. The framework of dance competition facilitated the transformation of Black dancing into blackface dancing and the displacement of Black performers by white minstrels. Ironically, the competitive rivalries among white blackface dancers (such as Brown, Sliter, and Warren) placed them in a performance genealogy extending back to the competition dances between the white blackface dancer John Diamond and the Black dancer William Henry Lane.[119] In 1841, Lane was managed by P. T. Barnum and performed under the stage name "Master John Diamond"—an explicit reference to John Diamond, who was the leading white blackface dancer of the time.[120] Within two years, in 1843, Lane performed under his more well-known stage name, Juba, in a competition dance against the actual John Diamond.[121] Such challenge dances were popular events and, in July 1844, "the two most renowned Dancers in the world, the Original JOHN DIAMOND, and the Colored Boy JUBA" competed in a "Public Trial" to determine "which is to bear the Title of the Champion Dancer of the World."[122] Lane won the title and frequently advertised himself as the winner of his trial dances "with John Diamond at the Chatham Theatre for $500, and at the Bowery Ampitheatre for the same amount" through which he "established himself as the King of All Dancers!!"[123] Attesting to his exceptional skill—and in contrast to many of his rival white blackface dancers—Lane became a transatlantic star on the minstrel stage, performing throughout Britain during the second transatlantic tour of Pell's Ethiopian Serenaders in 1848.[124] Though the archive is riddled with gaps, available sources indicate that Lane remained in the British Isles until his presumed death circa 1852.[125]

However, despite general recognition of Lane as a superlative dancer, his transatlantic fame was not without its ambivalences. Though it is unclear whether Lane wore blackface onstage, his performances were read alongside and taken up in the practices of blackface minstrelsy, and white spectators imaginatively transformed his body into an abject figuration of blackness. During his British tour, newspapers frequently cited Charles Dickens's famous passage describing a dancer in New York's Five Points who was almost certainly Lane:

> Single shuffle, double shuffle, cut and cross-cut: snapping his fingers, rolling his eyes, turning in his knees, presenting the backs of his legs in front, spinning about on his toes and heels like nothing but the man's fingers on the tambourine; dancing with two left legs, two right legs, two wooden legs, two wire legs, two spring legs—all sorts of legs and no legs—what is this to him?[126]

In Dickens's metaphorical language, Juba becomes an automaton as his jig dance transforms his dancing body into a machine. His legs become "wooden legs," "wire legs," "spring legs," "all sorts of legs and no legs." In Dickens's interpretation, even Lane's laughter resounds as the minstrel cacophony of "a million counterfeit Jim Crows." Moreover, Dickens's account marks the corporeality of Juba as essentially different from the everyday "walk of life" or "dance of life" of whiteness.[127] Juba was imagined to be uncannily enlivened and not, mechanized and not, and therefore indistinguishable from the proliferating blackface minstrel figures and automatons circulating throughout the British Empire.[128]

Troping on this discursive framing, London newspapers such as the *Morning Post* introduced Lane as "a genuine nigger" and emphasized his corporeality as distinctly unhuman, for "[h]is limbs seem[ed] to be formed of catouchouc [*sic*] slightly diluted with gutta percha [two forms of natural rubber]—hence his elasticity and aplomb."[129] Other British papers reiterated these tropes, proclaiming, "Surely [Lane] cannot be flesh and blood, but some more subtle substance," for his limbs were presumably able to "lengthen out and wrap round the lamp post—or fall in pieces like Maffey's marionettes."[130] The racializing language of the popular press traced the racial anxieties animating the arena of blackface competition dance. While acknowledging and even celebrating Lane's exceptional skill, critics, audiences, and rival performers imagined Lane as beyond the category of "the human" and frequently excluded him from public blackface dance challenges in explicitly racist terms. In the wake of Lane's victory over John Diamond, white blackface dancers literalized this exclusionary practice by refusing to compete against Black performers. To wit, Sliter replied to a challenge from Warren by announcing "that [Sliter] would dance [Warren] or any other man a straight jig for from $500 to $1000, or will dance any *white man* (not excepting Mickey Warren) four dances he (Dick Sliter) can name."[131] Sliter's racially exclusionary challenge signals how Lane's victories over John Diamond haunted the succession of white blackface dancers who claimed to be champions of Black dancing. The competition dances of blackface minstrelsy were fashioned as something of a compensatory fantasy of white supremacy in Black dancing in the wake of Lane's victories, ensuring that the "champion dancer of the world" would always be a white man.

Brown's claims to be "champion dancer" and to have defeated Sliter were therefore doubly specious—first, because Brown never won a victory over Sliter; and second, because such a victory was always already imagined within a white supremacist and racially exclusive arena of competition. Moreover, far from shaming Brown or otherwise disciplining him for his fabulations, the performance culture of blackface minstrelsy reveled in such white masculinist self-fashioning and swaggering braggadocio. Within a year of Warren's accusations of Brown's misrepresentations, Brown was listed alongside Warren and Sliter as one of the three "best jig dancers of the present day"—a list that tellingly identified John Diamond "as a champion dancer in his best days" but that erased Lane from its popular history of blackface dancing.[132] As this example demonstrates, competition dancing was structured by what Jayna Brown terms "the property of *erasure*, the effort to contain the agency of racialized expressive bodies" by which the "black subject is evacuated, removed."[133]

Brown's "champion" silver belt circulated as a material property of Black erasure. In its travels to Cape Town in August 1862, the belt extended the ambit of blackface dancing across the Anglophone world while positing Brown as the "origin" of Black dancing throughout the British Empire. The racial choreographies and scripts of Joe Brown's "Silver Belt Jig" were immensely popular throughout the transoceanic tours of Christy's Minstrels. Brown's preeminence in this troupe was such that Cape politician R. W. Murray remembered Brown thirty years afterward as "the champion jig-dancer of the world," and the Christy's Minstrels as "Joe Brown's Minstrels" and "Joe Brown's Band of Brothers."[134] Across these celebrations of Brown's unique and singular talent, the earliest reportage on the silver belt jig in the colonial world traces the racializing work of Brown's "Silver Belt Jig" and of white blackface dance.

Brown's "Silver Belt Jig," as a newspaper in Sydney later reported, involved his "appear[ance] in his costume, encircled by a magnificent belt."[135] Adorning his white dancing body with a material prop that furnished forth the latent scripts of blackface dance, Brown embodied the "wild," "out-of-control" dancing Black body of minstrelsy while simultaneously enacting white corporeal mastery and control over "blackness."[136] As journalistic reportage attests, far from being viewed as inhuman, Brown's excellence in blackface dance was understood to derive from his "skil[l]" and "clever[ness]."[137] Here, Brenda Dixon Gottschild's landmark analysis of Lane's Black dancing is instructive in apprehending how white blackface dancers rechoreographed the Black body through minstrel performance. Per Gottschild, Lane's jig dancing exemplified his signature style of Black dance in which he balanced a "hot" active lower body with a "cool" composed torso and positioned himself as simultaneously corporeal and cerebral.[138] By marked contrast, Brown's delineation of blackface dance in the "Silver Belt Jig" was "clever" and "skil[l]ful" insofar as Brown usurped rationality as a racialized marker of whiteness and embodied white racial control over corporeal "blackness." If Lane's dancing presented audiences with a Black body that balanced "cool" cerebral rationality with "hot" corporeality, Joe Brown's silver belt symbolically linked *and* racially segregated the white blackface dancing body. Above the waist, stillness and control embodied Brown's "cool" white rationality; below the beltline, Brown's steps animated the Black body in the mode of Dickens's description of Lane's dancing as intricate racialized machinery. Symbolically, the silver belt both bifurcated and bound together the racialized blackface body. The belt affirmed the white blackface dancer's supremacy over other white blackface dancers and, by extension, over the thingified Black figure at the center of the performance economy of blackface dancing. Blacked up and belted, Brown presented audiences with a racially segregated yet unified body—a corporeal effigy of the Anglophone empire. Worn onstage, the belt materialized "proof" of white supremacy in Black dancing while the dancer performed bodily control over blackness that replicated the control that colonial society exerted over colonized and racialized subjects.

Beyond its dramaturgical function within Nish's Christy's Minstrels performances, the silver belt also figured as a condensation of the racializing performance economy of blackface minstrelsy. The silver belt condensed the discourses, repertoires, and genealogies of blackface minstrel dancing into a singular material object, which scripted portable racial dramaturgies that facilitated the proliferation of blackface dancing throughout the Anglophone empire. Throughout its travels, the silver belt indexed not only Brown's claims to global supremacy in blackface dance but also a thingly biography of imperial travel. Indeed, newspaper biographies of Brown often dedicated more space to the biography of the silver belt.[139] The silver belt's biography took a surprising turn on October 13, 1862, when the steamship *Waldensian* was shipwrecked and sunk at Struys Point, South Africa, with the Christy's Minstrels on board. No lives were lost in the wreck—the casualty most mourned was Joe Brown's silver belt.[140] Brown's silver belt enacted something typically reserved for persons and other living things: it was drowned. The white residents of the Cape Colony mourned its loss and set to finding its replacement. On November 19, 1862, just over a month after the untimely loss of the silver belt, the colonial inhabitants of Cape Town presented Joe Brown with a new silver belt:

> The belt (which was manufactured by Mr. Gangain, silversmith, of this city, is quite as handsome as the one which was lost, being set with amethysts, topazes, aquamarines, and garnets, and engraved by Mr. J. A. Crew) was enclosed in a neat stinkwood box, manufactured by Mr. P. J. Stigant, and presented by Mr. John Rowe. The inscription on the front of the belt is "The Cape Presentation Belt," and on the inside "Presented to Mr. Joe Brown of the Christy's Minstrels, by His Excellency the Governor and the inhabitants of Cape Town, to replace the Champion Belt (won by him at Chicago in the year 1856) which was lost in the wreck of the steamer *Waldensian* in October, 1862, and also to mark their appreciation of his gallant conduct on that trying occasion.—Cape Town, 19th Nov., 1862."[141]

"The Cape Presentation Belt" was intended "to replace as nearly as local circumstances permit the one (now beneath the waves)."[142] It was explicitly fashioned as an effigy of the lost one that, in the words of Joseph Roach, "fill[ed] by means of surrogation a vacancy created by the absence of an original."[143] As an effigy surrogating the lost belt, Brown's "Cape Presentation Belt" cited the performance histories of the original, replacing the lost belt and thereby memorializing Brown's fabricated victory over Sliter.

Onstage and off, both silver belts functioned as what Robin Bernstein terms "scriptive things," hailing present and future persons into relation with past performances, thereby prompting and scripting future performances.[144] The silver belt traces the global circulation of blackface minstrelsy and its racial dramaturgies through the "social life" of a lively stage prop.[145] The scripts of blackface dance were animated by and through such material objects, which, per Bernstein, attain their "thingness" by "invit[ing] . . . person[s] to dance."[146] The loss of Brown's "original" belt also prompted Cape colonists to invest an expenditure of wealth and material in order to reconstitute the performance assemblage of Joe Brown's blackface dance. The press coverage of the Cape Presentation Belt offered colonial white subjects the opportunity to fashion themselves and the Anglophone imperial community of blackface performance that gathered to invite Brown to resume his white supremacist dance. The *Cape Argus* account names various colonial actors in relation to the roles they took in fashioning the Cape Presentation Belt: the engraver, the silversmith, the presenter, the carver of the stinkwood box in which the belt was presented, the governor, and the many subscribers who funded the fashioning of the belt. The thick description of the Cape Presentation marks how the drowning of the silver belt hailed Cape colonists into a collective performance of material reproduction.

As evident in the dedication of the "Cape Presentation Belt," local colonial publics played a significant role in remaking the affective and material lifeworlds of transoceanic blackface minstrelsy and imperial white supremacy. Cape colonists fashioned themselves as members of the Anglophone empire through their contributions to the fashioning of the new silver belt. In other words, they fashioned themselves by fashioning a blackface thing, binding their social statuses in relation to racialized matter. Simultaneously, this expenditure allowed the Cape colonists to fashion themselves as respectable members of the Anglophone empire and its cultural traffics. The new silver belt bore the site of its genesis in its new name, "The *Cape* Presentation Belt." Dedicated "as a badge of [Brown's] professional abilities and as a *souvenir* of the Cape," the new belt placed the Cape at the center of a new circulation of transoceanic blackface and imperial whiteness.[147] As a souvenir, the belt fashioned an imperial imagined community around the collective memory of the lost object and its subsequent replacement. In this way, the Cape Presentation Belt materially manifested the transoceanic networks of blackface minstrelsy. It was a material thing, made of matter gathered through British imperialism, collected by colonists, and expended in support of a performance form explicitly aimed at reperforming white supremacy throughout the transoceanic Anglophone world. Here, Aimé Césaire's equation, "colonization = thingification" appears in strikingly economical form.[148]

Indexing these economies in their broad circulations, the silver belt became a paradigmatic scriptive thing. The belt danced when danced with, it invited others to dance, and it demonstrated the performative ability of effigies to proliferate themselves. Brown's silver belts not only prompted Brown's dancing but also hailed future audiences and future surrogate jig dancers. In June 1863, after nearly a year of successful performances in southern Africa and Australia, Brown left Nish's Christy's Minstrels and briefly performed as a solo act in Melbourne.[149] He soon sailed to London, where he assembled a new troupe. In yet another example of minstrel puffery and irony, the troupe performed under the name "The Original Christy's Minstrels."[150] These "Original" Christy's Minstrels, like Nish's troupe, featured Brown's "Silver Belt Jig" at their premiere performance in Mumbai in November 1863.[151] After a successful two-month tour in Mumbai, the troupe traveled to Kolkata in 1864, where Brown performed his "American Prize Dance" at the request of his Kolkata audience.[152] Such performances were propped up by the Cape Presentation Belt and evidently lost nothing in the exchange of the original belt for its surrogate—Brown and his new belt "were enthusiastically and deservedly applauded."[153] Indeed, the new belt received an honor unmatched by the original when a rival minstrel impresario, Dave Carson of the San Francisco Minstrels, performed a parody of Joe Brown titled "The Electro-Plated Silver-Gilt Toothpick Jig."[154] Through these tours, Brown and his silver belt attained "world-wide celebrity."[155]

Brown's silver-belted celebrity furnished other blackface dancers with a repeatable choreography and a durable script for white supremacy in blackface dance. In the wake of Brown's departure from Nish's Christy's Minstrels, he was surrogated by his former company member, Washington ("Wash") Norton, who performed his own "Silver Belt Jig." Brown's belt was replaced as well. In 1864, Australian colonists presented Norton with his own silver belt, explicitly naming him as "the best prize jig and burlesque dancer that had ever visited Australia."[156] A full notice recounting the dedication of the silver belt was published in the Sydney newspaper *Empire*:

> The address ran thus:—"Presented to Mr. Washington Norton, of the Christy's Minstrels, by his friends and admirers in Sydney, New South Wales, as a mark of their appreciation of his abilities as the best prize Jig and burlesque dancer that has ever visited Australia, March 4th, 1864," to which was appended the names of the subscribers, numbering thirty-four. Mr. Norton expressed his gratitude amidst enthusiastic applause. The belt is of Australian manufacture, and made of silver, being lined with morosco. In the inside of it is a plate, on which is engraved the words forming the heading of the before-mentioned address. On the outside is a representation of the Australian arms, the kangaroo and emu. At either end are embossed the English and American flags. In the centre of the belt is a cairngorm, surrounding which in a circle is inscribed, "Presented to Washington Norton, of the Christy Minstrels, by his friends in Sydney, N.S.W., March 4, 1864." Two amethysts are tastefully arranged at the ends of the belt, which is so formed of scales as to be perfectly pliable, and thus easy for wear. The whole is the workmanship of Mr. Julius Hogarth, of Hunter-street, whose artistic handy work is so frequently the subject of much attention. The exquisite taste and neatness in the design of the belt, and the chasteness of the execution in its formation, especially the manner in which it is embossed and engraved, would redound credit upon any first-rate London establishment.[157]

In its woozy prose and repetitious detail, the *Empire*'s thick description of Norton's belt mimicked and cited prior accounts of Brown's belt much as Norton's belt mimetically reproduced Brown's. Yet, the description also noted how Norton's belt superseded Brown's. In contrast to Brown's belt and its numerous gemstones, Norton's silver belt featured not only "precious stones" but also an embossing of Australian flora and fauna alongside national emblems of Britain and the United States. Kangaroos, emus, the Stars and Stripes, and the Union Jack appear together as shared impressions of white imperial dominion. Tracing new transoceanic routes, Norton's silver belt functioned as an Anglo-American-Australian emblem, condensing symbols of the Anglophone empire in a singular object that performatively asserted Norton's global supremacy in blackface dance.

Norton's surrogate belt was also marked by its different entry point into the transoceanic circulations of blackface dance. A report on Norton's belt in the *Empire* noted the belt's "Australian manufacture" as well as the inscribed names of the belt's thirty-four colonial Australian subscribers on centerpiece of the belt. Fashioned as distinctively Australian, the belt animated the competing colonial investments underpinning British imperialism—a competitive rivalry among British colonies that mimicked the theatrical rivalries of blackface competition dancing. Norton's belt and its attendant discourses traveled widely, functioning as a material prop for Norton's self-promotion. Four years after he was awarded the belt in Australia, he toured the Cape Colony, where the *Eastern Province Herald* again described Norton's Australian belt and its presentation in exacting detail.[158] As with the Sydney *Empire*'s thick description, the Cape colonial newspaper's description of Norton's belt insisted on localizing the global contest between Brown and Norton. In Gqeberha (Port Elizabeth), newspaper coverage dwelled on the memorialization of Norton's gold medal, which he received from Cape colonists at the same ceremony at which Brown was awarded his silver belt. Cape colonists thus emphasized their local investments in the transoceanic economy of competitive blackface dancing. The Cape newspaper's descriptive passage ended by advertising the display of Norton's belt in a local store, further enticing Cape colonists to invest themselves in the belt as though it were a sacred relic. In this way, Norton's belt manifested the affective economies of transoceanic blackface dance.

Moreover, Norton's belt extended the chain of surrogations one move further from Lane, recentering contests over Black dance on racially exclusive competitions between blackfaced white male performers. An Australian reviewer opined, "Norton was very funny in his negro eccentricities, his dancing we have not seen equalled since the days of Bos's 'Juba,' and we question very much if Juba could dance so well in Norton's peculiar style. His 'Silver Belt Jig' was inimitable."[159] For this colonial critic, Norton had surpassed Lane without ever competing with him directly. Gone was Lane's claim to be the "King of All Dancers"; in his place was Norton's "inimitable" jig and his champion silver belt.

Norton's belt and its implicit scripts of imperial white supremacy circulated throughout the Anglophone empire and beyond, traveling from Australia to the Cape Colony, then to Brazil by way of St. Helena.[160] Norton was the first "champion dancer" to tour Latin America and the Caribbean, including stops in Brazil, Uruguay, Paraguay, Argentina, Chile, Panama, Jamaica, Barbados, and Guyana.[161] During Norton's transoceanic tours, in March 1870 he competed against Joe Brown in a challenge dance in Shoreditch, winning the title of England's champion blackface dancer as well.[162] In 1871, Norton completed another tour to Bahia, Brazil, before returning to perform at the Opera Comique in London.[163] The following year, he performed in Jamaica, touring the island with his "Silver

Belt Jig," which was rapturously received by its white colonial audience.[164] Following these several global tours, a Chicago newspaper offered a history of blackface minstrelsy, proclaiming that Norton had "won the belt of England and Australia as the champion jig dancer" and that he had "introduced minstrelsy and burlesque opera in Africa, India, China, South America, West Indies, Australia, and New Zealand"—yet the newspaper conspicuously refrained from any mention of Lane or of any other Black performer.[165] Lane was insistently displaced from the stage and social lives of competition dance, as minstrelsy's dance repertoires choreographed white supremacy throughout the Anglophone empire.

The Silver Belt and the Colonial Color Line

The circulations of minstrelsy's silver belts encapsulate the formation of an imperial circuit of ensemble blackface minstrelsy that bound together the United States, Britain, the British colonies, and Anglophone port cities throughout the globe. Indeed, in the wake of Brown's and Norton's dueling silver belt jigs, several white blackface dancers reanimated the scripts and repertoires of blackface competition dance in disparate imperial sites. In February 1866, Tommy (T.J.) Peel arrived in Aotearoa New Zealand advertising himself as an "unapproachable Jig Dancer, and winner of the Prize Belt from the united CHAMPIONS OF THE WORLD!"[166] In his tours throughout the antipodes, Peel claimed to be "the champion jig dancer of America, and [to hold] the silver belt as such."[167] Peel's obituary in the *New York Clipper* narrated his acquisition of the title and his silver belt in a trial dance with R. M. Carroll on April 16, 1862.[168] In contrast to this eulogistic account, an early history of blackface minstrelsy offers a contradictory version of this event that asserts, "It was never intended to give any other decision than that of a draw" between Peel and Carroll as the trial dance was a contrivance designed to generate fame and notoriety for both performers.[169] Following this stunt, Peel continued to advertise himself as a champion dancer. In 1864, Peel toured to San Francisco, where he defended his claim to superiority in dance when he won a trial dance against Otto Burbank (formerly of the Backus Minstrels and Dave Carson's San Francisco Minstrels).[170] As with Brown before him, Peel transformed an ersatz victory into a transoceanic claim to supremacy in blackface dancing. When he arrived in the antipodes, he surrogated Brown and Norton, embodying his claimed supremacy in blackface dancing as yet another white supremacist assertion of mastery in Black dance.

Other silver-belted surrogations regularly took the blackface stage throughout the Anglophone empire. In Gqeberha, 1865, a blackface trio of "Christys" (Charles Steele, Harry Leslie, and J. R. Taylor) performed a "Terpsichorean Competition, or Grand Burlesque Challenge Dance," likely in the mode of the Bryant's Minstrels' *Challenge Dance* sketch. The Christy Minstrel trio also featured "Harry Leslie's World-Renowned American Prize Jig," which cited Brown's and Norton's Silver Belt Jigs.[171] In 1869, an amateur white blackface minstrel company in Cape Town called the Amateur Coloured Troupe performed "the favourite Nigger Scene: The Challenge Dance," featuring adult and children blackface minstrel performers.[172] Between 1872 and 1874, Edward H. Harvey, who had performed previously in several Australian blackface troupes, also made the "American Prize Jig" a core element in his blackface repertoire during the Harvey-Dougherty-Leslie-Braham Minstrels' tour of southern Africa.[173] Throughout their reanimations of the challenge dance scenario, these variations on the Silver Belt Jig furnished forth embodied performances of Anglophone imperial white supremacy.

The colonized subjects and subalterns of southern Africa were acutely aware of the epistemic violence animated by the Silver Belt Jig and ensemble minstrelsy's proliferation of transoceanic blackface performance. Indeed, in colonial South Africa, Black and brown colonized subjects and subalterns directly experienced the imbrications between minstrelsy and their racial subjection: white colonists commonly referred to Africans as "Christy Minstrels," "Jim Crow," or simply "Jim."[174] Beyond this general and ubiquitous reanimation of minstrelsy as an everyday weapon of racist abuse, blackface minstrel material suffused public spaces where the colonized confronted its symbolic figurations of blackness.

One such encounter was recounted in the *Cape Argus* in 1872. The Harvey-Dougherty-Leslie-Braham Minstrels advertised their performances by mounting posters on the streets of Gqeberha featuring "a large representation of a nigger melodist" that troped on the figural economies of blackface visual culture.[175] According to a reporter for the *Cape Argus*, these derogatory representations became "the subject of a 'coloured grievance'" by "[t]hree benighted sons of Africa," who voiced their protest in Afrikaans:

> *Ja, neef, zoo is het met de verdoemde Englechman. Ons moet bij hem werk, werk alle de dagen van ons leven, en daarom stik hij ons op de muur zomaar voor een spotterij. De Engelschman is de slechtete natie onder de Hemel!! Toe maar, laat one gaan een soopie drink!*
>
> [Yes, cousin, so it is with the damned Englishman. We have to work for him, work all the days of our lives, and therefore he tacks us up on the wall just for ridicule. The Englishman is the worst race under the heavens. Well, let's go for a drink!][176]

The three African men in this scenario interpreted the minstrel figure not as a representation of Black Americans but rather as a derogatory figuration of colonized "sons of Africa." As Chinua Thelwell notes, this passage demonstrates that "Africans who were exposed to minstrel imagery understood they were being ridiculed by the performers."[177] Notably, the three African men were "leaders or drivers of wagons" who had recently arrived from "the country[side]," yet they nevertheless immediately perceived minstrelsy's denigrating functions. The account offers a rare transcript of how colonized subjects and subalterns experienced the ubiquity of blackface material culture. Moreover, it is suggestive of how colonized audiences might have understood minstrel performances and their circulation of imperial racial discourses throughout the Anglophone empire. Indeed, the three Africans were familiar enough with the racial repertoires of minstrelsy to play on them in their protest—their assertion that the "Englishman is the worst race under the heavens" inverted colonial racial hierarchies and thereby contested the colonial common sense of white supremacy.[178]

The Africans' familiarity with the visual codes of minstrel imagery suggests the extent to which transoceanic blackface saturated everyday colonial life. Yet, though this moment of public critique recounts a scenario of colonial resistance to the figural economies of transoceanic blackface, it arose only after colonial South Africa had been inundated with transoceanic blackface through decades of continuous performances by amateur and professional ensemble blackface minstrel troupes. While the account offers an instance of resistant subaltern protest against minstrelsy, it is important to note that it was a *rare* instance and that the circulation of transoceanic blackface continued unabated despite such protestations. Like other surviving examples of outright resistance, such as the Black Canadians who petitioned the mayor of Toronto to prohibit blackface minstrel shows, colonial subjects and subalterns did openly voice their disapprobation of minstrelsy's discursive violence. Nevertheless, the colonial state's nonresponsiveness to their appeals for racial equity outlines how the popular repertoires of transoceanic blackface were tacitly and explicitly supported by the structures and agents of the Anglophone empire.

Moreover, transoceanic blackface in many ways subsumed such acts of resistance—a dynamic also traced in the account of the three Africans' complaint. The tone of the account is deeply sardonic, referring mockingly to the Africans' "coloured grievance" as what "nigger complaints are in these days of pseudo-philanthropy called." The *Cape Argus* reporter's tone invites skepticism to the veracity of the scene recounted, particularly when considered alongside the scenario's burlesque conclusion: the scene ends when the three African men retire to the canteen to drink alcohol in a minstrel punch line that undercuts the sobriety of the Africans' complaint. Here, there is a remarkable similarity between this passage's mockery of the African critiques of minstrel ridicule and Mordecai Noah's antiblack "journalistic" accounts of Black New York and T. D. Rice's minstrelization of James Hewlett's appeal to his "brother actors" as a blackface joke about "brudder actors" (more on this in chapter 4). Therefore, though this passage might offer a trace of outspoken resistance, its similarities to scriptive blackface also indicate that such resistance was readily folded back into—if not in part scripted and produced by—the racial repertoires of blackface minstrelsy. The question of colonial resistance to minstrel abjection—including what forms of opposition were possible in the arena of imperial popular culture—remains bound up with the complexities of subjectivity and subjection, pitched between ambivalent records and archival silences.

Meanwhile, across the Indian Ocean from South Africa, the Silver Belt Jig continued its transoceanic circulations uninterrupted, as ensemble blackface minstrelsy choreographed imperial racial discourses throughout the Anglophone empire. Two members of the Australia-based troupe Hudson's Surprise Company danced versions of the "American Prize Jig" during tours of Kolkata in the 1880s.[179] In 1896, in Melbourne, Miss Connie Milne performed a "silver belt jig" as part of a Santa Claus pantomime at the Alexandra Theatre.[180] Through the wide circulation of ensemble blackface minstrelsy—epitomized by the silver belts and their social and stage lives—the actual lives of Black, brown, Asian, and Indigenous persons were increasingly subjected to minstrelsy's imperial racial repertoires. The silver belt materialized the global processes through which, in the words of W. E. B. Du Bois, "The Color Line Belts the World."[181] In the wake of the transoceanic traffic of the "Silver Belt Jig," the world was figured as an anthropomorphized minstrel body modeled on Joe Brown's silver belt jig, belted at the middle, and animated by the circulation of blackface minstrelsy and its material cultures.

The "Silver Belt Jig" was only one of countless blackface performances that scripted an extensive repertoire of imperial activity throughout transoceanic colonial popular culture. The dance and its titular stage prop exemplified how blackface minstrelsy worked itself into the everyday lives of Anglophone audiences across the globe. The ensemble form of blackface minstrelsy circulated by the Christy's Minstrels offered a capacious format for the exponential proliferation of blackface throughout Anglophone imperial popular culture. Unlike early blackface minstrelsy, the ensemble minstrel show was not limited to songs and song sheets, scripts and theatrical enactments, solo dances, and occasional competitions. Instead, ensemble blackface minstrelsy recombined these elements to produce polymodal performances of racialization that suffused theatrical and everyday life throughout the transoceanic Anglophone world. In addition to the vast majority of racial impressions on the blackface stage that continued to circulate the antiblack tropes, imagery, scenarios, and repertories underpinning the Anglophone empire's racial politics, the minstrel show's formal flexibility also afforded discursive space for the circulation of other racializing performances and the reification of imperial racial politics. The color line that belted the world—which Sylvia Wynter terms the "Color (cum) Colonial Line"—was not strictly one drawn in black and white.[182] It divided the globe into white imperial subjects and enslaved and colonized subjects and subalterns. It is to the capacious, variegated minstrel burlesques of Anglophone imperial subjects and subalterns that we now turn.

Chapter 4

✦

Othello Travestied

Edward Williams Clay's 1839 satirical engraving *The Fruits of Amalgamation* stages an antiabolitionist nightmare of interracial marriage, miscegenatory domesticity, and hybrid progeny. The image presents its viewer with a concatenation of inversions of the imperial racial order: an interracial couple lounges in familial repose; a white servant attends his Black master; a white mother nurses her interracial child; and a second interracial couple enters the threshold. Three embedded images function as keys to Clay's satirical commentary. In the foreground, a dog rests its head on Thomas Paine's *The Age of Reason*, positing abolitionist rationality as a bestial practice that upends natural laws. On the right side of the image, a framed illustration of William Lloyd Garrison overlooks the scene of amalgamation. This ghostly abolitionist presence is doubled by the Black father's choice of reading—Benjamin Lundy's antislavery newspaper the *Emancipator*, which inspired Garrison's *Liberator*. Last, above the contented couple sharing the sofa hangs an illustration of "Othello and Desdemona." This theatrical allusion refigures the scene's domestic bliss, in Tavia Nyong'o's analysis, "literarily under the sign of Othello" and therefore beneath the discursive frame of interracial tragedy.[1] Per its title, Clay's scene of amalgamation comically yet anxiously envisages the "fruits" of abolition as racial mingling and confusion.

Amid its lurid staging of antiabolitionist tropes, one aspect of Clay's image has eluded critical consideration: Othello's representation as visually Orientalized through the twinned symbols of his turban and scimitar. This figuration imagined the titular Moor in the mode of eighteenth-century frontispieces to published editions of *Othello* as well as Edmund Kean's early nineteenth-century Orientalized stage performance and the subsequent "so-called 'bronze age'" of "tawny" Othellos, during which the titular character was figured through shifting racial costuming and makeup.[2] *The Fruits of Amalgamation* figures Othello not only as a paradigmatic effigy of Black-and-white miscegenation but also as an ambiguously non-white yet non-Black figure racially linked to the primal scene of interracial amalgamation. The presence of an Orientalized Othello as the figuration

Fig. 13. Edward Williams Clay, *The Fruits of Amalgamation* (New York: J. Childs, 1839). Courtesy of the American Antiquarian Society. https://www.americanantiquarian.org/Exhibitions/Reading/5/5point20L.jpg.

of miscegenatory assaults on white womanhood signals the dizzying circulation of overlapping racial and theatrical discourses throughout the Anglophone empire. Far from epitomizing a distinctively US American racial formation around a uniquely anxious articulation of nationalistic antiabolitionism, *The Fruits of Amalgamation* symptomizes the insistent convergence of Anglophone imperial racial discourses at the conjuncture of global white supremacy, the biopolitical production of race, and the imperial-cum-racial management of sexuality.

This chapter traces global restagings of the "sign of Othello" as it circulated throughout the nineteenth-century British Empire in tragedies and travesties. Throughout the transoceanic Anglophone empire, *Othello* was one of the most frequently produced plays in Australia, Aotearoa New Zealand, the Cape Colony of southern Africa, South Asia, and the United States.[3] It was performed by white, Black, and South Asian actors, and the titular character was figured from "Black" to "tawny" to everything in between. British imperial stagings of *Othello* and its many burlesque versions in the Cape Colony, New South Wales, and Kolkata demonstrate that theatrical enactments of miscegenatory anxieties were not limited to the racial formations of the newborn United States of America but rather constituted a global, transoceanic phenomenon. The prolific performances of *Othello* and *Othello* burlesques forged multidirectional, citational relays through which white theatrical and print cultures fashioned racial sensibilities through affectively charged scenarios of interracial sexual contact.

If Frederick Timpson I'Ons's *The Freed Slave* (1840) imagined political freedom as an inherently white property in a scene of travestied liberation, then *Othello* and its many burlesques animated the greatest danger to the Anglophone empire's patriarchal racial hegemony as the sexual freedom of non-white men and white women. In the words of Ann Laura Stoler, these plays placed "sexuality at the center of imperial politics" and at the center of imperial racial formations.[4] Theatrical stagings of *Othello* offered white audiences a site to engage with sexuality as what Michel Foucault identifies as "an especially dense transfer point for relations of power" that functioned as a "linchpin" for transnational racial formations throughout the Anglophone empire.[5] These various articulations of *Othello* were remarkably fungible, and the play was often adapted to encompass other interracial scenarios and attendant anxieties in accordance with popular white imperial racial sensibilities. The broad array of Orientalized and blackface Othellos constituted a mutable yet stable theatrical repertoire that assured white audiences—and especially white male audiences—of their "flexible *positional* superiority" over the Anglophone empire's racial others.[6]

Eighteenth- and nineteenth-century performances of *Othello* figured the bodies of Othello and Desdemona as fantastical sights and sites of imperial "contact zones," which Mary Louise Pratt defines as "social spaces where disparate cultures meet, clash, and grapple with each other, often in highly asymmetrical relations of domination and subordination—such as colonialism and slavery."[7] White performers enacted miscegenatory scenes that staged encounters in which contact animated and mediated imperial white anxieties about the Anglophone empire's manifold colonized, racialized subjects through dramaturgies that tacitly reified the imperial horizon of racialized heteronormativity. As a response to fears of racial amalgamation, transoceanic performances of *Othello* transformed the Moor of Venice into a series of burlesque figures, alternately segregating and recombining blackness and brownness while indexing both to social abjection and abasement.

Travesty functioned at the center of this imperial economy of racial feeling, transmogrifying anxieties over racial propriety into scenarios of burlesque impropriety. In other words, travesties of *Othello* reworked the serious matters of interracial tragedy into the "grotesque" and "debased" (i.e., high-to-low) inversions of blackface burlesque.[8] Circulations of *Othello* and its nineteenth-century burlesques such as Maurice Dowling's *Othello Travestie* (1834) trace the global racialization of the character *Othello* as an icon of racial abjection. Across these transoceanic circulations, the race of Othello slipped from "Black" to "tawny" to "Black" again as he was refigured from noble Black Moor to a noble Orientalized figure and then into a Black, brown, or Asian minstrel clown—all the while remaining the enduring, paradigmatic sign of interracial sexuality.

The Anxious Amalgamations of Empire

In 1770, British theater critic Francis Gentleman published his recollection of James Quin's eighteenth-century embodiment of Othello (ca. 1738), in which Quin performed

> in a large powdered major wig, which, with the black face, [and which] made such a magpye appearance of his head, as tended greatly to laughter; one stroke however, was not amiss, coming on in white gloves, by pulling off which the black hands became more realized.[9]

Gentleman's narration of Quin's performance hinged on an affective braid of laughter and sensation. Quin's misfiring attempt to embody Othello as a noble Moor staged, in Gentleman's recollection, an unintentionally comic scenario due to the "magpye" appearance of his black-and-white head. Simultaneously, Gentleman noted Quin's success in sating the British audience's desire to see Othello's blackened hands that might besmirch Desdemona's white womanhood. In Gentleman's account, the interracial contact zone appeared as the site of affective intensities—either as a comic absurdity or as sensationally "realized." Elsewhere, Gentleman recounted a similar transformation of interracial desire and disgust into racial denigration in response to David Garrick's 1745 embodiment of an Orientalized, beturbaned, Black Othello, which Gentleman sardonically interpreted as a reincarnation of the comically out-of-place Black servant figure Pompey from William Hogarth's *A Harlot's Progress* (1732).[10] While leading British performers attempted to "realize" Othello racially amid a period of imperial expansion and deepening racial entrenchment, Gentleman's responses signal the affective ambivalences already circulating among eighteenth-century British audiences, who greeted the sight of Orientalized (and) Black Othellos alternately with fascination and derision.

Such affective matrixes of racial response were not limited to London. Throughout the Anglophone world, critical commentators on *Othello* articulated white anxieties about racial amalgamation. For instance, a 1786 London production at the Theatre Royal, Drury Lane, prompted antiblack comic ripostes, as in the *Public Advertiser*'s rhetorical question, "Is it necessary the Moor should be as *black* as a native of Guiney?"[11] In a less comic vein, in March 1786, Abigail Adams, the future First Lady of the United States, recounted her experience of this *Othello* production in a private letter to her sister:

> I lost much of the pleasure of the play, from the sooty appearance of the Moor. Perhaps it may be early prejudice; but I could not separate the African color from the man, nor prevent that disgust and horror which filled my mind every time I saw him touch the gentle Desdemona.[12]

By contrast to comic commentary that emphasized the humorousness British audiences found in the staging of blackened skin, Adams's apprehension of the play fixated on the tragic potential of miscegenatory contact—Othello's "touch[ing] the gentle Desdemona"—as a source of deep racial anxiety that overwhelmed her with physical revulsion.

John Quincy Adams evidently shared his mother's affective response to the play. After his single term as president of the United States, Adams published a series of articles of Shakespearean criticism, including several on *Othello* wherein he rationalized his feelings of disgust at the sight of interracial contact as the purpose of the play. Despite Adams's avowed abolitionism, he voiced profoundly antiblack interpretations of Shakespeare's play, attributing his anxieties about the play to the figuration of Othello as a "rude, unbleached African soldier."[13] Visualizing interracial contact and the "intermingl[ing]" of "black and white blood" as the central dramatic crisis animating *Othello*, Adams articulated a contorted vein of criticism that posited the ostensible dangers of racial amalgamation as the "great moral lesson of the tragedy."[14]

Throughout his essays, Adams explicitly outlined the ways in which sexuality animated Anglophone racial formations, castigating Desdemona for her "violations" of "Nature"—that is, of the Anglophone social and racial order.[15] Adams substantiated this argument by emphasizing Desdemona's willful entry into an interracial relationship with Othello. He viewed Desdemona as upending the decorum of courtship rituals because she acted as an agent in her own sexual life. Most "disgusting," for Adams, was the physical contact between the Black Othello and the white Desdemona enacted "upon the stage."[16] In his view, this scene of interracial "fondling" figuratively expelled Desdemona from the family of respectable whiteness.[17] In a second essay, Adams defended his attribution of blame to Desdemona by making explicit the racial underpinnings of his critique: "The passion of Desdemona for Othello is *unnatural*, solely and exclusively because of his color."[18] Adams's anti-amalgamationist critique redounded on Desdemona, whom he criticized as "not only very deficient in delicacy, but totally regardless of filial duty, of female modesty, and of ingenuous shame."[19] Adams interpreted Desdemona's desire for Othello and her disobedience of her father as a moral stain, one that ought to produce a racialized and gendered shame in her but that, in failing to do so, instead served as a moral lesson of the inevitable ends of interracial intimacy. His loathing of interracial sex was such that he welcomed Desdemona's death: "This character takes from us so much of the sympathetic interest in her sufferings, that when *Othello* smothers her in bed, the terror and the pity subside immediately into the sentiment that she has her deserts."[20] In this way, Adams reimagined *Othello* as a tragedy in which poetic justice manifested as the restoration of the sexual orders of whiteness.

The passions exhibited throughout the Adamses' criticisms of *Othello* were commonplace in early nineteenth-century Shakespearean commentary. Abigail Adams's critique anticipated (and John Quincy Adams's essays echoed) Charles Lamb's 1811 interpretation of Othello as a "*coal-black Moor*" who produced "something extremely revolting in the courtship and wedded caresses of Othello and Desdemona."[21] Like Adams, Lamb passionately asserted that the bodily presence of interracial contact between Othello and Desdemona on a theatrical stage necessarily produced a singular, intense affective response: revulsion. In a paradigmatic case of both antitheatrical and antiblack prejudice, Lamb named "body and bodily action"—specifically, the corporeal contact between an embodiment of Black masculinity and a white female body—as the singular moral problem in performing *Othello*.[22]

In response to the affective intensities animated by these "monstrous" threats posed by the physical union of Othello with Desdemona, Samuel Taylor Coleridge reimagined the play's anxious interracial scenarios by inverting the Adamses's and Lamb's interpretations of *Othello*, proclaiming, "entirely by the best moral feelings that Desdemona attached herself to Othello and Othello to Desdemona."[23] However, in order for Othello's and Desdemona's affections to be legible as morally propitious, Coleridge imagined an emphatically non-Black Othello: "Othello must not be conceived a negro, but a high and chivalrous Moorish chief."[24] Coleridge distinguished these two Othellos as belonging to different categories in a clearly defined racial schema. Echoing the antiblack and antiabolitionist discourses that T. D. Rice staged in his London adaptations of "Jim Crow," Coleridge asserted that a "barbarous *negro*" could not legitimately "plead royal birth"; by contrast, a Moor could be a "warrior," and therefore presumably could be an appropriate object for Desdemona's desires.[25] Coleridge promoted Kean's 1814 figuration of a "tawny" Othello made up in a "deep copper colour" rather than in burnt cork—an affectively tempered, civilized, and chromatically lightened surrogate in accordance with the Anglophone empire's racial sensibilities.[26] Coleridge's endorsement of Kean prompted a wave of "tawny" Othellos. In the United States, Othello was interpreted in a wide array of racializations, including "octoroon," "warrior Moor," and "Persian suitor," while the globe-trotting German

Shakespearean actor Daniel Bandmann modeled his Othello after an upper-class, upper-caste Bengali philosopher and social reformer named Keshub Chunder Sen, proclaiming Sen to be his "*beau ideal* of an 'Othello make-up.'"[27] Despite their differing interpretations and figurations of Othello's race, the complex and contradictory criticisms of *Othello* animated discourses of antiblackness and reified imperial anxieties about interracial amalgamation. As the contact zones of the Anglophone empire proliferated, so did the felt intensities about the permeability of whiteness, the fragility of racial boundaries, and the tenuousness of white racial rule. In response, the tragic Othello was whitewashed into a "tawny" figure, while many white Anglophone theater makers removed the play's explicitly sexual language and de-emphasized the bodily aspects of Othello and Desdemona's stage relationship.[28]

Contemporaneously, in the 1820s, Black performers began to embody Othello and to stage scenes of interracial contact and intimacy. William A. Brown's succession of "African" theaters in New York City served as the earliest site of such performances, where James Hewlett took the stage as the earliest known Black American performer of Othello.[29] Though Hewlett's performance as Othello was paired with "a very handsome copper-colored woman" as Desdemona, the appearance of a Black Othello with a figuratively "white" Desdemona on the New York stage was greeted by a white crowd who noisily disrupted the performance by hurling food at the actors in a social performance akin to the "rough music" of charivari used by groups of young white men to regulate sexual morality.[30] Such riotous white audiences, bolstered by Mordecai Noah's antiblack attacks on Hewlett in the New York press, forced Brown to close his theaters.

Nevertheless, Black performers adapted their stagecraft to play on white sexual and racial anxieties. In 1825, Ira Aldridge, a young performer in Brown's theaters, fled the violently maintained embargo on Black theatrical performance in the United States for the ostensibly freer stages of Britain. When Aldridge arrived, he stepped into a British theatrical culture rife with white anxieties about interracial contact, such as those articulated in Lamb's and Coleridge's criticisms.[31] Across his British performances, Aldridge featured stagings of *Othello* in which he embodied an amalgam of racial figurations. Performing under the pseudonym "Mr. Keene," Aldridge styled his interpretation on Edmund Kean's "tawny" Othello and ornamented himself in "Oriental" garb. Nevertheless, audiences fixated on his skin as an indelible sign of blackness rather than on his Keanesque attire.[32] Theatrical commentators drew from the repertoires of scriptive blackface to denigrate Aldridge's performance, as in an 1825 London *Times* review of his performance that called him "a *genuine* nigger . . . Mr. Keene, the *African Roscius*."[33] The *Times*' derisive epithet evoked Charles Mathews's burlesque of James Hewlett as the "Kentucky Roscius," tracing yet another link in the citational chain of scriptive blackface. In response to the British press's denigration, Aldridge negotiated the contradictions of his new theatrical life by playing with and against white expectations and conventions for theatrical blackness. Aldridge performed regularly under the billing "The AFRICAN ROSCIUS," signifying ironically on the *Times*' racist invective by transforming an attempt at denigration into his theatrical signature.[34]

Despite (or because of) his inventive and savvy negotiations of Anglophone racism and his challenge to the unspoken racial exclusivity of the British stage, Aldridge became the target of white anxieties and animus during his 1833 London debut at Covent Garden. His embodiment of Othello onstage with the white British actress Ellen Tree as Desdemona touched off a flurry of antiblack criticism. The London *Athenaeum* greeted his performance by protesting that the production subjected "an interesting actress and lady-like girl . . . to the indignity of being pawed about by [Aldridge]."[35] In his later performances of Othello (and perhaps in his earliest ones), Aldridge seemed intent on staging such scenes of interracial contact to provoke rather than temper racial anxieties. For instance, the anonymously authored *Memoir and Theatrical Career of Ira Aldridge, the African Roscius* (ca. 1848) narrated his initial meeting with his first wife, Margaret Gill, as a theatrical scene in which Gill "played, to some extent, a modern Desdemona to Mr. Aldridge's Othello."[36] Here, Aldridge's biographer adorned him in the figural trappings of Othello and its racial associations, blurring the boundaries between the stage figure and the performer and thereby suggesting that the permeability of the color line onstage led directly to the transgression of the Anglophone sexual-racial imperial order offstage.

Aldridge developed similar strategies onstage for provoking his critics by playing on white Londoners' disgust at—and desire for—the sight of interracial contact. As Dame Madge Kendal reported in her memoir of an 1865 production of *Othello*,

> Mr. Ira Aldridge was a man who, being black, always picked out the fairest woman he could to play Desdemona with him, not because she was capable of acting but because she had a fair head. One of the great bits of "business" that he used to do was where, in one of the scenes he had to say, "Your hand, Desdemona," he made a very great point of opening his hand and making you place yours in it, and the audience used to see the contrast. He always made a point of it and to a round of applause, how I do not know.[37]

Aldridge appears to have drawn from the British theatrical repertoire to restage James Quin's spectacle of drawing the "contrast" between Othello's hand and whiteness. Moreover, Aldridge may have been responding to the British press's explicit fascination with "his hands ungloved, and the finger-nails expressively apparent," which allowed the audience "to perceive the play and action of the hand."[38] With his ungloved hand, Aldridge savvily touched off Anglophone white anxieties by staging miscegenatory contact as theatrical choreography. He not only removed a white glove to reveal the sight of his Black skin but also placed his Black hand in direct contact with Kendal's white one. Though Kendal does not theorize "how" Aldridge provoked such a consistent response through this bit of racial business, it is no stretch to conclude that Aldridge's staging enlivened the affective crux of *Othello* for nineteenth-century Anglophone audiences: the transgression of the anxiously maintained boundary between Black male and white female bodies as a metonymic condensation of the Anglophone imperial contact zone.

Aldridge's stage manipulations of *Othello*'s primal scenes of interracial contact explicitly challenged the tacit color line circumscribing the British stage while also embodying Aldridge's anti-racist humanism. Offstage, antislavery activists championed Aldridge as a figurehead for their movement because his performances demonstrated that he was, in the slogan of antislavery activism, "A man and a brother" of white Anglophone subjects.[39] Aldridge openly advocated for racial equality in Britain, as when he gave a public speech in which he declared his opposition to the belief that anyone "should be deprived of a hearing on the stage, because his face was of another colour, seeing [as] the black man and the white were both the work of the same Creator."[40] White Anglophone audiences would have interpreted Aldridge's gestural byplay with reference to his antislavery politics—that is, as a corporeal enactment of his radical politics, which provoked the empire's anxious white publics by challenging the foundations of imperial white supremacy.

While Aldridge succeeded in tuning imperial racial anxieties to a fever pitch, white Anglophone theater makers responded to the presence of Black performers on the circum–North Atlantic stage by fashioning a proliferation of burlesque Black versions of *Othello*. These many *Othello* travesties inverted the affective dynamics of the Othello-Desdemona scenario, transforming the imperial interracial contact zone into a comic sketch of absurdity, incongruity, and farcical dissolution. In the numerous published *Othello* travesties, Othello did not transform from "Black" to "tawny." Indeed, if we consider blackface burlesques in the same frame as Shakespeare's *Othello*, the nineteenth-century "bronze age" of Othello never occurred. As the Kean tradition transformed the tragic Othello from "Black" to "tawny," burlesques of *Othello* concurrently altered Orientalized, Black, and Orientalized Black Othellos from tragic to comic figures. The simultaneous racial transmogrifications of Othello—the lightening-cum-civilizing of the tragic Othello and the denigration of the burlesque

Othello—were not independent processes. They constituted a shared global Anglophone racial discourse premised on a clear bifurcation: they preserved blackness as social abjection while simultaneously positioning "tawny" races as nearer to whiteness and therefore as superior on the civilizational chain of being.

Othello, Travestied

When Charles Mathews premiered his monopolylogue *A Trip to America*, he included an extended blackface routine mocking William A. Brown's stagings of Black Shakespearean productions in New York City, including a burlesque of Hamlet's famous soliloquy ("To-*by* or not to-*by*, dat is de question"). Despite drawing from extant blackface repertoires for his sketch, Mathews's characterization of the "Kentucky Roscius" was widely interpreted by circum–North Atlantic Anglophone audiences as a direct mockery of James Hewlett and Ira Aldridge.[41] In order to defend his reputation, Hewlett penned a retort in which he directly addressed Mathews:

> You have, I perceive by the programme of your performance, ridiculed our *African Theatre in Mercer-street*, and burlesqued me with the rest of the negroe actors, as you are pleased to call us—mimicked our styles—imitated our dialects—laughed at our anomalies—and lampooned, O shame, even our complexions. Was this well for a brother actor?[42]

Hewlett mobilized the abolitionist language of brotherhood to defend himself from racist shaming by signifying on the abolitionist interrogative, "Am I not a Man and a Brother?" in his rhetorical question: "Was this well for a *brother* actor?" Despite Hewlett's eloquent articulation of his grievances against Mathews, his claims to political and artistic equality were countered by the well-rehearsed antiblack tropes of scriptive blackface that transformed his ethical plea to his "brother actor" into yet another trope of racial burlesque. Nearly a decade after Hewlett published his letter, in an editorial in the *Morning Courier and New-York Enquirer* dated October 11, 1833, T. D. Rice authored a dizzying article of scriptive blackface in the voice of "Jim Crow" in which Rice compared the Jim Crow character to "his *brudder* actors"—that is, Hewlett and others in Brown's company.[43] This series of relays—from Mathews's derisive parody to Hewlett's enunciation of racial brotherhood to Rice's mockery of Hewlett's articulation—presents a concise synopsis of the circum–North Atlantic performance genealogy that furnished forth blackface burlesques of *Othello*. White Anglophone performers insistently rearticulated Black voicings of "high," "refined," and "respectable" speech into "low" burlesque, composting Black performative claims to racial equality to fertilize the grounds of transoceanic white supremacy.

It is therefore unsurprising that multiple burlesques of *Othello* focused on Othello's oration to the Venetian Senate and the ironic potential of its spectacle of self-making through performative utterances. Through his famous speech, Othello narrates his heroic capacities to gain acceptance into white, Christian Venice and to prove himself worthy of the civic trust. The oration relies on Othello's eloquence as a successful performance of selfhood that demonstrates his racial exceptionality. The Venetian oration provided grist for the blackface mill, which churned out numerous burlesques of its articulation of Black speech. It functioned as a critical site for white revanchist denials of political claims of Black equality and for travestying anxious scenarios of racial amalgamation.

For instance, in an 1825 "At Home" performance contemporaneous to Aldridge's arrival in England, Mathews shifted his Shakespearean burlesque from *Hamlet* to *Othello*, with a West Indian caricature named Chingaree performing "Othelly speech to him father-in-law":

> Most patented sir reverences!
> My very good massas! dat I take away
> Old buckra man him daughter,
> It all true, true, no lie was;
> Den she marry, I make her my Chumchum,
> Dat all I do, cause I do no more was![44]

Explicitly ineloquent and inarticulate, Mathews's mockery insisted that the West Indian "Chingaree" was no tragic Othello. The scene transmits the tacit racial script that only white performers could imbue Othello with nobility. Indeed, Mathews elaborated this trope in his 1829 Adelphi staging of W. H. Moncrieff's *Monsieur Mallet; or, My Daughter's Letter*, in which the Black character Oroonoko is abased from a tragic hero in Aphra Behn's novel *Oroonoko; or, The Royal Slave* (1688) to a blackface buffoon who "play wid him Tragic Muse ebbery night in de Niggar playhouse," including rehearsals of "Otelly."[45] As Bernth Lindfors has noted, Mathews's blackface burlesque *Othello, the Moor of Fleet Street* (1833) further expanded on these scenes and their racial scripts, combining them with several others rehearsed on London's stages, such as Frederick Henry Yates's performances as "Mister Othello Hoe-and-Scrape" in Yates's *Reminiscences; or, Etchings of Life and Character* (1829) and Richard Alfred Milliken's *The Anaconda, the Terrific Serpent of Ceylon* (1826), which features the Black caricature Smoki who mispronounces the Venetian oration "Most impurent, grave & irreverent Cinders, mine werry wathy and improved good massas."[46] In Mathews's 1833 burlesque, Othello offers a variation on this trope, beginning his speech by pronouncing a passable

Shakespearean oration ("Most potent, very reverend, grave, / My noble and approved good masters") before devolving into a bawdy song in which he announces:

> Once upon a time
> I touched the maid so nearly
> That she forgot my clime
> And owned she loved me dearly.[47]

With stage directions instructing the passage be "*spoken in the manner of Kean*," this Othello speech directed its mockery at Aldridge, who was then performing throughout Britain as "Mr. Keene" in the Orientalized style of Edmund Kean while "touch[ing]" white British actresses "so nearly" as to arouse white Londoners' anxieties.[48] Mathews's burlesque punned on the intimacy implicit in Othello's narration, suggesting that he "won" Desdemona not through his speech but rather through his sexual touch.[49] Abasing the potency of Othello's oratory, Mathews refashioned Othello from an eloquent noble to a crude libertine as he troped on blackface's prolific scripts of Black freedom as an immediate step toward interracial amalgamation.

In 1834, Maurice G. Dowling, the superintendent of police in Liverpool, elaborated extensively on these antiblack scripts in his blackface burlesque *Othello Travestie*.[50] Dowling's burletta was popular enough with British audiences that in 1836, London's Strand Theatre produced a revised version of *Othello Travestie* for a phenomenal run of over six hundred performances, with Charles Rice declaring it "unquestionably the best burlesque that has ever appeared."[51] As with Mathews's version, Dowling's travestied *Othello* placed both the Venetian oration and the scene of Othello and Desdemona's interracial contact at the center of his comedic inversions. Simultaneously, he introduced Othello as the "*Moor of Venice, formerly an independent nigger from the republic of Hayti*," figuring the "Moor" as an unquestionably Black specter of revolutionary racial liberation, evoking and defusing Anglophone racial anxieties aroused by the imminent abolition of slavery throughout the empire.[52] Though Dowling continued Mathews's tradition of mocking contemporary Black actors, his racial humor troped expansively on the circum–North Atlantic circulations of scriptive blackface and concomitant Anglophone scenarios of interracial sexual contact. In other words, while referencing Aldridge, Dowling broadly subjected the romance between Othello and Desdemona to withering ridicule, inverting Othello from a "noble Moor" into a dialect-speaking caricature of impossible freedom unworthy of Desdemona's affections.

Centrally, Dowling rearticulated the theatrical repertoires of *Othello* burlesque by transforming Othello's Venetian oration from an exhibition of Othello's nobility and valor into a scene of blackface abjection set to the tune of "Yankee Doodle":

> Potent, grave, and rev'rend sir,
> Very noble massa—
> When de maid a man prefer
> Den him no can pass her.
> Yes, it is most werry true
> Him take dis ole man's daughter,
> But no by spell, him promise you,
> But by fair means him caught her.[53]

Dowling's version of the titular character spoke in a Mungoesque, West Indian articulation of scriptive blackface reminiscent of Charles Dibdin's blackface songs. The titular character referred to himself as "Otello," suggesting that he could not pronounce his own name in a citation of Mathews's "Kentucky Roscius" who called himself "Othelly."[54] Further derogating Othello's capacity for self-fashioning speech, Dowling's burlesque abjected the character by figuring him as a formerly enslaved Black fool who called the white authorities of the Venetian Senate his "very noble massa." *Othello Travestie*'s doggerel verse reduced the proud general to a subordinate figure whose blackness functioned as evidence of his axiomatic abjection within the Anglophone white imperium. Situated in a long genealogy of blackface burlesques that linked blackness to servility, inferiority, and comic failure, Dowling's Othello was bound to broken speech, corporeal impropriety, and unintentional irony.

Othello's abjection boomeranged to denigrate Desdemona's desire. Whereas in Coleridge's whitewashing the anxious interracial scenarios staged in *Othello* exhibit "the best moral feelings," Dowling's *Othello Travestie* staged a scene in which the worst moral feelings of interracial amalgamation attach the pair.[55] Dowling's burlesque insisted on the comedy of interracial attachments, emphasizing the physical—rather than moral—affections of Othello and Desdemona's union. Central to his seduction of Desdemona, Othello "tell[s] . . . lilly lie[s]" while "look[ing] [in] de eye of miss," to which Desdemona responds with an invitation to join her "all alone," where he will promise to join their "hearts" and "hear her sigh" in a scenario rife with sexual innuendo.[56] Dowling's refashioning of the courtship scene amplified the intimacies enacted between Othello and Desdemona, eliciting an audience's anxieties at the prospect of a white woman "all alone" wooed by a Black man, while subverting this scenario by framing the seduction as one of comic deception.

The visual archive of *Othello Travestie* staged these inversions of the couple's union through scenes of interracial contact designed to be read as comically ludicrous. In the frontispiece to the Lacy acting edition of

Fig. 14. Frontispiece to Maurice Dowling, *Othello Travestie* (London: Lacy, 1859). Courtesy of the British Library.

Othello Travestie (1859) (see fig. 14), Othello is adorned in an ornate white military officer's uniform with a white powdered wig and blackened face and hand in a possible reference to James Quin's eighteenth-century "magpye" appearance in the role as well as to Aldridge's 1829 performance as King Christophe.[57] Desdemona is sketched in a line drawing without any shading on her face or hands. In contrast, Othello appears so visibly black that it is difficult to discern his facial features. In a subtle amplification of

Fig. 15. John William Gear, *Mr. W. J. Hammond and Miss Daly as Othello and Desdemona at the New Strand Theatre* (1836). Folger Shakespeare Library Shelfmark: ART File H229.5 no.1 (size M). Used by permission of the Folger Shakespeare Library. https://luna.folger.edu/luna/servlet/detail/FOLGERCM1~6~6~303845~123827.

the scenario's interracial dramaturgy, Othello's left hand is gloved in white (in marked contrast to his black hat), while his right hand is markedly black in juxtaposition to Desdemona's white skin. Moreover, Desdemona drapes her torso over Othello's blackened right arm, pressing her chest against him while gazing adoringly at his nearly imperceptible blackfaced visage. This staging of Othello's blackness and Desdemona's affectionate embrace layers the burlesque's verbal racial economy of scriptive blackface with the condensed visual codes of interracial contact.

J. W. Gear's 1836 souvenir lithograph from the London Strand Theatre production reiterated this ironic theatricalization of racial touching (see fig. 15). As in the frontispiece image, W. J. Hammond as Othello wears the same "magpye" costume that emphasizes his blackness by contrast to his white sartorial adornments. Circulating beyond the theater, Gear's lithograph stages what Robin Bernstein might call a "nearly palpable vision" of interracial contact.[58] At the center of the image, Othello's visibly blackened left hand—darker than any other part of his visible body—holds the white, nearly unshaded right hand of Desdemona. The pair also make eye contact, staging Othello's claim to "look de eye of miss," while Desdemona's left hand touches her white breast in a gesture of pronounced feeling. This staging of the characters' interlocked gaze proliferates the central sight of Black and white contact, relaying the site of interracial touching through an embodied constellation of erogenous zones: eyes, hands, breasts.

Gear's lithograph manifests the complex visual economy of *Othello Travestie*—what Nicole Fleetwood terms "the relationship between the audience's looking practices, the looks among the staged performers, and the visual markings of the performers' bodies."[59] In order for audiences to interpret this scene as humorous rather than tragic, they must have been intimately familiar with circum–North Atlantic racial "regime[s] of looking," sensitized to perceive the slightest nuances in habituated practices of racialization through acts of making bodily contact through one's gaze.[60] As bell hooks notes in *Black Looks*, the enslaved and recently emancipated alike were subjected to punishment if they violated racial codes of looking at white bodies—throughout the circum–North Atlantic, "to look directly was an assertion of subjectivity, equality."[61] Gear's image stages Othello gazing directly into Desdemona's eyes, asserting his equality in a condensed embodiment of Black freedom. The lithograph envisions the horizon of Black liberation as a scenario of interracial eye contact, a mode of intimacy fixated on the bodies of white women who appear vulnerable to such seduction.

Simultaneously, the lithograph interrupts the scene by contrasting the "looks" of Othello and Desdemona. Desdemona gazes longingly into Othello's eyes, yet Othello's return gaze appears ambivalent, perhaps expressing his characteristic jealousy through his furrowed brow and accusatory finger-pointing. Furnishing an embodied repertoire for potential stage business for *Othello Travestie*, this image offers insight as to how the characters' bodily contact was choreographed to stimulate the anxieties of audience members by staging Lamb's dreaded sight of "the courtship and wedded caresses of Othello and Desdemona."[62] Moreover, the burlesque performance of scenes of miscegenatory contact parodied and potentially defused the very provocation that Aldridge likely intended by prominently holding Desdemona's white hand. Whereas Samuel Taylor Coleridge imagined a "monstrous" matrimony in which "this beautiful Venetian girl [falls] in love with a veritable Negro," *Othello Travestie* made such monstrosities into mockeries by framing any such racial amalgamation as absurd.[63] Thus, the image manifests how blackface burlesques staged affectively intense interracial scenarios within the comedic frame of travesty and its structures of bathetic failure: Othello might look whiteness in the face and Desdemona might return his gaze lovingly, but he would remain foolishly suspicious of her virtue as both would be revealed to be comic cautionary figures denigrated by their violation of habituated racial codes. Dowling's *Othello Travestie* presented audiences with a frame through which interracial contact and its associations with sexual amalgamation were insistently and ironically interrupted by the structures of comedy. Collectively, this performance repertoire functioned as a racial pedagogy for Anglophone audiences. These stage figures entrained audiences to anticipate the restoration of the imperial racial order promised by comedic plot structures. In other words, *Othello Travestie* parodied Black Othellos and their embodied threat to the social and sexual sanctity of white women by putting Othello back in his racially ordained place.

Following its immense popularity in Liverpool and London, *Othello Travestie* circulated widely throughout the Anglophone empire. Within a year of its 1836 London premiere, Dowling's burletta received stagings across the British provincial theater circuit.[64] *Othello Travestie* was also quickly taken up by blackface performers—for instance, Edward "Ned" Harper, who had previously attained transatlantic fame for his performance of "Jim Along Josey," performed the burlesque during his touring performances in Cork in 1841.[65] Across the Atlantic, *Othello Travestie* also received full performances in US American theaters immediately following its London successes. Beginning in August 1836, it entered the theatrical repertories of New York City, Boston, Philadelphia, and New Orleans, where it was frequently staged alongside excerpts from Shakespeare's *Othello*.[66] Sometimes billed as *Othello; or, The Jealous Nigger*, several productions of Dowling's burletta featured early blackface minstrel Thomas H. Blakely in the titular role (which he reprised as late as 1847), while others starred T. D. Rice.[67] Concurrent with Rice's antiabolitionist tour of "Jim Crow" to London, Dowling's script relayed British anti-amalgamationist articulations of *Othello* to US American audiences, tracing the prolific, multidirectional circulations of blackface throughout the circum–North Atlantic.

In 1844, Rice seized on *Othello Travestie*'s potential for blackface burlesque by drawing directly from Dowling's script to fashion his own version, titled *Otello: A Burlesque Opera*.[68] Rice's *Otello* did not significantly alter the antiabolitionist dramaturgical structures of Dowling's burletta, as Rice merely interpolated additional references and blackface jokes drawn from the repertoires of scriptive blackface. Rice's Otello, for instance, announces in the murder scene in the bedroom, "Yes, she must die, dat is plain, / Else more niggers she'll betray again" in a citation of the popular 1834 London print series *Tregear's Black Jokes*, which burlesqued Othello's closing speech: "Yet she must die, else, she'll betray more *Niggers*."[69] In his most significant revision of Dowling's burletta, Rice introduced Desdemona and Otello's child, "Young Otello," who appears with one side of his face "marked black, the other white," the apparent progeny of a "dis 'malgamation."[70] The chromatically binary makeup of

"Young Otello" featured prominently in production, with a playbill for an 1846 production at the National Theatre, Cincinnati, describing him as "eldest son of Otello, and that there may be no partiality, nature has colored him half and half."[71] This imagination of the "fruits of amalgamation" was yet another act of cribbing from the intertheatrical blackface repertoire: Rice's "Young Otello" played on popular familiarity with Edward Williams Clay's antiblack imagery and with George Cruikshank's figuration of a Black man and white woman holding their visually half-Black, half-white child in his antiabolitionist print *The New Union Club* (see fig. 3). Finally, Rice frequently changed the burlesque's title to incorporate citations of other popular blackface burlesques, as in his 1849 advertisement at Chanfrau's National Theatre in New York of *Otello; or, The Moor of Orange Street*.[72] Citing Charles Mathews's *Othello, The Moor of Fleet Street* (1833), Rice translocated Othello from central London to New York's Five Points neighborhood. Rice's adaptation of Dowling's burlesque and his copious citations of British blackface humor signal the dense entanglements of ostensibly disparate national discourses on race, abolitionism, and amalgamation.

In turn, both Dowling's *Othello Travestie* and Rice's *Otello* prompted numerous additional blackface *Othello* burlesques that animated and assuaged white anxieties over interracial amalgamation. In 1850, a pseudonymous British author published an illustrated comic poem titled *Othello: An Interesting Drama, Rather!* in London using the pen name "Alexander Do Mar" in a mocking reference to French Creole writer Alexander Dumas, père (see fig. 16).[73] This poetic travesty in rhyming couplets transforms Othello into a blackface minstrel who sings the popular songs "Old Joe" and "Dan Tucker" and plays the "banjo and bones."[74] Reinforcing the minstrelization of Othello, illustrations figure him as a "black serenader" whose banjo accompanies him as he seduces Desdemona and when he commits suicide. Though this artifact of scriptive blackface concludes tragically with the deaths of both Desdemona and Othello, it offers its reader an emphatic comic "MORAL" accompanied by multiple references to blackface minstrelsy:

> While for poor Lucy Neal's fate you drop a salt tear,
> Or wonder at what uncle Gabriel will say,
> Or list to other songs Ethiopians play,
> Remember that, though they are all pleasant fellows,
> Yet, like Mister Othello, all Blacks are jealous.
> Believe me, the banjo that produces such tones,
> Is made, from Mistress O's skin and Mister O's bones.[75]

This ghoulish conclusion imagines blackface minstrelsy as the amalgamation of instruments grotesquely fashioned from the corpses of the

Fig. 16. Alexander Do Mar, *Othello: An Interesting Drama, Rather!* (London: T.L. Marks, 1850), plate 1. Folger Shakespeare Library, PR2829.A72 D7 1850 Cage. Used by permission of the Folger Shakespeare Library. https://luna.folger.edu/luna/servlet/detail/FOLGERCM1~6~6~51835~103854.

Anglophone world's most famous miscegenatory couple. Here, "Do Mar" draws from Dowling's *Othello Travestie*, which sets Othello's act 5 speech ("It is the cause") to A. W. Humphreys's popular song "The King of the Cannibal Islands" (1830), which itself furnished forth the Black island despot Poonoowingkeewang as an ignoble savage who exhibits excessive sexual passions and beheads his wives.[76] *Othello: An Interesting Drama, Rather!* retraces this terrain of Black sexuality as inherently "jealous" and violent, weaving the threat of interracial sex into the figuration of Black music and sexuality as akin to cannibalism.

Meanwhile, on the US American minstrel stage, *Othello* was a regular object of blackface travesty in the free-form model of Rice's burlesque. In 1862, Eph Horn and Frank Brower of Wood's Minstrels in New York City staged *Othello; or, Dere's de Money*.[77] Published in 1880 as *Dar's de Money*, this burlesque enacts a metatheatrical travesty of *Othello* by staging two blackface figures in their failed attempt to stage the play tragically.[78] In 1870, George W. H. Griffin published *"Othello" Ethiopian Burlesque*, which condenses the plot to seven pages while retaining many of the hallmarks of previous versions: characters repeatedly emphasize Othello's blackness, Othello and Desdemona's courtship receives a musical burlesque set to Dan Emmett's famous blackface song "Dixie," and the murder scene is played for humor.[79] In 1874, Griffin published another minstrel burlesque, *Desdemonum*, in which "dat nigger Oteller" is accompanied by banjo interludes and breakdown jig dances.[80] These versions separately restaged the bathos buttressing all blackface *Othello* burlesques: the minstrel stage insistently figured Black tragedy as travesty, transforming the anxious specter of interracial sexuality into comic absurdity.

Othello's Transoceanic Travesties

While US American audiences engaged with a proliferation of *Othello* burlesques on and off the minstrel stage, Anglophone audiences throughout the British Empire primarily encountered Dowling's *Othello Travestie*. Local amateur theaters in Australia and the Cape Colony frequently staged the blackface burlesque as one of the first pieces in the imperial theatrical repertoire.[81] The immense popularity of this anti-amalgamationist, antiblack burlesque throughout the colonial world signals the consistency with which the spectacle of interracial sexuality functioned as a dense transfer point in furnishing forth Anglophone discourses of imperial white supremacy.

Sydney's Theatre Royal staged the earliest known performance of *Othello Travestie* in the colonies on March 20, 1837. Though Henry Melville introduced blackface to the Australian stage through the Aboriginal caricatures in his *Bushrangers; or, Norwood Vale* (1834), Dowling's burlesque was the first to circulate circum–North Atlantic figurations of Black caricature to Australian audiences. Staged a year prior to the earliest known Australian performance of "Jump Jim Crow," *Othello Travestie* transmitted early blackface minstrelsy avant la lettre. The performances appear to have been closely modeled after the London and Liverpool productions, and responses echoed the critical reception of its metropolitan premieres. Colonial critics and audiences responded enthusiastically to the production, as it received subsequent performances throughout the Australian continent—at Adelaide, Ballarat, Bendigo, Geelong, Hobart, Launceston, Maitland, Melbourne, and Sydney.[82]

Australia's leading theater impresario, George Coppin, ensured that *Othello Travestie* remained in the repertoire for the ensuing two decades. The proverbial "father of the Australian theatre," Coppin "seemed to have a particular weakness" for the "extravaganza *Othello Travestie*," which he frequently staged as an afterpiece to conclude an evening's entertainment.[83] Coppin typically took the role of Othello, which he performed in the manner of a "rale [real] genuine nigger," in the words of a local Australian reviewer.[84] An Australian performer's recollection of an 1851 Adelaide production starring John Lazar in the title role traces how Australian embodiments of Othello's blackness involved similar physical stage business as the London premiere: "When Desdemona fell on his neck and said 'I'll cut you all for this, my blackamoor,' Lazar, as Othello, flapped her several times on the back with his cocked hat and feathers, indecently."[85] The apprehension of indecency in Lazar's performance of Othello arose during a moment of physical contact between Othello and Desdemona, specifically upon Othello's "indecent" touching of Desdemona's "back[side]." The burlesque's staging of interracial contact also prompted a critic reviewing an 1838 Australian production to proclaim that its "sufficiency of vulgarity" and its "blotches . . . no virtuous female can witness without feeling the blush of shame tingle on her cheek."[86] As in its circum–North Atlantic circulations, *Othello Travestie* in its Australian performances aroused white anxieties over interracial sexuality as much as they contained them.

Despite its reception as improperly sexual and morally "indecent" by some colonial critics, Dowling's burlesque quickly became a staple in the Australian repertoire and was often staged alongside blackface minstrelsy. For instance, an August 1838 production of *Othello Travestie* at Sydney's Royal Victoria Theatre featured "Jim Crow" as an entr'acte.[87] Similarly, in 1845, Coppin performed as Othello in Dowling's burlesque and as "the 'Old Kentucky Nigger,' . . . 'Jim Brown'" in the evening's entr'acte at the Queen's Theatre Royal, Melbourne.[88] Moreover, in 1854 and 1855, Rainer's Original Ethiopian Serenaders incorporated *Othello Travestie* into their minstrel program during their Australian tour.[89] Soon thereafter, a reviewer of an 1857 production of *Othello Travestie* in the mining town of Ballarat proclaimed that Mr. Grenville's performance as Othello "might challenge Backus as a Blackamoor . . . [because] he tosses the *hagony* [agony] in true Ethiopian style."[90] The comparison of a local Australian performer to Charles Backus, one of the first globally touring blackface minstrels, signals the intimacy with which Dowling's *Othello* burlesque was entangled with the wider repertoires of minstrelsy. The convergences between *Othello Travestie* and blackface minstrelsy demonstrate the enduring stability of circum–North Atlantic figurations of blackness as part of the furniture of Anglophone imperial racism.

In South Africa's Cape Colony, *Othello Travestie* was similarly popular with white colonial audiences. In the Cape Colony on May 26, 1836, an amateur Dutch company staged *Othello, or De Jaloersche Zwart* [*Othello, or the Jealous Black*], which may have been a Dutch translation of the Shakespearean text or a translation of *Othello Travestie*—the latter more likely given the title's resonances with the alternate title of Dowling's burletta: *Othello; or, The Jealous Nigger*.[91] A review of *De Jaloersche Zwart* emphasized the morally dangerous possibilities of staging *Othello* in colonial South Africa, whether as tragedy or burlesque:

> In frequenting the theatre, do not professing Christians pointedly violate their baptismal vows? . . . In listening to Othello, do they not necessarily contract a horrible familiarity with passions and deeds of the most fiendish character . . . and give up their minds to be polluted by language so gross? Is not the guilt of such persons great, and their danger imminent?[92]

Echoing the moral and racial panic of *Othello*'s circum–North Atlantic critics, this South African reviewer associated Othello with "pollut[ion]" and "danger," citing the threat of "horrible familiarity" with the "fiendish character" as a vector for contagious "passions." The emphasis on the "danger" latent not in the play *Othello* but in the character of Othello signals an early white colonial construction of the perceived *swart gevaar* (Afrikaans for "Black danger" or "Black peril") of African militancy, sexuality, and anticolonial revolt as well as the racialization of such danger as determinately "Black."[93] Othello, a military general and a non-white figure in the Venetian court, easily evoked widespread fears of rebellious Black Africans beyond the Cape's frontier, embodying a threat to the absolute supremacy of the white British colonial enterprise.

Despite (or because of) its capacity to elicit such anxieties, *Othello Travestie* received its English-language Cape premiere on May 13, 1842, with a repeat performance on May 19, only a month after the earliest known South African printing of the lyrics to "Jim Crow."[94] By contrast to its stagings in Britain, the United States, and Australia, in the Cape production, both Othello and Desdemona were played by male actors because women were not yet actors on the Cape stage due to prevalent Calvinist antitheatrical prejudice.[95] An anonymous review in the *Cape Town Mail* celebrated the performance, praising Mr. MacDonald's acting in the role of Desdemona: "The drollness of his little endearments toward his black '*Hobby*' called forth bursts of applause."[96] The reviewer's attention to the travesty performance of Desdemona's (likely physical) affections toward

Othello suggests the critic's and the audience's shared enjoyment of the comic abjection of interracial amalgamation through a blackface burlesque drag. In contrast to the 1836 London production in which Miss Daly performed the role of Desdemona, the amateur Cape Town production presented its audiences with a complex assemblage of gendered and racialized performances. MacDonald's cross-dressing deflated the sexual threat that Othello's Black masculinity posed to white women by precluding any white female performers from the stage. Though the play's resultant all-male racial and gender masquerade permitted the possibility of homoeroticism, such queer possibilities were delimited by the commonsense conventions of imperial drag performance as a site for the rehearsal of heteronormativity and the containment and policing of nonnormative sexualities and presentations of gender. Indeed, the Cape stage's prohibition of female performers stemmed from broader colonial investments in delimiting women from public space in the ostensible interest of public racial-sexual morality. Though the drag performance of *Othello Travestie* afforded a scene of potential queer byplay, it would have been most important to colonial audiences that the performance did not threaten the imperial racial project with the prospect of interracial reproductive sex or resultant miscegenated progeny. The felt exigency of policing the racial-sexual boundaries in order to prevent interracial reproduction was so intense that two decades later, the Cape Colony witnessed "a painful case of infanticide" when a "new-born child, the offspring of a native and a white woman" was strangled to death; the newspaper report noted that the "European concerned" in the case was akin to Desdemona as she "[was] said to have occupied a highly respectable position in society."[97] In lieu of such a tragic enactment of the colonial necropolitics governing "who may live and who must die," the Cape performance of *Othello Travestie* as a drag show explicitly promised its audience that there would be no "piccaninnies" resulting from the central couple's "affections."[98] The cross-dressing reinforced the mandates of comedic burlesque, whereby physical contact between Othello and Desdemona could touch on racial anxieties without threatening the audience with imaginings of an amalgamated future or of the violent reprisals visited on those who transgress the imperial racial bounds.

Othello Travestie's capacity to provoke white anxieties was key to its theatrical appeal and broad circulation. Attesting to its popularity in the Cape Colony, after an 1861 production, the *Cape Argus* review of the production printed the entirety of Othello's travestied Venetian oration.[99] In this circulation beyond the performance event, Dowling's burlesque reentered the domestic economy of scriptive blackface. The *Argus* invited audience members and novice readers to recite the script aloud in the comfort of their own homes, where they could rehearse Othello's transformation into a minstrel fool. This transmission of blackface scripts from theatrical stages into colonial homes signals how intimately trans-oceanic circulations of burlesques and other minstrel materials scripted colonial laughter and pleasure at the abjection of blackness. In the familial home, blackface scripts facilitated what Ann Laura Stoler identifies as "the *learning* of place and race," redoubling the racial pedagogies of the popular stage by furnishing the parlor with lessons in the affective habits of empire.[100]

Though *Othello Travestie* was written at least in part as a direct mockery of Ira Aldridge, the laughter of colonial audiences and readers was not contingent on their familiarity with the interpersonal theatrical rivalries between Aldridge and the white British theatrical community or between other circum-Atlantic performers such as James Hewlett and Charles Mathews. Instead, white audiences in Australia and the Cape Colony encountered Othello as a Black Haitian whose hardships centered on his having been "sold for slavey."[101] Combined with the later parody of Othello's "It is the cause" speech set to "King of the Cannibal Islands," the burlesque defused any threats that Othello embodied by transforming him into a mockery of a colonized subject of the empire. Amid rebellions of enslaved peoples in Haiti (1791–1804) and Jamaica (1831–1832) as well as the 1833 abolition of slavery in the colonies, audiences throughout the Anglophone empire were inclined to view Othello as a representative of the specter of violent rebellion by enslaved and colonized people.[102] *Othello Travestie* invited colonial audiences to laugh at the popular impression that this "independent" Othello remained an unthreatening colonial subject and a burlesque fool.

Anglophone imperial audiences were deeply invested in viewing Othello as a blackface buffoon. In March 1861, the amateur Royal Alfred and Cape Town Dramatic Club produced Dowling's *Othello Travestie*. This production of "the Musical Extravaganza of OTHELLO" was an "IMMENSE SUCCESS" and received repeat performances by popular acclaim.[103] The *Cape Argus* review of the production reassured potential future audiences that this burlesque *Othello* was "very far removed from Shakespeare" because "the Moor [was] more musical than G. Brooke, and tells his tale in less forcible but more agreeable strains."[104] As this review suggests, the production's appeal likely arose in part from the representation of the noble Moor as a singing, dancing, blackfaced minstrel fool. The reviewer specifically referenced the 1855 Cape Town production of Shakespeare's *Othello* starring G. V. Brooke and Fanny Cathcart, preferring the "musical" burlesque to the Shakespearean tragedy.[105] Contemporaneous trends emerged in London, where the *Illustrated London News* observed that burlesques had "gone far to modify the taste of modern audiences," placing all Shakespearean performance in relation to travesty.[106] The preference for comic Othellos in southern Africa endured for much of the century. When Sefton Parry staged Shakespeare's *Othello* in September

1861, four months after a successful production of *Othello Travestie*, his attempts "managed mainly to give very high tragedy the effect of low—very low—comedy."[107] This unintentional comedic effect could have been due to the ever-present possibility of theatrical failure. However, it is also likely that colonial audiences were no longer willing to take *Othello* seriously.

Throughout the Anglophone empire, *Othello* functioned as a charged site of affective imbrications about race, gender, and sexuality. The play's burlesque inversions facilitated the transformation of imperial anxieties into racialized travesties. This dramaturgical effect was epitomized by the earliest known performance of *Othello* featuring a non-white colonial subject of British India. In August 1848, a "Native Gentleman" named Baishnav Charan Adhya performed the title role in *Othello* at the Sans Souci Theatre in Kolkata.[108] In this singular example of a non-white performer enacting a Shakespearean role in the colonies, the presence of a non-white subject on the colonial stage threatened the hegemony of imperial whiteness.[109] Mid-nineteenth-century colonial theaters uniformly prohibited stage performers of color from performing so as to prevent any theatrical contact between white and non-white bodies. Nevertheless, the Kolkata theater staged a public engagement with interracial theatricality that promised a tantalizing spectacle for its predominantly white colonial audience and an opportunity for protonationalistic pride for its smaller Bengali audience.[110]

Adhya's presence on the colonial stage played on imperial racial ambivalences, staging a non-white Othello who resisted the racial discourses through which *Othello* had been interpreted. Adhya's performance in the role was supported by "the patronage of several distinguished Native Rajahs."[111] These upper-class South Asian individuals published their collective support in the local newspaper, announcing that the performance was produced:

> Under the Patronages of Maharajah Radakaunt Bahadur; Maharajah Buddinauth Roy; Maharajah Aupurvokrishna Bahadur; Maharajah Jadubkissen and Brothers; Maharajah Brejendronarain Roy; Maharajah Purtaub Chunder Singh and Brother; Baboos Prawnkissen Mullick and Brothers; Baboos Greeschunder Dutt and Brothers; and Baboo Hurrownauth Mullick.[112]

Though there is scanty documentation recounting how South Asian audiences experienced Adhya's performance, this public endorsement by several upper-class and upper-caste Bengalis demonstrates that South Asians were affectively invested in his endeavor. The *Bengal Hurkaru*, a British newspaper, reported that "[t]he friends of Young Bengal mustered in considerable numbers" at the Sans Souci Theatre on opening night.[113]

These Bengalis likely viewed the production as an opportunity for a Bengali actor to prove his capacity to perform Shakespeare and thereby to challenge the racial hierarchies of the Anglophone empire.

In turn, the predominantly white imperial audience was all too aware of the threat posed by Adhya's successful performance of Othello, as indicated by the *Hurkaru*'s anxious usage of military language to describe the "muster[ing]" masses of Young Bengal in attendance. White imperial audiences knew that Adhya's theatrical success would have placed him in the agential position of the white colonial subject rather than in the subordinated position of the racialized hierarchy on which the Anglophone imperial order relied. Indeed, one notice advertising the production explicitly compared Adhya to "Mr. Ira Aldridge, an African, [who] has played Othello, Zanga, Mungo and other characters with great success."[114] As in Aldridge's famous enactments of Othello, Adhya's performance opposite a white female performer in the role of Desdemona confronted white Anglophone audiences with an embodiment of potential interracial contact. At the same time, the scandalous and transgressive potential of this performance excited white colonists, who flocked to the theater for the "debut of the real unpainted nigger 'Othello,' who had for so many days set the whole world of Calcutta agog."[115] As this comment notes, white Anglophone imperial subjects were tantalized by the prospect of seeing a "real" Othello. In a similar vein as the circum–North Atlantic performances of James Hewlett and Ira Aldridge, the "reality" of racial difference here took center stage, animated by imperial racial discourses and concomitant affective economies. However, likely due to the threat it posed to the imperial order, Adhya's premiere performance was canceled. A military order barred British soldiers in the production from taking their parts, thus making the performance impossible.[116] This state intervention eerily restaged New York City sheriff Mordecai Noah's policing of William Brown's attempts to stage Shakespeare at his African theaters in New York.[117] Half a world apart, these twinned actions by imperial states demonstrated how such states relied on the insistent policing of the colonial color line to maintain their white supremacist imperial racial orders.

Paradoxically, the assertion of state order enforcing the color line circumscribing the colonial theater stage produced a scene of riotous confusion in the streets outside. In an anonymous satirical letter to the editor of the *Calcutta Star* in the style of *Punch*, a "Mr Cheeks" narrated a scene of bewildered audience members who learned of the play's cancellation as they approached the theater's shuttered doors:

> What do they say?—No play, said stout gentleman—What? said the multitude. Othello's sick!! No—he ain't painted! Gammon! Ask again—Desdemona inebriated! [James] Barry drunk! Iago not

> come—one gentleman in a white choker roared out, how could you expect him when his very name tells you Aya a go? Ha ha!! The choker's turned joker—no, but what is it?—'an incident—Othello in drawing his sword stuck himself instead of Desdemona, and so now they've stuck the public'—no, no, it is not a laughing matter, I paid for my ticket;—dere's de money, said another.[118]

The Othello imagined by "Mr Cheeks" bears striking similarity to blackface burlesque Othellos whose threats of violence were always already defused by his hapless ineptitude. Moreover, in its punning language and in the chaotic, carnivalesque scene it imagined, the editorial reimagined Adhya's canceled performance as a blackface Shakespearean burlesque, complete with a bumbling, ignoble Othello and a reference to "dere's de money" decades prior to the staging and publication of the *Othello* burlesques *Dere's de Money* (1862) and *Dar's de Money* (ca. 1880).[119] In addition to this burlesque catalog of puns and inversions, "Mr Cheeks" offers an account of the colonial public's marked anticipation of—and desire for—Adhya's failure. The desire for Adhya to be at fault for the play's cancellation is most evident in the joke that Othello "stuck himself instead of Desdemona," which requires a complete forgetting of the plot of the play, wherein Othello does stab himself and not Desdemona. In this travestied scene of an imagined *Othello*, the carnivalesque atmosphere of blackface minstrelsy spilled outside the theatrical stage and onto the streets of colonial Kolkata. Though the show was intended as a serious performance, the white colonial audience interpreted Adhya's unperformed *Othello* as a burlesque, restoring the colonial racial order by asserting their social authority over the theater itself. Through its minstrelized narration of this street scene, the editorial articulates the canceled production as a scenario of scriptive blackface.

Despite the withdrawal of several actors at the command of a colonial authority, Adhya's *Othello* premiered with new actors the following week. As with the canceled performance, the audience at the premiere included "English ladies and gentlemen from Calcutta . . . [and] also quite a number of Bengali baboos, including princes."[120] The Bengali press celebrated Adhya's performance, with *Sambad Pravakar* declaring that he "was able to charm the audience with his excellent delivery and expressive gestures."[121] By contrast, Adhya's performance was greeted with ambivalence in the British colonial press, which tempered faint praise of his racial exceptionalism with evident enjoyment of his theatrical missteps.[122] Whatever successes Adhya enjoyed in his debut were brief. A repeat performance on September 12 received the following dismissive review in the *Englishman*: "Whether our Native friend juggled wisely or well in selecting so difficult a task we will not venture to discuss, but that he failed, in every sense of the word, both in conception and execution, we think everybody present must admit."[123] As promised by the jokes made in anticipation of the performance, Kolkata's white imperial audiences expected Adhya to fail. No amount of individual theatrical virtuosity could allow Adhya to undo the deeply embedded dramaturgies of blackface burlesque that positioned him as yet another comically ineffectual "*black* Othello."[124] Indeed, a reviewer for the *Calcutta Star* compared Adhya's physical embodiment of Othello's turn to exit the stage as "something between the Jem Crow and Polka fling," a derisive critique that drew Adhya into the minstrel fold.[125] Letters to the editor reinforced the theatrical color line, with one denouncing "the whitey brown specimen of Young Bengal" whose "speech to the [Venetian] Senate was delivered as tamely as if given by a sniveling urchin at a grammar school."[126] Framed as a misfiring attempt at tragedy transmuted into travesty, Adhya's performance appeared to his white Anglophone audience as a yet another incarnation of minstrelized racial abjection—an objectified ethnological display of a racial "specimen" attempting and failing to adequately enunciate his claim to subjecthood.

Unlike the several Black actors who followed Ira Aldridge's path on the London stage (e.g., Samuel Morgan Smith and Paul Molyneaux Hewlett), there were no more South Asian Othellos on the white imperial stages of South Asia. All-white productions of *Othello* continued throughout the nineteenth century while midcentury Bengali and Parsi theater companies began to incorporate Shakespearean drama into their repertoires and to adapt *Othello* for their South Asian troupes.[127] However, though these South Asian troupes developed an early intercultural Shakespearean theater on the subcontinent, it was not widely patronized by white imperial audiences, who favored the Shakespearean productions of all-white colonial theaters.[128]

Amid this segregated theater scene, the burlesque Othello made several repeat appearances on India's white imperial stages. Most notably, Othello circulated through Dave Carson's caricature "Othello Sahib Bahadoor" (Master Othello, the Brave Warrior). The title of Carson's *Othello* burlesque suggests that he parodied Coleridge's vaunted "warrior Moor" as a South Asian caricature, much as he minstrelized upper-class Bengalis in his "Bengalee Baboo" caricature (more on this in chapter 5). Like most touring blackface performers, Carson regularly performed *Othello* burlesques, as in his 1861 Kolkata sketch parodying G. V. Brooke's *Othello* as "G. V. Brooky" and his 1863 Mumbai performance of "Othello, a Musical Burlesque."[129] By contrast to these stock blackface burlesques that mocked leading Shakespearean performers and *Othello* broadly, "Othello Sahib Bahadoor" translocated blackface *Othello* burlesques to the Indian subcontinent, making South Asian colonized subjects the target of racial scorn. Carson's "Othello Sahib Bahadoor" was a solo minstrel sketch in which Carson "call[ed] on the audience to *imagine* such and such circumstances of the plot and transformations of the scenes" that featured "burlesque weeping" and a comic conclusion of Othello's "self immolation" by "dash[ing] himself on the floor."[130] The earliest known version of "Othello Sahib Bahadoor" was performed at the town hall of Kolkata on December 27, 1864, when it was advertised as a "grand oriental, venetian, Shakespearean, Tragical, Comical, Musical, Burlesque, scena."[131] Led by Kuvarjī Sorābjī Nājar (Cooverjee Sorabjee [C. S.] Nazir), the Parsi Elphinstone Dramatic Society staged a production of *Othello* in Mumbai in October 1864, just two months prior to Carson's invention of "Othello Sahib Bahadoor," and it is plausible that Carson's 1864 *Othello* burlesque took aim at such South Asian performances of *Othello* much as the white imperial audience burlesqued Adhya's earlier performance.[132]

In 1889, at the end of his career, Carson claimed to have performed his Othello "over 4,000 consecutive times at Her Majesty's Theatre, Dum Dum," in a parody of extravagant claims of Shakespearean actors such as Daniel Bandmann, who toured Kolkata and drew inspiration for his "noble Moor" from Bengali reformer Keshub Chunder Sen.[133] Carson's assertion of four thousand consecutive performances was hardly serious. Nevertheless, his exaggerated boasting aptly accounted for the massive popularity of travestied Othellos throughout the Anglophone empire. Indeed, the racial travesty of Black, brown, and Asian peoples throughout the imperial white world was common enough to qualify as an "art." To wit, an 1867 article in the *Pioneer* (Prayagraj) reprinted an essay titled "The Art of Burlesque" from the London *Pall Mall Gazette*, which defined burlesque as an explicitly racialized performance form that

> fits appropriate words to nigger melodies, so as to afford opportunities for the introduction of idiotic choruses and utterly demented dancing, after the manner of that accursed people whom Homer, in his ignorance, calls "the blameless Aethiopians." It is a great point, too, in casting the piece to transpose the races as far as possible.
>
> The puns, jokes and smart dialogue of the piece afford a certain amount of grave satisfaction, but when there comes a parody of some charming lyric of the Christy-Minstrel school . . . followed by a dance intended to outnigger the nigger buffoonery of the Ethiopian Serenaders, then the delight of the intelligent audience knows no bounds.[134]

As an "art," racial travesty and burlesque transformed non-white subjects into abjected racial figures in order to animate and contain white anxieties about interracial amalgamation under the comic "sign of Othello" as they circulated throughout the Anglophone world.

Travestied Othellos initially formed a distinct transoceanic performance repertoire in parallel to the nineteenth-century tragic "tawny"

Fig. 17. "Othello! Othello! Everywhere. There is no getting away from Othello." *Moonshine* (London), May 28, 1881, 253. Courtesy of Harvard University Libraries.

Othello tradition. Nevertheless, by the end of the century, these two performance strands met in South Asia, where they amalgamated into a new racialized burlesque that abjected "tawny" South Asians as kin to the Ethiopian Serenaders and the blackface burlesque Othellos of the minstrel stage. The amalgamation of differently racialized Othellos epitomized a process central to the racial discourses of the Anglophone empire. Returning to Clay's *Fruits of Amalgamation* (1839), we may trace how the inclusion of the Orientalized Othello within a scene mocking the domestic civility of Black-white miscegenation effectively burlesqued any and all scenes of racial mixing. Indeed, an 1881 satirical print in the London magazine *Moonshine* envisioned a proliferation of Othellos ranging from Edwin Booth's "tawny" example to G. W. Moore's blackface burlesque Othello ornamented with a pseudo-Japanese topknot, which altogether threatened to overwhelm the Anglophone stage (see fig. 17). Dave Carson's "Othello Sahib Bahadoor" condensed these many Othellos into a new racialized burlesque assemblage encompassing the Anglophone empire's Black, brown, and Asian subject populations in a singular racial travesty. These travestied Othellos sowed the seeds of anti-amalgamation discourse around the globe. In turn, the affective economies animated by Othello burlesques furnished forth the racial formations of the Anglophone empire as the most fecund and enduring fruit of amalgamation.

Chapter 5

✦

The Racial Makeup of Empire

On March 7, 1863, US American blackface minstrel Charles Backus donated 114.3 taels in proceeds from a minstrel performance in Shanghai, China, for the benefit of the cotton workers of Manchester, England.[1] Two decades prior, Shanghai was forcibly opened to British trade after the First Opium War and the signing of the Treaty of Nanjing, with US-Chinese trade beginning shortly thereafter, following the Treaty of Wanghai. Anglo-American gunboat diplomacy conscripted China into the trade networks of global capitalism, forging new routes through which transoceanic blackface quickly trafficked. Backus made his early career as a leading minstrel impresario in the resultant "Pacific circuit" that connected China to Australia, Japan, Aotearoa New Zealand, and the United States.[2] Within this transpacific network of performance, Backus developed the earliest known yellowface act on the minstrel stage. As the *Pioneer; or, California Monthly Magazine* recounted in 1854, "There is no single Ethiopian Minstrel in California who can be compared with the great Backus. His 'China Washerman' is immense."[3] In 1855, following his successes in California, Backus toured his minstrel troupe and his yellowface act to Australia, where he would return on Pacific tours that also brought him to Shanghai.[4]

Following Backus's tours of the Pacific circuit and his popularization of yellowface minstrel performance, the racial cast list of minstrelsy expanded to enfold Asian caricatures. The ensemble minstrel show proved capacious enough to stage East Asian figures in yellowface and South Asian caricatures in brownface alongside its vast repertoires of blackface burlesque. This conjuncture of Orientalist performance and Black abjection elaborated new "racial geometries" beyond minstrelsy's foundational binary of Black and white.[5] The overlapping and intersecting repertoires of blackface, yellowface, and brownface trace the "racial triangulation" not only of Asian migrants in the United States but also of differently racialized Asian subjects and subalterns throughout the Anglophone empire.[6] These various modes of racialized performance coalesced through the transoceanic traffics of blackface minstrelsy and the performance form's investments in racial capitalism and imperial violence across what Lisa Lowe terms "the intimacies of four continents."[7]

The racialized performances of the minstrel stage were not segregated into discrete categories but rather formed intertwined braids that incorporated white male performances of blackface, yellowface, and brownface; male and female caricatures; and white female and Black male performers as well. Through its expanding racial repertoire, transoceanic blackface staged a complex repertoire of blackface, Orientalism, and gender drag, the enduring entanglement of which Christian DuComb has illustrated as characteristic of racialized performance in the United States.[8] Studies of minstrel drag have analyzed its mediation of racial and sexual politics within national contexts. By contrast, this chapter maps the imbrications of racialized gender performance and the "scattered hegemonies" of Anglophone imperial culture—that is, how the repertoires of transoceanic blackface were bound up with what Inderpal Grewal and Caren Kaplan identify as interlocking "global economic structures, patriarchal nationalisms, 'authentic' forms of tradition, local structures of domination, and legal-juridical oppression on multiple levels."[9] I trace the entanglements of minstrelsy's plural modes of racialized and gendered performance beyond the national boundaries of the United States to outline how the transoceanic traffics of minstrelsy furnished popular sites for acting out and managing the racial and sexual anxieties of the Anglophone empire.

The Burlesque Chinaman and Transpacific Yellowface

Backus's "Burlesque Chinaman" was a transoceanic hit. Throughout the Pacific circuit, Anglophone audiences cheered his derogation of Asian migrant workers who crossed oceans to labor in California, Hawaii, and Australia. Though several recent studies have analyzed the consolidation of yellowface as an anti-Asian performance form in the mode of minstrelsy, they typically narrate the popularization of the yellowface figure beginning with Bret Harte's "heathen Chinee" figure of Ah Sin (1870) and his many theatrical reappearances.[10] By contrast, Backus's yellowface act usually appears as a brief precursor or antecedent, in part due to its development in mining camps along the California coast rather than in metropolitan New York.[11] By situating Backus's California performances of his "Burlesque Chinaman" alongside his many Pacific tours, I map the transpacific formation of yellowface minstrel caricature more than a decade prior to Harte's ambivalent yellowface figure. As Matthew Wittmann observes, "The Chinese performances of Charley Backus were so enjoyable for both American and Australian audiences . . . [because] stages reflected and reified racial differences across the Pacific and ultimately helped engender very similar policies regarding Asian immigration and racial exclusion."[12] The transpacific popularity of Backus's yellowface act demonstrates the imbrication of US American and British imperial racial orders and the intimate ways in which ostensibly discrete national modes of white supremacy were intertwined.

Throughout the Anglophone empire's expansion across the Pacific, Asian subjects were conscripted into the racial repertoires of imperial common sense. In California, anti-Chinese sentiment was tightly entangled with antiblackness. In a diary entry dated May 4, 1852, a white Californian gold miner named Alfred T. Jackson declared,

> Chinamen are getting altogether too plentiful in the country . . . . They are not to be looked upon as human beings and have no rights that a white man is bound to respect, except in protecting them in their titles to grounds that they have regularly bought under agreed conditions.[13]

Jackson mobilized this declaration of Chinese rightlessness to justify the actions of white mobs that threatened to remove Chinese settlers by force unless they purchased claims to the land for white profit. Five years prior to the US Supreme Court decision in *Dred Scott v. Sandford* that would make the phrase infamous, Jackson's articulation of this de facto "miners' law" proclaimed that Chinese in California were like Black Americans throughout the country insofar as they had "no rights that a white man [was] bound to respect."[14] Jackson's de facto legal reasoning departed from Chief Justice Roger B. Taney's in that Jackson allowed that Chinese miners might legally own property whereas Taney insisted that Black Americans were themselves property—"that the negro might justly and lawfully be reduced to slavery for his benefit."[15] The distinction relied on a hierarchy of unfreedom. Black Americans prior to the passage of the Thirteenth Amendment could legally be considered property and were therefore devoid of freedom altogether. Asian Americans were legally free but substantively rightless and inhabited the abject zone of unfreedom shared by other non-white subjects of the Anglophone empire. Chinese Americans specifically were, in the terms of Andrew Markus, "regarded not as equals but as 'burlesques on humanity'" who were subjected to "the sporadic use of force" by white mobs.[16]

Chinese miners in Australia fared little better than in California. As Charles Wentworth Dilke notes in his aptly titled 1869 survey of the white Anglophone empire, *Greater Britain*:

> In America, as in Australia, there is a violent prejudice against John Chinaman. He pilfers, we are told; he lies, he is dirty, he smokes opium, is full of bestial vices—a pagan, and—what is far more important—yellow! . . . In both countries they [Chinese men] take out mining licenses from the State, which is bound to protect them in the

> possession of the rights thus gained, but which is powerless against the rioters of Ballarat, or the "Anti-Chinese mob" of El Dorado.[17]

Dilke directly linked the yellowface minstrel figure of "John Chinaman" to anti-Chinese violence much as blackface minstrelsy entangled abject Black figurations with antiblack violence. Perhaps most importantly, it was in mining regions in California and Australia (El Dorado County, Ballarat) that the imbricated practices of minstrelsy and white masculine mob violence forged these entanglements.[18] Yellowface minstrelsy was fashioned as a differently colored but substantively similar piece of the imperial furniture of white supremacy.

Though Backus performed yellowface widely, he did not leave significant evidence that indicates how he embodied his "Burlesque Chinaman" caricature. Theatrical reviews across continents repeatedly cited the applause and approbation of audiences without providing details of the performance. For instance, the Honolulu newspaper the *Polynesian* simply declared, "People who have not seen his Chinese personation are to be pitied."[19] The strongest evidence of Backus's performance style arises from reviews that refer to "the eccentricities of Backus in his burlesque Chinese."[20] The language of "eccentricities" and "burlesque" situate Backus's "Chinese personation" among the solo blackface character sketches that populated the "olio" section of the minstrel show.[21] The fullest description available refers to "his personation of a Chinaman, which included a Chinese Song and an appeal to the audience in the same dialect (or something dreadfully like it)."[22]

The only known version of Backus's yellowface songs, "The Chinee Laundryman," was published in 1880. It is unlikely that this was the same version that Backus performed on his earliest tours of the Pacific, but it nonetheless gives a sense of his oeuvre:

> Me come from Hong Kong Chinee
> To workee for de Mellican man,
> Me no can talkee much english,
> Me speakee you de best I can.
> Me workee all day in laundry,
> For ching chong dat's his name,
> Me catchee de rats in de market,
> Makee pot-pie all a same.
> All same! All same! All same!
>
> CHORUS.
> Oh ching chong opium, taffy on a stick,
> No likee brass band, Makee very sick.
> Mellican man listen, sing you littee song,
> With a chinee fiddle, and a shanghai gong.[23]

In his caricature of "The Chinee Laundryman," Backus enfolded Asian peoples into the minstrel repertoire by animating several tropes of scriptive blackface. Central to Backus's yellowface act was a mishearing of Chinese speech. As with early blackface minstrelsy's insistent figuration of Black speech as marked by sonic difference, Backus's yellowface speech articulates as a source of humor the presumptive incapacity of Chinese people to speak English. The nonsense chorus "ching chong opium, taffy on a stick" exemplifies the insistent mishearing of Asian diasporic speech as nonsensical—a minstrel figuration that abjected Asian diasporic people as unthinking and, ultimately, less than human. Core motifs of Asian abjection recurred throughout Backus's early yellowface, as in the popular trope that Chinese people ate dogs, cats, and rats, which situated the eating habits of Asian and Asian diasporic peoples as beyond the pale of Anglophone whiteness and its alimentary codes of civility. In a finishing touch that placed the "Chinee Laundryman" firmly in the minstrel fold, the final verse of the song centers on the Laundryman's desire to "gettee nice littee wife," which implied a desire for racial amalgamation with a white woman. Taken together, these reanimated minstrel tropes forged popular impressions of Chinese racial difference by adapting blackface scripts for yellowface performance.

Backus's "Burlesque Chinaman" quickly prompted imitations and variations throughout the Pacific circuit and beyond. The minstrel stage was a critical site for the transmission of the early yellowface caricature, circulating anti-Chinese songs as well as yellowface enactments fashioned on Backus's model.[24] As early as September 1857, Eph Horn—who had performed in a rival troupe to the Backus Minstrels in California in 1855—staged what was likely a variation of Backus's yellowface act on Broadway. His performance of "The Chinese Wash Man" enacted what is perhaps the earliest yellowface act in a New York minstrel show.[25] Contemporaneously, minstrel songbooks published the earliest known print version of a yellowface minstrel act in S. S. Steele's "A Chinaman's Tail (Tale)" (1857), which alluded to the "Chinese" hairstyle of the queue that Sean Metzger identifies as "the dominant visual signifier of Chineseness in the late nineteenth and early twentieth centuries."[26] Steele's yellowface song took the form of a narrative recounting a comic brawl between a British "John Bull" and a Chinese "Joss" featuring the nonsense chorus:

> Ching ring, chow chow, ricken chicken, a chow,
> Chinaman loves big bow wow and little puppies too.[27]

The year following the publication of Steele's song, Joe Murphy performed in Honolulu with the California Minstrels as the troupe toured the Pacific circuit. Reviewers made special note of his "Chinese washerwoman" act—"a striking and laughable imitation of that class of celestials which abounds in San Francisco and Honolulu."[28] Murphy's variation would ultimately share the stage with Backus himself when Murphy performed his "Chinese Impersonations" in Backus's minstrel show.[29] These several examples of early yellowface characters and songs signal the central role of minstrelsy's Pacific circuit in promulgating the "Burlesque Chinaman" as a new entry in the racial repertoires of the Anglophone empire.

Even as yellowface roles proliferated widely, early yellowface caricature remained tightly entangled with the repertoires of blackface minstrelsy. For instance, Frank Curtis's "The Artful Chinee" (ca. 1870) transformed the chorus of Steele's "Ching ring, chow chow, ricken chicken, a chow" into an explicit citation of early blackface minstrel songs: "Chingaring chi, and chingaring chee, / Chingaring chi for the young Chinee."[30] Altering "Ching ring, chow chow" into "Chingaring chi," Curtis placed "The Artful Chinee" in a performance genealogy extending back to Charles Dibdin's blackface song "Negro Philosophy" ("Chingaring, Chingaring, never mind") and the anonymously authored early blackface hit "Ching-A-Ring-Chaw" or "Sambo's 'Dress to He Bred'ren" ("Chinger ringer, ring ching, ching, Ho ah, ding ah ding kum darkee").[31] This performance genealogy forged early figurations of Black plantation life across the Caribbean and the United States as a harmonious, banjo-laden scene of contented labor that naturalized and explicitly excused acts of corporal and sexual violence against Black captives. Caroline H. Yang further notes that this genealogy was reanimated in midcentury blackface "Topsy" songs featuring the "wicked" Black girl character from *Uncle Tom's Cabin*, which featured lyrics such as "Ching a ring a ring a ricked."[32] These several blackface songs circulated transoceanically, furnishing forth blackface performance material that Curtis refashioned to elaborate yellowface caricature in the minstrel mold.

Another wave of yellowface caricature crested—particularly on the US American stage—following the publication of Bret Harte's "Plain Language of Truthful James" and its figuration of Ah Sin, the "heathen Chinee" (1870). Though Harte crafted his poem as a rebuke to the anti-black and anti-Chinese racism of the minstrel stage, he wrote within a broadly minstrelized mode of caricature, and his poem ultimately functioned to popularize the "heathen Chinee" as a new yellowface role.[33] Harte posited the "heathen Chinee" as a typical cardplayer insofar as he and his competitors all cheat by keeping cards up their sleeves. Nevertheless, the popular reception of the poem and song figured the "heathen Chinee" as a uniquely villainous swindler.[34] In brief, Harte's ironic claim that "for ways that are dark / And for tricks that are vain, / The heathen Chinee is peculiar" was quickly flattened into the defining characteristic of the yellowface "heathen Chinee" role (see fig. 18).[35]

Harte's later story of "Wan Lee, the Pagan" (1876) attempted to dispel readers' common-sense impressions of Chinese Americans, specifically

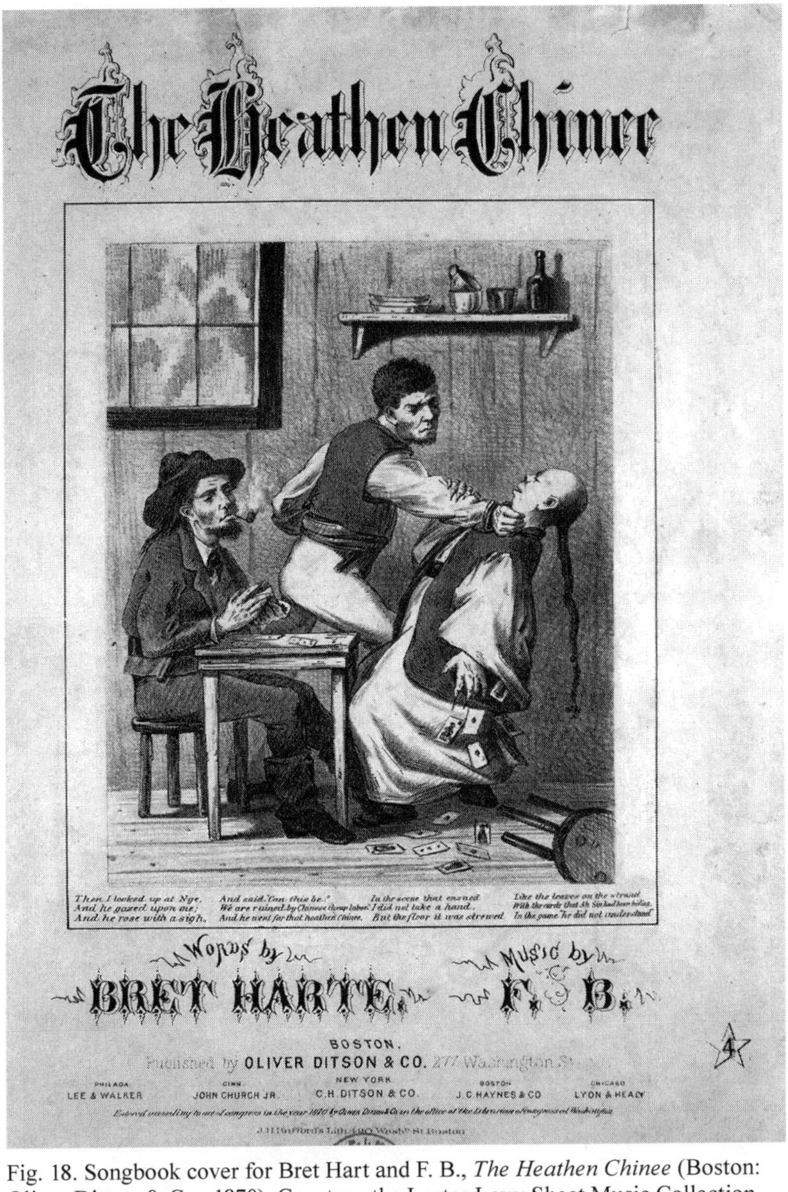

Fig. 18. Songbook cover for Bret Hart and F. B., *The Heathen Chinee* (Boston: Oliver Ditson & Co., 1870). Courtesy the Lester Levy Sheet Music Collection, Sheridan Libraries, Johns Hopkins University.

those forged through the yellowface performance.[36] In "Wan Lee," Harte's white narrator introduces a new Chinese figure, Hop Sing:

> Before I describe him I want the average reader to discharge from his mind any idea of a Chinaman that he may have gathered from the pantomime. He did not wear beautifully scalloped drawers fringed with little bells—I never met a Chinaman who did; he did not habitually carry his forefinger extended before him at right angles with his body, nor did I ever hear him utter the mysterious sentence, "Ching a ring a ring chaw," nor dance under any provocation.[37]

Amid the popularization of his character of Ah Sin on the minstrel stage, Harte's rebuke of the yellowface figuration of Chinese character signals the impact of the popular stage in shaping popular impressions of Asian peoples. Most strikingly, Harte cites the yellowface "Ching a ring a ring chaw" trope and the caricature's comic dancing, situating the origins of the "Chinaman" stereotype firmly on the minstrel stage. While Harte labored to extricate his Chinese characters from the vortices of minstrelsy, the circulations of transoceanic yellowface whorled, churning out abject performances of Asian-ness on antiblack themes. Indeed, by 1871, Backus had established himself as a leading minstrel performer and impresario, staging his blackface and yellowface acts with the San Francisco Minstrels on Broadway. He continued to perform in yellowface, staging his "Chinese Laundryman" through 1891.[38] However, to compete with emergent rivals in yellowface performance, he also interpolated the "Comic Ditty, 'Bret Harte's Heathen Chinee'" into his repertoire.[39] The "Heathen Chinee" also went global, as it was performed by G. H. Henri in Dave Carson's minstrel show during an 1875 tour to Singapore.[40] That same year in Sydney, the theatrical couple of Mr. Williamson and Miss Maggie Moore regularly performed "The Chinese Question," "in which they impersonate[d] a pair of Celestials in a style which elicit[ed] convulsions of laughter."[41] Minstrel variations on the "heathen Chinee" crowded the stage and, by the end of the nineteenth century, the Anglophone imperial stage was awash in waves of yellowface.

Throughout the transoceanic circulations of early yellowface performance, Asian subjects appeared in abject, minstrelized form. It is unclear the extent to which minstrel performers applied racializing makeup in order to appear "yellow," though Harte's rebuke of the "pantomime" suggests the prevalence of yellowface makeup on the minstrel stage. Harte asserts of "Wan Lee" that "[h]is complexion, which extended all over his head except where his long pig-tail grew, was like a very nice piece of glazed brown paper-muslin."[42] Here, Harte tacitly critiques a form of theatrical makeup that did *not* extend the Asian character's complexion "all over his head" and that appeared not like "glaze brown paper-muslin"—instead, the yellowface makeup he describes seems to follow the conventions of blackface by emphasizing the face as the site of racial identity and by de-emphasizing verisimilitude in theatrical representation. Nevertheless, as Metzger has demonstrated with regard to Charles Parsloe's "Chinaman" character, yellowface did not necessarily involve yellow face paint so much as it relied on the ornamentation of gesture and fashion that signified Asian-ness to Anglophone imperial audiences.[43] Appearing in varying form across transoceanic stages, yellowface was a mutable form of racialized performance—one that was flexible enough to enfold non-Black racialized figures into the repertoires of minstrel abjection.

The Bengalee Baboo and the Brownface Repertoire

The capaciousness and fungibility of yellowface is perhaps best exemplified by its transmutation into brownface. In 1859, during his second tour of Australia, Backus joined a company featuring blackface minstrel Dave Carson.[44] Though this professional alliance was short lived, Carson almost certainly had opportunity to study Backus's yellowface caricature as they performed together as leading "endmen" of the company. Two years later, in 1861, Carson and his new San Francisco Minstrels troupe toured South Asia, including long stays in Kolkata and Mumbai. During this tour, which began a mere four years after the Indian Rebellion of 1857, Carson "attained Hindostanese" and developed brownface impressions "in which he mimicked and caricatured a certain class of the native people."[45] By December 1864, Carson had elaborated his "Hindostanese" into a brownface caricature, "The Bengalee Baboo," which mocked anglicized Bengali men.[46] Adapting the tropes and techniques of blackface and yellowface minstrelsy to South Asian subjects, Carson popularized abject racial impressions of South Asian peoples and furnished forth novel repertoires for enacting the racialized "brown" subjects of the Anglophone empire.[47]

By contrast to the yellowface caricatures populating Australian and US American stages, Carson's brownface figures did not target migrant subjects who labored in predominantly white settler spaces. Instead, his extensive repertoire of brownface caricatures ostensibly was drawn from the non-white majority populations of South Asia. Throughout his subcontinental career, Carson not only fashioned a singular, enduring brownface archetype but also developed several popular South Asian caricatures. As Sir Dinesh Wacha notes in his memoir, "Dave Carson himself was a facetious actor, of ready wit and humour and knew how to catch his audience, specially with local topics of interest and many a topical song."[48] The earliest known example of Carson's localized, South Asian topical pieces, "I'm

Off to Charlestown with Original Hindoostanee Chorus" (later "Hum Jata Challstown") laid out the formula for much of his ensuing repertoire of brownface minstrelsy.[49] Carson developed an extensive cast of brownface songs and caricatures, including "The Delhi Mummy" (originally, "The Virginia Mummy"), "That's So (with New Local Verses)," "Hold Your Ghoras" ("Hold Your Horses"), "The Calcutta Swell" ("The Dandy Broadway Swell"), and "The Belles of Calcutta" ("The Belle of Broadway" or "Belle of Baltimore").[50] In the "Calcutta Swell," for instance, Carson burlesqued the nouveau riche Bengali as an absurdly affluent, tea plantation–owning, dandified "swell" who

> Lives in Chowringhee [an upper-class area of Kolkata]
> Keeps a bolio [large sailing boat] and dinghy
> Has large estates in Chittagong
> And grows no end of tea.[51]

In keeping with the dramaturgies of the blackface and yellowface repertoire, Carson's brownface caricatures such as his "Calcutta Swell" targeted South Asian aspirations to social and political advancement, particularly when manifest as the attainment of wealth, status, or rights that were understood to be racial properties of whiteness.

In May 1865, Carson added to his brownface repertoire a burlesque of upper-class Parsis, "Davejee Carsonbhoy's Dream," to capitalize on a wave of popular anti-Parsi sentiment among his white Anglophone audiences.[52] During his 1865 tour of Mumbai, Parsi audiences frequented performances of Dave Carson's San Francisco Minstrels, and his fashioning of minstrelized Parsi caricatures responded directly to Parsi audience members' active contestation over public space in the theater.[53] After two Parsi audience members refused to give up their seats to white British subjects, Carson directed a "scathing side hit" at the two Parsi men. The drama among the audience spilled into the press as the *Times of India* breathlessly reported on the weekslong controversy of the "Race Question" in Mumbai.[54] The climactic moment of this series of colonial racial confrontations arose when Dave Carson introduced a new South Asian caricature, Davejee Carsonbhoy, whose moniker mocked a prominent Parsi named Jamsetjee Jejeebhoy and whose purpose was to continue his "scathing side hits" against Mumbai's Parsis. Though no script nor songbook for this Parsi act has yet been recovered, the *Times of India* offers a detailed description of Carson's caricature:

> Dave will shew well also in his inimitable character as a "Parsee," with the peculiar turban of the race inclining at the same angle with the nose—white cotton collar-less body coat, red silk trousers, white stockings, and shoes with the toes turned up like

> the prows of a venetian gondola. Dave has the true Parsee cast of features—sloping forehead—long full nose, on an elongated face—full lips, large mouth, with chin slightly receding—long neck, and shoulders falling.[55]

This passage omits any mention of racializing makeup, instead outlining Carson's "Parsee" costume and physical comportment in extensive detail, indicating how Anglophone imperial audiences perceived brownface minstrel caricature primarily through sartorial adornment, embodiment, and gesture. The racial mask of brownface was not the only nor the primary theatrical signifier of brownface performance. Instead, as evident in the retinue of brownface Othellos circulating across the transoceanic stage, the Orientalist signifiers of a turban and pointed shoes were sufficient to animate Anglophone impressions of the empire's Asian subjects and to draw such subjects into the minstrel fold.

The centerpiece of Carson's extensive brownface repertoire was his "Bengalee Baboo" or "Ram Jam Thandah Ghose" (see fig. 19).[56] Carson was so closely associated with this role that he was referred to not as a "Negro-minstrel" but as a "Bengali-minstrel."[57] Carson's minstrel caricature of aspirational Bengalis invited audiences, in the terms of one of his advertisements, to laugh at "the buffooneries of the Bengalee Baboo."[58] Carson's fame extended throughout and beyond the Indian subcontinent, and he established himself as a leading performer and theatrical impresario in Kolkata and Mumbai. He also toured the "Bengalee Baboo" widely throughout the subcontinent and the Pacific circuit.[59] By 1875, an advocate for British education in India explicitly cited Carson as a primary mechanism for the dissemination of knowledge of Bengalis throughout South Asia, claiming that the "ordinary Bombay man knows but little more what a Bengalee Baboo is really like than he may have gleaned from Dave Carson's famous caricature."[60] Though Carson frequently revised his performance over his thirty-year career in and beyond South Asia, his performances instantiated the minstrel figuration of the "Bengalee Baboo" as the popular archetype of an aspirational South Asian subject who sought social advancement as well as entry into the upper classes of imperial society.

One of two extant full-length printings of Carson's "Bengalee Baboo" survives via the logbook of Captain W. H. Angel of the clipper ship *Sheila*, which sailed from Kolkata to the Caribbean transporting a cargo of indentured South Asians, or "Indian coolies."[61] Angel stayed in Kolkata for three months in 1877, and while there he evidently acquired a song sheet of Carson's popular brownface act. Here, the entanglements among the racial repertoires of transoceanic blackface and the "coolie trade" are remarkably dense. Carson's song, however, did not attempt to represent "coolies" but instead staged the figure of the Bengali shopkeeper:

Fig. 19. Carte de visite of Dave Carson as "The Bengalee Baboo" (undated). Courtesy of Françoise Mazza.

I very good Bengalee Baboo,
In Calcutta a long time e-stop;
Ram Jam Tundah Ghose my name;
In Radah Bazaar I keep it e-shop.
Very good Hinodo, smoke my *hookah*, (native pipe)
Eat my *dhall-bat* every day; (pan-cake)
Night time come, make plenty *poojah*, (fun)
Hear *Nauch-wallah* on tom-tom play. (dancing girls).
Chorus.
Kautch-per-wanee, good time coming; (never mind)

Sing Britannia rules the waves,
Jolly good-e-fellow, go home in the morning—
Babboo how he can make slaves.[62]

Like Backus's "Burlesque Chinaman," Carson's "Bengalee Baboo" was a racialized character song in which the titular character introduces himself to the audience in accented, "broken" English. Attesting to Carson's lack of interest in accurate representation of South Asian people, his song mistranslates several words—perhaps most egregiously, he defines "puja," an act of Hindu ritual, as a form of evening "fun." Instead of attempting theatrical verisimilitude, Carson cited the intertheatrical repertoire of transoceanic blackface and its tropes of broken speech, through which he drew anglicized South Asians into the minstrel fold. To this end, Carson's "Baboo" narrates a sequence of burlesque scenarios across eleven verses that culminate in his embarrassment and abjection. In the first third of the song, the "Baboo" attempts to sell a white patron ("Sahab") the various wares available in his shop. In the second third, he embarks on an overseas journey to a foreign ("Balattee") country, where he becomes a middle-class "good civil servant." In the final third, he becomes a high-ranking subject of the British Empire, receiving the "Star of India" as well as invitations to fancy balls, where he enacts the cultural scripts of Englishness by eating beef, drinking champagne, and attempting (and failing) to seduce a white woman ("Mem-Sahab"), who throws a mustard pot in his face.[63] In his racial and class aspirations, Carson's "Bengalee Baboo" appears not only as an adaptation of Backus's "Burlesque Chinese" but also as a brownface variation on the blackface dandy. Moreover, the "Baboo" embarrasses himself in his attempt to court a white woman in a minstrel burlesque of interracial sexuality, simultaneously animating and defusing Anglophone imperial anxieties about racial amalgamation while figuring South Asian men as less desirable than white men. Braiding together yellowface and blackface, Carson's brownface burlesque troped on minstrelsy's well-worn mockery of racialized subjects of the Anglophone empire who attempted (and failed) to attain the trappings of whiteness.

Carson's brownface performances demonstrate how theatrical enactments mediated public feelings, transformed popular racial discourses, and animated white supremacist common sense throughout the subcontinent. As with the early caricatures of scriptive and theatrical blackface, Carson did not necessarily develop his performance in imitation of actual Bengalis; nor did he invent the "Bengalee Baboo" out of whole cloth. The figure of the "babu" was already circulating within Bengali literary and performance culture prior to Carson's performances.[64] Over the course of the nineteenth century, the babu transformed from a nouveau riche snob who preferred traditional music into the English-educated, social-climbing colonial functionary exemplified by Carson's "Bengalee Baboo." By contrast to its early nineteenth-century Bengali meaning, its late nineteenth-century English connotation shifted from a "term of respect attached to a name" to an appellative tinged with "a slight savour of disparagement, as characterizing a superficially cultivated, but too often effeminate, Bengali."[65] As Mrinalini Sinha notes, the putative effeminacy of the Bengali babu was a racial marker of the colonial South Asian male subject's difference from the "manly English man." Carson's performance as the "Bengalee Baboo" played an integral role in the circulation and consolidation of the imperial iteration of the babu stereotype. Sinha cites Carson's "Bengalee Baboo" song as symptomatic of the emergent class and gender discourses constitutive of colonial South Asian subjecthood—its "social-climbing or money-grubbing" theme burlesqued "the economic acquisitiveness of the *babus* as shopkeepers, petty traders, clerks, and so on," in order to discipline South Asian men into imperial discourses of colonial masculinity.[66] The broad circulation of Carson's brownface caricature signals that the minstrel stage was a vital corollary to what Homi Bhabha terms the "English book" in forging colonial authority over the Anglophone empire's subjects.[67] Carson's brownface act insistently furnished forth the "Bengalee Baboo" in derogatory contrast to white Anglophone subjects, mocking the so-called mimic man for his failures to attain whiteness, Englishness, or imperial masculinity.[68]

Carson's mockery of the "Bengalee Baboo" as a "mimic man" took up the mode of vertiginous racial enactment endemic to blackface minstrelsy: a white performer abjecting a racialized caricature as incapable of performing white masculinity. Many Bengali performers, writers, and critics engaged with Carson's "Bengalee Baboo," responding to the ubiquity of his racial burlesque. Most famously, Ardhendu Śekhar Mustafi performed a riposte to Carson's brownface act titled *Mustafī sahib kā pakkā tamāśā* [*Mr. Mustafi's Great Skit*] (1873)—a direct parody of Carson's minstrel show "Dave Carson Sahib Ka Pucka Tumasha"—in which Mustafi "paid [Carson] back in his own coin through songs and mimicry."[69] South Asian theater practitioner and critic Girish Chandra Ghosh wrote of Mustafi's "Sahib" caricature, "Just as Dave Carson used to joke that he was a Bengali babu, Ardhendu also appeared at the first performance at National Theatre dressed as a Saheb with a fiddle in hand and sang: 'I am the greatest Saheb in the world, none can be compared with me.'"[70] Ghosh further opined that though Carson was a skilled performer on the Anglophone stage who was "singlehandedly responsible for pleasing the audience," Carson "had a lower level of this talent" than Mustafi.[71] Here, Mustafi and Ghosh demonstrate their awareness of the theater as a site of colonial contestation in which Bengali male subjects could enact muscular, nationalist reclamations of their agency and masculinity by tactically subverting Carson's racist oeuvre.[72]

Despite these retorts that asserted Mustafi's superiority to Carson, the derogatory minstrel figuration of the "Bengalee Baboo" proved enduring.

Many upper-class Bengalis such as Shib Chunder Bose took pleasure in Carson's "humorous performance" of the caricature's "anglicised taste, habits and bearing."[73] Bose cited Carson's minstrel caricature in his critique of the modern Bengali subject who was "composed of very heterogenous elements . . . [,] disdaining almost everything Indian, and affecting a love of European aesthetics."[74] Through such nationalist critiques, the "Bengalee Baboo" stuck as a "burlesque figure" who did not adequately perform proper cultural embodiments of Bengali masculinity.[75] Indeed, Amrita Lal Bose's *Babu: A Society Sketch*, a Bengali-language play that premiered at the Star Theatre in Kolkata in 1894, reanimated Carson's "Bengalee Baboo" in the figure of Shashtī Krishna Vatavyāl, an upper-class, over-anglicized "'philanthropic' Bābu (and a *poseur*)."[76] The anxieties animated by the brownface derogation of the "Baboo" centered on nationalist fears of inauthenticity, emasculation, and cultural shame—all of which aggregated around minstrelsy's repertoires of racial theatricality and mimicry ("poseur"). The early nationalist theater of Bengal responded forcefully to Carson and his brownface act. Nevertheless, in the wake of Carson's three decades of minstrel performance, his "Bengalee Baboo" continued to animate protonationalist anxieties and to solidify essentialist gender identities.

Beyond such ambivalent accounts of subaltern opposition, transoceanic blackface regularly enfolded colonized peoples into its performance economies. For example, James Arthur, who performed in one of Carson's minstrel troupes, remarked of a Kolkata audience that "the dusky faces of many attendant native swells [i.e., wealthy Bengalis] were in striking contrast to the fairer faces of their European brethren."[77] While Arthur's account demonstrates that interracial audiences were commonplace at South Asian minstrel shows, it is important to note the classed exclusivity of these performances that ensured that only "native swells" and not the colonized masses were included in the economies of minstrelsy. It is therefore of little surprise that Bengali discourses on Carson's brownface figure of the "Bengalee Baboo" were centered on upper-class Bengali debates about bourgeois nationalism and respectability. The missionary-educated Shib Chunder Bose identified the "Bengalee Baboo" as a satire of insufficiently civilized and otherwise unrefined Bengali subjects. By contrast, bourgeois Bengali nationalist theater makers such as Ardhendu Śekhar Mustafi staged responses that disidentified with Carson's minstrel figure in order to lay the groundwork for a Bengali national theater. These several discursive and theatrical responses figured the minstrel caricature of the "Bengalee Baboo" as a prism through which to refract a respectable, classed Bengali subjectivity and a redemptive Bengali nationalism. In invoking José Esteban Muñoz's theory of "disidentification," I want to emphasize his attention to the classed exclusivity of the politics of performance that emerged in the wake of minstrelsy, for Muñoz is clear that the "strategies and practices that constitute disidentification are, for the most part, more readily available to subjects whose class privilege gives them access to systems of representation."[78] In attending to the classed positionalities of South Asian audiences and critics of transoceanic blackface, it becomes more apparent that only select South Asian subjects—mostly men and mostly those from higher class positions—publicly protested, critiqued, resisted, or disidentified with Carson's racial denigration of South Asians.

By contrast to these classed acts of disidentification, most colonized subjects and subalterns who engaged with racialized performances left minimal evidence as to how they experienced the racial repertoires of transoceanic blackface. The majority of surviving accounts that attest to subaltern audiences' enjoyment of minstrel performances were authored by white Anglophone writers such as the white correspondent for the *Times of India* who praised Carson's "wonderful power in the delineation of native Indian character, which amused the natives themselves, and never offended them."[79] This example highlights how the distortions and omissions that characterize colonial archives more broadly also bear on the archives of transoceanic minstrelsy. Such omissions and misrepresentations should therefore not be ignored, nor should colonial accounts be taken at face value. Instead, interpretations of such imperial reportage of interracial harmony at blackface minstrel shows might better begin by reading them critically for their gaps and aporias. Through this critical approach, the correspondent's anxious assertion that Carson's minstrelsy "never offended" South Asian subjects manifests the evident need to make such an imperious claim in order to represent the feelings of those who lacked the capacity to represent themselves.

Shifting away from acts of resistance and outright opposition brings other possible responses into focus, particularly the ways in which transoceanic blackface afforded Black, brown, Asian, and Indigenous subjects and subalterns opportunities for multidirectional identification. In particular, the capacious racial repertoires of transoceanic blackface not only prompted non-white audiences to engage in acts of self-identification but also facilitated their identification of other colonized subjects and subalterns as the object of minstrel denigration. For instance, Joseph Charles Parkinson celebrated Carson's popularity in South Asia by claiming that he made "the Parsee laugh at his caricature of the Hindoo, while the Hindoo is convulsed at his clever skits on the Parsee."[80] Far from being a transparent account of subaltern enjoyment, however, Parkinson's account traces the ways in which Carson's brownface minstrel show animated regional, protonationalistic antagonisms, as when he ventriloquized racial insults targeting Parsis through his performances of the "Baboolah accent" of the "Bengalee Baboo."[81] It is plausible that Bengali audiences enjoyed Carson's figurations of Parsi caricatures or the ubiquitous staging of Black abjection, that Parsi audiences found pleasure in his mockeries of the "Bengalee

Baboo," and that the colonized subjects and subalterns of the Anglophone empire navigated minstrelsy's racial repertoire through similar acts of identification and counteridentification. Indeed, the Parsi theater modeled the ease with which South Asians took up the repertoires of minstrelsy in the frequent incorporation of blackface into its performance economies. For instance, the Parsi Stage Players incorporated "'Ethiopian' songs, and 'Ethiopian' farces in English" into their performance repertoire as early as 1865, and an 1870 Parsi concert opened with a burlesque "Ethiopian ballet."[82] Similarly, in 1875, Parsi theater maker Kuvarjī Nājar staged a series of collaborations with Carson's minstrel troupe in Kolkata that featured a blackface "Ethiopian Delineation" and a yellowface "Characteristic Chinese Representation" of "The Celebrated 'Heathen Chinee.'"[83] Such triangulations of minstrelsy's racial masquerade conscripted the racialized subjects and subalterns of the Anglophone empire into an affective economy of comedic divide and rule.

Among the contested, classed, interracial, and predominantly male audiences of South Asian theaters, colonial gender anxieties were central to minstrelsy's mediation of imperial racial anxieties. It is therefore unsurprising that Carson also fashioned several brownface drag roles that mocked South Asian women. For instance, his song "The Belles of Calcutta" articulated a "scathing satire" of Bengali women.[84] His "Burlesque Hindoostanee Nautch" (also performed as "Zuleika, the Pearl of the Punjaub," "Zuleika, the Pearl of Dum Dum," and "Zuleika, the Pearl of Chinchpoogly") parodied female South Asian nautch dancers.[85] As with Carson's satire of Bengali women, Carson's "Zuleika" explicitly mocked South Asian performance as "perfectly ear-splitting."[86] Nevertheless, white Anglophone audiences readily interpreted this burlesque nautch as an accurate representation, with a review in the *Pioneer* proclaiming the satire "was exactly like the real thing."[87] Carson also fashioned a "Comic Anglo-Indian Interlude" titled "Coochperwani Mari Jhan, or She Lived with her Mother in Bow Bazaar."[88] First performed in Kolkata in January 1868, this "new English Hindustani Song" quickly became a staple of Carson's brownface repertoire.[89] A surviving verse suggests that this female brownface act was likely a burlesque romance ballad in which the character of the "Babu Ramjam Thunda Ghose, B. A. (failed)" (i.e., the "Bengalee Baboo") addressed "Mari Jhan," which means "my darling" in Hindi:

> Here today and gone tomorrow
> In this vale of tear and sorrow;
> Never lend but always borrow,
> Kuchpurwani Mari Jan![90]

In a similar vein, the most famous and enduring of Carson's brownface drag acts was his "Ratae Madam," in which he travestied the courtship of the Parsi "girl of the period."[91] Such brownface drag acts extended the performance genealogy of blackface minstrelsy and its repertoires of gendered burlesque.

Minstrelsy's Wenches and Aunties

Racialized drag and gendered burlesque were core elements of transoceanic blackface since its inception. From "Cloe" in *High Life below Stairs* (1759) through "African Sal" in *Tom and Jerry; or, Life in London* (1821), and across the circulations of Edward Williams Clay's scriptive blackface imagery, Black female figures were frequent targets for racialized derision and desire in the earliest waves of blackface performance culture. Early blackface minstrelsy prominently featured the blackface "wench" role, as evident in the highly popular song "Coal Black Rose" (1829) made famous by George Washington Dixon and its several theatrical adaptations by T. D. Rice.[92] The dramaturgy of "Coal Black Rose" inaugurated a central element of the minstrel repertoire—what blackface hagiographers Dailey Paskman and Sigmund Spaeth term the "dark triangle," a burlesque love triangle among a Black female figure and two Black male rivals for her affection.[93] Prior to the formation of the ensemble minstrel show, Black romance served as a frequent scenario of blackface burlesque.

Whereas "Coal Black Rose" spoke and sang, blackface minstrelsy quickly transformed the blackface female role into the silent spectacle of the blackface drag "wench." Eric Lott summarizes the staging of the "wench" figure, in which a male performer was costumed as a Black female caricature and "exhibit[ed] himself in time with the [song's] grotesque descriptions."[94] A prime example of the early blackface "wench" was "Lucy Long" (1842), a song popular enough throughout the Anglophone empire to be sung in the streets of Cape Town within four years of its publication.[95] Sung by a white male minstrel in blackface while the blackface "wench" performed silently alongside, the lyrics of "Lucy Long" describe the blackface female character to the audience:

> Miss Lucy, she is handsome,
> And Miss Lucy, she is tall;
> To see her dance Cachucha,
> Is death to Niggers all.[96]

"Lucy Long" was an obvious burlesque of the desirability of Black women. The role of "Miss Lucy" was performed in drag, and the singer's descriptions of her as "handsome" and "tall" were potential laugh lines that drew physical humor from the perceived disjuncture between the male minstrel's body and Lucy's blackface drag costume.[97] This kind of physical humor was a common feature of blackface drag in minstrel shows, as one reminiscence on E. P. Christy recalled the typical "Southern darky scene in which muscular mammies in red bandanas . . . never failed to figure."[98] Other blackface "wench" songs such as the "Belle of Broadway" played upon inversions of love ballads: proclaiming "Lubly Rosa" to be a woman who "dresses neat when in de street, And wears an alligator," the singer of "Belle of Broadway" mocked Black female aspirations to fashionability as indelibly linked to animality and the grotesque.[99] As with the broader repertoires of transoceanic blackface, the blackface "wench" trafficked in denigration, abjecting Black female figures as undesirable and absurd.

Another line of minstrel burlesque drag coalesced through the broad minstrelization of *Uncle Tom's Cabin* into "Tom Shows" and their spectacular abjection of the novel's female characters.[100] In this vein, Charles Backus performed in Melbourne as "Aunt Chloe" in an "Operatic Burletta, in two acts, entitled Uncle Tom's Cabin."[101] Through such "Tom Shows," the blackface "wench" role returned to a speaking and acting part in the minstrel show's burlesque.[102] Backus's "Aunt Chloe" transformed Stowe's figuration of Uncle Tom's faithful wife—already bound up with the romantic racialism of the minstrel repertoire—into an ambivalently sentimental and comic minstrel "Old Auntie" figure who was interchangeable with the plantation "Mammy."[103] Joining the ranks of minstrel "wench" figures who were sentimentally mourned after they were "kidnapped or sold or died," such as "Poor Aunt Dinah" and "Old Aunty Neal," Backus's "Aunt Chloe" staged a complex enactment of blackface drag in which Black female characters functioned as comic targets of racial humor while also eliciting sympathy as faithful servants of the patriarchal plantation household.[104] Such blackface embodiments of maternal Black figures signal the enduring appeal of the plantation fantasy—particularly as they refigured Stowe's reformist antislavery narrative into a burlesque, comic restoration of the Anglophone imperial racial order. In brief, "Aunt Chloe" functioned as a figure of minstrel enjoyment insofar as she acted out scripts of Black contentment and docility for white Anglophone audiences.

Blackface minstrel shows incorporated these derogatory figurations of Black women throughout their economy of burlesque, particularly in their showstopping operatic burlesque finales. Operatic burlesques took a similar form to the Shakespearean burlesques that parodied refined performance through minstrel dramaturgies of denigration. For instance, Francis Leon ("The Only Leon"), a minstrel performer specializing in drag roles, printed a carte de visite in costume as a blackface opera ballet corps member (see fig. 20).[105] Adorned in tights and a knee-length skirt rather than a floor-length hoopskirt, Leon embodied a Black ballerina in an act that exemplified the ambivalence of minstrelsy's racial drag. Staged within a broad burlesque of ballet that hinged on the perceived incongruity between "refined" European dance and blackface performance, Leon's

Fig. 20. Carte de visite of "Leon the Great" in blackface opera burlesque costume (undated). Courtesy of the Harry Ransom Center, University of Texas at Austin.

ballerina nevertheless offered a minstrel leg show—a titillating spectacle of racialized femininity.[106]

Minstrelsy's operatic burlesques not only staged ambivalently erotic spectacles of blackface drag but also mocked opera broadly and female opera singers in particular. For instance, Washington Norton regularly performed a mockery of Adelina Patti in his minstrel impersonation of a prima donna, Mademoiselle Oyster Pattie.[107] Norton's opera burlesque drag was a hit with audiences throughout the Anglophone empire. While performing with Nish's Christy's Minstrels in Australia in 1863, Norton performed his standard operatic burlesque, with a Melbourne reviewer praising his "imitation of the vocal powers of a prima donna," while another from the same year in Sydney praised "his high falsetto," which he used to enact "a capital immitation [*sic*] of Lucy Escott," a US American opera singer who performed across Australia concurrent with the Christy's Minstrels' global tour.[108] Reviewers declared Norton's "imitations of a prima donna [to be] something remarkable, and so successful is he in his efforts in some of the operatic airs, that it almost ceases to be burlesque, at least upon some of the singers who have appeared upon the same stage."[109] Such burlesque drag proved effective in abjecting white women who performed beyond the minstrel stage, placing prominent female performers in unflattering comparison to the minstrel "wench." To wit, during a subsequent Christy's Minstrels troupe's tour of southern Africa in 1869, the *Cape Argus* wrote that Norton's "prima donna was inimitable. The affected negro lady was personated so admirably—so naturally to the life, that had it not been announced that Mr. Norton would sustain this character, the audience would have believed that a veritable negress was before them."[110] This Cape Town reviewer suggests that the minstrel prima donna was sometimes—if not often—understood as a blackface burlesque of "veritable negress[es]" on the operatic stage, and therefore as a mockery of early Black female operatic singers such as Elizabeth Taylor Greenfield.[111] As with the racial repertoires of minstrelsy's Shakespearean burlesque, Norton's operatic burlesque drag collapsed any distinction between "refined" opera singers and the blackface "wench," denigrating both within minstrelsy's performance economies of racialized inversion.

Though blackface burlesques predominantly staged drag roles as mockeries of Black femininity, the minstrel stage also furnished forth parodies of white women and, especially, white female social reformers. When not performed in blackface, minstrelsy's "wench" acts abjected white women by conscripting white female figures into minstrelsy's economies of enjoyment. The proslavery significances of blackface drag radiated beyond caricatures of happy Black captives to dramatize a race/sex/gender system in which any threat to the stability of the white domestic idyll of the patriarchal plantation was subjected to burlesque scorn.[112] Minstrelsy's misogynistic imbrications with reactionary politics were perhaps most clearly manifest in its antagonisms with social reform movements such as abolitionism. Following the publication of *Uncle Tom's Cabin*, the book's author was a common target of blackface burlesque, as in the minstrel song "Aunt Harriet Becha Stowe," which admonished Stowe for traveling to Britain to advocate for the antislavery cause while "forget[ting] de WHITE SLAVES ober dere."[113] Troping on proslavery discourses that figured white "wage slavery" as worse than chattel slavery, the song ended by chastising "Aunt" Stowe for neglecting her downtrodden white brethren for the benefit of "happy niggers."[114] As evident in this concluding moral, "Aunt Harriet Becha Stowe" shares a significant amount of material with the Christy's Minstrels' song "Pompey's Trip to New York," which narrated the abandonment of a fugitive slave, Pompey, by the abolitionist "Aunty Sarah Rowe" and Pompey's consequent desire to return to the southern plantation among the "happy darkies."[115] While targeting white female abolitionists, minstrelsy's anti-antislavery "Aunt" figures also implicitly enfolded Black female abolitionists such as Mary Webb into the blackface intertheatrical repertoire.[116] Such minstrel critiques of antislavery reform affixed a derogatory figuration of "Aunt" to female activists, channeling white working-class resentments toward female reformers while also blaming them for disrupting the racial fantasy of the harmonious plantation.

Women's rights activists were also a frequent target for minstrel scorn, with minstrels refashioning the antiabolitionist "Aunt" figure into an antifeminist effigy. By midcentury, social reform movements for women's rights coalesced in the United States and Britain, with minstrels responding by performing parodies of feminist "stump speeches," often without racializing makeup.[117] This line of misogynistic satire circulated widely throughout the transoceanic minstrel network, and by 1855, W. A. Porter of the Backus Minstrels incorporated a "Women's Rights, Lecture" into the company's repertoire on their Australian tour.[118] When Dave Carson performed with Porter in Sydney with the New Orleans Serenaders, Carson took over this specialty act, renaming it "The Rights and Wrongs of Woman" or, later, "Aunty Smith's Lecture on Women's Rights."[119] Carson featured variations on this "Burlesque on the Rights of Women," often in the form of "Aunty Smith, in Defence of the Ladies" or "Aunty Smith in Defence of the Fair Sex," which he performed regularly throughout his decades-long career in South Asia.[120] In "Aunt Harriet Becha Stowe" and Carson's "Aunty Smith," the white female reformist "Aunt" caricature appeared as a threat to the sentimental image of the bourgeois ideal of domestic femininity. The feminist "Aunt" caricature was a woman who, in the lyrics of one minstrel song that burlesqued women's rights, threatened to break her marital vows by "mak[ing] [her] home [t]o ev'ry lover free," to invest in her public appearance at the expense of her domestic role by "dress[ing] as gay [a]s she can well afford," and to invert patriarchal gender hierarchies by "rul[ing] the head and treat[ing] him as her slave."[121] Though authorship of the minstrel song is attributed to a woman named Kate Horn, it nevertheless models how minstrelsy's antifeminism troped on discourses of "wage slavery" and "white slavery," imagining any threat to white male supremacy as akin to white enslavement.[122]

Horn's authorship also signals how minstrelsy enfolded white women into its performance economies by staging nonnormative female caricatures as objects of denigration. Indeed, the burlesques of white female reformers and Black women in general were intimately proximate to one another on the minstrel stage. Moreover, they often intertwined, as in Harry Seymour's temperance drama *Aunt Dinah's Pledge* (1850), and Harry Leslie's performance of "Aunty Chloe, in His Celebrated Burlesque Lecture on the Rights of Women" during his 1865 tour of South Africa.[123] Both of these acts troped on the minstrelized maternal "Aunty" figure and the antifeminist minstrel "Aunt." The convergence of the blackface "wench" role ("Aunt Dinah," "Aunty Chloe") with both reformist drama and antireformist parody demonstrates that the "Aunt" or "Aunty" was a slippery signifier that was nevertheless bound to minstrel dramaturgies of denigration. It consistently framed a certain kind of female figure imagined as the constitutive outside of the race/sex/gender system of white bourgeois domestic reproduction. If "Aunt Chloe" exemplified the minstrel ideal of a racialized and desexualized "Aunt" devoted to serving the white bourgeois family, then white women engaged in the antislavery and women's rights movements represented inattentive, unmaternal "Aunts" whose public activism threatened to upend the racial-sexual order of the Anglophone empire.

The Girls of the Period

As evident in minstrelsy's proliferating stagings of drag, the mid-nineteenth-century Anglophone empire was deeply anxious about the stability of its imperial apparatuses of race and gender. Beyond the minstrel stage, this anxiety coalesced around the popular discourse surrounding the "girl of the period," who, like the female social reformer, was figured as a threat to the imagined "traditional" race/sex/gender system of the past. In March 1868, Eliza Lynn Linton—the first woman to be a salaried writer for a major British daily newspaper—anonymously published a jeremiad on modern women titled "The Girl of the Period."[124] In her essay, Linton excoriated the titular modern English girl for a multitude of sins: "The Girl of the Period" emasculated English men; she besmirched her "innate purity and dignity" with her "vanity and ostentation"; and, in ceasing to behave like the "fair young English girl" of the past, she betrayed her nation and her "race" by becoming "far too fast . . . to be stopped by these slow old morals."[125] Performance looms large in Linton's figuration. She painted the "Girl of the Period" as a fallen woman who aped the styles of the demimonde and who by her "imitation" prostituted herself for the fripperies of fashion. In markedly antitheatrical language, Linton defined the "girl of the period" as "only a poor copy of the real thing"—a "continual weak imitation" of the demimondaine.[126] In this figuration, the modern girl appears as a theatricalized travesty of Platonic womanhood—a bad copy of the bad fashions of bad women. At the same time, Linton decried that the wayward girl's "imitation[s]" despoiled her reputation and her social and sexual worth in the eyes of her audience of English male suitors. By contrast, Linton begged young women to conform to an explicitly national embodiment of womanhood: "The old English ideal, at once the most beautiful, the most modest, the most essentially womanly in the world."[127] Pitched between appropriate behaviors and sartorial customs in courtship rituals, discourses of national and racial purity, and the embodiment of constitutive acts of gender, Linton's vision of the "essentially womanly" woman perversely anticipated social constructionist theories of gender, tacitly advancing an understanding of white womanhood as a performative enactment.

Linton's "Girl of the Period" furnished critics of white womanhood with an enduring yet malleable transnational construct that Gayle Rubin might term a "demonology"—one that invented the racial innocence of the prelapsarian national "girl" through the construction of a demonic, fallen "girl of the period."[128] Linton articulated the demonic threat to English feminine innocence in explicitly racialized terms, describing the hairstyling of the "girl of the period" as akin to that of "a negress or a maniac."[129] Elsewhere, Linton bemoaned that the modern girl adorned herself in "pinchbeck" fashion—that is, she decorated herself in seeming value "according to the pattern of a Sandwich islander," but in actuality appeared cheap, tawdry, and "hideous."[130] For Linton, the modern girl debased her role as progenitor of the white English race by adorning her body with modern fashions that, according to Linton, brought the white English girl perilously close to primitiveness and blackness. This paradox, by which the "girl of the period" betrayed her cultural inheritance and became simultaneously "modern" and "primitive," carved out a space for the English "tradition" as a lost past prior to the degradation of colonial modernity. This paradox cohered as imperial common sense through a reactionary, isolationist impulse to confine the "girl" within the boundaries of the English domestic scene. In sum, Linton sought to restore the English girl to her rightful place in the race/sex/gender system by embracing gendered propriety and racial and sexual purity.

Linton's impressions of the "girl of the period" traveled widely. Across many refigurations in print and performance, numerous national and racial "girls of the period" were imagined along the binarized axes of prelapsarian racial innocence and modern falls from feminine grace.[131] Attesting to the quick circulation of the "Girl of the Period" throughout the Anglophone empire, Dave Carson further signaled the imbrication of the "girl of the period" with imperial racial and gender anxieties when he premiered his antifeminist drag act "The Girl of the Period (after the *Saturday Review*)" in Kolkata, less than seven months after Linton published her essay.[132] Given that minstrelsy's antifeminist burlesques ridiculed modern women's fashions symbolized by "bloomers" (a sartorial object whose name evoked women's rights activist Amelia Jenks Bloomer), it is plausible that Carson and other minstrels might have played on the perception of such modern fashion as inherently unfeminine by staging the "girl of the period" as yet another minstrel "wench" and by drawing the audience's attention to the male performer beneath the drag.[133] Regardless of the specific performance tactics, Carson's embodiment of the "girl of the period" signals the consonance between minstrelsy's antifeminism and Linton's reactionary figuration of the abject modern woman. In each case, the "girl of the period" appeared as an object of scorn who also served as a cautionary image warning of modernity's threats to racial purity and feminine respectability.

Carson and other male blackface minstrels were not the only performers of "girl of the period" caricatures. As early as September 1871, US American actress Nellie Hosmer performed as the "Girl of the Period" in Kolkata while touring with the Eureka Variety Troupe.[134] Hosmer was one of several white female performers on the transoceanic stage who also took up the role in complex stagings of white femininity in early variety shows. One of the most successful of these actors was Grace Egerton, an Englishwoman whose performance career charted itineraries throughout the British Empire. Specializing in comic caricatures, Egerton featured in quick-change acts modeled on Charles Mathews's monopolylogues, which Jane R. Goodall terms "protean farce."[135] Her virtuosic embodiments of multiple characters on a single bill regularly drew critical praise and robust attendance. At the Egyptian Hall in London, she frequently staged her solo spectacles of gendered and racialized play, enacting male and female roles as well as blackface caricatures—such as a "Young Lady of colour" named "Miss Susyanna Angelina Boss" who sang "two nigger melodies": a plantation "carry-me-back" and a blackface burlesque love ballad titled "Nigger Life."[136]

Though Egerton was a successful performer who traveled widely, she and other early female variety performers necessarily navigated imperial anxieties about the respectability of women onstage. As Tracy C. Davis has demonstrated, Victorian actresses were familiars of working women (i.e., sex workers): they were "autonomous professionals" and were closely associated with Linton's demonic demimondaine.[137] As "working women," Victorian actresses negotiated the gaps and tensions between the persona of the public, sexually available pornographic object and the figure of the socially and sexually respectable white woman—that is, as both the "girl of the period" and the "fair, young English girl." Though Egerton was a solo performer and a headliner, her acts were always structured as joint affairs between Egerton and her husband, Mr. George Case. Onstage and in their cartes de visite, Egerton appeared alongside George Case, or, at the very least, alongside his name, as Egerton's billing often attributed her two names: "Grace Egerton (Mrs. George Case)."[138] Touring through Australia, Aotearoa New Zealand, Britain, South Asia, South Africa, and the United States, Egerton took center stage while her husband played second fiddle—or rather, the concertina—in support of her performances. Given that the ideal British imperial woman was "her husband's silent partner," Egerton's performances inverted imperial gender norms while maintaining her familial, Victorian respectability.[139] Mr. George Case (and his legitimating name) was a central prop for Egerton's imperial, transoceanic tours. Egerton savvily negotiated her identities as a working woman and a married woman to carve out space in the competitive performance economies of the Anglophone empire.

Beyond the paratheatrical performance of marital domesticity that undergirded her theatrical persona, Egerton also engaged directly with contemporary discourses on womanhood at home and abroad. For instance, while on tour in Chicago in 1870, Egerton herself performed a song titled "The Girl of the Period" written by local resident Mrs. J. G. Burnett on Linton's model.[140] Egerton also famously imitated Sairey Gamp, the drunken nurse from Charles Dickens's *Martin Chuzzlewit*, evincing her consistent comedic interest in satirizing disreputable women. In each case, Egerton's performances signal a strategy of securing her own respectability by demonizing socially abject modern women who appeared as dissolute or frivolous. In her performances in South Asia, this strategy extended to racialized embodiments of colonized women, most centrally in Egerton's popular impersonation of the "Parsee Girl of the Period."

In Mumbai in 1873, Egerton premiered "The Parsee Girl of the Period," in which she sang a satirical song written specially for her by Parsi theater impresario Kuvarjī Nājar.[141] The *Times of India* reported that "[t]he words and the song—'Ratae Madame is my name'—written by Mr. Cooverjee Sorabjee Nazir, were full of local allusions which took the fancy of the audience immensely."[142] Despite its local allusions, the first stanza of the song exhibits pronounced similarities between the English and Parsi girls of the period:

> I've seen a deal of gaiety, and lead a jolly life,
> My name is Ratai Madame, the Parsee Doctor's wife,
> The thing I most excel in, is dressing neat and tight,
> In silken suits and patent boots, the brightest of the bright.[143]

Drawing from scripts of female impersonation common to the Parsi theater, Nājar's lyrics satirized the Parsi girl of the period while furnishing forth "new norms of Indian womanhood."[144] Mocking Ratae Madame for dressing in contemporary European fashions, Nājar's song admonished Parsi women who wore flashy, form-fitting European clothing and modern, ostensibly unfeminine attire. Performed by Egerton, the song staged a vertiginous spectacle of race and gender typical of minstrelsy. In other words, Egerton's performances of the "Parsee Girl of the Period" enacted what Jayna Brown terms "female minstrelsy," with a white woman performer enacting the role of a brown woman mimicking white women's style.[145]

Upon debuting the song in Mumbai, Egerton announced that "she would take the Bombay Girl of the Period with her wherever she went, and make her known all over the world."[146] Egerton kept her promise by prominently advertising the "Parsee Girl of the Period" in her 1874 tour of the subcontinent.[147] Farther afield on her transoceanic tours, audiences in Auckland, Aotearoa New Zealand, enthusiastically applauded "'The Parsee Girl of the Period,' which character was dressed in costume."[148] In Egerton's performances of this role, she emphasized the character's sartorial fashion. Her advertisements for performances in southern Africa's diamond fields and the Natal Colony promoted the "splendid Eastern costume" of "Ratae Madame," asserting its authenticity as it was "presented to [Egerton] by Parsee Ladies during her sojourn in Bombay."[149] Appearing in an "Eastern Costume" while singing about being dressed in silken slacks and patent boots, Egerton furnished forth an Orientalized exotic-erotic spectacle for predominantly white male audiences. Egerton's brownface caricature was popular throughout the Anglophone empire. She reperformed it throughout South Asia as well as in South Africa and the antipodes. Moreover, several other white women such as Madge Antoinette and Victoria Loftus later performed as "the Parsee Girl of the Period" at Nājar's Gaiety Theatre.[150] "Ratae Madame" later became a fixture of Carson's brownface minstrelsy, with Sir D. E. Wacha recalling that Carson "donned the garb of the Parsi masher [seducer] of the period and made love to 'Rati Madam.'"[151] Across its many reappearances, the "Parsee Girl of the Period" consolidated a reactionary figuration of essentialized femininity that extended minstrelsy's antifeminist attacks against reformist, "modern" white women to denigrate "modern" South Asian women.

The "Parsee Girl of the Period" animated a racial script endemic to late nineteenth-century South Asia, in which bourgeois male figures such as Nājar imagined South Asian women as guardians of national traditions, suggesting that South Asian women were morally and spiritually superior to white British memsahibs.[152] Nājar's conflation of the promiscuous, modern, bad South Asian woman with the English demimondaine tacitly imagined the "good" nationalist South Asian woman as a domestic figure of "tradition." In other words, the "Parsee Girl of the Period" fashioned the modern Parsi woman as a female counterpart to Carson's "Bengalee Baboo" and his Parsi figure "Davejee Carsonbhoy." The "Parsee Girl of the Period" appeared as a mimic woman who betrayed her racial and national heritage in her aspirational yet failed performance of anglicization. The surface-level comedy of the racial caricature abjected colonized women as failed imitators of white women. Thus, Egerton and her imperial audiences could take comfort in the reassurance that the "Parsee Girl" could not quite attain English whiteness. Audiences could also find more humor in the minstrelized juxtaposition of a colonized woman in modern fashions. Here, Egerton's brownface performance inscribed the racial binaries of imperialism in a familiar double bind: like her English counterpart, any Parsi woman who aspired to modernity could be seen as an impure traitor to her own "national" traditions. Moreover, and by contrast to English women, Parsi "girls of the period" also appear as almost-but-not-quite-white demimondaines. Parsi "girls of the period" were demonized both for their failure to adhere to national tradition and for their inability to attain whiteness. The "Parsee Girl of the Period" conflated the critique of modern South Asian womanhood with that of racy, young, Victorian white women, thereby incorporating South Asian women into the Victorian discourse on the "woman question" about gender roles and appropriate public display. Ironically, Nājar's song placed South Asian women's bodies under public surveillance and scrutiny by staging the "Parsee Girl of the Period" through the performing body of white women and, eventually, white male blackface minstrels. Here, Egerton and Nājar acted as coconspirators in a project that Gayatri Spivak might call white women and brown men saving brown women from themselves.[153]

Throughout the circulation of the "Parsee Girl of the Period" onstage and in print, Parsi women had limited opportunities to challenge or subvert the discourse of the "modern" Parsi woman in public. Instead, the "Parsee Girl" mediated white female performers' agency and South Asian, male-authored gender discourses, furnishing forth what Kathryn Hansen identifies as "the new gendered code of conduct for women" by disciplining "the external markers of femininity—the armor of correct sari style, hairdo, and jewelry, together with appropriate gestures."[154] Yet, Parsi audiences could interpret Egerton's performance against the grain, subverting the act's racial abjection and recontextualizing its demonic discourses of gendered propriety. For instance, in his surrogation of the "Parsee Girl of the Period" for the English "Girl of the Period," Nājar embedded a hidden transcript that inverted the racial economy of Linton's essay. In Nājar's protonationalist middle-class gender discourse, Parsi culture was abased and degraded when Parsi women adopted *English* sartorial culture and behaviors. Nājar invented a pristine, pure Parsi national "tradition" prior to British colonialism and ensuing processes of imperial transculturation.[155] Perhaps this tacit nationalistic critique of the influence of British imperialism on Parsi gender performance accounts for the *Times of India*'s observation that "none seemed to enjoy the fun of the piece more than the Parsee ladies who were present, in pretty fair numbers, to see their fast sister reproduced on the stage."[156] The Parsi audience likely viewed Egerton's performance as an example both of the national-cultural inauthenticity of modern Parsi women and of a white woman who appeared on display before desiring audiences.[157] Egerton, intentionally or not, enacted tropes of the excessively liberated English memsahib even as her performance critiqued the libertine "Parsee Girl of the Period." Structurally, this role was scripted for Egerton in advance by bourgeois nationalist proscriptions against South Asian women performers in and beyond the Parsi theater, which permitted white women to act in public while delimiting "respectable" South Asian women to the domestic space of the home.[158] In other words, Egerton's performance acted out a subversive irony of imperial racial and gender discourses insofar as she necessarily staged herself as a white, public, working woman while preserving the absent, idealized Parsi woman from moral danger: it was Egerton—and not a Parsi woman—who appeared as an actress and therefore as a sort of demimondaine.[159]

Amid these entangled scripts of race and gender, Egerton's enactment traced the imbrications of liberal discourses on freedom and equality with colonial practices of racial subjection. Egerton distinguished herself as a globe-trotting white woman performer—always under threat of abjection and disrepute—while also staging scenes of theatrical subjection of other women. If Nājar attempted to restore cultural authority to Parsis, he did so by disciplining the gender performance of Parsi women, evidently with the approbation of middle-class Parsi women in the audience. If Nājar fashioned an opportunity for white women performers, their agency was premised on the abasement of "modern" English and Parsi women alike. Egerton's performances of the role were similarly complex in their entanglements of gendered agency and racialized abjection. Egerton's agency as a performer hinged on her ability to navigate complex codes of bourgeois respectability. At the same time, her performance of the "Parsee Girl" relied on the colonial racial order to secure the exotic-erotic non-white woman as the necessary precondition for white English women's agency. Egerton acted within an imperial performance economy that traded in abject figurations of women while requiring female performers to body forth such effigies. Egerton's drama played out through the performing body of an English woman, who herself displaced actual Parsi women from the field of representation and public discourse. Meanwhile, the colonized women of the period remain offstage, spoken for and silenced, imitated and abjected in discourses that celebrated their purity so long as they were neither seen nor heard.

Attesting to the impact of the "Girl of the Period" on South Asian gender discourses, the London *Morning Star* correspondent in South Asia reported that Linton's essay was "translated into Hindustani, and the people are all saying, why should they educate their women if that is the result of education on Englishwomen?"[160] Hardly an expression of disinterested concern for South Asian women, this rhetorical question indicates how British nationalist print culture shared similar investments in managing the sexual and gendered discourses governing the conduct of women as South Asian nationalists. In 1875, *Punch* published a comic short story about "the daughter of Mr. Manockji Framji" attending the annual Masonic Ball in Karachi, in which "the Parsee Girl of the Period" attracted the attention of white male attendees. Nevertheless, the story concluded by warning the Parsi woman to "be sure that she does not aspire to imitate the 'making-up' devices of her European sisters."[161] *Punch*'s admonishment found a South Asian corollary in 1884, when Nasarvānji Sohrābjī Jīnvālā (N. S. Ginwalla) published an essay in the *Times of India* denouncing the "Parsee Girl of the Period."[162] Though the *Times* introduced Jīnvālā's essay through a comparison with Linton's original essay, it is quite likely that Nājar's song and Egerton's performances were integral in familiarizing Jīnvālā and his readers with the figure. As in Nājar's song, Jīnvālā specifically critiqued the "modern Parsee girl" for "affect[ing] all the airs and manners of a dainty young English lady, whom she in her heart of hearts wishes to equal or imitate."[163] Jīnvālā mocked the "Parsee Girl of the Period" as a mimic woman much as Egerton's performances staged a female counterpart to Carson's mockery of the "Bengalee Baboo" as a mimic man. Jīnvālā's essay prompted numerous responses over the succeeding weeks in which the "Parsee Girl of the Period" became a central topic of debate in the *Times of India*.[164] Several respondents disputed the prevalence of this figure in Mumbai, while others critiqued the accuracy of Jīnvālā's description. Nevertheless, even when Doseebai C. Jussawalla, a Parsi woman, replied with a corrective to Jīnvālā's characterization, she relied on the discursive frame that opposed "traditional" Parsi to "modern" English culture in order to affirm women's adoption of English and European fashions as a sign of "progress."[165] Jussawalla was able to publish a critique of Jīnvālā's essay in the leading paper of Mumbai while remaining effectively barred from performing on the city's stages. Her response remained bound up with Anglophone imperial discourses of race and gender enacted throughout South Asia's colonial theaters—especially the figure of the idealized, nontheatrical yet performatively enacted innocent woman of nationalist "tradition."

Coda: Baby Benson and the Children of the Anglophone Empire

Throughout the Anglophone empire, the trope of prelapsarian female innocence found its most potent distillation in the figure of the white girl child. In September 1875, US American female child performer "Baby Benson" (Marguerite Fish) made her Australian debut at the age of six while touring the Pacific circuit, where she performed as "The Girl of the Period."[166] Performing alongside her mother Jennie Benson as the star actor of the Benson American Troupe, "Baby Benson" surrogated the line of female child stars that preceded her, such as Cordelia Howard, Lotta Crabtree, and other juvenile actors such as the children of the Marsh Troupe.[167] As Robin Bernstein notes, the performance of childhood in the nineteenth century was densely entangled with racial discourses that figured white girls as innocent "tender angels" in contrast to abject figurations of Black girls as grotesque "insensate pickanninies."[168] Howard's career centered on her embodiment of the angelic "Little Eva" from *Uncle Tom's Cabin* as an idealized representation of white childhood innocence in contrast to the minstrelized figuration of "Topsy."[169] By contrast, Crabtree departed from this singular mode of performing white racial innocence by staging spectacular acts of multiple impersonation akin to Egerton's "protean farce."[170] Crabtree's performance career, also like Egerton's, frequently intersected with minstrelsy, as in her many enactments of young male characters and in her performance with Backus's San Francisco Minstrels in Northern California in 1856, when, at the age of nine, she "black[ed] up" to enact her signature blackface "Topsy act."[171]

Benson's early career braided together the racial scripts of Howard's white innocence and Crabtree's "rambunctious" racial and gender play.[172] Benson toured the British colonies in southern Africa in 1877–1878, where she prominently featured her ethnic and racial impersonations, such as her blackface "Negro Comedian"—sometimes billed as an imitation of blackface minstrel Hughey Dougherty, who toured South Africa from 1872 through 1874—and her "lightning change from a Black Face to a White Face."[173] Such enactments staged the uncanny juxtaposition of white girlhood and blackface caricature, through which Benson performed her racial innocence by demonstrating that blackface could "slide by without sticking" to her or otherwise tarnishing her purity.[174] In other words, such anxious performances remained safely within the conventions of blackface burlesque, which framed these juxtapositions as momentary transgressions of a stable imperial racial order. Onstage and off, Benson played on sentimental figurations of childhood innocence, repeatedly staging pathetic ballads such as "Please Give Me a Penny" and acting in roles such as the "Shoeless Orphan Girl" through which she raised charitable donations in support of local orphanages.[175] Her charitable donations notwithstanding, performing white girlhood was good business, and Benson's company earned £12,000 on its 1877–1878 tour of South Africa.[176] As demonstrated in her profitably sentimental staging of charity, Benson was well versed in the scripts of bourgeois respectability, and she calibrated her performances of racial innocence to elicit and defuse anxieties about the Anglophone empire's white girls.

Benson's performances gave theatrical form to broader racial discourses about imperial childhood. As Ann Laura Stoler observes, "Children had to be taught both their place and their race, and the family was the crucial site in which future subjects were to be made and loyal citizenship was to be learned."[177] Benson's global tours with her family's troupe functioned as object lessons in white girlhood in which Benson staged pedagogical performances of racial innocence. Simultaneously, Benson invested herself in the repertoires of Anglophone imperial performance, learning how to mobilize imperial racial discourses throughout her career. After a decade as a star child performer, Benson reimagined herself as a vaudevillian and theatrical performer who shared the stage with her husband, Charles Warren, in transoceanic tours that reproduced the itineraries of Grace Egerton and George Case.[178] Performing under her given name, Marguerite Fish, she maintained a successful career on the variety stage.

Despite her change in stage name, Fish continued to draw on the repertoires of racialized performance, as in her 1902 London performance as a "Japanese Cherry Blossom."[179] Written by Edgar Smith in 1901, "My Japanese Cherry Blossom" adapted the character of Cho-Cho-San from David Belasco's *Madame Butterfly* (1898), scripting her as a yellowface role within the minstrel repertoire:

> I have what you callee "sweetheart,"
> He's Unite' States man,
> Big moustache like this,
> It allee samee nicee, little Cho Cho San;
> Tickle when he kiss.
> The firstee time I meetee him he wink this way,
> And 'fore I know he near,
> He sittee down beside me and I hear him say
> All these nice words in my ear—
>
> CHORUS.
> I love you, my Jap'nese Cherry Blossom,
> Your lips are sweeter than pone or possum,
> Nestle close against your ragtime "Mel"-can man,
> You can't shake me, my Cho Cho San.

Fish's performance as a "Japanese Cherry Blossom" intertwined several threads of Orientalism, minstrel drag, and blackface balladry. Citing Backus's yellowface tropes of "allee samee" and "'Mel'-can [American] man," Fish's performances drew the tragic figure of Cho-Cho-San into the minstrel fold. Moreover, the chorus's voicing of a male figure's desire for the "Jap'nese Cherry Blossom" took the form of blackface speech, praising Cho-Cho-San as "sweeter than pone or possum." Fish's yellowface act thereby reanimated the discursive structures of blackface "wench" routines with Cho-Cho-San voicing a white male fantasy of Asian women's desires within a broader racial burlesque. Staged within an extravagant "special scene represent[ing] a lovely Japanese garden" adorned with "masses of flowers," "prettily arranged lanterns," and a "number of Geishas," Fish's act staged the convergence of the minstrel repertoire and Orientalist fantasy.

Affirming the tight imbrications between these forms of racialized performance, Fish announced that her ensuing performance would be "a realization of 'Down South,'" which her interviewer speculated would entail "the soothing melody of the 'coon' and 'plantation' order, and another pretty and specially painted scene." At the advent of the twentieth century, Fish drew on her racial education in the performance networks of transoceanic blackface to furnish forth novel articulations of old imperial spectacle. Staged in London, Fish's yellowface act traces how apparently "new" metropolitan modes of racialized performance such as fin de siècle Orientalism were forged through transoceanic theatrical traffic. The figural forms of colonial-imperial blackface, yellowface, and brownface returned to imperial metropoles, where they furnished racial pedagogies to entertain and entrain ensuing generations of the Anglophone empire.

Epilogue

✦

Blackface Backwash

Marguerite Fish was not the only performer who brought the racial repertoires of the Anglophone empire home to metropolitan theaters. As the twentieth century began, transoceanic blackface continued to circulate across the multidirectional relays of empire. Despite the fact that there is no evidence of Dave Carson ever performing in England, "The Bengalee Baboo" found its way to the London stage at the 1904 premiere of the musical comedy *The Cingalee*. A South Asian correspondent for Kolkata's *Amrita Bazar Patrika* viewed this production and offered a fulsome critique of the musical's racist caricatures while also noting their remarkable familiarity. The reporter drew a direct link between the London production of *The Cingalee* and Carson's brownface empire in South Asia, asserting that *The Cingalee*'s "caricature of a Bengali Babu at which a thousand people are laughing every night" was a self-evident surrogate of Carson's "derisive song concerning the Bengal Babu."[1] Protesting *The Cingalee* for "the harm to Indian character and reputation which [its South Asian] caricature . . . will do to make difficult the right appreciation of educated Indians by their British fellow-subjects," this reporter critiqued the musical's racist figurations of South Asians and asserted the equality of South Asians and British as "fellow-subjects" of the Anglophone empire. Moreover, this account succinctly analyzed the detrimental effects of racialized performance on colonized subjects while also outlining how Anglophone theater makers exploited minstrelsy's racist figurations for capitalist profit, tracing the interrelationship of the epistemic "harm" of brownface performance and its effectiveness in "making much money for a theatre proprietor." Thus, the reporter's critique of *The Cingalee* underscored the mechanisms by which the racial repertoires forged in the colonies washed back to the imperial metropole, where they furnished London's stages with the extensive catalog that constituted transoceanic blackface.[2]

The reappearance of Carson's signature caricature in London therefore models how the repertoires of transoceanic blackface continued circulating into the twentieth century, wherein they furnished enduring dramaturgies of racialized performance throughout the Anglophone empire. Crucially,

The Cingalee's reanimation of Carson's repertoire in London and Fish's successful return to the London stage following her South African career as "Baby Benson" both signal that the colonial theaters of the Anglophone empire were sources for new performance material rather than merely serving as receiving houses for the dissemination of metropolitan performance culture. In this epilogue, there is not sufficient space—nor, at present, evidence—to trace the extensive performance genealogies of twentieth- and twenty-first-century transoceanic blackface in detail. Nevertheless, the examples of Carson and Fish complicate the current scholarship on the global traffics of blackface following the demise of the minstrel show.

Much more research is necessary to continue mapping the prolific and enduring circulations of transoceanic blackface, particularly as it manifested in sites across the Global South. It is my hope that this book prompts others to seek out and trace such performance genealogies in greater detail. In the remainder of this epilogue, I sketch three vignettes that outline potential areas of future inquiry into the enduring global remains of transoceanic blackface. First, I revise prevailing framings of twentieth-century blackface in television and film as US American exports by outlining the multidirectional, transnational circulation of mediatized blackface in the twentieth and twenty-first centuries. Second, I attend to the national theaters of the Global South as underrecognized sites for the continued transmission of minstrelsy's racial repertoires. Whereas I began this book with a call to deprovincialize minstrelsy studies by mapping circulations of blackface performance beyond the United States, I here call to deprovincialize the historiography of other national theaters by tracing their heretofore unmarked investments in transoceanic blackface. To this end, I focus on early South African playwright Stephen Black to trace his frequent recourse to minstrelsy as he forged a new South African national theater. Third, I highlight a significant gap in studies of global blackface minstrelsy. Much extant scholarship on global blackface rightly attends to the "representational agency" of colonized and subaltern performers who engage with the vexed repertoires of transoceanic blackface.[3] Yet, such studies do not adequately consider how blackface minstrelsy functioned as a key vector of imperial racial discourse or how it furnished the very terms of racial subjectivity that later subaltern performers worked to subvert and resist. I therefore consider how transoceanic blackface and its afterlives have shaped transnational discourses of whiteness and blackness under colonial modernity by racializing colonial and imperial subjects across the globe. Here, I follow Jemima Pierre's call for greater attention to "the occurrence of racialization in purportedly unusual or unsuspecting places," particularly in colonial sites beyond the juridical boundaries of nation-states of the Global North.[4] I conclude this epilogue (and this book) with two figures whose racial subjectivities were forged through the racial repertoires of transoceanic blackface. These examples trace how the "forgotten but not gone" racial repertoires of transoceanic blackface not only furnished historical performance cultures with imperial scripts but also continue to animate transnational popular culture and global racial discourses.[5]

The Black and White Minstrel Show Goes Global

Minstrel scholarship focusing on the United States and Britain has established how the decline of the minstrel show in the 1890s led not to the disappearance of blackface from popular culture but rather to its diffusion across multiple media and modes of performance. After the heyday of the minstrel show, performers continually drew on minstrelsy in new forms of popular music, vaudeville, musical comedy, and dance. Beyond the stage, blackface minstrelsy provided an extensive, foundational repertoire for new media such as radio, film, and television. Chinua Thelwell has further demonstrated that the early repertoires of blackface were regularly refurbished, revised, and expanded on across five successive waves of blackface that made minstrelsy global. Thelwell provides a useful framework to parse shifts from the large nineteenth-century ensemble minstrel show to the mediatized blackface of Hollywood films.[6] In particular, this approach offers insight into the ways in which blackface (and) minstrelsy functioned as mass media, with each wave tracing global blackface as it adapted to new modes of transmission such as vaudeville, radio, film, and television. Yet, this approach tacitly posits US blackface minstrelsy as the prehistory of any non-US American or non-Anglophone form of blackface—such as blackface in German film or the Ghanaian Concert Party theater.[7] It therefore remains bound to already-existing histories of blackface minstrelsy that center on US American media and archives, framing other forms of blackface in tacit or explicit comparison with US American "originals."

By contrast, I reiterate that histories of blackface minstrelsy must become more attuned to the multidirectional circulations of blackface. Simply put, the United States has never been the sole source of blackface performance—neither in the eighteenth and nineteenth centuries nor in the twentieth and twenty-first centuries. Though the global cultural hegemony of the United States during the so-called American century solidified its dominant role in disseminating blackface via radio, film, and television, critical attention to such twentieth-century US blackface has obscured other lines of transmission. Notably, the British Broadcasting Corporation (BBC) produced a succession of blackface programs in the mid-twentieth century. First, the BBC radio program *The Kentucky Minstrels* (1933–1950) served as a British alternative to the popular US American blackface radio show *Amos 'n' Andy* (1928–1955).[8] Second, the BBC television program *The Black and White Minstrel Show* (1958–1978) aired weekly in parallel to a celebrated London stage show.[9] These distinctively British forms of blackface were not mere imports of US programming; nor were they derivative imitations. Instead, they reanimated the repertoires of transoceanic blackface still in circulation throughout Britain and its empire.

In turn, the BBC's *Black and White Minstrel Show* played a significant role in disseminating minstrelsy across the British Commonwealth throughout the mid- to late twentieth century. In Australia, *The Black and White Minstrel Show* was rebroadcast by the Australian Broadcasting Corporation until 1982.[10] There, it inspired popular Australian television programs including *Hal Lashwood's Alabama Jubilee* (1958–1960) and *Hal Lashwood's Minstrels* (1960–1961).[11] Additionally, a touring company of the London stage version—also titled *The Black and White Minstrel Show*—performed in Australia and Aotearoa New Zealand in 1962–1964, 1984, and 1987 to popular reception.[12] Inspired by the popularity of the television program and the success of these touring productions, local Australian theater makers also mounted their own minstrel show variations, such as a 1980 production simply titled *Minstrels*.[13] Meanwhile, in apartheid-era South Africa, which did not permit television broadcasting until 1976 and therefore did not air the BBC's programming, *The Black and White Minstrel Show* spurred a wave of South African minstrel shows and a concomitant minstrel craze amid the white supremacist apartheid government's crackdown on anti-apartheid activism in the 1960s and 1970s. In addition to Brian Brooke and John Kavan's *Minstrel Show* (1966) and Adam Leslie's *Merry Minstrel Show* (1966), Joan Brickhill and Louis Burke staged a trilogy of theatrical minstrel spectacles modeled directly on the stage version of the BBC television and stage shows: *Minstrel Scandals* (1966); *All-New, Non-Stop Minstrel Scandals* (1970); and *Minstrel Follies* (1974).[14] These several theatrical productions trace the global dissemination of *The Black and White Minstrel Show*'s twentieth-century brand of British blackface through both televisual broadcasts and a series of globally touring and locally produced stage shows. They exemplify how minstrelsy circulated across multiple media throughout the Anglophone empire.

This reframing opens critical ground to consider more contemporary appearances of blackface in popular culture. For instance, given the Australian theater's long-standing investments in blackface minstrelsy and its more recent investments in televisual blackface, it is worth reconsidering Australian pop star Iggy Azalea and what Matthew D. Morrison terms her "somewhat caricatured 'black'-sounding, southern-influenced rap voice."[15] Since attaining global fame for her 2014 hit "Fancy," Azalea has received criticism for rapping in a "blaccent"—a purportedly "Black" accent that differs starkly from her Australian-accented speaking voice.

Though there is no question that Azalea's sonic blackface takes southern US hip-hop as its model, focusing solely on her appropriation of contemporary Black American music obscures how her performances surrogate more than a century of white Australian blackface minstrelsy. How does Azalea's sonic blackface engage with the performance genealogies of Australian minstrelsy extending back to the early minstrel shows produced by George Coppin, the proverbial father of Australian theater? What other forms of blackface aurality and mediatized minstrelsy might Azalea have drawn on in fashioning her twenty-first-century hip-hop persona? Attending to these lines of transmission does not minimize the significant role of US-based minstrelsy in the globalization of blackface. Rather, tracing other performance genealogies demonstrates that US American minstrelsy is one of numerous forms of blackface that were sustained by transoceanic traffics of performance culture. There remain other histories of blackface globalization remaining to be told.

Transoceanic Blackface and the Birth of National Theaters

Whereas mediatized minstrelsy reproduced and transmitted the racial repertoires of transoceanic blackface in spectacularly global fashion, the scripts and scenarios of minstrelsy were also taken up in more localized theater cultures. In the aftermath of minstrelsy's heyday, theater makers in British colonies and newly established independent nations forged early, national theaters from the repertoires of transoceanic blackface. These theaters continually reanimated and refashioned imperial racial repertoires already in local circulation, further adapting and reimagining them in response to new political conjunctures. Such early nationalistic enactments remained local productions, circulating in smaller orbits within the broader economies of Anglophone imperial traffic. Their seeming provincialism has allowed their entanglements with global performance cultures to remain underrecognized.

Consider South African playwright Stephen Black, whose *Love and the Hyphen* (1908) has been hailed as "the first English play to be written by a born and bred South African."[16] According to South African theater scholar Stephen Gray, the premiere of *Love and the Hyphen* was a "watershed event" wherein "an indigenous theatre was planned, launched and acclaimed in South Africa."[17] In such nationalistic framings, the playwright appears as a local hero who transformed South Africa from a dependent outpost of the British Empire into a site of "indigenous"—that is, white South African—Anglophone cultural production. Indeed, Black's *Love and the Hyphen* was an unparalleled success on the early twentieth-century South African stage, receiving over six hundred performances to full audiences in Cape Town, Johannesburg, and throughout the railway hubs of southern Africa including colonial Rhodesia (modern-day Zimbabwe and Zambia).[18]

In *Love and the Hyphen*, Black adapted the theatrical conventions of late Victorian and Edwardian social comedies to fashion a "satire of pretentious masters and cheeky servants" tailored to the particularities of turn-of-the-century South African social formations.[19] To wit, a South African critic wrote in 1925 that the play comprised "an amusing picture of 'life below stairs.'"[20] While this commentary highlighted *Love and the Hyphen*'s stylistic similarities to contemporaneous London theater, it also noted that Black's dramaturgy was densely entangled with a performance genealogy extending back to the eighteenth-century blackface play *High Life below Stairs*. In keeping with the play's investments in blackface dramaturgies, the two primary "below stairs" characters in *Love and the Hyphen* are Cape Colored servant figures drawn from the minstrel repertoire: Sophie Wijnbek, "the Cape 'slavey'"; and Frikkie Schaapkop, a Cape "boy," or servant.[21] Both roles were performed in blackface, and the role of Sophie was also acted in drag. As a blackface drag role, Sophie furnished forth the "Dutch 'tante'" (Dutch aunt) caricature—indeed, a *Cape Argus* reviewer described Sophie as "a grotesque caricature of the old aunt which a very male Italian played in the style of a wrestler."[22] Such commentary indicates that South African audiences understood Sophie as a more contemporary surrogate of minstrelsy's misogynistic blackface wench roles and situated *Love in the Hyphen* in relation to the performance genealogies of transoceanic blackface.

In addition to reanimating the minstrelsy's "Aunty" caricature, Black also interpolated an old set piece from the blackface repertoire. In a comic routine, Sophie and Frikkie use their mistress's grand piano to perform a choral interpretation of Henry Wadsworth Longfellow's poem "The Village Blacksmith":

> Under der spreading chestnut tree
> Der willage blacksmith stens
> Der smit a mighty men is he
> Wid large en sinervee hens
> And der muscles of his broany arms
> Is like Salvation Army bens.[23]

Sophie and Frikkie's burlesque of Longfellow's poetry was hardly an original invention as it followed the well-worn template of blackface burlesque. More to the point, touring blackface minstrels staged blackface burlesques of "The Village Blacksmith" in South Africa as early as October 6, 1862, in Gqeberha, when Nish's Christy's Minstrels introduced one such parody during their global tour.[24] Though Black may have known of the Christy's popular version from the transoceanic blackface repertoire, Stephen Gray notes that Black likely had a more proximate blackface inspiration for his burlesque "Village Blacksmith." Turn-of-the-century British minstrel G. H. Chirgwin, "The White-Eyed Kaffir," popularized his own burlesque of the poem, which may have served as a model for Black's scenario of unintentional musical comedy.[25] Here, it is important to note that Chirgwin's burlesque was also fashioned from the repertoires of transoceanic blackface, and he may have drawn from the Christy's Minstrels version (or a derivative thereof) for his parody "Village Blacksmith." Regardless of whether Black drew inspiration from Chirgwin or the still-circulating repertoires of transoceanic blackface, his comic characters and their signature burlesque were drawn directly from minstrel material.

Black's indebtedness to transoceanic blackface signals that—far from originating an "indigenous" South African national theater—his theatrical oeuvre hinged on the reanimation of blackface burlesque and minstrelsy's wench caricatures from Andrew Geddes Bain's *Kaatje Kekkelbek* to *Love and the Hyphen*'s Sophie Wijnbek.[26] In other words, *Love and the Hyphen* did not invent this South African burlesque scenario but rather retraced the entanglements among repertoires of blackface minstrelsy and the South African theater's Cape Colored caricatures. Black's variations on local South African blackface in *Love and the Hyphen*—and in his second play, *Helena's Hope Ltd.*—remained firmly entangled with the circuits of transoceanic blackface and minstrelsy's dramaturgical structures of racial abjection.[27] Though they drew from globally circulating repertoires of transoceanic blackface, Black's plays were not produced beyond the stages of southern Africa. Nevertheless, his protonationalist dramas drew from the transoceanic blackface repertoire and remained in local circulation, where they furnished the grounds for a new national performance culture—one that remained invested in blackface throughout the twentieth century.

By attending to the endurance of blackface in colonial and early national theaters, we might better grasp the centrality of racialized performance to colonial and postcolonial performance cultures. Indeed, the endurance of transoceanic blackface may be traced throughout—and beyond—the Anglophone empire. Rashna Darius Nicholson's research on the Parsi theater has demonstrated the prolific entanglements among that early national theatrical form and blackface minstrelsy. As we saw in the introduction to this book and in Kuvarjī Nājar's "Parsee Girl of the Period," the Parsi theater borrowed extensively from the repertoires of transoceanic blackface. These entanglements between the Parsi theater and transoceanic blackface warrant further consideration. Given the Parsi theater's role in inspiring other forms of South and Southeast Asian theater such as Bangsawan, Komedie Stamboel, Konkoni tiatr, and Nurti, more research is necessary to trace whether and how the Parsi theater relayed scripts and repertoires of racialized performance to other national theater forms.[28] Did the Parsi theater stage transoceanic blackface solely for white Anglophone audiences? Might it also have circulated blackface minstrelsy among colonized audiences during its tours of South and Southeast Asia? If the latter, did other theatrical forms take up the repertoires and dramaturgies of blackface, minstrelsy, and racial burlesque? These questions point to only a few of the many potential avenues for future research into the enduring legacies of transoceanic blackface and its repertoires of racialized performance across numerous, ostensibly disparate, national and linguistic performance cultures.

The Racial Educations of Dave and Eliza

Mediatized minstrelsy transmitted spectacular scenes of blackface abjection globally, and national performance cultures furnished forth minstrelsy's racial repertoires into the twentieth century. Simultaneously, transoceanic blackface also endured in unspectacular facets of everyday life. The prolific circulations of transoceanic blackface routinely refurbished, restored, and reified the common sense of race at the level of racialized subjectivity. Throughout the Anglophone empire, imperial subjects invested themselves in whiteness in an ongoing process, evincing that whiteness was not an essence of British and US American subjects that inhered in colonial and imperial bodies throughout their travels. Nor did colonized subjects and subalterns possess any racial essence prior to their subjection within imperial racial orders. Instead, the subjectivities of colonized peoples were forged in relation to the racial discourses of empire and the racial repertoires of transoceanic blackface. Blackface, minstrelsy, and related forms of racialized performance furnished critical sites of subject formation, interpellating white colonial subjects and non-white colonized subjects and subalterns into imperial racial discourses.

To grasp the globality of these processes, let us return one final time to Dave Carson. Carson was born in New York City as David Nunez Cardoza, the son of a Jewish father and a Spanish émigré mother.[29] As the US American son of Spanish and Jewish parents, Carson would not necessarily have been racialized as "white" in the United States. His given name marked him as non-white or as a white ethnic—that is, as a racialized subject with provisional but precarious access to the comforts of whiteness. From his earliest blackface performances in Australia, he performed under the name "Dave Carson" rather than his ethnically marked given name.[30] In adopting a stage name, Carson took up a well-rehearsed practice among Irish and Irish American blackface minstrels who also performed under Anglo-derived stage names to downplay their tenuously non-white ethnic identities: Jerry Bryant was born Jerry O'Brien; Dan Bryant was born Daniel Webster O'Brien; J. W. Raynor was born J. W. Rea; T. J. Peel was born Thomas Jefferson O'Reilly.[31] Like Al Jolson (born Asa Yoelson) or his character from *The Jazz Singer*, Jack Robin (born Jakie Rabinowitz), Carson fashioned himself a white subjectivity through his minstrel performances of blackness as the definitive sign of non-white racial difference.[32]

Yet, Carson's career differed in one significant way from those of his fellow precariously (non)white blackface minstrels. Whereas minstrelsy studies has long posited blackface as a critical site for the formation of whiteness as a national US American racial project, Carson did not begin his career by working toward whiteness on minstrel stages within the nation-based racial formations of the United States.[33] Instead, his performance of minstrelsy's scripts of whiteness unfolded through his studies of the transoceanic blackface repertoire during his decades-long career in Australia and South Asia and throughout the Pacific circuit. Indeed, there is no evidence that Carson identified—or was identified—as white prior to his minstrel performances on the Australian goldfields. In other words, Carson attained whiteness not as a national US American subject but rather as a transnational subject of the Anglophone empire. Through his prolific stage career, Carson's Jewish and Spanish ethnic identifications were overwritten by the itinerant, imperial form of whiteness that he performed under the theatrical mask of "Dave Carson." Beyond the binarized racial logics through which US American blackface minstrels performed their whiteness in contradistinction to Black Americans, Carson enacted his whiteness through his manifold performances of blackface *and* brownface, forging an imperial whiteness in contradistinction to the Black, brown, and Asian subjects of the Anglophone empire. Carson's performances thus trace the tacit racializing work of transoceanic blackface, which allowed touring minstrels to performatively fashion whiteness on the global stage.

Transoceanic blackface forged a transnational formation of whiteness through the reinscription of the colonial color line around the world. It also occasioned the subjection of colonized peoples into the racialized subjectivities of empire. By contrast to Carson's case, in which a decades-long career produced copious archival material, transoceanic blackface's role in the intimate processes of colonial racial subjection remains mostly obscure, muted by archival silences. Nevertheless, a rare account survives that traces a microhistory of how colonized subjects understood themselves in relation to the ubiquitous transoceanic performance cultures of blackface minstrelsy.

On September 10, 1863, the *King William's Town Gazette and Kaffrarian Banner* newspaper published a translation of the journal of an unnamed "Kafir girl" who traveled from St. Matthew's Mission—an Anglican mission in the Eastern Cape Colony—to Cape Town.[34] Drawing from archival sources, historian C. C. Saunders identifies the girl as "Eliza," a student at the St. Matthew's mission school who was likely named in reference to a Black female character from *Uncle Tom's Cabin*.[35] Her published journal relates her experiences witnessing the celebration of the royal wedding of Prince Albert and Princess Alexandra. According to the *South African Advertiser and Mail*, "The most successful of the various novelties of the Fancy Fair" at the wedding celebration were "the performances of the Darkie Minstrels," an amateur troupe who modeled their concert on Nish's company of Christy's Minstrels that featured Joe Brown and Washington Norton.[36] Eliza observed the performance, and her journal entry described the amateur concert as well as several other racialized performances and encounters.

Eliza's journal presents what is the earliest known account of blackface minstrelsy authored by a Black South African spectator:

> We . . . went to see white people smeared with soot, they went into a house made of a tent where there were stools, and two came out and spoke to the people saying, "Ladies and gentlemen, come in and see what we have got here inside." Some went in and others did not, afterwards they opened that the people might see; there were black people sitting on chairs and singing.

The passage traces Eliza's confusion at her first encounter with racialized performance. Immediately prior to entering the minstrels' tent, she observed "white people smeared with soot"; yet, inside the minstrel tent, she recounted seeing "black people sitting on chairs and singing." The discrepancy between soot-faced "white people" outside the tent and "black people" singing onstage offers a compelling testament to the racializing work of blackface performance. Why did Eliza differentiate between the "black people" onstage and the "white people" outside the tent? Was the theatrical performance of blackface sufficient to produce the impression that the amateur minstrels were actually "black people"? What aspects of blackface performance prompted her to slip into language that ascribed blackness to the minstrels?

Eliza's journal does not answer these questions. Instead, it supplements her interpretation of the minstrel tent performance with another blackface enactment. Her second encounter with blackface occurred outside the theatrical space and in the streets of Cape Town amid the "Carnival Procession":

> I have seen today another thing which I did not know of, that thing which is said to be always done by white people in this month of May. They make themselves black people, they smear themselves with something black, with red patches on the cheeks; a thing is made with evergreens, and a man is put inside, and two people carry it, and another man carries a pan, and goes begging for money.

Here, Eliza describes the carnivalesque performance of "Jack-in-the-Green and Attendants," a May Day procession commonly performed by chimney sweeps who blackened their faces with soot.[37] Once again, Eliza's description traces the ambivalences and confusions that blackface performance prompted in spectators unfamiliar with its conventions and racial meanings, as she refers to the participants in the May Day folk ritual as "white people" who "make themselves black people." Across these two blackface performances—a minstrel show and a street parade—Eliza twice encountered white people who "make themselves black people . . . [by] smear[ing] themselves with something black." In neither case does Eliza use language of pretense or representation to describe the alchemical work of blackface. Instead, in each case, she describes the transformation of "white people" into "black people" through blackface performance.

Eliza's two encounters with blackface also functioned as pedagogical moments during which Eliza wrote herself into colonial racial discourses. A third scene from Eliza's journal further demonstrates her comprehension of race as a discursive system structuring colonial society. Upon her arrival in Cape Town, Eliza "saw black people, and [she] thought they were [her] kind, but they are not; they are Slams, called in English, Malays." In this passage, Eliza signals her colonial education in racial discourses, categorizing both herself and Cape Malay (or Cape Colored) people as "black" before noting that she and the Malays on the street were not the same "kind." In between Eliza's first impression and her recategorization of the "Slams," an offstage voice subtly prompted Eliza with the "correct" racial categories and the proper ways to understand the colonial racial order of the Cape and the differences between racial "kind[s]." This scene offers a faint glimpse as to how Eliza understood herself to be "black": it documents the colonial racial education that subjected her as both "black" and "a Kafir girl," linked to the "Slams" yet indelibly different from the "white people" into whose "English" categories she was interpellated.

In sum, Eliza's journal presents an archive of Eliza's encounters with blackface while also placing blackface minstrelsy as an everyday element in the pedagogies of Anglophone imperial racial discourse. Her account traces the ways in which blackface mediated processes of racialization—not only among the white subjects of the Anglophone empire but also among colonized subjects and subalterns. Notably, in Eliza's encounter with blackface, she does not mention any minstrel tropes of racial abjection, burlesque, or denigration that typified the repertoires of transoceanic blackface. Instead, Eliza simply identifies herself and Cape Malays as "black people" while using the same term to describe blackface minstrels. Perhaps Eliza did not have the vocabulary in her language to parse the intricacies of Anglophone racial discourses and practices. Perhaps some nuance was lost in translation. Nevertheless, Eliza's account gives credence to Catherine M. Cole's assertion that colonial African engagements with blackface were "on some level *about* race . . . or at least about racial identification."[38] Indeed, Eliza's account documents a brief moment in which she identified with amateur blackface minstrels—an identification that necessarily entailed Eliza's understanding both herself and the minstrels as "black." Moreover, she referred to herself in such racializing terms rather than or in addition to other modes of identification (e.g., ethnicity or tribal affiliation) that remain unspecified in her journal.

I conclude this book with this banal moment of racial education because it offers a microhistory of the everyday practices involved in a transoceanic process that Jemima Pierre calls "making race global."[39] Eliza's writing, buttressed by an unspectacular offstage pedagogy at her mission school, signals how her understanding of blackness was mediated through numerous cultural enactments performed by "white people . . . who smear themselves with something black." It provides primary evidence in support of Zine Magubane's assertion that minstrelsy "was one of the first means whereby Africans in South Africa came to know blackness."[40] Indeed, Eliza's account narrates her encounters with "black people"—that is, Cape Malays, carnival revelers, and blackface minstrels—in the understated language of colonial common sense, signaling the unremarkable ways in which transoceanic blackface furnished forth the racial orders of the Anglophone empire. Perhaps most importantly, Eliza's encounter with blackface offers a rare transcript of how the antiblack racial repertoires of minstrelsy worked to mold the racial subjectivities of colonial subjects in large part because they were not necessarily perceived, interpreted, or resisted as antiblack articulations of white supremacy. Rather, they were familiar elements of colonial performance culture, as unremarkable and commonplace as pieces of imperial furniture. This microhistory, then, encapsulates the racializing work of transoceanic blackface—not only by furnishing forth whiteness as a privileged racial category in its imperial ordering of the world but also by conscripting colonized peoples into the racial discourses of the Anglophone empire.

My primary goal in this book has been to challenge and revise orthodox understandings regarding the imbrications among performance, race, and empire. To this end, I have drawn together an expansive material archive of transoceanic blackface that cuts across the epistemic divisions that have delimited analyses of racialized performance within discrete national contexts or under the apparatuses of area studies and their Cold War–era mappings of the world. The segregation of knowledges into disciplinary silos has imposed significant limitations on theater and performance studies. Despite the oft-proclaimed interdisciplinary origins of performance studies, much of its interdisciplinary work accepts the epistemic foundations of other disciplines unquestioningly. My contention is that working deeply and reflexively across disciplinary divides allows new questions to arise. If we no longer presume blackface to be the privileged preserve and national shame of US American popular culture, how might we apprehend the racializing work of contemporary transnational articulations of blackface and minstrelsy? If we account for the ubiquity of racialized performance throughout the Anglophone imperial world and for its attendant animation of colonial structures of feeling, how might we reconceptualize racialized performance as constitutive of racial subjectivity and subjecthood not only in the United States, Britain, and the circum-Atlantic but also throughout Africa, the Americas, the antipodes, and Asia? How might grappling with the global popularity of blackface performance allow us to grasp the ongoing transnationality of whiteness that facilitates the reanimation and reification of white supremacy beyond national borders? These questions offer a mere sketch of possible directions for future research into the complex and prolific transnational materialization of race animated by imperial performances of blackface, minstrelsy, and related forms of racialized enactments. To paraphrase Cedric J. Robinson, this project has not attempted to exhaust the subject of transoceanic blackface, only to suggest that it is there.[41]

ACKNOWLEDGMENTS

This project would not have been possible without the financial support of multiple institutions and the generous mentorship and camaraderie of several advisers, colleagues, and friends. The earliest research for this book was funded by the Stanford University Department of Theatre & Performance Studies, the Stanford University Center for African Studies, and the Stanford University Center for South Asia, which facilitated months of on-site archival research in Cape Town, eThekwini, Kolkata, and London. An Andrew W. Mellon Postdoctoral Fellowship at Dartmouth College supported the revision of this manuscript, and an Alfred A. and Blanche W. Knopf Fellowship allowed me to conduct research at the Harry Ransom Center at the University of Texas at Austin. Florida State University and the University at Buffalo, State University of New York, provided additional support that was critical to its completion.

Numerous research librarians, archivists, and curators have been instrumental in locating materials and directing me to other possible lines of inquiry. I would like to thank the staffs at Stanford University's Cecil H. Green Library, the National Library of South Africa Cape Town Campus, the Killie Campbell Africana Library, the National Library Kolkata, the British Library, Dartmouth College's Baker-Berry Library and Rauner Special Collections Library, Trinity College's Watkinson Library, the American Antiquarian Society, the University of Texas at Austin's Harry Ransom Center, Harvard University's Houghton Library, Florida State University's Strozier Library, the Folger Shakespeare Library, the Library Company of Philadelphia, the Library of Congress, New York Public Libraries, Johns Hopkins University Libraries, Yale University Libraries, Oxford University's Bodleian Libraries, and the University at Buffalo, SUNY's Lockwood Memorial Library. Particular thanks are owed to Melanie Geustyn at the National Library of South Africa, Eric Colleary at the Harry Ransom Center, and Matthew Wittmann at Houghton Library. I am also especially grateful to the staff of the Rauner Special Collections Library for scanning material for this project when an on-site visit became impossible due to the COVID-19 pandemic. Additionally, countless unnamed library staff have made digital versions of historical newspapers available via the National Library of Australia's TROVE collection, the National Library of New Zealand's Papers Past collection, Gale Historical Newspapers, Readex Historical Newspapers, and Newspaper SG (Singapore); my sincere thanks to those workers and their institutions for their contributions to public knowledge.

I would like to thank Northwestern University Press, especially Faith Wilson Stein, Patrick Anderson, and Nick Ridout, for their support of this project. My deep thanks as well to the anonymous reviewers of this manuscript for their constructive comments. The care and critical generosity they extended to this work granted me fresh perspectives and led me to new insights and connections. Moreover, as this book was completed during the COVID-19 pandemic, I extend my sincere and enduring gratitude to those who offered their time and energy to support this work during a particularly trying period in academic publishing. An earlier version of chapter 2 was originally published in *Theatre Journal*, and part of chapter 5 was originally published in *Mimetic Desires: Impersonation and Guising across South Asia*; my thanks to the Johns Hopkins University Press and the University of Hawai'i Press for permitting them to be reproduced here. At Florida State, my research assistant Rebecca Curran helped to secure image reproduction permissions, for which I am very grateful. Additional thanks to Elliott Turley for helping me access materials at Harvard University during the COVID-19 pandemic, and to Michelle Liu Carriger for doing the same at the University of California, Los Angeles. I have also been fortunate to meet Françoise Mazza, who has generously shared her family collections of material relating to Dave Carson and granted permission for them to be reproduced; she has my sincere gratitude.

This project has benefited immensely from the support and care of my mentors and teachers, to whom I owe enduring thanks for their advice, guidance, and wisdom. Jisha Menon was a remarkable mentor and adviser, and I am thankful for her critical engagement with and support of my work. Special thanks are owed to Harry Elam, who guided me through the first inklings of this project; it would not have begun—much less have been completed—without his mentorship. Jennifer Brody generously offered her advice and critical insights as well as her continued support of this project. Last but certainly not least, Catherine Cole shared additional feedback that proved instrumental in identifying new lines of inquiry that have enriched this book.

I am grateful to my friends, colleagues, and acquaintances who have offered their support, camaraderie, and critical insights during this project's long development. My deep thanks to the faculty and staff in the Dartmouth College Department of Theater, the Florida State University School of Theatre, and the University at Buffalo, SUNY, Department of Theatre and Dance who have provided me with material support and scholarly community. I would also like to express my enduring gratitude to Chari Arespacochaga, Trina Nileena Banerjee, Rimli Bhattacharya, James Bradbury, Michelle Bumatay, Michelle Liu Carriger, Sukanya

Chakrabarty, Partha Chatterjee, Gibson Alessandro Cima, Meredith Conti, Amanda Culp, Mary Karen Dahl, Kimberley Dawn, Rebecca Eacho, Laura Edmondson, Julia Fawcett, Willemien Froneman, Kathryn Hansen, Sonia Hazard, Amy Huang, Yizhou Huang, Laura Hubbard, Lindsay Brandon Hunter, Lisa Jackson-Schebetta, Paige Johnson, Harshita Mruthinti Kamath, Kareem Khubchandani, Summer Kim Lee, Margaret Kirby, Eero Laine, Carla Lever, So-Rim Lee, Megan Lewis, Pamela Lothspeich, Rishika Mehrishi, Sean Metzger, Derek Miller, Tarini Mookherjee, Eman Morsi, Gianna Mosser, Vivek Narayan, Heather Nathans, Noémie Ndiaye, Ariel Nereson, Beth Osborne, Lakshmi Padmanabhan, Claire Pamment, VK Preston, Emily Raymundo, Tatiana Reinoza, Aileen Robinson, Tara Rodman, Jennifer Row, Kris Salata, Analola Santana, Rudrani Sarma, Bryan Schmidt, April Sizemore-Barber, Kristina Straub, Lakshmi Subramanian, Chinua Thelwell, Elizabeth Timbs, Richard Waterhouse, E. J. Westlake, Joshua Williams, and Derek Woods. Special thanks are owed to Rebecca Chaleff, Doug Eacho, Aaron C. Thomas, and Elliott Turley for generously reading all or part of this manuscript and offering their wisdom and sage advice.

I have shared excerpts of this project at numerous conferences, where audiences and interlocutors offered constructive feedback; my thanks to the African Studies Association, American Society for Theatre Research (ASTR), the Annual Conference on South Asia at the University of Wisconsin, Madison, the Association for Asian Performance, the Association for Theatre in Higher Education, and the Mellon School of Theater and Performance Research at Harvard University. The ASTR working group on Performance in/from the Global South has been a critical space and supportive home for me to develop my research. Similarly, the working group on "Global Blackface" has offered a challenging and dynamic space for refining and deepening this work. My gratitude to Doug Jones for co-convening this group with me and for both his friendship and mentorship.

I have been at work on this project in one form or another for more than a decade. I would not have completed it without my family, all of whom have extended themselves in spectacular and subtle ways to support me. Profound thanks to my parents, who have always encouraged—and endured—my tendency to question everything. My endless gratitude is owed to Rebecca Chaleff, who has been my partner throughout this decade-long journey, and has always shared her love, care, and intellectual support.

NOTES

Note on Terminology

1. Koritha Mitchell, "Teaching & the N-word: Questions to Consider," *KorithaMitchell.com*, March 23, 2018, http://www.korithamitchell.com/teaching-and-the-n-word/.

Introduction

1. *Straits Times Overland Journal* (Singapore), July 21, 1881, 7.

2. See Rashna Darius Nicholson, *The Colonial Public and the Parsi Stage: The Making of the Theatre of Empire (1853–1893)* (Cham, Switzerland: Palgrave Macmillan, 2021).

3. *Straits Times Overland Journal* (Singapore), July 21, 1881, 7.

4. Daphne A. Brooks, *Bodies in Dissent: Spectacular Performances of Race and Freedom, 1850–1910* (Durham, NC: Duke University Press, 2006), 28, 352n44. See also Hazel Waters, *Racism on the Victorian Stage: Representation of Slavery and the Black Character* (Cambridge: Cambridge University Press, 2007), 127, 215n55; cf. "St. James's Theatre," *The Man in the Moon* 3 (1847): 182. For John W. Smith's *The Quack Doctor*, see *Darkey Plays, A Collection of Ethiopian Dramas, Farces, Interludes, Burlesque Operas, Eccentricities, Extravaganzas, Comicalities, Whimsicalities, etc. etc.: As Played by the Principal "Burnt Cork" Performers All Over the Union*, vol. 3 (New York: Happy Hours Company, 1874); reprinted in Gary D. Engle, ed., *This Grotesque Essence: Plays from the American Minstrel Stage* (Baton Rouge: Louisiana State University Press, 1978), 28–40. For *The Black Doctor*, see James V. Hatch and Ted Shine, eds., *Black Theatre USA: Plays by African Americans: The Early Period, 1847–1938*, revised and expanded edition (New York: Free Press, 1996). 3–24; Keith Byerman, "Creating the Black Hero: Ira Aldridge's *The Black Doctor*," in *Ira Aldridge: The African Roscius*, ed. Bernth Lindfors (Rochester, NY: University of Rochester Press, 2007), 205–15.

5. Nicholson, *Colonial Public*, 6, 85n118; Rashna Darius Nicholson, "'A Christy Minstrel, a Harlequin, or an Ancient Persian'? Opera, Hindustani Classical Music, and the Origins of the Popular South Asian 'Musical,'" *Theatre Survey* 61, no. 3 (2020): 331–50.

6. *Times of India* (Mumbai), December 16, 1873, 1; *Times of India* (Mumbai), December 18, 1873, 2.

7. As I discuss in chapter 5, "yellowface" did not necessarily require yellow face paint, as Orientalist costuming was often sufficient to produce the desired racializing effect.

8. *Straits Times Overland Journal* (Singapore), July 21, 1881, 7; Saw Swee-Hock, "Population Trends in Singapore, 1819–1967," *Journal of Southeast Asian History* 10, no. 1 (1969): 36–49, at 41.

9. Nicholson, *Colonial Public*, 108–13.

10. *Straits Times Overland Journal* (Singapore), July 21, 1881, 7.

11. Amitav Ghosh, "The Anglophone Empire," *New Yorker* 79, no. 7 (April 7, 2003): 46–47.

12. For prehistories of these transoceanic theatrical networks throughout the long eighteenth century, see Elizabeth Maddock Dillon, *New World Drama: The Performative Commons in the Atlantic World, 1649–1849* (Durham, NC: Duke University Press, 2014); Kathleen Wilson, *Strolling Players of Empire: Theater and Performances of Power in the British Imperial Provinces, 1656–1833* (Cambridge: Cambridge University Press, 2022).

13. Antonio Gramsci, *Selections from the Prison Notebooks*, ed. and trans. Quintin Hoare and Geoffrey Nowell Smith (New York: International Publishers, 1971), 421–23. See also Stuart Hall, "Gramsci's Relevance for the Study of Race and Ethnicity," *Journal of Communication Inquiry* 10, no. 5 (1986): 5–27; Ann Laura Stoler, *Along the Archival Grain: Epistemic Anxieties and Colonial Common Sense* (Princeton, NJ: Princeton University Press, 2009); Douglas A. Jones, *The Captive Stage: Performance and the Proslavery Imagination of the Antebellum North* (Ann Arbor: University of Michigan Press, 2014), 3 and passim.

14. Raymond Williams, "Structures of Feeling," in *Marxism and Literature* (Oxford: Oxford University Press, 1977), 128–35; Raymond Williams, *Drama from Ibsen to Brecht* (New York: Penguin, 1952), 1–14; cf. Catherine Hall, "Introduction: Thinking the Postcolonial, Thinking the Empire," in *Cultures of Empire: Colonizers in Britain and the Empire in the Nineteenth and Twentieth Centuries: A Reader*, ed. Catherine Hall (London: Routledge, 2000), 1–33.

15. Ann Laura Stoler, *Carnal Knowledge and Imperial Power: Race and the Intimate in Colonial Rule*, 2nd ed. (Berkeley: University of California Press, 2010), xii.

16. Tavia Nyong'o, *The Amalgamation Waltz: Race, Performance, and the Ruses of Memory* (Minneapolis: University of Minnesota Press, 2009), 105.

17. Lisa Lowe, *The Intimacies of Four Continents* (Durham, NC: Duke University Press, 2015), 11.

18. Michael Rogin, *Blackface, White Noise: Jewish Immigrants in the Hollywood Melting Pot* (Berkeley: University of California Press, 1998), 5.

19. Brander Matthews, "The Rise and Fall of Negro Minstrelsy," *Scribner's Magazine* 57 (1915): 754–59, quote on 754.

20. See Charlotte M. Canning, "Dramatic Criticism's Imperial Ambitions: Brander Matthews and the Establishment of Theatre in US Higher Education," *Journal of Dramatic Theory and Criticism* 32, no. 2 (2018): 53–65. For other foundational contributions to blackface minstrel studies as a US American national project, see Carl Wittke, *Tambo and Bones: A History of the American Minstrel Stage* (1930; repr. Westport, CT: Greenwood Press, 1968); Constance Rourke, *American Humor: A Study of the National Character* (1931; repr. New York: New York Review of Books, 2004), 70–90.

21. Robert C. Toll, *Blacking Up: The Minstrel Show in Nineteenth-Century America* (Oxford: Oxford University Press, 1974); Jean H. Baker, *Affairs of Party: The Political Culture of Northern Democrats in the Mid-Nineteenth Century* (Ithaca, NY: Cornell University Press, 1983), 213–57; Alexander

Saxton, *The Rise and Fall of the White Republic: Class Politics and Mass Culture in Nineteenth-Century America* (New York: Verso, 1990), 165–82; David R. Roediger, *The Wages of Whiteness: Race and the Making of the American Working Class*, rev. ed. (New York: Verso, 2007), 95–131; Eric Lott, *Love and Theft: Blackface Minstrelsy and the American Working Class* (Oxford: Oxford University Press, 1993).

22. Lott, *Love and Theft*, 38–62.

23. Matthews, "Rise and Fall of Negro Minstrelsy," 754.

24. Dale Cockrell, *Demons of Disorder: Early Blackface Minstrels and Their World* (Cambridge: Cambridge University Press, 1997), ix; W. T. Lhamon Jr., *Raising Cain: Blackface Performance from Jim Crow to Hip Hop* (Cambridge, MA: Harvard University Press, 1998), 63. See also W. T. Lhamon Jr., *Jump Jim Crow: Lost Plays, Lyrics, and Street Prose of the First Atlantic Popular Culture* (Cambridge, MA: Harvard University Press, 2003); Christopher J. Smith, *The Creolization of American Culture: William Sidney Mount and the Roots of Blackface Minstrelsy* (Urbana: University of Illinois Press, 2013).

25. Catherine M. Cole, *Ghana's Concert Party Theatre* (Bloomington: Indiana University Press, 2001); Jill Lane, *Blackface Cuba, 1840–1895* (Philadelphia: University of Pennsylvania Press, 2005).

26. Robert Nowatzki, *Representing African Americans in Transatlantic Abolitionism and Blackface Minstrelsy* (Baton Rouge: Louisiana State University Press, 2010).

27. Richard Waterhouse, *From Minstrel Show to Vaudeville: The Australian Popular Stage, 1788–1914* (Kensington, Australia: New South Wales University Press, 1990); Matthew W. Wittmann, "Empire of Culture: U.S. Entertainers and the Making of the Pacific Circuit, 1850–1890" (PhD diss., University of Michigan, 2010); Chinua Thelwell, *Exporting Jim Crow: Blackface Minstrelsy in South Africa and Beyond* (Amherst: University of Massachusetts Press, 2020).

28. Brian Rouleau, *With Sails Whitening Every Sea: Mariners and the Making of an American Maritime Empire* (Ithaca, NY: Cornell University Press, 2015), 46–50; Victor Fell Yellin, "Mrs. Belmont, Matthew Perry, and the 'Japanese Minstrels,'" *American Music* 14, no. 3 (1996): 257–75, at 266.

29. *New York Evening Post*, March 23, 1841, 3; *New York Evening Post*, March 24, 1841, 2.

30. Playbill, April 13, 1844, container 44.9, Minstrel Show Collection, Harry Ransom Center, University of Texas at Austin.

31. Roediger, *Wages of Whiteness*, 116; Toll, *Blacking Up*, 58–59n12; cf. Stewart McCauley, *Songs of Kunkel's Nightingale Opera Troupe* (Baltimore: 1854), v. Lincoln exhibited "an insatiable fondness for negro minstrelsy," even once demanding an encore of Dan Emmett's "Dixie" prior to its instantiation as the de facto anthem of the Confederacy (Jesse W. Weik, *The Real Lincoln: A Portrait* [New York: Houghton Mifflin, 1922], 75, 85–86).

32. Samuel S. Sanford, "Personal Reminiscences of Himself Together with the History of Minstrelsy from the Origan [*sic*] 1843 to 1893 with a Sketch of All the Celebrities of the Past and Present," 19, manuscript held in container 32.11, Minstrel Show Collection, Harry Ransom Center, University of Texas at Austin.

33. *Morning Chronicle* (London), January 20, 1846, 5; *Illustrated London News*, January 24, 1846, 61. Polk's letter, reprinted in the *Morning Chronicle* (London), also includes an endorsement of the Ethiopian Serenaders by Dolly Madison, the widow of former US president James Madison.

34. Zine Magubane, *Bringing the Empire Home: Race, Class, and Gender in Britain and Colonial South Africa* (Chicago: University of Chicago Press, 2004), 153.

35. Richard Waterhouse, "The Internationalisation of American Popular Culture in the Nineteenth Century: The Case of the Minstrel Show," *Australasian Journal of American Studies* 4, no. 1 (1985): 1–11, at 3; Stephen Johnson, "Death and the Minstrel: Race, Madness, and Art in the Last (W)rites of Three Early Blackface Performers," in *Burnt Cork: Traditions and Legacies of Blackface Minstrelsy*, ed. Stephen Johnson (Amherst: University of Massachusetts Press, 2012), 85; *Sunday Times* (London), October 25, 1868, 3.

36. *Graham's Town Journal* (Makhanda, South Africa), December 4, 1868, 2.

37. For instance, colonial governors attended blackface minstrel performances in colonial South Africa and South Asia: *Cape Monitor* (Cape Town), September 6, 1862, 2–3; *Times of India* (Mumbai), May 17, 1865, 2; *Cape Argus* (Cape Town), November 14, 1865, 2; November 21, 1872, 2; *Supplement to the Bengal Hurkaru* (Kolkata, India), February 5, 1866, 1; *Ceylon Observer* (Colombo, Sri Lanka), April 23, 1870, 157; *Indian Daily News* (Kolkata), January 17, 1871, 1; *Era* (London), April 30, 1871, 11; *New York Clipper*, November 25, 1871, 268; *Natal Mercury* (eThekwini, South Africa), March 24, 1874, 3; *Diamond Field* (Kimberley, South Africa), April 30, 1873, 3; August 15, 1874, 3.

38. *Colonial Standard* (Kingston, Jamaica), February 10, 1872, 3.

39. *Colonial Standard* (Kingston, Jamaica), February 17, 1872, 2.

40. Sara Ahmed, "Affective Economies," *Social Text* 79, no. 2 (2004): 117–39, quote on 119.

41. These letters are reprinted in Edna Bradlow, ed., *Life at Natal a Hundred Years Ago* (Cape Town: C. Struik, 1972). On questions of authorship, see Bradlow, 7–8.

42. Bradlow, *Life at Natal*, 92, 93.

43. Bradlow, *Life at Natal*, 92.

44. Sarah Meer, *Uncle Tom Mania: Slavery, Minstrelsy, & Transatlantic Culture in the 1850s* (Athens: University of Georgia Press, 2005). See also Tracy C. Davis and Stefka Mihaylova, eds., *Uncle Tom's Cabins: The Transnational History of America's Most Mutable Book* (Ann Arbor: University of Michigan Press, 2018).

45. Joseph Roach, *Cities of the Dead: Circum-Atlantic Performance* (New York: Columbia University Press, 1996), 4–5; see also Paul Gilroy, *The Black Atlantic* (Cambridge, MA: Harvard University Press, 1993).

46. Eric Williams, *Capitalism & Slavery* (1944; Chapel Hill: University of North Carolina Press, 1994), 123.

47. Adam Smith, *The Wealth of Nations*, ed. Edwin Cannan (New York: Modern Library, 2000), 675.

48. Karl Marx and Friedrich Engels, *The Communist Manifesto*, trans. Samuel Moore (New York: Penguin Books, 2002), 220. Importantly, as Cedric

Robinson observes, the "transnational character was not only true for mature capitalism as Marx and Engels indicated in *The Communist Manifesto*; it also characterized capitalism from its inception" (Cedric J. Robinson, *An Anthropology of Marxism* [Aldershot, UK: Ashgate, 2001], 12).

49. Ngũgĩ wa Thiong'o, *Globalectics: Theory and the Politics of Knowing* (New York: Columbia University Press, 2014), 45–46.

50. Lowe, *Intimacies of Four Continents*. See also Immanuel Wallerstein, *The Capitalist World-Economy* (Cambridge: Cambridge University Press, 1979); *The Modern World-System III: The Second Era of Great Expansion of the Capitalist World-Economy, 1730s–1840s* (Berkeley: University of California Press, 2011); *The Modern World-System IV: Centrist Liberalism Triumphant, 1789–1914* (Berkeley: University of California Press, 2011).

51. Walter Rodney, *How Europe Underdeveloped Africa* (1972; repr. Baltimore: Black Classic Press, 2011), 199; Aníbal Quijano and Immanuel Wallerstein, "Americanity as a Concept, or the Americas in the Modern World-System," *International Journal of Social Science* 134 (1992): 549–59; Aníbal Quijano, "Coloniality of Power, Ethnocentrism, and Latin America," trans. Michael Ennis, *Nepantla* 1, no. 3 (2000): 533–80; Ann Laura Stoler, *Race and the Education of Desire: Foucault's "History of Sexuality" and the Colonial Order of Things* (Durham, NC: Duke University Press, 1995); Stoler, *Carnal Knowledge*; Lowe, *Intimacies of Four Continents*.

52. Giovanni Arrighi, *The Long Twentieth Century: Money, Power and the Origins of Our Times*, new and updated ed. (New York: Verso, 2010).

53. *Era* (London), April 25, 1847, 11.

54. E. Stirling, *The Buffalo Girls*, British Library Add MS 43003, 288.

55. "Jim Crow's Personal History," in *The Humorous Adventures of Jump Jim Crow* (Glasgow: [1840?]), 6; BL 11621.b.19.14. See also reprint as "Jim Crow," in *The British Minstrel, A Collection of Popular Songs* (London: Thomas Allman, 1848), 97.

56. Playbill, Virginia Minstrels, Brinley Hall, Worcester, March 20, 21, and 22, 1843, American minstrel show collection, 1823–1947, MS Thr 556 (607), Virginia Minstrels, Playbills, 1843–1870, Harvard Theatre Collection, https://iiif.lib.harvard.edu/manifests/view/drs:424935963$5i.

57. Stephen C. Foster, *Old Folks at Home, Ethiopian Melody, as Sung by Christy's Minstrels. Written and Composed by E. P. Christy*, 15th ed. (New York: Firth, Pond, 1851), 4.

58. Jones, *Captive Stage*, 56.

59. Édouard Glissant, *Poetics of Relation*, trans. Betsy Wing (Ann Arbor: University of Michigan Press, 1997), 67.

60. Cedric J. Robinson, *Black Marxism: The Making of the Black Radical Tradition* (1983; repr. Chapel Hill: University of North Carolina Press, 2000).

61. Edward W. Said, *Orientalism*, 25th anniversary ed. (1979; New York: Vintage Books, 2004), 49; Dillon, *New World Drama*; Wilson, *Strolling Players of Empire*.

62. W. E. B. Du Bois, "The Souls of White Folk," in *Darkwater: Voices from within the Veil*, ed. Henry Louis Gates Jr. (Oxford: Oxford University Press, 2007), 22.

63. Gramsci, *Selections from the Prison Notebooks*, 421–23.

64. Catherine Hall, *Civilising Subjects: Colony and Metropole in the English Imagination, 1830–1867* (Chicago: University of Chicago Press, 2002), 8.

65. Catherine Hall, "Narratives of Empire: A Reply to Critics," *Small Axe* 7, no. 2 (2003): 168–78, quote on 173.

66. Raymond Williams, *Marxism and Literature* (Oxford: Oxford University Press, 1977), 133; italics in the original. Indeed, as Gramsci notes, common sense itself is "not rigid and immobile," nor is it ephemeral: it "creates the folklore of the future, a relatively rigidified phase of popular knowledge in a given time and place" (*Selections from the Prison Notebooks*, 326n5).

67. Laura Doyle, *Freedom's Empire: Race and the Rise of the Novel in Atlantic Modernity, 1640–1940* (Durham, NC: Duke University Press, 2008), 3; cf. Hartman, *Scenes of Subjection*, esp. 115–24.

68. Said, *Orientalism*, 7; italics in the original.

69. Denise Ferreira da Silva, *Toward a Global Idea of Race* (Minneapolis: University of Minnesota Press, 2007); Kyla Schuller, *The Biopolitics of Feeling: Race, Sex, and Science in the Nineteenth Century* (Durham, NC: Duke University Press, 2018); Xine Yao, *Disaffected: The Cultural Politics of Unfeeling in Nineteenth-Century America* (Durham, NC: Duke University Press, 2021).

70. Charles W. Mills, "Racial Liberalism," *PMLA* 123, no. 5 (2008): 1380–97.

71. Stoler, *Race and the Education of Desire*; Stoler, *Carnal Knowledge*.

72. My use of "abject" and "abjection" owes a significant debt to Saidiya Hartman's analysis of the "pervasiveness of the spectacle of black contentment and abjection" (Saidiya V. Hartman, *Scenes of Subjection: Terror, Slavery, and Self-Making in Nineteenth-Century America* [Oxford: Oxford University Press, 1997], 56). I also draw on the work of Karen Shimakawa, who theorizes the abject as that which "does not achieve a (stable) status of *object*—the term often used to describe the position of (racially or sexually) disenfranchised groups in analyses of the politics of representation" and which "must be both made present and jettisoned" in order for the normative position to cohere (*National Abjection: The Asian American Body Onstage* [Durham, NC: Duke University Press, 2002], 3). See also Judith Butler, *Bodies That Matter: On the Discursive Limits of "Sex"* (1993; repr. New York: Routledge, 2011), xiii.

73. Hershini Bhana Young, *Haunting Capital: Memory, Text, and the Black Diasporic Body* (Hanover, NH: Dartmouth College Press, 2006), 11–13; see also Jemima Pierre, *The Predicament of Blackness: Postcolonial Ghana and the Politics of Race* (Chicago: University of Chicago Press, 2013).

74. Jenny Sharpe, *Allegories of Empire: The Figure of Woman in the Colonial Text* (Minneapolis: University of Minnesota Press, 1993), 5.

75. Roderick A. Ferguson, *Aberrations in Black: Toward a Queer of Color Critique* (Minneapolis: University of Minnesota Press, 2004), 4.

76. Nyong'o, *Amalgamation Waltz*, 83.

77. See Michel Foucault, *History of Sexuality*, trans. Robert Hurley, vol. 1, *An Introduction* (New York: Pantheon Books, 1978), 103.

78. Stoler, *Carnal Knowledge*, 7.

79. *The London Mathews; Containing an Account of This celebrated Comedian's Trip to America, Being an Annual Lecture on Peculiarities, Characters, and Manners, Founded on His Own Observations and Adventures, to Which*

Are Prefixed, Several Original Comic Songs (Philadelphia: Morgan & Yeager, ca. 1824), 11; italics in the original.

80. Marvin McAllister, *White People Do Not Know How to Behave at Entertainments Designed for Ladies and Gentlemen of Colour* (Chapel Hill: University of North Carolina Press, 2003), 160.

81. Jacky Bratton, *New Readings in Theatre History* (Cambridge: Cambridge University Press, 2003), 37.

82. Tracy C. Davis, "Repertoire," *Nineteenth Century Theatre and Film* 36, no. 2 (2009): 8. See also Tracy C. Davis, "Introduction: Repertoire," in *The Broadview Anthology of Nineteenth-Century British Performance*, ed. Tracy C. Davis (London: Broadview Press, 2012), 13–26.

83. Diana Taylor, *The Archive and the Repertoire: Performing Cultural Memory in the Americas* (Durham, NC: Duke University Press, 2003), 2 and passim.

84. Taylor, *Archive and the Repertoire*, 46. Though death looms large in Joseph Roach's theory of "surrogation," he also notes departure can take the form of many absences—through disappearance but also through "diasporic diffusions" and "displaced transmissions" (*Cities of the Dead*, 30, 36); see also Rebecca Schneider, *Performing Remains: Art and War in Times of Theatrical Reenactment* (New York: Routledge, 2011), 96.

85. Harry Reynolds, *Minstrel Memories: The Story of Burnt Cork Minstrelsy in Great Britain from 1836 to 1927* (London: Alston Rivers, 1928), 85; Michael Pickering, *Blackface Minstrelsy in Britain* (Aldershot, UK: Ashgate, 2008), 85–88.

86. "Glut of Ethiopians," *Punch, or the London Charivari* 12 (1847): 122.

87. Rev. H. R. Haweis, *Music and Morals* (New York: Harper & Brothers, 1872), 472.

88. Haweis, *Music and Morals*, 472.

89. Victor Turner, *From Ritual to Theatre: The Human Seriousness of Play* (New York: PAJ Publications, 1982), 79.

90. Roach, *Cities of the Dead*, 3, xi.

91. William Shakespeare, *The Tragedy of Hamlet, Prince of Denmark: The First Folio (1623)*, in *Hamlet: The Texts of 1603 and 1623*, Arden Shakespeare Third Series, edited by Ann Thompson and Neil Taylor (London: Arden Shakespeare, 2006), 1.2.177–78; italics mine. References are to act, scene, and line. Though Roach makes frequent reference to *Hamlet*, noting that it "dramatizes the cultural politics of memory, particularly as they are realized through communications between the living and the dead," he does not cite this paradigmatic passage on "furnish[ing] forth" (*Cities of the Dead*, 34).

92. Roach's ghostly Shakespearean citation from a play fixated on spectral succession ironically encapsulates Roach's concept of "surrogation" as central to the interplay of performance, culture, and memory (*Cities of the Dead*, 3). Signaling the success of Roach's surrogate definition, Taylor attributes "to furnish forth" to Turner (*Archive and the Repertoire*, 3).

93. Roach, *Cities of the Dead*, 27.

94. Roach, *Cities of the Dead*, 36.

95. For canonical performance studies texts that engage with Shakespeare's *Hamlet*, see, for instance: Herbert Blau, *Take Up the Bodies: Theatre at the*

Vanishing Point (Urbana: University of Illinois Press, 1982); Richard Schechner, *Between Theater and Anthropology* (Philadelphia: University of Pennsylvania Press, 1985), esp. 100–123; Bert O. States, *Great Reckonings in Little Rooms: On the Phenomenology of Theater* (Berkeley: University of California Press, 1985); Marvin Carlson, *The Haunted Stage: The Theatre as Memory Machine* (Ann Arbor: University of Michigan Press, 2003); Schneider, *Performing Remains*.

96. Roach, *Cities of the Dead*, 110–12.

97. W. B. Worthen, "Antigone's Bones," *TDR* 52, no. 3 (2008): 10–33, at 15.

98. Here, I am thinking alongside Soyica Colbert, Doug Jones, and Shane Vogel, who have called for an "accounting [of] all performance as racialized" (*Race and Performance after Repetition*, ed. Soyica Colbert, Douglas A. Jones Jr., and Shane Vogel [Durham, NC: Duke University Press, 2020], viii).

99. My usage of "conscripting" owes a debt to David Scott, *Conscripts of Modernity: The Tragedy of Colonial Enlightenment* (Durham, NC: Duke University Press, 2004).

100. Hartman, *Scenes of Subjection*, 55. See also Saidiya Hartman, "Venus in Two Acts," *Small Axe* 12, no. 2 (2008): 1–14.

101. *Cape Argus* (Cape Town): September 2, 1862, 3; September 13, 1862, 2; *Graham's Town Journal* (Makhanda, South Africa), September 27, 1862, 1; *Eastern Province Herald* (Gqeberha, South Africa), November 10, 1868, 2; November 25, 1873, 3; *Standard & Mail* (Cape Town), November 26, 1872, 3; *Port Elizabeth Telegraph* (Gqeberha, South Africa), December 27, 1872, 2; November 21, 1873, 2; *Natal Mercury* (eThekwini, South Africa), April 2, 1874, 2; *Natal Witness* (Pietermaritzburg, South Africa), May 1, 1874, 3.

102. *Standard & Mail* (Cape Town), December 5, 1872, 3.

103. Hartman, *Scenes of Subjection*, 7, 23.

104. bell hooks, *Black Looks: Race and Representation* (Boston: South End Press, 1992), 120. Italics in the original.

105. hooks, *Black Looks*, 120.

106. José Esteban Muñoz, *Disidentifications: Queers of Color and the Performance of Politics* (Minneapolis: University of Minnesota Press, 1999). Muñoz defines disidentification as "descriptive of the survival strategies the minority subject practices in order to negotiate a phobic majoritarian public sphere that continuously elides or punishes the existence of subjects who do not conform to the phantasm of normative citizenship" (4).

Chapter 1

1. John Adams, "John Adams to Abigail Smith, September 30, 1764," in *Adams Family Correspondence*, ed. L. H. Butterfield, vol. 1, *December 1761–May 1776* (Cambridge, MA: Belknap Press of Harvard University Press, 1963), 47–49, quote on 48–49.

2. Rogin, *Blackface, White Noise*, 5.

3. Lynn Fauley Emery, *Black Dance from 1619 to Today*, 2nd rev. ed. (Hightstown, NJ: Princeton Book Company, 1988), 180.

4. S. Foster Damon, "The Negro in Early American Songsters," *Papers of the Bibliographical Society of America* (1934): 133; cf. *New-York Journal; or, The General Advertiser*, April 9, 1767, 3.

5. Lott, *Love and Theft*, 55; cf. Constance Rourke, *American Humor: A Study of the National Character* (1931; repr. New York: New York Review Books, 2004), 70–90.

6. Walter Benjamin, *The Origin of German Tragic Drama*, trans. John Osborne (London: NLB, 1977), 45.

7. *Diary of Cadet Robert Ramsay: Voyage to Calcutta 1825*, Caird Library, National Maritime Museum, Greenwich, UK, JOD 5, 39–41.

8. *Diary of Cadet Robert Ramsay*, 39–40.

9. Simon J. Bronner, *Crossing the Line: Violence, Play, and Drama in Naval Equator Traditions* (Amsterdam: Amsterdam University Press, 2006).

10. Nicole R. Fleetwood, *Troubling Vision: Performance, Visuality, and Blackness* (Chicago: University of Chicago Press, 2011), 234n29.

11. *Diary of Cadet Robert Ramsay*, 45–46.

12. Wilson, *Strolling Players of Empire*, 274.

13. *The London Stage Database*, https://londonstagedatabase.uoregon.edu/, accessed March 22, 2023; cf. George Winchester Stone Jr., *The London Stage*, part 4, vol. 1 (Carbondale: Southern Illinois University Press, 1962), clxvi. Additionally, the Harry Ransom Center's playbill collections for London theaters contain records of 101 productions of *High Life below Stairs* at Drury Lane, Haymarket, and Covent Garden from 1780 to 1850 (see London Playbills Collection, Harry Ransom Center, University of Texas at Austin); note that these statistics refer only to productions at licensed theaters in London and exclude productions in the British provinces.

14. Data on British colonial and US American productions have been compiled from George O. Seilhamer, *History of the American Theatre*, vols. 1–3 (Philadelphia: Globe Printing House, 1888–1891); George C. D. Odell, *Annals of the New York Stage*, vols. 1–6 (New York: Columbia University Press, 1927–1931).

15. George O. Seilhamer, *History of the American Theatre*, vol. 1, *Before the Revolution* (Philadelphia: Globe Printing House, 1888), 154.

16. Wilson, *Strolling Players of Empire*, 472–73; "Madras Theatricals of the Ton," (London) *Times*, August 11, 1788; cf. David Worrall, *Harlequin Empire: Race, Ethnicity and the Drama of the Popular Enlightenment* (London: Pickering & Chatto, 2007), 32.

17. *African Theatricals: Being a Collection of Play Bills, Prologues, Epilogues, and Songs, as They Were Performed at Cape Town, Cape of Good Hope, in the Year, 1807, by the Officers of the Garrison*, National Library of South Africa, Cape Town, MSB 940.1.5.

18. Odell, 6:217. Indeed, *High Life below Stairs* continued to receive productions across the nineteenth-century United States, including three separate productions in New Orleans in the 1820s–1830s (April 24, 1829; February 15, 1837; February 21, 1837). See Nelle Smither, "A History of the English Theatre at New Orleans, 1806–1842 (Concluded from January 1945 Quarterly)," *Louisiana Historical Quarterly* 28, no. 2 (April 1945): 361–572, at 391, 435.

19. Gretchen Holbrook Gerzina, *Black London: Life before Emancipation* (New Brunswick, NJ: Rutgers University Press, 1995), 29–67.

20. James Townley, *High Life below Stairs. A Farce of Two Acts. As It Is Performed at the Theatre-Royal in Drury-Lane* (London: J. Newberry, 1759), 24.

21. Jan Nederveen Pieterse, *White on Black: Images of Africa and Blacks in Western Popular Culture* (New Haven, CT: Yale University Press, 1992), 128.

22. Townley, *High Life*, 26.

23. Townley, *High Life*, 41.

24. Townley, *High Life*, 43.

25. *The London Stage Database*, https://londonstagedatabase.uoregon.edu/, accessed March 22, 2023; cf. Stone, *London Stage*, part 4, 1:clxvi.

26. *New-York Gazette, and Weekly Mercury*, May 29, 1769, 3; *Pennsylvania Gazette*, November 16, 1769; *Pennsylvania Chronicle* (Philadelphia), December 4–11, 1769, 379. Printed scripts of *The Padlock* were advertised for sale in the British American colonies as early as April 1769 (*Pennsylvania Journal*, April 6, 1769, 3). As with *High Life below Stairs*, data have been compiled for the mainland British American colonies and the United States from 1769 to 1840 from Seilhamer, *History of the American Theatre*, vols. 1–3; Odell, *Annals of the New York Stage*, vols. 1–4.

27. Wilson, *Strolling Players of Empire*, 274, 472; P. W. Laidler, *The Annals of the Cape Stage* (Edinburgh, UK: William Bryce, 1926), 27.

28. Gerzina, *Black London*, 10; Heather S. Nathans, *Slavery and Sentiment on the American Stage, 1787–1861: Lifting the Veil of Black* (Cambridge: Cambridge University Press, 2009), 24.

29. Monica L. Miller, *Slaves to Fashion: Black Dandyism and the Styling of Black Diasporic Identity* (Durham, NC: Duke University Press, 2009), 29.

30. Joyce Green MacDonald, "Acting Black: *Othello*, *Othello* Burlesques, and the Performance of Blackness," *Theatre Journal* 46, no. 2 (1994): 231–49, at 239–40.

31. Odell, *Annals of the New York Stage*, 1:171; cf. *Rivington's Gazetteer*, August 5, 1773.

32. Jennifer Stiles, "Import or Immigrant? The Representation of Blacks and Irish on the American Stage from 1767–1856," *Journal of American Drama and Theatre* 12 (2000): 38–56, at 47.

33. Charles Dibdin, *The Professional Life of Mr. Dibdin, Written by Himself*, 4 vols. (London: Charles Dibdin, 1803), 1:70.

34. Odell, *Annals of the New York Stage*, 1:151.

35. David Dabydeen, *Hogarth's Blacks: Images of Blacks in Eighteenth Century English Art* (Manchester, UK: Manchester University Press, 1987), 18.

36. Diana Donald, *The Age of Caricature: Satirical Prints in the Reign of George III* (New Haven, CT: Yale University Press, 1996), 5.

37. Kay Dian Kriz, *Slavery, Sugar, and the Culture of Refinement: Picturing the British West Indies, 1700–1840* (New Haven, CT: Yale University Press, 2008), 72.

38. Dabydeen, *Hogarth's Blacks*, 64.

39. Laurence Hutton, *Curiosities of the American Stage* (New York: Harper & Brothers, 1891), 94.

40. As Monica L. Miller aptly notes, the potential inversion of blackface comedy into abolitionist tragedy remained latent within *The Padlock*, where savvy performers such as Ira Aldridge activated the possibility of pathos by

imbuing the comically drunken Mungo with fuller humanity (*Slaves to Fashion*, 33). Yet, to attribute abolitionist sentimentality as characteristic of this image or of Dibdin's comic opera not only distorts *The Padlock*'s dramaturgy and politics but also minimizes the artistic and political work performed by Aldridge.

41. For instance, two additional images of interracial sexual contact drew directly from the racial discourses animated by *High Life below Stairs*: James Bretherton, *High Life below Stairs: As It Was Represented at Cashiobury, the Seat of the Earl of Essex* (London: February 23, 1774); Robert Cruikshank, *High Life below Stairs* (London: G. Tregear, 1825). Numerous additional prints similarly parodied Julius Soubise, a Black servant to Catherine Hyde, the Duchess of Queensbury, as yet another variation on Mungo—as in M. Darly's *A Mungo Macaroni* (1772) and William Austin's *The D—of—Playing at FOILS with Her Favorite lap dog Mungo after Expending near £10000 to Make Him a*—(1773). The latter image directly quotes Mungo's catchphrase from *The Padlock*—"Mungo here Mungo dere Mungo Every where"—as Soubise's épée touches the Duchess's chest. Darly's image cites Hogarth's and Humphrey's reiterated scenario of interracial sexuality sited at the juncture of a Black male figure touching a white woman's breast (Gerzina, *Black London*, 54–57; Miller, *Slaves to Fashion*, 69–76).

42. Charles Dibdin, "Rondeau [the Negro and His Banjer]," in *Professional Life of Mr. Dibdin*, 3:78.

43. Charles Dibdin, "Negro Duet—the Sun Go Down," in George Hogarth, *The Songs of Charles Dibdin, Chronologically Arranged, with Notes, Historical, Biographical, and Critical; and the Music of the Best and Most Popular of the Melodies, with New Piano-Forte Accompaniments* (London: G. H. Davidson, 1818), 1:174–75.

44. Charles Dibdin, "Ballad [Negro Philosophy]," in *Professional Life of Mr. Dibdin*, 4:21–22. Future quotations from the same.

45. Oscar George Theodore Sonneck, *A Bibliography of Early Secular American Music* (Washington, DC: H. L. McQueen, 1905), 98; Odell, *Annals of the New York Stage*, 2:146.

46. Isaac Jackman, *The Divorce: A Farce. In Two Acts. As It Is Performed at the Theatre-Royal, Drury-Lane* (London: G. Kearsley, 1781), 34.

47. Jackman, *Divorce*, 34.

48. Hartman, *Scenes of Subjection*, 29.

49. William Macready, *The Irishman in London; or, The Happy African. A Farce. In Two Acts. Performed at the Theatre-Royal, Covent-Garden* (London: T. N. Longman, 1799), 13.

50. Macready, *Irishman in London*, 31.

51. Prince Hoare, *The Prize; or, 2, 5, 3, 8, a Musical Farce in Two Acts, as Performed by His Majesty's Company. Written by Prince Hoare, Esq. The Music by Storace. Correctly Taken from the Manager's Book* (Dublin: F. Farquhar, 1793), 6–7.

52. Hoare, *Prize*, 7.

53. Hoare, *Prize*, 7.

54. Frederick Reynolds, *Laugh When You Can: A Comedy, in Five Acts. As Performed at the Theatre Royal, Covent-Garden* (London: T. N. Longman and O. Rees, 1799), 58.

55. Reynolds, *Laugh When You Can*, 58.

56. David Brion Davis, *The Problem of Slavery in the Age of Revolution, 1770–1823* (Oxford: Oxford University Press, 1999), 373.

57. Seilhamer, *History of the American Theatre*, 3:301; Odell, *Annals of the New York Stage*, 1:454; Odell, *Annals of the New York Stage*, 2:57, 191, 255, 274, 289, 322, 387; Odell, *Annals of the New York Stage*, 3:77, 250, 355, 406, 416, 465, 500, 506, 516; West T. Hill Jr., *The Theatre in Early Kentucky: 1790–1820* (Lexington: University Press of Kentucky, 1971), 59, 112, 176; William B. Hamilton, "The Theater in the Old Southwest: The First Decade at Natchez," *American Literature* 12, no. 4 (1941): 471–85; at 476.

58. Sam Dennison, *Scandalize My Name: Black Imagery in American Popular Music* (London: Garland, 1982), 11.

59. Cockrell, *Demons of Disorder*, 16, 173n7.

60. Seilhamer, *History of the American Theatre*, 2:207, 342, 345; Odell, *Annals of the New York Stage*, 1:324.

61. Nathans, *Slavery and Sentiment*, 48.

62. John Murdock, *The Triumphs of Love; or, Happy Reconciliation. A Comedy. In Four Acts. Written by an American and a Citizen of Philadelphia. Acted at the New Theatre, Philadelphia* (Philadelphia: R. Folwell 1795), 69.

63. L. Beach, *Jonathan Postfree; or, The Honest Yankee. A Musical Farce, in Three Acts* (New York: David Longworth, 1807), 28.

64. Nowatzki, *Representing African Americans*, 72.

65. James C. Scott, *Domination and the Arts of Resistance: Hidden Transcripts* (New Haven, CT: Yale University Press, 1990), 15.

66. Andrew Barton [pseud. of Thomas Forrest], *The Disappointment, or, The Force of Credulity*, ed. David Mays (Gainesville: University Press of Florida, 1976). The identity of the author remains uncertain despite Mays's assertion of Thomas Forrest as the playwright.

67. Seilhamer, *History of the American Theatre*, 1:177.

68. *Pennsylvania Chronicle*, April 20–27, 1767, 56; Seilhamer, *History of the American Theatre*, 1:177–78.

69. *New-York Journal; or, The General Advertiser*, April 9, 1767, 3; the American Company premiered *The Padlock* on May 29, 1769 (Odell, *Annals of the New York Stage*, 1:151). It is possible that *The Disappointment* was inspired at least in part by *High Life below Stairs*, which was performed twice at the Southwark Theatre, Philadelphia, on January 26 and February 6, 1767, a few months prior to the abortive performance of *The Disappointment* at the same theater.

70. Barton, *Disappointment*, 45.

71. Hugh F. Rankin, *The Theater in Colonial America* (Chapel Hill: University of North Carolina Press, 1965), 117. See also Frederick W. Bond, *The Negro and the Drama: The Direct and Indirect Contribution Which the American Negro Has Made to Drama and the Legitimate Stage, with the Underlying Conditions Responsible* (Washington, DC: Associated Publishers, 1940), 20.

72. David Mays, introduction to *The Disappointment*, by Barton, 19–20; Carolyn Rabson, "*Disappointment* Revisited: Unweaving the Tangled Web. Part I," *American Music* 1, no. 1 (1983): 12–35; William Torbert Leonard, *Masquerade in Black* (Metuchen, NJ: Scarecrow Press, 1986), 159. As Mays

was the editor of the 1976 edition of *The Disappointment*, his assertion of Raccoon's non-Black identity has significantly impacted subsequent analysis of the play (see Patricia H. Virga, *American Opera to 1790* [Ann Arbor, MI: UMI Research Press, 1982], 24, 35; Roediger, *Wages of Whiteness*, esp. 97–100).

73. Barton, *Disappointment*, 63.

74. Nederveen Pieterse, *White on Black*, 25.

75. Barton, *Disappointment*, 58.

76. Raccoon preceded Mrs. Malaprop from Richard Brinsley Sheridan's *The Rivals* (in print, if not on the stage) by eight years.

77. Barton, *Disappointment*, 93.

78. Col. Robert Munford, *The Candidates, a Comedy in Three Acts*, in *A Collection of Plays and Poems, by the Late Col. Robert Munford, of Mecklenburg County, in the State of Virginia. Now First Published Together* (Petersburg, VA: William Prentis, 1798), 9–51, quote on 16.

79. *The Trial of Atticus, before Justice Beau, for a Rape* (Boston: Isaiah Thomas, 1771), 22.

80. Samuel Low, *The Politician Out-Witted, a Comedy, in Five Acts. By an American* (New York: W. Ross, 1788); Hugh Henry Brackenridge, *Modern Chivalry*, ed. Claude M. Newlin (New York: American Book Company, 1937), 2:114–18. Low acknowledged that his play was not staged, but nonetheless advertised the script for sale (*Daily Advertiser* [New York], May 8, 1789, 2; May 18, 1789, 4). For a discussion of *Modern Chivalry*, see David Waldstreicher, *In the Midst of Perpetual Fetes: The Making of American Nationalism, 1776–1820* (Chapel Hill: University of North Carolina Press, 1997), 209n51.

81. *Occurrences of the Times. Or, The Transactions of Four Days. [Viz.— From Friday the 16th, to Monday the 19th January, 1789. A Farce. In Two Acts* (Boston: 1789), 9. *Herald of Freedom and the Federal Advertiser* (Boston), February 27, 1789, 196.

82. Jeffrey H. Richards traces several additional early American closet dramas with Black characters, including the anonymously authored *The Downfall of Justice* (1777), St. Jean de Crèvecoeur's unpublished "Landscapes" (ca. 1777), and Royall Tyler's *May Day in Town* (1787) (*Drama, Theatre, and Identity in the American New Republic* [Cambridge: Cambridge University Press, 2005], 24–25, 71).

83. Catherine Burroughs, "The Stages of Closet Drama," in *The Oxford Handbook of The Georgian Theatre, 1737–1832*, ed. Julia Swindells and David Francis Taylor (Oxford: Oxford University Press, 2014), 442–56, quote on 446.

84. See Abigail Williams, *The Social Life of Books: Reading Together in the Eighteenth-Century Home* (New Haven, CT: Yale University Press, 2017), esp. 169–203. See also Norman Philbrick, introduction to *Trumpets Sounding: Propaganda Plays of the American Revolution*, ed. Norman Philbrick (New York: Benjamin Blom, 1972), 1–26, at 9.

85. William Paterson, *Glimpses of Colonial Society and the Life at Princeton College 1766–1773*, ed. W. Jay Mills (Philadelphia and London: Lippincott, 1903), 35; cf. Virga, *American Opera*, 19–21.

86. William MacPherson Horner, "Extracts from the Letters of John MacPherson, Jr., to William Patterson, 1766–1773," *Pennsylvania Magazine of History and Biography* 23, no. 1 (1899): 51–60, quote on 52.

87. Alexander Graydon, *Memoirs of a Life Chiefly Passed in Philadelphia within the Last Sixty Years* (Harrisburg, PA: 1811), 15; italics mine.

88. This relationship is key to my theorization of "scriptive blackface," which insists on written modes of blackface as both archive and repertoire. For related theorizations, see "literary blackface" (Waldstreicher, *In the Midst of Perpetual Fetes*, 209, 230, 327, 337); "performative texts" (Jones, *Captive Stage*, 14, 49); "discursive blackface" (Lane, *Blackface Cuba*, 20 and passim); "oral blackface" (Jenna M. Gibbs, *Performing the Temple of Liberty: Slavery, Theater, and Popular Culture in London and Philadelphia, 1760–1850* [Baltimore: Johns Hopkins University Press, 2014], 43–44).

89. Ngũgĩ wa Thiong'o, *Penpoints, Gunpoints, and Dreams: Towards a Critical Theory of the Arts and the State in Africa* (Oxford: Clarendon, 1998), 119. See also Roach, *Cities of the Dead*, 11–12; Ngũgĩ wa Thiong'o, *Homecoming: Essays on African and Caribbean Literature, Culture, and Politics* (New York: Lawrence Hill, 1972), 67–77; Pio Zirimu and Austin L. Bukenya, "Oracy as a Skill and as a Tool for African Development," in *The Arts and Civilization of Black and African Peoples*, ed. Joseph Okpaku, vol. 4, *Black Civilization and African Languages* (Lagos: Third Press International, 1986), 89–106; Mĩcere Gĩthae Mũgo, *African Orature and Human Rights* (Roma, Lesotho: Institute of Southern African Studies, National University of Lesotho, 1991); Ngũgĩ wa Thiong'o, *Globalectics*, 71–85.

90. Houston A. Baker Jr., *Modernism and the Harlem Renaissance* (Chicago: University of Chicago Press, 1987), 18, 21; italics in original.

91. Mĩcere Gĩthae Mũgo, "The Woman Artist in Africa Today: A Critical Commentary," *Africa Development / Afrique et Développement* 19, no. 1 (1994): 49–69, quote on 57.

92. Jeffrey H. Richards, introduction to *Early American Drama* (New York: Penguin, 1997), ix–xxxvii, quote on xii.

93. Nathans, *Slavery and Sentiment*, 48n98.

94. John Murdock, *The Politicians; or, A State of Things. A Dramatic Piece* (Philadelphia: 1798), 30.

95. Alan W. C. Green, "'Jim Crow,' 'Zip Coon': The Northern Origins of Negro Minstrelsy," *Massachusetts Review* 11, no. 2 (1970): 385–97, at 387. See also Jones, *Captive Stage*, 27.

96. *National Advocate* (New York), August 3, 1821, 2.

97. *National Advocate* (New York), August 3, 1821, 2.

98. Dillon, *New World Drama*, 228–29.

99. Samuel A. Hay, *African American Theatre: A Historical and Critical Analysis* (Cambridge: Cambridge University Press, 1994), 13. On Noah's campaign against Black voting as a crucial context in his parallel campaign against William Brown's African Grove and the African Theatre, see Hay, *African American Theatre*, 5–11; see also Shane White, *Stories of Freedom in Black New York* (Cambridge, MA: Harvard University Press, 2002); McAllister, *White People*.

100. Shane White and Graham White, *Stylin': African American Expressive Culture from Its Beginnings to the Zoot Suit* (Ithaca, NY: Cornell University Press, 1998), 108; see also Waldstreicher, *In the Midst of Perpetual Fetes*, 201–16; Jones, *Captive Stage*, 40.

101. I take the term "figural economies" from Judith Hamera, *Unfinished Business: Michael Jackson, Detroit, and the Figural Economy of American Deindustrialization* (Oxford: Oxford University Press, 2017), xii, 4–9.

102. Jones, *Captive Stage*, 23; see also Waldstreicher, *In the Midst of Perpetual Fetes*, 323–35.

103. Sol Smith, *Theatrical Management in the West and South for Thirty Years* (New York: Harper & Brothers, 1868), 12.

104. Leonard Richards, *"Gentlemen of Property and Standing": Anti-Abolition Mobs in Jacksonian America* (Oxford: Oxford University Press, 1970); Roediger, *Wages of Whiteness*, 105–11.

105. Roediger, *Wages of Whiteness*, 101–3.

106. For an elaboration of this point, see Jones, *Captive Stage*, 29–30. On pre-emancipation Black celebratory practices, see Shane White, "'It Was a Proud Day': African Americans, Festivals, and Parades in the North, 1781–1834," *Journal of American History* 81, no. 1 (1994): 13–50; Sterling Stuckey, *Going through the Storm: The Influence of African American Art in History* (Oxford: Oxford University Press, 1994), 53–80. By contrast to White's assertions of Pinkster's interracial mutuality and syncretism, Gabriel Furman's account of Pinkster—authored ca. 1824–1838, but published in 1874—makes clear that pre-emancipation rituals such as Pinkster remained structured by dominant racial practices: "The frolickings on that occasion were not confined to the negroes, but the younger portion of the white population also shared in them, and had frequent balls and dances, *not with the blacks, however, although at the same time*" (Gabriel Furman, *Antiquities of Long Island*, ed. Rank Moore [New York: J. W. Bouton, 1874], 269; italics mine). Instead, as Stuckey maintains, race structured and segregated social practices, even in ostensible enactments of interracial contact and exchange.

107. Baker, *Affairs of Party*, 225.

108. Philip Lapsansky, "Afro-Americana: Inventing Black Folks," *Annual Report of the Library Company of Philadelphia for the Year 1997* (Philadelphia: Library Company of Philadelphia, 1998), 29–46; Corey Capers, "Black Voices, White Print: Racial Practice, Print Publicity, and Order in the Early American Republic," in *Early African American Print Culture*, ed. Jordan Alexander Stein and Lara Langer Cohen (Philadelphia: University of Pennsylvania Press, 2012), 107–26; Jones, *Captive Stage*, 49; Christian DuComb, *Haunted City: Three Centuries of Racial Impersonation in Philadelphia* (Ann Arbor: University of Michigan Press, 2017), 101.

109. Grand Jubelum!!! Order 12f Annebersary ob Affricum Bobalition (1827), Brown University Digital Repository, Providence, RI. https://repository.library.brown.edu/studio/item/bdr:40145/.

110. Hortense Spillers, "Mama's Baby, Papa's Maybe: An American Grammar Book," *Diacritics* 17, no. 2 (1987): 64–81, quote on 66.

111. Jones, *Captive Stage*, 41.

112. Hartman, *Scenes of Subjection*, 6.

113. Phillip Lapsansky, "Graphic Discord: Abolitionist and Antiabolitionist Images," in *The Abolitionist Sisterhood: Women's Political Culture in Antebellum America*, ed. Jean Fagin Yellin and John C. Van Horne (Ithaca, NY:

Cornell University Press, 1994), 216; cf. Joshua Sharp, *Country Almanack, for 1820* (Charleston, SC: 1819), 23.

114. *National Advocate*, August 27, 1823, 2.

115. *National Advocate*, August 27, 1823, 2. In his parodic citation of *Hamlet* ("making night hideous"), Noah further mocked Brown's theater for its frequent stagings of Shakespeare.

116. Toll, *Blacking Up*, 27.

117. McAllister, *White People*, 160; Robert Hornback, "Black Shakespeareans vs. Minstrel Burlesques: 'Proper' English, Racist Blackface Dialect, and the Contest for Representing 'Blackness,' 1821–1844," *Shakespeare Studies* 38 (2010): 125–60; Robert Michael Lewis, "Speaking Black, 1824: Charles Mathews's *Trip to America* Revisited," *Nineteenth Century Theatre and Film* 43, no. 1 (2016): 43–66.

118. Hornback, "Black Shakespeareans," 135; Lewis, "Speaking Black," 48.

119. Hans Nathan, *Dan Emmett and the Rise of Early Negro Minstrelsy* (Norman: University of Oklahoma Press, 1962), 48–49.

120. On reprintings of Noah's accounts of the African Theatre, see *Miscellanies Selected from the Public Journals* (Boston: J. T. Buckingham, 1822), 1:243–46. On Faux, see Shane White, *Stories of Freedom*, 200–201, and Tracy C. Davis, "*Trip to America* (1824)," in *The Broadview Anthology of Nineteenth-Century British Performance*, 163–72, at 163n1.

121. W[illiam]. Faux, *Memorable Days in America: Being a Journal of a Tour to the United States* (London: W. Simpkin and R. Marshall, 1823), 9.

122. "Matthews in America," *Blackwood's Edinburgh Magazine* 15, no. 87 (April 1824): 424–29, at 424.

123. See, for instance, Tracy C. Davis, "Acting Black, 1824: Charles Mathews's *Trip to America*," *Theatre Journal* 63, no. 2 (2011): 163–89, at 183–84; Gibbs, *Performing the Temple of Liberty*.

124. George Cruikshank, *Lowest "Life in London"—Tom, Jerry and Logic, among the Unsophisticated Sons and Daughters of Nature, at "All Max" in the East* (London: Sherwood, Neely & Jones, May 1, 1821); British Museum 1864,0611.398, https://www.britishmuseum.org/collection/object/P_1864–0611–398. The lithograph was used as an illustration to Pierce Egan, *Life in London; or, the Day and Night Scenes of Jerry Hawthorn, Esq., and His Elegant Friend Corinthian Tom, Accompanied by Bob Logic, the Oxonian, in Their Rambles and Sprees through the Metropolis* (London: Sherwood, Jones, 1823), 286.

125. Peter R. Reed, *Rogue Performances: Staging the Underclasses in Early American Theatre Culture* (Basingstoke, UK: Palgrave Macmillan, 2009), 127.

126. Jan Marsh, ed., *Black Victorians: Black People in British Art, 1800–1900* (London: Lund Humphries, 2005), 110; Gibbs, *Performing the Temple of Liberty*, 124.

127. Nancy Reynolds Davison, "E. W. Clay: American Political Caricaturist of the Jacksonian Era" (PhD diss., University of Michigan, 1980), 85; Nyong'o, *Amalgamation Waltz*, 79.

128. On Clay's *Life in Philadelphia* as theatrical, see Davison, "E. W. Clay," 90; Nyong'o, *Amalgamation Waltz*, 77; Gibbs, *Performing the Temple of Liberty*, 134.

129. Jones, *Captive Stage*, 46.

130. "Life in Philadelphia," in *The New Comic Annual for 1831*, ed. Thomas Hood, (London: Hurst, Chance, 1830), 147–61. See also the several plates republished in *Tregear's Black Jokes, Being a Series of Laughable Caricatures on the March of Manners amongst the Blacks. Twenty Plates* (London: G. S. Tregear, 1834).

131. DuComb, *Haunted City*, 61.

132. As Shane White notes, in slaveholding New York, "[t]ypically, slaves lived in cellars or cellar kitchens located partially underground and had separate access to the street" (*Somewhat More Independent: The End of Slavery in New York City, 1770–1810* [Athens: University of Georgia Press, 1991], 92).

133. "Life in Philadelphia," 150.

134. DuComb, *Haunted City*, 65.

135. On the role of circus clowns in the popularization of blackface, see Russel Sanjek, *American Popular Music Business: The First Four Hundred Years*, vol. 2, *From 1790 to 1909* (New York: Oxford University Press, 1988), 163, 166–70.

136. Playbill, December 25, 1835, Davis-Kendall Collections, Hoblitzelle Theatre Arts Library, University of Texas: Programs 1830s, New York Franklin Theatre.

137. *Sambo's 'Dress to He' Bred'ren, As Sung with the Most Enormous Applause, at Mr. Davis' Musical Parties, on Friday Evenings, Broadway House, by Mr. Brower, the Celebrated Comic Singer . . . Arranged . . . by James B. Taylor* (New York: 1833); reprinted in Nicholas Tawa, ed., *American Solo Songs through 1865* (Boston: G. K. Hall, 1989), 109–11.

138. S. Foster Damon, *Series of Old American Songs. Reproduced in Facsimile from Original or Early Editions in the Harris Collection of American Poetry and Plays, Brown University* (Providence, RI: Brown University Library, 1936), no. 17.

139. The scenario also echoes Charles Mathews's parody of "a *black* Methodist" (Mathews, *Memoirs*, 3:390; italics in the original).

140. The references to Washington and Lafayette were also intertheatrical citations of Micah Hawkins's 1824 blackface song, "Massa Georgee Washington and General Lafayette."

Chapter 2

An earlier version of this chapter first appeared in *Theatre Journal* 72, no. 4 (December 2020). Published with permission by Johns Hopkins University Press.

1. J. Kennard Jr., "Who Are Our National Poets? By Our 'Salt-Fish Dinner' Correspondent," *Knickerbocker; or, New York Monthly Magazine* 26, no. 4 (October 1845): 331–41, quote on 331. On "impossible purities," see Jennifer DeVere Brody, *Impossible Purities: Blackness, Femininity, and Victorian Culture* (Durham, NC: Duke University Press, 1998).

2. Kennard, "Who Are Our National Poets?," 333. See also Lott, *Love and Theft*, 57–60, 99; Meer, *Uncle Tom Mania*, 27–28.

3. Kennard, "Who Are Our National Poets?," 334.

4. See especially Roediger, *Wages of Whiteness*, 95–131; Hartman, *Scenes of Subjection*, 17–48; Nyong'o, *Amalgamation Waltz*, 103–34; Jones, *Captive Stage*, 50–74.

5. C. Vann Woodward, *The Strange Career of Jim Crow* (1955; Oxford: Oxford University Press, 2002), 13.

6. Woodward, *Strange Career*, 13.

7. Catherine M. Cole, "American Ghetto Parties and Ghanaian Concert Parties: A Transnational Perspective on Blackface," in *Burnt Cork: Traditions and Legacies of Blackface Minstrelsy*, ed. Stephen Johnson (Amherst: University of Massachusetts Press, 2012), 223–57, quote on 224.

8. Lhamon, *Raising Cain*; Lhamon, *Jump Jim Crow*; Waters, *Racism on the Victorian Stage*, 89–129; Pickering, *Blackface Minstrelsy in Britain*.

9. For the best analysis of blackface in the circum–North Atlantic to date, see Nowatzki, *Representing African Americans*, 60–79.

10. Lowe, *Intimacies of Four Continents*, 3; see also Uday Singh Mehta, *Liberalism and Empire: A Study in Nineteenth-Century British Liberal Thought* (Chicago: University of Chicago Press, 1999); Mills, "Racial Liberalism."

11. Here, I offer a small yet significant revision to Chinua Thelwell's analysis of the transnational traffics of early blackface minstrelsy in *Exporting Jim Crow* (see Thelwell, *Exporting Jim Crow*, 28–31).

12. Lhamon, *Jump Jim Crow*, 33, 36, 412n56; cf. *Louisville (KY) Public Advertiser*, May 21, 1830. Rice reprised the song during his return to Louisville in fall 1830 (Cockrell, *Demons of Disorder*, 64; cf. *Louisville (KY) Public Advertiser*, September 22, 1830).

13. Damon, *Series of Old American Songs*, no. 15. On adaptations and variations, see Lhamon, *Jump Jim Crow*.

14. Cockrell, *Demons of Disorder*, 65; James H. Dorman, "The Strange Career of Jim Crow Rice (with Apologies to Professor Woodward)," *Journal of Social History* 3, no. 2 (1969–70): 109–22, at 111; Nelle Smither, "A History of the English Language Theatre in New Orleans, 1806–1842," *Louisiana Historical Quarterly* 28, no. 1 (1945): 84–276, at 197–98, 202, 267.

15. *New York Clipper*, February 19, 1910, 3; Playbill, February 4, 1837, Davis-Kendall Collections, Hoblitzelle Theatre Arts Library, University of Texas, Programs 1830s, New York Franklin Theatre.

16. Lhamon, *Raising Cain*, 48–49.

17. Lhamon, *Jump Jim Crow*, 3.

18. Robert P. Nevin, "Stephen C. Foster and Negro Minstrels," *Atlantic Monthly* (November 1867): 608–16, quote on 608.

19. Nevin, "Stephen C. Foster," 609–10. See also Francis Courtney Wemyss, *Twenty-Six Years of the Life of an Actor and Manager* (New York: Burgess, Stringer, 1847), 1:206.

20. Noah Miller Ludlow, *Dramatic Life as I Found It* (St. Louis: G. I. Jones, 1880), 392. See also "The Origin of Jim Crow," *Public Ledger*, May 27, 1841, 4.

21. Lhamon, *Raising Cain*, 153; Lott, *Love and Theft*, 51.

22. Joseph Jefferson, *The Autobiography of Joseph Jefferson* (New York: Century, 1889), 7–8.

23. Jefferson, *Autobiography of Joseph Jefferson*, 7.

24. Rebecca Schneider, "Hello Dolly Well Hello Dolly: The Double and Its Theatre," in *Psychoanalysis and Performance*, ed. Patrick Campbell and Adrian Kear (London: Routledge, 2001), 94–114, quote on 96.

25. Schneider, "Hello Dolly Well Hello Dolly," 96.

26. Cockrell, *Demons of Disorder*, 76; Lhamon, *Jump Jim Crow*, 34–35.

27. Dibdin, *Professional Life of Mr. Dibdin*, 1:70. On Moody's theatrical activity in Jamaica, see Errol Hill, *The Jamaican Stage, 1655–1900: Profile of a Colonial Theatre* (Amherst: University of Massachusetts Press, 1992), 21–23, 76–77.

28. Kathleen Wilson, "Introduction: Three Theses on Performance and History," *Eighteenth-Century Studies* 48, no. 4 (2015): 375–90, quote on 382.

29. William Dunlap, *A History of the American Theatre* (New York: J. & J. Harper, 1832), 31. On Hallam's theatrical activity in Jamaica, including productions of *The Padlock*, see Hill, *Jamaican Stage*, 23–25, 28–30, 78–79.

30. Wilson, *Strolling Players of Empire*, 274.

31. See Roach's axiom, "Memory is a process that depends crucially on forgetting" (*Cities of the Dead*, 2).

32. Cockrell, *Demons of Disorder*, 65–66; Lhamon, *Jump Jim Crow*, 61–70; Pickering, *Blackface Minstrelsy in Britain*, 7.

33. *The Origin of Jim Crow: Being an Authentic Account of the Life and Adventures of That Comic American Nigger* (London: J. Hodson, 1837), text held at Watkinson Library, Trinity College, Hartford, Connecticut. See also "Jump Bob Peel," *Figaro in London*, December 31, 1836, 215; the following texts reprinted in Lhamon, *Jump Jim Crow*: "The Life of Jim Crow," 386–98, and "A Faithful Account of the Life of Jim Crow the American Negro Poet," 399–404.

34. "Jim Crowism," *New York Spirit of the Times*, February 4, 1837, 402.

35. Pickering, *Blackface Minstrelsy in Britain*, 11–12; Meer, *Uncle Tom Mania*, 150–51; Waters, *Racism on the Victorian Stage*, 98–113.

36. Meer, *Uncle Tom Mania*, 150.

37. William Leman Rede, *Flight to America* (1836; British Library Add MS 42939, ff. 444–79), reprinted in Lhamon, *Jump Jim Crow*, 246.

38. Rede, *Flight to America*, 247.

39. Lhamon, *Jump Jim Crow*, 431n1.

40. White, "'It Was a Proud Day,'" 44; Waters, *Racism on the Victorian Stage*, 106.

41. On *Obi*, see Waters, *Racism on the Victorian Stage*, 26–28; Frances R. Botkin, *Thieving Three-Fingered Jack: Transatlantic Tales of a Jamaican Outlaw, 1780–2015* (New Brunswick, NJ: Rutgers University Press, 2017), 68–88.

42. The act stipulated that all formerly enslaved persons complete a six-year apprenticeship period initially scheduled to end on August 1, 1840, but the apprenticeship was amended to a four-year term that concluded with the manumission of all enslaved persons in the British Empire on August 1, 1838.

43. Reprinted in the *Mississippi Free Trader and Natchez Gazette*, April 8, 1836, 141.

44. Rice quoted (approximately) in the *Sun* (Baltimore), November 9, 1837, 2. See also "The Theatre," *Colored American*, December 9, 1837, 2–3; cf. Jones, *Captive Stage*, 67–68, 186n64.

45. Quoted in the *Sun* (Baltimore), November 9, 1837, 2.

46. Lhamon, *Jump Jim Crow*, 65.

47. William Leman Rede, *The Foreign Prince: A Burletta in One Act*; reprinted in Lhamon, *Jump Jim* Crow, 318–20.

48. Rede, *Foreign Prince*, 315. On discourses of racial amalgamation, see Nyong'o, *Amalgamation Waltz*.

49. Rede, *Foreign Prince*, 320.

50. Thomas Landseer, *Monkey-ana, or Men in Miniature* (London: Moon, Boys & Graves, 1827); see also Hugh Honour, *The Image of the Black in Western Art*, vol. 4, part 2 (Cambridge, MA: Harvard University Press, 1989), 58.

51. *Canadian Correspondent* (Toronto), July 13, 1836, quoted in Gerald Lenton-Young, "Variety Theatre," in *Early Stages: Theatre in Ontario, 1800–1914*, ed. Ann Saddlemyer (Toronto: University of Toronto Press, 1990), 176.

52. Quoted in Stephen Johnson, "'Shield Us from This Base Ridicule': The Petitions to Censor Blackface Circus Clowns, Toronto, 1840–43," in *Canadian Performance Histories and Historiographies*, ed. Heather Davis-Fisch (Toronto: Playwrights Canada Press, 2017), 254–79, quote on 256. The 1840 protest responded to the arrival of the "National Circus, from the City of New York," which advertised in the *British Colonist*, July 15, 1840, 3.

53. Quoted in Johnson, "'Shield Us from This Base Ridicule,'" 258.

54. Quoted in Johnson, "'Shield Us from This Base Ridicule,'" 259. The 1841 circus advertised the performances of "Mr. S. W. Seely, the greatest delineator of Ethiopian character" (*British Colonist* [Toronto], October 13, 1841, 3).

55. Hosea Easton, *To Heal the Scourge of Prejudice: The Life and Writings of Hosea Easton*, ed. George R. Price and James Brewer Stewart (Amherst: University of Massachusetts Press, 1999), 106–7; cf. Nyong'o, *Amalgamation Waltz*, 19–22. See also Martin Delany's account of an instance in Marseilles, Ohio, on May 28, 1848, at which he gave an abolitionist speech that an antiabolitionist white mob proclaimed "a darkey burlesque" before they threatened Delany and his associates: "Burn them alive!—kill the niggers!—they shall never leave this place!" (Martin Delany, "Sandusky, June 1st, 1848," *North Star* (Rochester, NY), July 14, 1848, 3).

56. See Jones, *Captive Stage*, 50–74.

57. Despite these protests, theaters in Ontario and Quebec continued to serve as regular stops on the North American blackface minstrel circuit throughout the nineteenth century, and amateur blackface troupes were ubiquitous from Ontario to Quebec to Newfoundland into the twentieth century. See Franklin Graham, *Histrionic Montreal: Annals of the Montreal Stage* (Montreal: John Lovell and Son, 1902); Stephen Johnson, "Uncle Tom and the Minstrels: Seeing Black and White on Stage in Canada West prior to the American Civil War," in *(Post)Colonial Stages: Critical & Creative Views on Drama, Theatre & Performance*, ed. Helen Gilbert (London: Dangaroo Press, 1999), 55–63; Lorraine Le Camp, "Racial Considerations of Minstrel Shows and Related Images in Canada" (PhD diss., University of Toronto, 2005); Joan Nicks and Jeannette Sloniowski, "Entertaining Niagara Falls, Ontario: Minstrel Shows, Theatres, and Popular Pleasures," in *Covering Niagara: Studies*

in Local Popular Culture, ed. Joan Nicks and Barry Keith Grant (Waterloo, ON: Wilfred Laurier University Press, 2010), 285–310; Colleen Quigley and Melissa Templeton, "Performing Blackface on the Newfoundland Stage: The Rossleys, Transnational Connections, and Early Twentieth Century Theatre in St. John's," *Theatre Research in Canada / Recherches théâtrales au Canada* 41, no. 1 (2020): 64–87.

58. *Colonial Times* (Hobart, Tasmania), January 9, 1838, 2; *True Colonist Van Diemen's Land Political Despatch* (Hobart, Tasmania), January 12, 1838, 4.

59. *Australian* (Sydney), April 9, 1839, 3.

60. Benjamin Miller, "'Come Be Off with You': White Spatial Control in the Representation of Aboriginality in Early Australian Drama," *Journal of Commonwealth Literature* 52, no. 2 (2015): 365–81.

61. David Burn, *The Bushrangers*, ed. W. and J. E. Heiner (Richmond, Australia: Heinemann Educational Australia, 1971), vii.

62. Burn, *The Bushrangers*, 30. Future quotations from the same.

63. Henry Melville, *The Bushrangers; or, Norwood Vale*, in *Australian Plays for the Colonial Stage, 1834–1899*, ed. Richard Fotheringham (St. Lucia, Australia: University of Queensland Press, 2006), 3–38, quote on 19.

64. *Sydney Herald*, March 20, 1837, 1.

65. "The Life in 'Summonsing' Courts," *Sydney Herald*, November 6, 1837, 5.

66. *Englishman* (Kolkata), March 3, 1838, 5.

67. Partha Chatterjee, *The Black Hole of Empire: History of a Global Practice of Power* (Princeton, NJ: Princeton University Press, 2012), 6–7.

68. *Englishman* (Kolkata), March 3, 1838, 421.

69. *Bengal Hurkaru* (Kolkata), March 29, 1838, 3, and April 23, 1838, 3. A contemporaneous court case in Kolkata involved a defendant who used the pseudonym "Jim Crow"; see "Coolie Serang v. J. A. Foster, W. H. Foster, and Jim Crow," *Englishman* (Kolkata), July 31, 1838, 1454.

70. Cockrell, *Demons of Disorder*, 17; *Baltimore Gazette and Daily Advertiser*: May 17, 1833, 2, and October 29, 1832, 3.

71. *Englishman* (Kolkata), April 26, 1838, 795.

72. Hill, *Jamaican Stage*, 90; cf. *Morning Journal* (Kingston, Jamaica), October 15, 1840, cited in Errol Hill Papers (1960–2002), Rauner Special Collections Library, Dartmouth College, ML-77, box 30, folder 5, p. 3. On the constitution of Kingston's theater audiences in the 1840s, see Hill, *Jamaican Stage*, 87. Hill notes that *The Padlock* was the most popular farce on the eighteenth-century Jamaican stage (*Jamaican Stage*, 78–79); therefore, Jim Crow surrogated Mungo in Kingston as he did in Britain and the United States. Other early blackface figures also circulated in colonial Jamaica prior to the arrival of "Jim Crow" through scriptive blackface printed in periodicals such as *A West India Scene* (1824) and *Jamaica: A Comedy* (1824–1825); see Hill, *Jamaican Stage*, 163–67 (and cf. *Jamaican Journal and Kingston Chronicle*, December 4, 11, and 18, 1824, and January 8, 1825).

73. T. P. Taylor, *Jim Crow; or, The Creole Ball*, in *Pattie's Modern Stage: A Collection of the Most Approved and Popular Dramas*, Vol. 3 (London: J. Pattie, 1839); "English Theatricals," *New York Spirit of the Times*, May 6, 1837, 89.

74. Taylor, *Jim Crow*, 15–16.

75. Hill, *Jamaican Stage*, 90; cf. *Morning Journal* (Kingston, Jamaica), January 30, June 4, and December 17 and 24, 1841, cited in Errol Hill Papers, ML-77, box 30, folder 5, pp. 6, 7b, 9.

76. Hill, *Jamaican Stage*, 90; cf. *Morning Journal* (Kingston, Jamaica), October 14, 22, and 29, and November 5, 1842, cited in Errol Hill Papers, ML-77, box 30, folder 5, pp. 15–16. The named title interpolates Rice's *The Virginia Mummy* with its source text, William Bayle Bernard's *The Mummy; or, The Liquor of Life* (1833), suggesting familiarity with both pieces; see Lhamon, *Jump Jim Crow*, 46–52, 159–77.

77. *De Verzamelaar* (Cape Town), April 19, 1842, 1.

78. *De Natalier* (eThekwini, South Africa), January 16, 1846, 2; February 6, 1846, 4; August 11, 1846, 1.

79. *De Natalier* (eThekwini, South Africa), January 16, 1846, 2.

80. Jan Bouws, "Ook Minstrel Skyn die Ewige Lewe te Hê," *Die Burger* (Cape Town), November 2, 1966, 2, trans. Gerald Stone in Denis-Constant Martin, *Coon Carnival: New Year in Cape Town, Past and Present* (Cape Town: David Philip, 1999), 80.

81. Charles Étienne Boniface, "La Mort de Latanier" [November 1846], in *Bluettes*, ed. Gabriel Stephanus Nienaber (Durban, South Africa: University of Natal, 1963), 46.

82. *Sam Sly's African Journal* (Cape Town), November 9, 1848, 1.

83. Playbill, Drury-Lane Theatre, Constitution Hill, Cape Town, August 21, 1852, in National Library of South Africa, Cape Town campus, file g.16.c.100.002.

84. Patrick Bernard Anthony O'Neill, "A History of Theatrical Activity in Toronto, Canada—from Its Beginnings to 1858" (PhD diss., Louisiana State University, 1973), 468.

85. *Graham's Town Journal* (Makhanda, South Africa), November 1, 1838, 4; November 8, 1838, 4.

86. Reprinted in *Sam Sly's African Journal* (Cape Town), August 20, 1846, 4. Future quotations from the same.

87. On the Kat River Settlement, see Robert Ross, *The Borders of Race in Colonial South Africa: The Kat River Settlement, 1829–1856* (Cambridge: Cambridge University Press, 2014).

88. In 1828, the Khoekhoe of the Kat River Settlement had attained greater freedom relative to other colonial subjects under Ordinance 50, which proscribed Khoekhoe enslavement and permitted Khoekhoe landownership so long as as it did not displace white colonists (Ross, *Borders of Race*, 30–34). Many white colonists resented the policy and worked to delimit Khoekhoe freedom through reactionary legislation such as the 1834 Vagrancy Ordinance (Ross, *Borders of Race*, 80–90).

89. On the "circum-Atlantic fold," see Nyong'o, *Amalgamation Waltz*, 18–22.

90. Damian Shaw, "Two 'Hottentots,' Some Scots and a West Indian Slave: The Origins of *Kaatje Kekkelbek*," *English Studies in Africa* 52, no. 2 (2009): 4–17. See also Marisa Keuris, "The Representation of Khoisan Characters in Early Dutch-Afrikaans Dramas in South Africa," in *African Theatre*

9: *Histories, 1850–1950*, ed. Yvette Hutchison (Suffolk, UK: James Currey, 2010), 107–21; Elizabeth Elbourne, "Sara Baartman and Andries Stoffels: Violence, Law and the Politics of Spectacle in London and the Eastern Cape, 1809–1836," *Canadian Journal of African Studies* 45, no. 3 (2011): 524–64; P. R. Anderson, "'Never Luff to Meddle mit Politics, Sir': Errant Satire and Historical Gainsaying in A. G. Bain's 'Kaatje Kekklebek, or, Life among the Hottentots,'" *Journal of Southern African Studies* 38, no. 1 (2012): 217–32; Ross, *Borders of Race*, 139–43.

91. *Origin of Jim Crow*, 34–35. This version of "Jump Jim Crow" from *The Origin of Jim Crow* circulated widely enough that Henry Reynolds's 1928 history of British blackface reproduced it in full, along with several other songs and items from the chapbook, including "The Nigger and the Planter" (*Minstrel Memories*, 78–82, 52).

92. Richards, *"Gentlemen of Property and Standing,"* 61.

93. George Cruikshank, *All among the Hottentots Capering Ashore!! The Blessings of Emigration to the Cape of Good Hope; i.e., to Be Half Roasted by the Sun* (London: Thomas Tegg, 1819), Library of Congress Prints and Photographs, https://www.loc.gov/pictures/item/2006689007/.

94. Charles Dibdin the younger, "The Sailor-Boy Capering Ashore," in *The Universal Songster: Or, Museum of Mirth* (London: Jones, 1834), 3:401.

95. See V. A. February, *Mind Your Colour: The "Coloured" Stereotype in South Africa* (London: Kegan Paul, 1981), 23–28; Jill Fletcher, *The Story of South African Theatre, A Guide to Its History from 1780–1930* (Cape Town: Vlaeberg, 1994), 50–52, 64–66. Marisa Keuris cites Boniface's Khoekhoe character Grietje Drilboutin from *De Temperantisten* as a direct antecedent of "Kaatje" ("Representation of Khoisan Characters," 114).

96. Suggestive of the transoceanic scope of colonial articulations of blackface minstrelsy, a commemorative printing of *Kaatje Kekkelbek* remained in the Aotearoa New Zealand collection of Sir George Grey, who brought it with him when he left his post as colonial governor of the Cape Colony of southern Africa to become the governor (and later premier) of colonial New Zealand. See *Kaatje Kekklebek; or, Life among the Hottentots* (Cape Town: G. J. Pike, ca. 1846), Sir George Grey (Auckland) Collection, National Library of South Africa, MSB 223.9.2.

97. Nigel Worden and Clifton Crais, eds., *Breaking the Chains: Slavery and Its Legacy in the Nineteenth-Century Cape Colony* (Johannesburg: Wits University Press, 1994), cover image; Nigel Worden, Ruth Versfeld, Dorothy Dyer, and Claudia Bickford-Smith, *The Chains That Bind Us: A History of Slavery at the Cape* (Cape Town: Juta, 1996), cover image; "Emancipation Day," in Nigel Worden, Elizabeth Van Heningen, and Vivian Bickford-Smith, *Cape Town: The Making of a City* (Cape Town: David Philip, 1998), 106.

98. "Jim Along Josey," in Damon, *Series of Old American Songs*, no. 24.

99. W. J. Lawrence, "America in England: A Theatrical Retrospect," *Gentleman's Magazine* 270 (1891): 82–100, at 89. Harper also performed in Britain in 1838 and 1843, and in Cork, Ireland, in 1841 (Waters, *Racism on the Victorian Stage*, 212n81; Pickering, *Blackface Minstrelsy in Britain*, 12), and it is likely that he performed "Jim Along Josey" and *The Free Nigger of New York* during these tours as well. There is also evidence that "Jim Along Josey"

traveled to the British colonies, as Mr. Jordan performed the song and dance at the Royal Victoria Theatre in Kingston, Jamaica, on October 19, 1842 (*Morning Journal*, October 19, 1842, cited in Errol Hill Papers, ML-77, box 30, folder 5, p. 15).

100. See Harry J. Elam Jr., "The Device of Race: An Introduction," in *African American Performance and Theater History: A Critical Reader*, ed. Harry J. Elam Jr. and David Krasner (Oxford: Oxford University Press, 2001), 3–16.

Chapter 3

1. "The Hutchinson Singers," *Liberator* (Boston), December 30, 1842, 208.

2. Brian Roberts, *Blackface Nation: Race, Reform, and Identity in American Popular Music, 1812–1925* (Chicago: University of Chicago Press, 2017), 136.

3. *Albany (NY) Evening Journal*, August 13, 1842, 2; Dale Cockrell, *Excelsior: Journals of the Hutchinson Family Singers, 1842–1846* (Stuyvesant, NY: Pendragon Press, 1989), 81, 184, 202, 284, 301.

4. John Wallace Hutchinson, *Story of the Hutchinsons*, (Boston: Lee and Shepard, 1896), 1:35.

5. *Herald of Freedom* (Champlain, NY), January 13, 1843, 186; Hutchinson, *Story of the Hutchinsons*, 73.

6. Rogers quoted in Hutchinson, *Story of the Hutchinsons*, 77; cf. Roberts, *Blackface Nation*, 217.

7. Hutchinson, *Story of the Hutchinsons*, 70.

8. *New York Herald*, February 6, 1843, 3.

9. On Emmett's earlier usage of "Ethiopian Minstrel," see *New York Herald*, December 18, 1842, 3; on the prehistory of the Virginia Minstrels, see Nathan, *Dan Emmett*, 113–18.

10. Roberts, *Blackface Nation*, 5.

11. Pickering, *Blackface Minstrelsy in Britain*, 1 and passim.

12. Playbill, Virginia Minstrels, Brinley Hall, Worcester, MA, March 20, 21, and 22, 1843, American minstrel show collection, 1823–1947, MS Thr 556 (607), Virginia Minstrels, Playbills, 1843–1870, Harvard Theatre Collection, https://iiif.lib.harvard.edu/manifests/view/drs:424935963$5i.

13. Nathan, *Dan Emmett*, 138; "The Origin of Minstrelsy: Dan Emmett's History of the Wanderings of the First Troupe," *New York Clipper*, May 15, 1877, 5.

14. *Era* (London), July 9, 1843, 4; *Era* (London), August 20, 1843, 6.

15. *New York Herald*, February 25, 1843, 2; *New York Herald*, February 27, 1843, 3; Nathan, *Dan Emmett*, 120–21.

16. This partial list draws from Nathan, *Dan Emmett*, 147, and the *Sun* (New York), April 20, 1902, 3.

17. "The Hutchinson Family," *Turner's Comic Almanac for 1848* (Philadelphia and New York: Turner & Fisher, 1847), 32. Future quotations from the same.

18. Roberts, *Blackface Nation*, 230–34; Scott Gac, *Singing for Freedom: The Hutchinson Family Singers and the Nineteenth-Century Culture of Reform* (New Haven, CT: Yale University Press, 2008), 213–15.

19. Toll, *Blacking Up*, 197; Eileen Southern, *The Music of Black Americans: A History*, 3rd ed. (New York: W. W. Norton, 1997), 106–7.

20. See, for instance, "The Band of Niggers! From 'Ole Virginny State,'" in *The Georgia Melodies. As Sung by the Georgia Champions* (Boston: Henry Prentiss, 1844), https://levysheetmusic.mse.jhu.edu/collection/020/120.

21. Playbill, Christy's Minstrels, July 15, 1859, St. James's Hall, Piccadilly, London; Playbill, Christy's Minstrels, January 17, 1859, Athenaeum, Cork, Ireland; reprinted in Reynolds, *Minstrel Memories*, 251–52.

22. *Cape Monitor* (Cape Town), August 19, 1862, 2; *Bombay Gazette*, November 4, 1863; *Ballarat Star* (Ballarat, Australia), February 28, 1865, 2; *Maitland Mercury and Hunter River General Advertiser* (Maitland, Australia), April 28, 1866, 2.

23. Alec Bagot, *Coppin the Great: Father of the Australian Theatre* (Melbourne, Australia: Melbourne University Press, 1965), 55.

24. *Australian* (Sydney), October 24, 1843, 2.

25. *Sydney Morning Herald*, June 8, 1844, 1.

26. *Sydney Morning Herald*, June 14, 1844, 4.

27. Saxton, *Rise and Fall*, 167; Nathan, *Dan Emmett*, 143–46.

28. A. B. C. [pseud.], *Life in Sydney; or, The Ran Dan Club*, in *Australian Plays for the Colonial Stage, 1834–1899*, ed. Richard Fotheringham (St. Lucia, Australia: University of Queensland Press, 2006), 39–94, at 61.

29. *Sam Sly's African Journal* (Cape Town), September 10, 1846, 2.

30. *Sam Sly's African Journal* (Cape Town), September 14, 1848, 1.

31. *Sam Sly's African Journal* (Cape Town), September 21, 1848, 4.

32. *Sam Sly's African Journal* (Cape Town), September 21, 1848, 1; October 5, 1848, 1; December 21, 1848, 1; January 11, 1849, 3. *Cape Town Mail*, September 30, 1848, 1; January 6, 1849, 4.

33. Pickering, *Blackface Minstrelsy in Britain*, 18–20.

34. "The Ethiopian Serenaders," *Illustrated London News*, January 24, 1846, 61.

35. "Ethiopian Serenaders," 61.

36. Thomas Carlyle, "Occasional Discourse on the Nigger Question," in *Thomas Carlyle, the Nigger Question, and John Stuart Mill, the Negro Question*, ed. Eugene R. August (New York: Appleton-Century-Crofts, 1971), 1–37, quote on 3.

37. On "wage slavery" and "white slavery," see Pickering, *Blackface Minstrelsy in Britain*, 82; Roediger, *Wages of Whiteness*, 65–92, and passim; Jones, *Captive Stage*, 57–61.

38. John Stuart Mill, "The Negro Question," in August, *Thomas Carlyle, the Nigger Question*, 38–50, at 41.

39. Nowatzki, *Representing African Americans*, 96–97.

40. "Statement of Another Ethiopian Serenader," in Henry Mayhew, *London Labour and the London Poor* (London: Griffin, Bohn, and Company, 1861), 3:191.

41. "Glut of Ethiopians," *Punch, or The London Charivari* 12 (1847): 122; "Grand Combination of Talent," *Punch, or The London Charivari* 12 (1847): 153.

42. "Colonial Annuals," *Punch, or The London Charivari* 13 (1847): 180.

43. *Illustrated London News*, May 1, 1847, 287.

44. *Cape Town Mail*, January 6, 1849, 4; *Sam Sly's African Journal* (Cape Town), January 11, 1849, 3.

45. *Graham's Town Journal* (Makhanda, South Africa), February 16, 1850, 1.

46. Playbill, Drury-Lane Theatre, Constitution Hill, Cape Town, August 21, 1852, in National Library of South Africa, Cape Town campus, file g.16.c.100.002.

47. *Graham's Town Journal* (Makhanda, South Africa), August 15, 1857; *Cape Frontier Times* (Makhanda, South Africa), December 29, 1857, 1.

48. *Cape Town Mail*, January 13, 1858.

49. *Cape Argus* (Cape Town), September 6, 1860, 4; September 18, 1860, 2. *Cape Monitor* (Cape Town), September 19, 1860, 2; October 3, 1860, 2.

50. *Cape Argus* (Cape Town), March 9, 1861, 1.

51. Lily Wolpowitz, ed., *The Diaries of John Rose of Cape Town, 1848–1873* (Cape Town: Friends of the South African Library, 1990), 92. Rose continued his amateur blackface minstrelsy throughout his life, including performing in a minstrel show at the Cape Town Carnival and Fête celebrating the marriage of Prince Albert and Princess Alexandra (*Supplement to the Cape Argus* [Cape Town], May 21, 1863, 2). Rose also regularly attended professional touring productions of the Christy's Minstrels featuring Joe Brown and Washington Norton (1862) and the Harvey-Dougherty-Leslie-Braham Minstrels (1872–1874), as well as several amateur blackface minstrel concerts by the Darkie Minstrels and the Cape Town Christy Minstrels in Cape Town (Wolpowitz, *Diaries of John Rose*, 103, 114, 117, 135, 170–71).

52. *Natal Star* (eThekwini, South Africa), January 12, 1858, 2.

53. George S. Jackson, *Music in Durban: An Account of Musical Activities in Durban from 1850 to the Early Years of the Present Century* (Johannesburg: Witwatersrand University Press, 1970), 18–19.

54. *Falmouth Post* (Falmouth, Jamaica), March 24, 1846, cited in Errol Hill Papers, ML-77, box 30, folder 5, p. 25b.

55. *Cornwall Chronicle* (Launceston, Tasmania), May 2, 1846, 340.

56. *Sydney Morning Herald*, September 20, 1847, 2.

57. *Colonial Times* (Hobart, Tasmania), August 4, 1848, 1.

58. *Port Phillip Gazette and Settler's Journal* (Melbourne), July 24, 1849, 3.

59. *Sydney Morning Herald*, March 26, 1850, 1.

60. *Bell's Life in Sydney and Sporting Reporter*, April 6, 1850, 3.

61. *Sydney Morning Herald*, June 14, 1850, 3.

62. Peter Downes, *Shadows on the Stage: Theatre in New Zealand—the First 70 Years* (Dunedin, New Zealand: John McIndoe, 1975), 142; *Daily Southern Cross* (Auckland, Aotearoa New Zealand), May 4, 1852, 2; Wittmann, "Empire of Culture," 241–42.

63. *Maitland Mercury and Hunter River General Advertiser* (Maitland, Australia), September 11, 1850, 2.

64. *Bell's Life in Sydney and Sporting Reviewer*, November 9, 1850, 2.

65. Wittmann, "Empire of Culture," 23–24, 48–52.

66. *Sydney Morning Herald*, June 21, 1851, 1.

67. *Sydney Morning Herald*, June 25, 1851, 1.

68. *Bengal Hurkaru* (Kolkata), January 30, 1852, 3.
69. *Supplement to the Bengal Hurkaru* (Kolkata), January 31, 1852, 3.
70. *Bengal Hurkaru* (Kolkata), February 19, 1852, 3; February 21, 1852, 2.
71. *Bombay Times*, July 22, 1852.
72. *Bombay Times*, July 22, 1852, 1; *Bombay Times*, July 29, 1852, 703.
73. *Bengal Hurkaru* (Kolkata), March 5, 1853, 254.
74. *Bengal Hurkaru* (Kolkata), February 10, 1853, 162; February 23, 1853, 214.
75. Bayard Taylor, *A Visit to India, China, and Japan, in the Year 1853*, 16th ed. (New York: Putnam, 1855), 155–56.
76. *Bengal Hurkaru* (Kolkata), May 28, 1855, 507; July 13, 1855, 42.
77. *Bombay Times*, January 20, 1857, 129; January 28, 1857, 186; February 2, 1857, 217.
78. *Argus* (Melbourne), December 11, 1852, 5.
79. *South Australian Register* (Adelaide), January 26, 1855, 3.
80. *People's Advocate and New South Wales Vindicator* (Sydney), September 1, 1855, 15; see also Wittmann, "Empire of Culture," 56–62.
81. *Empire* (Sydney), October 27, 1855, 1.
82. *Empire* (Sydney), November 5, 1855, 1.
83. *Empire* (Sydney), November 26, 1855, 1.
84. *Age* (Melbourne), November 30, 1855, 8.
85. *Argus* (Melbourne), December 17, 1855, 8.
86. *Age* (Melbourne), December 4, 1855, 5.
87. *Age* (Melbourne), December 4, 1855, 5.
88. *Bell's Life in Sydney and Sporting Reviewer*, April 12, 1856, 2. For more on the Backus Minstrels, see Wittmann, "Empire of Culture," 62–69.
89. *Bell's Life in Sydney and Sporting Reviewer*, August 30, 1856, 3.
90. *Empire* (Sydney), April 29, 1857, 1.
91. *Sydney Morning Herald*, November 23, 1857, 1; *Empire* (Sydney), December 21, 1857, 1.
92. For instance, in August 1860, a San Francisco Minstrels performance featured Carson, Burbank, Boley, and Demerest alongside J. O. Pierce (formerly of the New York Serenaders) and T. P. Brower (formerly of Rainer's Serenaders) (*Sydney Morning Herald*, August 15, 1860, 1).
93. *Bengal Hurkaru* (Kolkata), October 5, 1861, 2.
94. *New York Clipper*, May 25, 1867, 49–50.
95. *Times of India* (Mumbai), March 12, 1863, 1.
96. See, for instance, Carson's 1875–1877 seasons: *Indian Daily News* (Kolkata), May 1, 1875, 1; February 17, 1877, 1; *Madras Mail* (Chennai), August 12, 1875, 3; August 26, 1875, 3; November 9, 1876, 1; *North-China Herald* (Shanghai), October 7, 1875, 355; *Japan Weekly* (Yokohama), November 20, 1875, 1081; *Ceylon Observer* (Colombo, Sri Lanka), February 18, 1876, 157; February 28, 1876, 88; *The Pioneer* (Prayagraj, India), February 28, 1877, 8; March 5, 1877, 10; March 12, 1877, 10; April 4, 1877, 17; May 3, 1877, 7; *Times of India* (Mumbai), May 11, 1877, 1.
97. *Otago (Aotearoa New Zealand) Witness*, October 20, 1883, 23.
98. John D. Drummond, *Choirs and Clogs, Mr. Ballads and Mr. Bones: Musical and Other Entertainments in Dunedin, 1860–1862* (Dunedin, New

Zealand: Hocken Library, 1991), 5; *Wellington (Aotearoa New Zealand) Independent*, July 12, 1861, 5.

99. Waterhouse, *From Minstrel Show to Vaudeville*, 100. See also Wilson, *Strolling Players of Empire*, 341–53.

100. *Supplement to the Bengal Hurkaru* (Kolkata), January 31, 1852, 3.

101. *Era* (London), August 2, 1857, 8.

102. Tracy C. Davis, "Christy's Minstrels (1857–61)," in *The Broadview Anthology of Nineteenth-Century British Performance*, 265–80, at 266; Thelwell, *Exporting Jim Crow*, 232n74.

103. On this and subsequent ensemble minstrel tours through South Africa, see Thelwell, *Exporting Jim Crow*, 37–95.

104. *Cape Monitor* (Cape Town), August 19, 1862, 2.

105. *Supplement to the Cape Argus* (Cape Town), November 20, 1862, 2.

106. *Cape Monitor* (Cape Town), August 19, 1862, 2.

107. *Cape Monitor* (Cape Town), August 23, 1862, 3.

108. *Cape Chronicle* (Cape Town), August 22, 1862, 2.

109. *Era* (London), September 13, 1857; Rice, *Monarchs of Minstrelsy*, 74.

110. *New York Clipper*, July 10, 1875, 116.

111. *New York Clipper*, August 23, 1856, 138; *New York Clipper*, September 6, 1856, 156.

112. *Morning Chronicle* (London), August 3, 1858; *New York Clipper*, August 28, 1858, 150.

113. Playbill, Queen's Theatre, Hull, England, October 1, 1859, American minstrel show collection, 1823–1947, MS Thr 556 (227), African Opera Troupe, Playbills, 1852–1859, Harvard Theatre Collection, Houghton Library, Harvard University, https://iiif.lib.harvard.edu/manifests/view/drs:45454189$6i.

114. *New York Clipper*, October 10, 1857, 194.

115. Arjun Appadurai, "Introduction: Commodities and the Politics of Value," in *The Social Life of Things: Commodities in Cultural Perspective*, ed. Arjun Appadurai (Cambridge: Cambridge University Press, 1986), 3–63, quote on 21.

116. Lhamon, *Raising Cain*, 20–23.

117. William J. Mahar, *Behind the Burnt Cork Mask: Early Blackface Minstrelsy and Antebellum American Popular Culture* (Urbana: University of Illinois Press, 1999), 19; cf. M. B. Leavitt, *Fifty Years of Theatrical Management* (New York: Broadway, 1912), 33.

118. "The Challenge Dance," in Engle, *This Grotesque Essence*, 13–20.

119. On Lane, see Marian Hannah Winter, "Juba and American Minstrelsy," *Dance Index* 6, no. 2 (1947): 28–48; Emery, *Black Dance*, 185–87; Brenda Dixon Gottschild, *Digging the Africanist Presence in American Performance: Dance and Other Contexts* (Westport, CT: Praeger, 1998), 81–128; James W. Cook, "Master Juba, the King of All Dancers! A Story of Stardom and Struggle from the Dawn of the Transatlantic Culture Industry," *Discourses in Dance* 3, no. 2 (2006): 7–20; Johnson, "Death and the Minstrel," 73–103.

120. Cook, "Master Juba," 10.

121. Cook, "Master Juba," 12.

122. *New York Herald*, July 8, 1844, 3.

123. June 18, 1845, Concert Hall, American minstrel show collection, 1823–1947, MS Thr 556 (454), Juba, Master, Playbills, 1845–1849, Harvard Theatre Collection, Houghton Library, Harvard University.

124. "Juba at Vauxhall," *Illustrated London News*, August 5, 1848, 77.

125. On Lane's death, see Johnson, "Death and the Minstrel," 75–82; Cook, "Master Juba," 18–19.

126. Charles Dickens, *American Notes* (New York: Penguin Books, 2000), 102.

127. Dickens, *American Notes*, 102.

128. As Douglas A. Lorimer recounts, "Juba" was actually made into blackface automatons (*Colour, Class and the Victorians: English Attitudes to the Negro in the Mid-Nineteenth Century* [Leicester, UK: Leicester University Press, 1978], 89). For an example of such advertisements for "Clockwork Juba Dancers," see *Queen* (London), July 3, 1875, 18.

129. *Morning Post* (London), June 21, 1848.

130. *Manchester (UK) Examiner*, October 17, 1848; *Manchester Times and Manchester and Salford (UK) Advertiser and Chronicle*, October 21, 1848, 5.

131. *New York Clipper*, October 4, 1856, 186; italics mine.

132. *New York Clipper*, March 27, 1858, 386.

133. Brown, *Babylon Girls*, 174.

134. R. W. Murray, *South African Reminiscences* (Cape Town: J. C. Juta, 1894), 208, 207. Early reviews also called the Christy's Minstrels a "Band of Brothers," troping on their burlesque of the Hutchinsons (*Cape Argus* [Cape Town], September 4, 1862, 2).

135. *Empire* (Sydney), March 30, 1863, 4.

136. Johnson, "Death and the Minstrel," 96–97.

137. *Cape Monitor* (Cape Town), August 23, 1862, 3.

138. Gottschild, *Digging the Africanist Presence*, 98–99.

139. *Illustrated Melbourne Post*, February 14, 1863, 5. I take the concept of a "thingly biography" from Igor Kopytoff, "The Cultural Biography of Things: Commoditization as Process," in *Social Life of Things*, 64–91.

140. *Cape Argus* (Cape Town), October 21, 1863, 3.

141. *Supplement to the Cape Argus* (Cape Town), November 20, 1862, 2. Elsewhere, the belt is described as follows: "It is of massive silver, in the shape of an inverted coronet, the front decorated with precious stones, the principal consisting of a rare Cape stone, with amethysts, rubies, and emeralds, in the shape of a cross, surrounded by a circle and the words 'Cape Presentation Belt'" (*Empire* [Sydney], March 30, 1863, 4).

142. *Supplement to the Cape Argus* (Cape Town), November 20, 1862, 2.

143. Roach, *Cities of the Dead*, 36.

144. Robin Bernstein, *Racial Innocence: Performing American Childhood from Slavery to Civil Rights* (New York: New York University Press, 2011), 73, 251n72.

145. Appadurai, *Social Life of Things*; Andrew Sofer, *The Stage Life of Props* (Ann Arbor: University of Michigan Press, 2003).

146. Bernstein, *Racial Innocence*, 73.

147. *Supplement to the Cape Argus* (Cape Town), November 20, 1862, 2; italics in the original.

148. Aimé Césaire, *Discourse on Colonialism*, trans. Joan Pinkham (New York: Monthly Review Press, 2000), 42.

149. *Argus* (Melbourne), June 2, 1863, 8; June 12, 1863, 8.

150. *Times of India* (Mumbai), November 2, 1863, 1; *South Australian Weekly Chronicle* (Adelaide), May 27, 1865, 5.

151. *Times of India* (Mumbai), November 9, 1863, 1. On a similar series of blackface minstrel troupes performing under the name "Original Christy's Minstrels" in colonial South Africa during the 1860s, see Thelwell, *Exporting Jim Crow*, 61–63.

152. *Bengal Hurkaru* (Kolkata), January 13, 1864, 1.

153. *Bengal Hurkaru* (Kolkata), January 23, 1864, 2.

154. *Bengal Hurkaru* (Kolkata), March 29, 1864, 1.

155. *South Australian Weekly Chronicle* (Adelaide), May 27, 1865, 5.

156. *Empire* (Sydney), March 5, 1864, 5; *Port Elizabeth Telegraph* (Gqeberha, South Africa), November 3, 1868, 3.

157. *Empire* (Sydney), March 5, 1864, 5.

158. *Eastern Province* (Gqeberha, South Africa), November 6, 1868, 3.

159. *Ovens and Murray Advertiser* (Beechworth, Australia), February 9, 1865, 3.

160. *Cape Argus* (Cape Town), May 1, 1869, 2; *Australasian* (Melbourne), July 3, 1869, 18; October 23, 1869, 18. During his 1869 tour, a sketch of Norton in his dancing apparel graced the cover of the French-language paper of Rio de Janeiro (*Ba-Ta-Clan: Journal Satirique Illustré*, August 28, 1869, 249).

161. *Jornal do Commercio* (Rio de Janeiro, Brazil), August 19, 1869, 4; August 23, 1869, 4; *Standard* (Buenos Aires, Argentina), July 13, 1869, 2; October 24, 1871, 2; November 16, 1871, 2; December 20, 1871, 2; *Diário do Rio de Janeiro*, August 22, 1869, 4; *Diario de S. Paulo*, September 10, 1871, 3; *Star and Herald* (Panama City, Panama), January 25, 1872, 2; *Colonial Standard* (Kingston, Jamaica), February 15, 1872, 2; March 16, 1872, 2; *Times* (Bridgetown, Barbardos), April 24, 1872, 3; *Barbados Globe*, July 1, 1872, 3. Some of the earliest reports of antiblack blackface performance in Argentina coincide with Norton's tours to Buenos Aires in the late 1860s and early 1870s (see Micol Seigel, "Cocoliche's Romp: Fun with Nationalism at Argentina's Carnival," *TDR* 44, no. 2 [2000]: 56–83, at 69).

162. *Era* (London), January 8, 1871, 4; *Jig, Clog, and Breakdown Dancing Made Easy, with Sketches of Noted Jig Dancers* (New York: Ed. James, 1873), 3.

163. *Era* (London), May 14, 1871.

164. *Colonial Standard* (Kingston, Jamaica), February 12, 1872, 3; February 15, 1872, 2.

165. *Inter Ocean* (Chicago), March 9, 1875, 2.

166. *New Zealand Herald* (Auckland), February 9, 1866, 1; *New Zealand Herald* (Auckland), February 10, 1866, 4.

167. *Leader* (Melbourne), August 7, 1869, 10; *Empire* (Sydney), February 28, 1866, 2.

168. *New York Clipper*, October 30, 1869, 7.

169. *New York Clipper*, March 1, 1890, 4.

170. *Newcastle Chronicle and Hunter River District News* (Newcastle, Australia), May 12, 1866, 2; *New York Clipper*, June 21, 1913, 2.

171. *Eastern Province Herald* (Gqeberha, South Africa), September 2, 1865, 2.

172. *Cape Argus* (Cape Town), May 1, 1869, 2; cf. Thelwell, *Exporting Jim Crow*, 228n8.

173. *Cape Argus* (Cape Town), December 7, 1872, 1; *Eastern Province Herald* (Gqeberha, South Africa), January 7, 1873, 1, 3; *Natal Mercury* (eThekwini, South Africa), April 10, 1874, 2; *Diamond Field* (Kimberley, South Africa), August 29, 1874, 2.

174. Veit Erlmann, *African Stars: Studies in Black South African Performance* (Chicago: University of Chicago Press, 1991), 31; Magubane, *Bringing the Empire Home*, 155; cf. J. W. Matthews, *Incwadi Yami, or Twenty Years' Personal Experience in South Africa* (New York: Rogers & Sherwood, 1887), 193.

175. *Cape Argus (Cape Town)*, November 19, 1872, 4. Future quotations taken from the same.

176. Italics in the original. My thanks to Megan Lewis for her translation.

177. Thelwell, *Exporting Jim Crow*, 68.

178. Thelwell, *Exporting Jim Crow*, 69.

179. *Indian Daily News (Kolkata)*, October 23, 1880, 1; October 3, 1885, 1.

180. *Age* (Melbourne), January 20, 1896, 6.

181. W. E. B. Du Bois, "The Color Line Belts the World," *Collier's Weekly*, October 20, 1906, 30; reprinted in *W. E. B. Du Bois on Asia: Crossing the World Color Line*, ed. Bill V. Mullen and Cathryn Watson (Jackson: University Press of Mississippi, 2005), 33–34.

182. Sylvia Wynter, "Unsettling the Coloniality of Being/Power/Truth/Freedom: Towards the Human, after Man, Its Overrepresentation—an Argument," *CR: The New Centennial Review* 3, no. 3 (2003): 257–337, at 322.

Chapter 4

1. Nyong'o, *Amalgamation Waltz*, 29. See also Elise Lemire, *"Miscegenation": Making Race in America* (Philadelphia: University of Pennsylvania Press, 2009), 97–99; Bernstein, *Racial Innocence*, 2–3.

2. Mylithi Kaul, "Background: Black or Tawny? Stage Representations of Othello from 1604 to the Present," in *Othello: New Essays by Black Writers*, ed. Mylithi Kaul (Washington, DC: Howard University Press, 1997), 1–19, quote on 8. See also H. D. Kaplan, "The Earliest Images of Othello," *Shakespeare Quarterly* 39, no. 2 (1988): 171–86; Michael Neill, "Unproper Beds: Race, Adultery, and the Hideous in Othello," *Shakespeare Quarterly* 40, no. 4 (1989): 383–412; Edward Ziter, *The Orient on the Victorian Stage* (Cambridge: Cambridge University Press, 2003, 55–64.

3. Lisa Warrington, "Acting the Moor: Critical Responses to Performances of Othello in Australia and New Zealand, 1834–1866," *Australian Studies* 6 (2014): 1–21; at 1; Eric Rosenthal, "Early Shakespearian Productions in South Africa," *English Studies in Africa* 7, no. 2 (1964): 202–16, at

209; Ania Loomba, "'Local-Manufacture Made-in-India Othello Fellows': Issues of Race, Hybridity and Location in Post-Colonial Shakespeares," in *Post-Colonial Shakespeares*, ed. Ania Loomba and Martin Orkin (London: Routledge, 1998), 143–63; and Tilden G. Edelstein, "Othello in America: The Drama of Racial Intermarriage," in *Region, Race, and Reconstruction: Essays in Honor of C. Vann Woodward*, ed. J. Morgan Kousser and James M. McPherson (Oxford: Oxford University Press, 1982), 179–97.

4. Stoler, *Carnal Knowledge*, 142.

5. Foucault, *History of Sexuality*, 103.

6. Said, *Orientalism*, 7.

7. Mary Louise Pratt, *Imperial Eyes: Travel Writing and Transculturation* (London: Routledge, 1992), 7.

8. Robert F. Willson Jr., *Their Form Confounded: Studies in the Burlesque Play from Udall to Sheridan* (The Hague: Mouton, 1975), x-xii. In the minstrel tradition of scriptive blackface, burlesque was itself travestied when "'burlesque' . . . [was] generally pronounced 'burly-cue'" (Dailey Paskman and Sigmund Spaeth, *Gentlemen, Be Seated! A Parade of Old-Time Minstrels* [Garden City, NY: Doubleday, Doran, 1928], 1).

9. Francis Gentleman, *The Dramatic Censor; or, Critical Companion* (London: J. Bell, 1770), 1:151–52.

10. Virginia Mason Vaughan, *Othello: A Contextual History* (Cambridge: Cambridge University Press, 1994), 121.

11. *Public Advertiser* (London), October 29, 1787; cf. Ruth Cowhig, "Actors, Black and Tawny, in the Role of Othello—and Their Critics," *Theatre Research International* 4, no. 2 (1979): 133–46, quote on 134.

12. Abigail Adams, "Letter to Mrs. Shaw, London, March 4, 1786," in *Letters of Mrs. Adams: The Wife of John Adams*, 4th ed. (Boston: Wilkins, Carter, 1848), 275–78, quote on 276.

13. John Quincy Adams, "Misconceptions of Shakespeare upon the Stage," *New England Magazine* 9 (1835): 435–40, quote on 438.

14. Adams, "Misconceptions," 438.

15. Adams, "Misconceptions," 439.

16. Adams, "Misconceptions," 439, 438.

17. Adams, "Misconceptions," 439.

18. John Quincy Adams, "The Character of Desdemona," *American Monthly Magazine* (1836): 209–17, quote on 215; italics in the original.

19. Adams, "Character of Desdemona," 215.

20. Adams, "Misconceptions," 439.

21. Charles Lamb, "Art. IX—*Theatralia*. No. 1," *Reflector* 2, no. 4 (June 1811): 298–313, quote on 309.

22. Lamb, "Art. IX," 309; see also Jonas Barish, *The Antitheatrical Prejudice* (Berkeley: University of California Press, 1981), 329–32.

23. Samuel Taylor Coleridge, "Notes on the Comedies of Shakespeare," in *Coleridge's Shakespearean Criticism*, ed. Thomas Middleton Raysor (Cambridge, MA: Harvard University Press, 1930), 1:92–137, quote on 124.

24. Samuel Taylor Coleridge, "Selections from 'Table Talk' [1835]," in *Coleridge's Shakespearean Criticism*, ed. Thomas Middleton Raysor (Cambridge, MA: Harvard University Press, 1930), 2:350–58, quote on 350.

25. Samuel Taylor Coleridge, "Notes on the Tragedies: *Othello* [1836]," in *Shakespearean Criticism*, 1:44–54, quote on 46.

26. Ziter, *Orient on the Victorian Stage*, 59; cf. Thomas Colley Grattan, "My Acquaintance with the Late Edmund Kean," *New Monthly Magazine* 39 (1833): 7–16; see also Cowhig, "Actors, Black and Tawny," 135, and Kaul, "Background: Black or Tawny?," 8.

27. Edelstein, "*Othello* in America," 184–86; Daniel E. Bandmann, *An Actor's Tour; or, Seventy Thousand Miles with Shakespeare*, ed. Barnard Gisby (Boston: Cupples, Upham, 1885), 136.

28. Nathans, *Slavery and Sentiment*, 184–85.

29. McAllister, *White People*, 78–82.

30. On this production of *Othello*, see Simon Snipe, *Sports of New-York. Containing an Evening at the African Theatre. Also a Trip to the Races! With Two Appropriate Songs* (New York, 1823), 3–16; cf. George A. Thompson Jr., *A Documentary History of the African Theatre* (Evanston, IL: Northwestern University Press, 1998), 114. On charivari and "rough music," see E. P. Thompson, "Rough Music Reconsidered," *Folklore* 103 (1992): 3–26. Given charivari's function as a ritual for enforcing social mores on sexuality, white mobs frequently enacted charivari as racial riots that aimed to entrench social distinctions of class, age, and gender while simultaneously policing interracial sexuality (see Lemire, "*Miscegenation*," 90; Nyong'o, *Amalgamation Waltz*, 71–75 and passim).

31. Bernth Lindfors, *Ira Aldridge*, vol. 1, *The Early Years, 1807–1833* (Rochester, NY: University of Rochester Press, 2011), esp. 79–85.

32. For an example of his costuming, see the print *Ira Aldridge as Othello* in Ira Aldridge, Harvard Theatre Collection theatrical portrait prints (visual works), TCS 43 (folder 24), Houghton Library, Harvard University, https://iiif.lib.harvard.edu/manifests/view/drs:491653400$3i. For reception of his performance, see Kaul, "Background: Black or Tawny?," 12; Lindfors, *Ira Aldridge* 1:66.

33. Lindfors, *Ira Aldridge*, 1:83; cf. *Times* (London), October 11, 1825, 2.

34. Lindfors, *Ira Aldridge*, 1:85, 266–67; *Athenaeum* (London), April 13, 1833, 236.

35. Lindfors, *Ira Aldridge*, 1:267; cf. *Athenaeum* (London), April 13, 1833, 236.

36. "Memoir and Theatrical Career of Ira Aldridge, the African Roscius," in *Ira Aldridge: The African Roscius*, 7–38, at 17; cf. Hazel Waters, "Ira Aldridge's Fight for Equality," in *Ira Aldridge: The African Roscius*, 98–125, at 100.

37. Mrs. [Madge] Kendal, *Dramatic Opinions* (Boston: Little, Brown, 1890), 28–29.

38. *Athenaeum* (London), July 31, 1858, 144; quoted in Waters, "Ira Aldridge's Fight for Equality," 118.

39. "Memoir and Theatrical Career of Ira Aldridge, the African Roscius," 8.

40. *Satirist, or The True Censor of the Times*, March 26, 1848, 102; quoted in Waters, "Ira Aldridge's Fight for Equality," 113.

41. *Account of Mr. Mathews' at Home* (London: Duncombe, 1824), 11; cf. Davis, "Acting Black, 1824," 172. There is no definitive text of Mathews's performance script; as Tracy C. Davis has demonstrated, "For each of the at

homes there are one or two souvenir texts pirated by hacks: all are illegitimate" ("Acting Black, 1824," 164).

42. *National Advocate* (New York), May 8, 1824, 2, italics in the original.

43. "Jim Crow" [T. D. Rice], letter to the editor, *Mourning Courier and New-York Enquirer*, October 12, 1833; italics in the original.

44. *Mathews in America! A New Dramatic At Home; Written for and Intended to Be Delivered by Mr. Mathews Abroad; Containing a New Budget of Songs, Tales, and Anecdotes* (London: Duncombe, ca. 1825), 16.

45. William T. Moncrieff, *Monsieur Mallet; or, My Daughter's Letter: A Gallo-American Drama, of National Manners and Peculiarities, in Three Acts* (London: Hailes Lacy, 1851), 2, 85.

46. *The Anaconda, Musical Burletta in Two Acts* (British Library Add MS 42875.5), 257–58; cf. Lindfors, *Ira Aldridge*, 1:245–47.

47. Charles Mathews, *Othello, the Moor of Fleet Street (1833)*, ed. Manfred Draudt (Tübingen, Germany: Francke Verlag, 1993), 55, 56.

48. Mathews, *Othello*, 55. As Robert Hornback notes, James Hewlett had also performed imitations of Edmund Kean, making it possible that Mathews's mockery was directed at both Aldridge and Hewlett, and Black actors generally ("Black Shakespeareans," 141).

49. William Shakespeare, *Othello*, Arden Shakespeare, third series, edited by E. A.J. Honigmann (London: Arden Shakespeare, 2004), 1.3.82. References are to act, scene, and line.

50. Bernth Lindfors, *Ira Aldridge*, vol. 2, *The Vagabond Years, 1833–1852* (Rochester, NY: University of Rochester Press, 2011), 61.

51. Charles Rice, "The Arab's Leap. Adelphi Theatre, Saturday March 11th 1837. *The Gamester Father, Hassan Pasha, The Wreck Ashore, Douglas*," in *The London Theatre in the Eighteen-Thirties* (London: Society for Theatre Research, 1950), 29–32, quote on 31–32. See also Lindfors, *Ira Aldridge*, 2:191n41.

52. Maurice G. Dowling, *Othello Travestie: An Operatic Burlesque Burletta* (London: Samuel French, 1859), 2.

51. Dowling, *Othello Travestie*, 9–10.

54. Dowling, *Othello Travestie*, 8.

55. Coleridge, "Notes on the Comedies of Shakespeare," 124.

56. Dowling, *Othello Travestie*, 10.

57. Lindfors, *Ira Aldridge*, 2:62.

58. Bernstein, *Racial Innocence*, 101.

59. Fleetwood, *Troubling Vision*, 79.

60. Kalpana Seshadri-Crooks, *Desiring Whiteness: A Lacanian Analysis of Race* (London: Routledge, 2000), 2.

61. bell hooks, *Black Looks: Race and Representation* (Boston: South End Press, 1992), 168.

62. Lamb, "Art. IX," 299.

63. Coleridge, "Notes on the Tragedies: *Othello* [1836]," 47.

64. Lindfors, *Ira Aldridge*, 2:67.

65. R. M. Sillard, *Barry Sullivan and His Contemporaries; A Histrionic Record* (London: T. Fisher Unwin, 1901), 86–87.

66. *Daily Pennsylvanian* (Philadelphia), August 22, 1836, 3; *National Gazette and Literary Register* (Philadelphia), August 26, 1836, 3; *Saturday Morning Transcript* (Boston), September 10, 1836, 6; *New York Herald*, June 4, 1839, 3; Odell, *Annals of the New York Stage*, 4:86–87, 160–61, 622; Joseph Patrick Roppolo, "Shakespeare in New Orleans, 1817–1865," in *Shakespeare in the South: Essays on Performance*, ed. Philip C. Kolin (Jackson: University Press of Mississippi, 1983), 112–27, at 124.

67. See Playbill, April 14, 1837, Davis-Kendall Collections, Hoblitzelle Theatre Arts Library, University of Texas, Programs 1836–39, New York American Theatre, Bowery Theatre; see also O'Neill, "History of Theatrical Activity," 469; White, *Stories of Freedom*, 155. On *Othello Travestie* in the US American repertoire, see Odell, *Annals of the New York Stage*, 4:103, 104, 189, 672; Joseph N. Ireland, *Records of the New York Stage, from 1750 to 1860* (New York: T. H. Morrell, 1867), 2:159, 501; Cockrell, *Demons of Disorder*, 173n8.

68. Thomas Dartmouth Rice, *Otello*, reprinted in Lhamon, *Jump Jim Crow*, 343–83.

69. Rice, *Otello*, 380; *Tregear's Black Jokes*, 9, italics in the original.

70. Rice, *Otello*, 362, 357.

71. Playbill, Cincinnati National Theatre, May 6, 1846, Harvard Theatre Collection, Houghton Library, Harvard University, https://iiif.lib.harvard.edu/manifests/view/ids:21933213.

72. Playbill, National Theatre, May 26, 1849, Harvard Theatre Collection, Houghton Library, Harvard University. See also Playbill, Broadway Theatre, May 14, 1858, Harvard Theatre Collection, Houghton Library, Harvard University, https://iiif.lib.harvard.edu/manifests/view/drs:424019356$2i.

73. Alexander Do Mar, *Othello: An Interesting Drama, Rather!* (London: T. L. Marks, 1850).

74. Do Mar, *Othello*, 1.

75. Do Mar, *Othello*, 5.

76. Anthony Bennett, "Rivals Unravelled: A Broadside Song and Dance," *Folk Music Journal* 6, no. 4 (1993): 420–45, at 420.

77. Playbill, October 18, 1862, container 34.1, Minstrel Show Collection, 1831–1959, Harry Ransom Center, University of Texas at Austin.

78. *Dar's De Money (Othello Burlesque)* (London: Samuel French, ca. 1880), 21–27.

79. George W. H. Griffin, *"Othello" Ethiopian Burlesque* (Clyde, OH: A. D. Ames, ca. 1870).

80. George W. H. Griffin, *Desdemonum: An Ethiopian Burlesque* (New York: Happy Hours, 1874), 5.

81. This pattern held in Jamaica as well: *Othello Travestie* was staged in Kingston on November 13, 1847 (*Morning Journal* [Kingston, Jamaica], November 13, 1847, cited in ML-77, box 30, folder 5, p. 28, Errol Hill Papers [1960–2002], Rauner Special Collections Library, Dartmouth College,).

82. Warrington, "Acting the Moor," 14, 20n65; cf. *Sydney Gazette and New South Wales Advertiser*, March 16, 1837, 3; March 25, 1837, 2; *Sydney Herald*, March 20, 1837, 1.

83. Bagot, *Coppin the Great*, 102; *South Australian* (Adelaide), February 5, 1847, 3; July 13, 1847, 2; August 17, 1847, 2; *Argus* (Melbourne), October 13, 1855, 8.

84. *South Australian Register* (Adelaide), July 9, 1851, 3. Here, the reviewer plays on blackface dialect, intentionally misspelling "real" in an approximation of the minstrel mispronunciation "rale."

85. Comedian John Gardner quoted in the *South Australian Register* (Adelaide), March 4, 1850, 3.

86. *Sydney Gazette and New South Wales Advertiser*, February 8, 1838, 2.

87. Warrington, "Acting the Moor," 14; *Sydney Gazette and New South Wales Advertiser*, August 30, 1838, 3. It was also advertised on the following dates: *Australian* (Sydney), February 13, 1838, 3; July 16, 1844, 2; July 25, 1844; *Sydney Herald*, February 19, 1838, 2; March 19, 1838, 3; *Sydney Monitor*, March 15, 1839, 3; *Colonial Times* (Hobart, Tasmania), January 11, 1842, 2; *Sydney Gazette and New South Wales Advertiser*, August 16, 1842, 3; *Cornwall Chronicle* (Launceston, Tasmania), August 20, 1842, 3; *Sydney Morning Herald*, June 1, 1843, 2; June 6, 1843, 2; *Maitland Mercury and Hunter River General Advertiser* (Maitland, Australia), August 12, 1843, 2; August 26, 1843, 3; September 16, 1843, 3; September 16, 1843, 3; June 22, 1844, 3; *Launceston Advertiser* (Launceston, Australia), July 26, 1844, 3.

88. *Port Phillip Patriot and Melbourne (Australia) Advertiser*, September 6, 1845, 3.

89. *Courier* (Hobart, Tasmania), August 22, 1854, 2; *Hobarton Mercury* (Hobart, Tasmania), August 26, 1854, 3; *Empire* (Sydney), May 26, 1855, 4.

90. *Star* (Ballarat, Australia), February 27, 1857, 2.

91. Rosenthal, "Early Shakespearian Productions," 210; F. C. L. Bosman, *Drama en toneel in Suid-Afrika*, deel 1, *1652–1855* (Pretoria, South Africa: J. H. de Bussy, 1928), 335. It is also likely that this Dutch translation cited Cervantes's *El Celoso Extremeño (The Jealous Extremeñan)*. The historical English translation was *The Jealous Husband*, which was itself the source for Charles Dibdin's *Padlock* and the blackface figure Mungo (K. Meira Goldberg, *Sonidos Negros: On the Blackness of Flamenco* [Oxford: Oxford University Press, 2019], 112–14).

92. Quoted in Rosenthal, "Early Shakespearian Productions," 210; cf. *Commercial Advertiser* (Cape Town), June 11, 1836. See also Bosman, *Drama en toneel*, 335, 352.

93. On *swaart gevaar*, see Sharpe, *Allegories of Empire*; Stoler, *Carnal Knowledge*, 58–60.

94. *Cape Town Mail*, May 17, 1842, 3–4; *De Verzamelaar* (Cape Town), May 17, 1842, 5–6; April 19, 1842, 1.

95. Stephen Gray, "Women in South African Theatre," *South African Theatre Journal* 4, no. 1 (1990): 75–87, at 75–76.

96. *Cape Town Mail*, May 17, 1842, 4.

97. *Cape Argus* (Cape Town), October 21, 1862, 3.

98. Achille Mbembe, "Necropolitics," trans. Libby Meintjes, *Public Culture* 15, no.1 (2003): 11–40, at 11; Dowling, *Othello Travestie*, 8.

99. *Cape Argus* (Cape Town), March 9, 1861, 2–3.

100. Stoler, *Carnal Knowledge*, 112.

101. Dowling, *Othello Travestie*, 2, 10.

102. MacDonald, "Acting Black," 232–33. There were also two notable uprisings in the Cape during the early nineteenth century: the 1808 revolt of the enslaved in Cape Town and the 1825 Bokkeveld farm uprising, in which the enslaved and indentured rebelled (Robert Ross, *Cape of Torments: Slavery and Resistance in South Africa* [London: Routledge, 1983], 97–116).

103. *Cape Argus* (Cape Town), February 28, 1861, 2; March 12, 1861, 2.

104. *Cape Argus* (Cape Town), March 9, 1861, 2.

105. *Cape Monitor* (Cape Town), January 13, 1855, 3. Brooke later staged his *Othello* at the Queen's Theatre in Melbourne, Australia, in February 1855 (Warrington, "Acting the Moor," 6).

106. *Illustrated London News*, December 7, 1861, quoted in Richard W. Schoch, *Not Shakespeare: Bardolatry and Burlesque in the Nineteenth Century* (Cambridge: Cambridge University Press, 2002), 85.

107. *Cape Argus* (Cape Town), September 7, 1862, 2.

108. *Calcutta Star*, August 4, 1848, quoted in Amal Mitra, *English Stage in India: 18th & 19th Century*, ed. Lab Kumar Bose, trans. Pratap Bonnerjee (1967; Kolkata: Dasgupta, 2012), 152. Cf. *Bengal Hurkaru* (Kolkata), August 9, 1848; August 12, 1848; August 16, 1848; August 17, 1848; August 19, 1848.

109. Though *Hicky's Bengal Gazette* (Kolkata) announced a 1781 performance of *Othello* and *The Padlock* by the Black gentleman Julius Soubise, it is more than likely that this "racist barb" (to use Kathleen Wilson's phrasing) was an imagined bill designed to scorn Soubise by associating him with Othello and Mungo. See Wilson, *Strolling Players of Empire*, 294.

110. On audience composition in Kolkata, see Jyotsna Singh, "Different Shakespeares: The Bard in Colonial/Postcolonial India," *Theatre Journal* 41, no. 4 (1989): 445–58, at 445.

111. *Bengal Hurkaru* (Kolkata), August 1, 1848, quoted in Mitra, *English Stage*, 153.

112. *Calcutta Star*, August 4, 1848, quoted in Mitra, *English Stage*, 152.

113. *Bengal Hurkaru* (Kolkata), August 12, 1848, 171.

114. *Calcutta Star*, August 10, 1848, quoted in Mitra, *English Stage*, 199.

115. *Calcutta Star*, August 12, 1848, quoted in Mitra, *English Stage*, 154.

116. *Bengal Hurkaru* (Kolkata), August 12, 1848, 171; *Calcutta Star*, August 11, 1848, quoted in Mitra, *English Stage*, 155–56.

117. McAllister, *White People*, 137–43; cf. MacDonald, "Acting Black," 236–37.

118. *Calcutta Star*, August 12, 1848, quoted in Mitra, *English Stage*, 155.

119. It is possible that "Mr Cheeks" derived this pun from a riddle in *Billy Black's Cabinet of Conundrums* that read, "What character in *Othello* does a Jew remind you of in paying you money? Dere's de mony (Desdemona)" (quoted in Lindfors, *Ira Aldridge*, 2:119).

120. *Sambad Pravakar* (Kolkata), August 21, 1848; quoted in Mitra, *English Stage*, 157.

121. *Sambad Pravakar* (Kolkata), August 21, 1848; quoted in Mitra, *English Stage*, 157.

122. *Bengal Hurkaru* (Kolkata), August 19, 1848, 98; see also Mitra, *English Stage*, 158–64.

123. *Englishman* (Kolkata), September 14, 1848, quoted in Mitra, *English Stage*, 162.

124. *Bengal Hurkaru* (Kolkata), August 19, 1848, 199; italics in the original.

125. *Calcutta Star*, August 19, 1848, quoted in Mitra, *English Stage*, 160.

126. *Calcutta Star*, September 14, 1848, quoted in Mitra, *English Stage*, 163.

127. Ania Loomba, "Shakespearian Transformations," in *Shakespeare and National Culture*, ed. John J. Joughin (Manchester, UK: Manchester University Press, 1997), 109–41, at 114–18; Somnath Gupt, *The Parsi Theatre: Its Origins and Development*, trans. and ed. Kathryn Hansen (Kolkata: Seagull Books, 2005), 41–42, 87–92. The earliest known all-Parsi performance of *Othello* in English was staged at Elphinstone College in July 1861 (Nicholson, *Colonial Public*, 3).

128. Gupt, *Parsi Theatre*, 41–42, 87–92.

129. *Bengal Hurkaru* (Kolkata), December 9, 1861, 2; *Times of India*, March 12, 1863, 1.

130. *Times of India* (Mumbai), April 17, 1865, 3; italics in the original.

131. *Bengal Hurkaru* (Kolkata), December 27, 1864, 1.

132. Kumudini Arvind Mehta, "English Drama on the Bombay Stage in the Late Eighteenth Century and in the Nineteenth Century" (PhD diss., University of Bombay, 1960), 179; cf. *Bombay Gazette*: October 22, 1864, October 28, 1864.

133. *Indian Daily News* (Kolkata), May 4, 1889, 1; May 9, 1889, 1.

134. *Pioneer* (Prayagraj, India), February 25, 1867, 9.

Chapter 5

1. *North-China Herald* (Shanghai), March 7, 1863, 39.

2. I take the term "Pacific circuit" from Wittmann, "Empire of Culture." On Backus's tours of the Pacific, see Richard Waterhouse, *From Minstrel Show to Vaudeville*, 33–40; Wittmann, "Empire of Culture," 62–69.

3. "Editor's Table," *Pioneer; or, California Monthly Magazine* 2, no. 6 (December 1854): 372. See also Krystyn R. Moon, *Yellowface: Creating the Chinese in American Popular Music and Performance, 1850s–1920s* (New Brunswick, NJ: Rutgers University Press, 2005), 43.

4. Playbill, Metropolitan Theatre, San Francisco, August 3, 1855, reprinted in the *New York Clipper*, March 27, 1875, 412; "Monthly Summary of Events," *Pioneer; or, California Monthly Magazine* 4, no. 5 (November 1855): 305. For instance, on his initial Pacific tour, Backus performed his "Chinese personation" or his "Burlesque Chinaman" in Honolulu, Sydney, Melbourne, and the mining town of Ballarat (*Polynesian* [Honolulu], September 8, 1855, 70; *Empire* [Sydney], October 31, 1855; *Age* [Melbourne], December 4, 1855, 5; *Geelong Advertiser and Intelligencer* [Geelong, Australia], March 12, 1856, 2). See also Playbill, Backus Minstrels at Coppin's Olympic (Australia), December 14, 1855, American minstrel show collection, 1823–1947, MS Thr 556 (243), Backus Minstrels, Playbills, 1854–1855, Harvard Theatre Collection, Houghton Library, Harvard University.

5. Shannon Steen, *Racial Geometries of the Black Atlantic, Asian Pacific, and American Theatre* (Basingstoke, UK: Palgrave Macmillan, 2010).

6. Claire Jean Kim, "The Racial Triangulation of Asian Americans," *Politics & Society* 27, no.1 (1999): 105–38.

7. Lowe, *Intimacies of Four Continents*, 1 and passim.

8. DuComb, *Haunted City*, 11 and passim.

9. Inderpal Grewal and Caren Kaplan, "Introduction: Transnational Feminist Practices and Questions of Postmodernity," in *Scattered Hegemonies: Postmodernity and Transnational Feminist Practices*, ed. Inderpal Grewal and Caren Kaplan (Minneapolis: University of Minnesota Press, 1994), 17.

10. James S. Moy, *Marginal Sights: Staging the Chinese in America* (Iowa City: University of Iowa Press, 1993); Sean Metzger, *Chinese Looks: Fashion, Performance, Race* (Bloomington: Indiana University Press, 2014); Caroline H. Yang, *The Peculiar Afterlife of Slavery: The Chinese Worker and the Minstrel Form* (Stanford, CA: Stanford University Press, 2020). Esther Kim Lee's *Made-Up Asians: Yellowface during the Exclusion Era* (Ann Arbor: University of Michigan Press, 2022) offers an intervention in this discourse by tracing an earlier genealogy of yellowface performance extending back to the enslaved Chinese figure of Kazrac in *Aladdin* pantomimes. Lee emphasizes the significant absence of Asian peoples in the United States and Britain amid the formation of yellowface. Yet, her circum-Atlantic genealogy of Anglophone yellowface maps a separate genealogy from Backus's caricature and its Pacific circulations. Backus's performances responded to the presence—rather than absence—of Asian people in California and Australia. Moreover, as Josephine Lee notes, Backus's "Chinese Personation" and other figurations of the "Burlesque Chinaman" that emerged from the Pacific circuit were "substantively different from the exotic curiosities and magical beings that had previously represented the theatrical Orient, instead presenting Chinese immigrant men as bumbling domestic servants, unintelligible laundrymen, or cunning villains" (*Oriental, Black & White: The Formation of Racial Habits in American Theater* [Chapel Hill: University of North Carolina Press, 2022], 79). Nevertheless, Backus's yellowface "Chinaman" was similar to *Aladdin*'s Kazrac insofar as both relied on the absence of actual Asian peoples on the Anglophone imperial stage.

11. Moon, *Yellowface*, 43.

12. Wittmann, "Empire of Culture," 69; cf. Andrew Markus, *Fear and Hatred: Purifying Australia and California, 1850–1901* (Sydney: Hale & Iremonger, 1979); Marilyn Lake and Henry Reynolds, *Drawing the Global Colour Line: White Men's Countries and the International Challenge of Racial Equality* (Cambridge: Cambridge University Press, 2008), 15–45.

13. Chauncey L. Canfield, ed., *The Diary of a Forty-Niner* (San Francisco: Morgan Shepard, 1906), 202.

14. Canfield, *Diary of a Forty-Niner*, 222.

15. "Dred Scott, Plaintiff in Error, v. John F. A. Sandford," https://www.law.cornell.edu/supremecourt/text/60/393, accessed May 10, 2023.

16. Markus, *Fear and Hatred*, 3, 6.

17. Charles Wentworth Dilke, *Greater Britain. A Record of Travel in English-Speaking Countries during 1866–7* (Philadelphia: J. B. Lippincott; London: Macmillan, 1869), 1:224–25.

18. Minstrelsy was commonplace in mining camps across the globe. After the Australian gold rush, itinerant miners brought minstrelsy to the gold mines of Aotearoa New Zealand and to the diamond and gold mines of southern Africa. See Downes, *Shadows on the Stage*; Drummond, *Choirs and Clogs, Mr. Ballads and Mr. Bones*; Magubane, *Bringing the Empire Home*; Thelwell, *Exporting Jim Crow*, 73–95.

19. *Polynesian* (Honolulu), September 8, 1855, 70.

20. *Empire* (Sydney), November 2, 1855, 5.

21. See, for instance, the playbill printed in *Empire* (Sydney), November 10, 1855, 1.

22. *Age* (Melbourne), December 4, 1855, 5.

23. Frank Dumont, "The Chinee Laundryman, Sung by Charles Backus" (Philadelphia: Chas. F. Escher Jr., 1880), https://levysheetmusic.mse.jhu.edu/collection/025/014. Cf. "The Chinese Laundryman," in *Birch and Backus' Songs of the San Francisco Minstrels*, ed. Frank Dumont (New York: DeWitt, 1881), 57.

24. For an early non-yellowface anti-Chinese song in Australia, see Charles Robert Thatcher, *Thatcher's Colonial Songster* (Melbourne: 1857), 5–6; quoted in Waterhouse, *From Minstrel Show to Vaudeville*, 107. Early yellowface roles also appeared in US American melodramas, especially those produced in California amid the gold rush. See Stuart W. Hyde, "The Chinese Stereotype in American Melodrama," *California Historical Society Quarterly* 34, no. 4 (1955): 357–67, at 359.

25. Odell, *Annals of the New York Stage*, 6:586. On Horn's time in California, see George R. MacMinn, *The Theater of the Golden Era in California* (Caldwell, ID: Caxton, 1941), 425–27; Edmond M. Gagey, *The San Francisco Stage: A History* (New York: Columbia University Press, 1950), 64–66.

26. Metzger, *Chinese Looks*, 21.

27. S. S. Steele, "A Chinaman's Tail (Tale)," in *Buckley's Ethiopian Melodies, No. 4, as Sung by Buckley's New Orleans Serenaders, at Their New Opera House, No. 585 Broadway, Opposite Niblos* (New York: J. Cozans, 1857), 66.

28. *Pacific Commercial Advertiser* (Honolulu), November 4, 1858.

29. Playbill, Backus, C., undated, American minstrel show collection, 1823–1947, MS Thr 556 (241). Backus, C. Playbills, 1862. Harvard Theatre Collection, Houghton Library, Harvard University, https://iiif.lib.harvard.edu/manifests/view/drs:45454203$2i. As the playbill lists Tom Maguire as the proprietor of the theater, this performance almost certainly occurred in Northern California.

30. Frank Curtis, "The Artful Chinee" (Cleveland: S. Brainard's Sons, ca. 1870); quoted in Moon, *Yellowface*, 42.

31. Charles Dibdin, "Ballad [Negro Philosophy]," in *Professional Life of Mr. Dibdin*, 4:21–22; Damon, *Series of Old American Songs*, no. 17.

32. Yang, *Peculiar Afterlife*, 44; cf. George Howard, "Oh, I'se So Wicked" (New York: Horace Waters, 1854), http://utc.iath.virginia.edu/songs/sowickedf.html. See also Bernstein, *Racial Innocence*, 49; Meer, *Uncle Tom Mania*, 39.

33. Yang, *Peculiar Afterlife*, 25–64.

34. Judy Tsou, "Gendering Race: Stereotypes of Chinese Americans in Popular Sheet Music," *repercussions* 6, no. 2 (1997): 25–62, at 58–61.

35. Bret Harte and F. B., *The Heathen Chinee* (Boston: Oliver Ditson, 1870), 2. See Yang, *Peculiar Afterlife*.

36. Metzger, *Chinese Looks*, 41.

37. Bret Harte, "Wan Lee, the Pagan," in *Bret Harte's Gold Rush: "Outcasts of Poker Flat," "The Luck of Roaring Camp," "Tennessee's Partner," and Other Favorites* (Berkeley, CA: Heyday Books, 1997), 81–82.

38. Playbill, Birch & Backus' San Francisco Minstrels, May 4, 1891, container 32.10, Minstrel Show Collection, Harry Ransom Center, University of Texas at Austin.

39. Playbill, San Francisco Minstrels, 585 Broadway, December 25, 1871, container 32.10, Minstrel Show Collection, Harry Ransom Center, University of Texas at Austin.

40. *Straits Observer* (Singapore), August 10, 1875, 2; August 13, 1875, 2.

41. *Sydney Mail and New South Wales Advertiser*, July 10, 1875, 47. See also *Sydney Morning Herald*, June 14 1886, 2.

42. Harte, "Wan Lee," 80–81.

43. Metzger, *Chinese Looks*, 42–43.

44. *New York Clipper*, May 25, 1867, 50. See also *Bendigo (Australia) Advertiser*, October 5, 1859, 5; October 12, 1859, 1.

45. *New York Clipper*, May 25, 1867, 50; cf. *Times of India* (Mumbai), March 12, 1863, 3.

46. *Bengal Hurkaru* (Kolkata), December 21, 1864, 1; *Times of India* (Mumbai), May 19, 1865, 3.

47. For a fuller discussion of Carson's brownface repertoire, see Kellen Hoxworth, "Racial Impressions, Capital Characters: Dave Carson Brownfaces the Empire," in *Mimetic Desires: Impersonation and Guising across South Asia*, ed. Harshita Mruthinti Kamath and Pamela Lothspeich (Honolulu: University of Hawai'i Press, 2022), 42–64.

48. Sir D. E. Wacha, *Shells from the Sands of Bombay: Being My Recollections and Reminiscences: 1860–1875* (Mumbai: Bombay Chronicle Press, 1920), 351.

49. *Times of India* (Mumbai), March 2, 1863, 1.

50. *Bengal Hurkaru* (Kolkata), March 10, 1864, 1; December 27, 1864, 1; January 17, 1865, 1; February 1, 1866, 1.

51. *Supplement to the Bengal Hurkaru* (Kolkata), February 12, 1866, 2.

52. *Times of India* (Mumbai), May 3, 1865, 2; May 4, 1865, 3; May 8, 1865, 3; May 15, 1865, 2; May 17, 1865, 2; May 18, 1865, 2; May 19, 1865, 3. Carson also performed as this character in his topical song on Mumbai land-reclamation schemes, "Tight Little Island" (*Bengal Hurkaru* [Kolkata], July 4, 1865, 1; *Indian Daily News* [Kolkata], July 6, 1865, 2).

53. For a fuller discussion of public debates surrounding the Parsi presence in Mumbai's theaters and the formation of minstrelized Parsi caricatures, see Hoxworth, "Racial Impressions, Capital Characters," 53–56.

54. *Times of India* (Mumbai), May 3, 1865, 2; May 4, 1865, 3; May 8, 1865, 3; May 15, 1865, 2; May 17, 1865, 2; May 18, 1865, 2; May 19, 1865, 3. See also Nicholson, *Colonial Public*, 75–76.

55. *Times of India* (Mumbai), June 6, 1865, 3.

56. *Indian Daily News* (Kolkata), July 6, 1865, 2. Carson also referred to his "Bengalee Baboo" caricature as "Baboo Dave Kar Sen" (*Indian Daily News* [Kolkata], August 8, 1868, 2; February 23, 1875, 1).

57. Mr. Dangle, "The Calcutta Stage," in *The Theatre: A Monthly Review of The Drama, Music, and the Fine Arts*, vol. 4, *July to December, 1881*, ed. Clement Scott (London: Charles Dickens & Evans, 1881), 91.

58. *Australasian* (Melbourne), May 25, 1872, 19.

59. See, for instance, the *North-China Herald* (Shanghai), October 7, 1875, 355, and April 4, 1878, 345, as well as the *Japan Weekly* (Yokohama), May 18, 1878, 456, all of which advertise his performances of the "Bengalee Baboo."

60. C. Wodehouse, "The Keatinge Rajk'umar College, Kathia' wa'r," *Calcutta Review* 60 (1875): 59–68, quote on 59. Wodehouse does not specify the racial identity of his "ordinary Bombay man," though it is likeliest that he was referring to white British subjects.

61. Captain W. H. Angel, *The Clipper Ship "Sheila," Angel—Master* (Boston: Charles E. Lauriat, 1923), 202. A second extant version is reproduced in Thomas W. R. McMahon, *My Reminiscences of a Picnic-Party at Penang, in the Year 1869* (Kolkata: P. S. D'Rozario, 1871), 49–51, which also traces the wide circulation of Carson's act. My thanks to Rudrani Sarma for alerting me to this second version. For versions of select verses, see Wacha, *Shells from the Sands*, 352; Lt.-Col. J. H. Leslie, "Dave Carson," *Notes & Queries* 181, no. 8 (1941): 105. The chorus of "The Bengalee Baboo" was also included in W. A. Fraser's short story "The Ace of Hearts," which was published in London's *Pall Mall* magazine and *Canadian Magazine* (W. A. Fraser, "The Ace of Hearts," *Pall Mall* 9, no. 40 [August 1896]: 592–97; W. A. Fraser, "The Ace of Hearts," *Canadian Magazine* 24, no. 1 [November 1904]: 147–51).

62. Angel, *Clipper Ship "Sheila,"* 129. The parenthetical translations are original to Angel's text and likely derive from Carson's published song sheet for "The Bengalee Baboo." The printed version in Angel's text makes a single reference to "coolies," who are identified as palkee bearers who carry the Baboo home after he becomes inebriated.

63. Angel, *Clipper Ship "Sheila,"* 129–32.

64. Sumanta Banerjee, *The Parlour and the Streets: Elite and Popular Culture in Nineteenth-Century Calcutta* (Kolkata: Seagull Books, 1998), 109, 180–82, 231n64; Rimli Bhattacharya, "Promiscuous Spaces and Economies of Entertainment: Soldiers, Actresses and Hybrid Genres in Colonial India," *Nineteenth Century Theatre and Film* 41, no.2 (2014): 50–75, at 67.

65. Sir Henry Yule and A. C. Burnell, *Hobson-Jobson: A Glossary of Anglo-Indian Colloquial Words and Phrases and of Kindred Terms*, ed. William Crooke (1886; London: John Murray, 1903), 44.

66. Mrinalini Sinha, *Colonial Masculinity: The "Manly Englishman" and the "Effeminate Bengali" in the Late Nineteenth Century* (Manchester, UK: Manchester University Press: 1995), 17.

67. Homi K. Bhabha, *The Location of Culture* (1994; New York: Routledge, 2004), 145.

68. Bhabha, *Location of Culture*, 121–31. See also Macaulay's "Minute on Indian Education," which figures centrally in Homi K. Bhabha's theorization of "colonial mimicry" (Thomas Babington Macaulay, "Indian

Education: Minute of the 2nd of February, 1835," in *Macaulay: Prose and Poetry*, ed. G. M. Young [Cambridge, MA: Harvard University Press, 1952], 719–30).

69. Playbill reprinted in the *New York Clipper*, November 25, 1871, 268; *Times of India* (Mumbai), December 4, 1871, 1; Sushil Kumar Mukerjee, *The Story of the Calcutta Theatres, 1753–1980* (Kolkata: K. P. Bagchi, 1982), 36. See also Prabhucharan Guha-Thakurta, *The Bengali Drama: Its Origins and Development* (London: Kegan Paul, Trench, Trubner, 1930), 105; Brajendra Nath Banerjee, *Bengali Stage, 1795–1873* (Kolkata: Ranjan Publishing House, 1943), 49–50; Hemendra Nath Das Gupta, *The Indian Stage*, rev. ed. (Kolkata: Metropolitan Print & Publishing House), 2:202–4; Bhattacharya, "Promiscuous Spaces," 67–68.

70. Girish Chandra Ghosh, "The Jewel of the Theatre: The Late Ardhendu Shekhar Mustafi (the Actor's Biography and Work in the Theatre)," in *Girish Rachanabali* (Kolkata: Sahitya Sansad, 1991), 5:340–56, quote on 343; my thanks to Taarini Mookherjee for the translation of this article from the Bengali. Cf. Guha-Thakurta, *Bengali Drama*, 105.

71. Ghosh, "Jewel of the Theatre," 343; translated by Taarini Mookherjee.

72. See Sinha, *Colonial Masculinity*; Parama Roy, *Indian Traffic: Identities in Question in Colonial and Postcolonial India* (Berkeley: University of California Press, 1998); Sikata Banerjee, *Make Me a Man! Masculinity, Hinduism, and Nationalism in India* (Albany: State University of New York Press, 2005).

73. Shib Chunder Bose, *The Hindoos As They Are: A Description of the Manners, Customs and Inner Life of Hindoo Society in Bengal* (London: Edward Stanford; Kolkata: W. Newman, 1881), 191.

74. Bose, *Hindoos*, 191.

75. Bose, *Hindoos*, 192.

76. Amrita Lal Bose, *English Translation of "The Babu,"* trans. Nibaran Chandra Chatterjee (Kolkata: Sanyal, 1911), vii. After its premiere on January 1, 1894, Bose's *Babu* received several repeat performances (*Indian Daily News* [Kolkata], January 1, 1894, 2; February 24, 1894, 2; October 2, 1895, 2).

77. J. Arthur, "News from India," *New York Clipper*, April 10, 1880, 3. As early as the 1863 tour of the San Francisco Minstrels to Mumbai, a critic for the *Times of India* advocated for offering half-price tickets to give "the poorer classes of English[-]taught natives an opportunity of seeing and hearing that vein of broad English humour which, although perhaps read of, has been seen by few or none" (*Times of India* [Mumbai], April 16, 1863, 3). Even this critic's advocacy, it should be noted, delimits attendance to an audience with a classed English-language education.

78. Muñoz, *Disidentifications*, 164.

79. *Times of India* (Mumbai), January 11, 1872, 3.

80. Joseph Charles Parkinson, *The Ocean Telegraph to India: A Narrative and a Diary* (Edinburgh, UK: Blackwood and Sons, 1870), 58.

81. *Times of India* (Mumbai), June 3, 1865, 3.

82. Nicholson, *Colonial Public*, 85n118; Nicholson, "'A Christy Minstrel, a Harlequin, or an Ancient Persian'?" 341; cf. *Bombay Gazette*, November 7, 1870, 3.

83. *Indian Daily News* (Kolkata), May 6, 1875, 1.

84. *Indian Mirror* (Kolkata), February 6, 1871 (reprinted in *Era* [London], April 30, 1871, 11).

85. *Bengal Hurkaru* (Kolkata), May 9, 1864, 1; *Indian Daily News* (Kolkata), December 27, 1864, 2; *Times of India* (Mumbai), April 10, 1865, 1, and April 30, 1874, 1; *Madras Mail* (Chennai), August 24, 1877, 4. Evidently, Carson took over the role of Zuleika from fellow company member J. O. Pierce: a Kolkata performance in December 1864 featured "Mr. Pearce figured as Zuleika, the Pearl of Dum Dum" (*Indian Daily News* [Kolkata], December 17, 1864, 3), whereas Carson was praised for his "'get up' and acting as 'Zuleika'" in Mumbai in April 1865 (*Times of India* [Mumbai], April 11, 1865, 3).

86. *Englishman* (Kolkata), December 19, 1864; quoted in Poonam Trivedi, "Performing the Nation: Dave Carson and the Bengali Babu," in *The Nation across the World: Postcolonial Literary Representations*, ed. Harish Trivedi, Meenakshi Mukherjee, C. Vijayasree, T. Vijay Kumar (Oxford: Oxford University Press, 2007), 246–69, at 259.

87. *Pioneer* (Prayagraj, India), June 14, 1865, 3; cf. Bhattacharya, "Promiscuous Spaces," 68.

88. Playbill, September 19, 1871, Secundrabad, India, reprinted in *New York Clipper*, November 25, 1871, 268; *Indian Daily News* (Kolkata), February 6, 1871, 1.

89. *Indian Daily News* (Kolkata), January 2, 1868, 2.

90. Major H. Hobbs, *John Barleycorn Bahadur: Old-Time Taverns in India* (Kolkata: Thacker, Spink, 1944), 284.

91. Wacha, *Shells from the Sands*, 351.

92. Cockrell, *Demons of Disorder*, 56; Lhamon, *Jump Jim Crow*, 42–46; DuComb, *Haunted City*, 76–79.

93. Paskman and Spaeth, *Gentlemen, Be Seated!*, 91.

94. Lott, *Love and Theft*, 160.

95. *Sam Sly's African Journal* (Cape Town), September 10, 1846, 2.

96. "The Celebrated Song: Miss Lucy Long" (New York: James L. Hewitt, 1842); reprinted in Damon, *Series of Old American Songs*, no. 31.

97. DuComb, *Haunted City*, 123; cf. Olive Logan, "The Ancestry of Brudder Bones," *Harper's New Monthly Magazine* 58, no. 347 (1879): 687–98, at 698. See also Meer, *Uncle Tom Mania*, 37.

98. Undated clipping, container 4, file 23, Minstrel Show Collection, Harry Ransom Center, University of Texas at Austin. Cf. "Death of George Primrose," *Two Step* 29, no. 11 (November 1919): 19.

99. "Belle of Broadway, Sung by Dan Bryant, at 472 Broadway, N. Y." (Chatham, NY: H. De Marson, n.d.), https://levysheetmusic.mse.jhu.edu/sites/default/files/collection-pdfs/levy-193–020.pdf.

100. On "Tom Shows," see Meer, *Uncle Tom Mania*, 105–93, and Bernstein, *Racial Innocence*, 49, 113, and passim.

101. *Argus* (Melbourne), December 17, 1855, 8.

102. On "Topsy" as an early blackface female speaking and singing role, see Meer, *Uncle Tom Mania*, 37.

103. On the "Old Auntie," see Toll, *Blacking Up*, 79. On the interchangeability of the "Aunty" and "Mammy" roles, see Bernstein, *Racial Innocence*, 176.

104. Stephen Johnson, "Gender Trumps Race? Cross-Dressing Juba in Early Blackface Minstrelsy," in *When Men Dance: Choreographing Masculinities across Borders*, ed. Jennifer Fisher and Anthony Shay (Oxford: Oxford University Press, 2009), 220–47, at 225. I omit "Aunt Jemima" from this list because this figure was initially a white character who later surrogated the blackface "aunt" figures of the mid-nineteenth century, particularly through Black minstrel performer Billy Kersands's performance of the song "Old Aunt Jemima" beginning in 1875. See Samuel S. Sanford, *Aunt Jemima's Plaster* (Philadelphia: Lee & Walker, 1855); Toll, *Blacking Up*, 259; M. M. Manring, *Slave in a Box: The Strange Career of Aunt Jemima* (Charlottesville: University of Virginia Press, 1998), 61.

105. On "The Only Leon," see Toll, *Blacking Up*, 142–44; Lott, *Love and Theft*, 164–65.

106. Beyond such blackface ballet burlesque, Leon made a career in the female impersonator specialty role, often performing his drag roles without racialized makeup and thereby, in the words of Eric Lott, "taking drag seriously" by whitewashing minstrelsy's spectacles of interracial desire (*Love and Theft*, 164). Nevertheless, Leon continually staged blackface and yellowface female roles, the latter most evident in his yellowface "Fe-An-Nich-Ton" in an 1870 production of Jacques Offenbach's opéra bouffe *Ching Chou Hi* (undated clipping, container 12, file 33, Minstrel Show Collection, Harry Ransom Center, University of Texas at Austin).

107. *Empire* (Sydney), March 20, 1863, 1.

108. *Freeman's Journal* (Sydney), March 21, 1863, 3.

109. *Age* (Melbourne), February 26, 1863, 5. Minstrel burlesques of opera's "prima donna" offer a forgotten genealogy of the minstrel "prima donna," which Annemarie Bean notes was a "highly stylized" feature of the "'afterpiece' of the minstrel show" ("Transgressing the Gender Divide: The Female Impersonator in Nineteenth-Century Blackface Minstrelsy," in *Inside the Minstrel Mask: Readings in Nineteenth-Century Blackface Minstrelsy* [Middletown, CT: Wesleyan University Press, 1996], 245–56, quote on 249).

110. *Cape Argus* (Cape Town), April 22, 1869; quoted in Thelwell, *Exporting Jim Crow*, 42.

111. Brooks, *Bodies in Dissent*, 312–13; Kristin Moriah, "'A Greater Compass of Voice': Elizabeth Taylor Greenfield and Mary Ann Shadd Cary Navigate Black Performance," *Theatre Research in Canada / Recherches théâtrales au Canada* 41, no.1 (2020): 20–38.

112. Here, I extend Gayle Rubin's foundational theorization of the "sex/gender system" to attend to the racial economies undergirding minstrelsy; see Gayle Rubin, "The Traffic in Women: Notes on the 'Political Economy' of Sex," in *The Second Wave: A Reader in Feminist Theory*, ed. Linda Nicholson (London: Routledge, 1997), 27–62, at 28.

113. Charles Soran and John H. Hewitt, *Aunt Harriet Becha Stowe* (Baltimore: Henry McCaffrey, 1853), 4.

114. Soran and Hewitt, *Aunt Harriet*, 4.

115. "Pompey's Trip to New York," in Edwin P. Christy, *Christy's Plantation Melodies, No. 3. The Only Authorized Edition of Genuine Christy's*

Songs, as Sung at Christy's Opera House, New York (Philadelphia: Fisher & Brother, 1853), 19.

116. Meer, *Uncle Tom Mania*, 185–93.

117. Mahar, *Behind the Burnt Cork Mask*, 59, 268–328.

118. *Empire* (Sydney), November 23, 1855, 1.

119. *Empire* (Sydney), July 17, 1857, 1; *Moreton Bay Courier* (Brisbane), August 8, 1857, 2; *South Australian Register* (Adelaide), May 21, 1860, 3.

120. *Bengal Hurkaru* (Kolkata), August 18, 1865, 1; *Indian Daily News* (Kolkata), August 18, 1865, 3; August 7, 1869, 1; *Times of India* (Mumbai), November 21, 1877, 1.

121. Kate Horn, "*Womans Rights": A Right Good Ballad "Rightly Written" for the "Womans Rights Conventions"* (Boston: Geo. P. Reed, 1853), 3–4, https://levysheetmusic.mse.jhu.edu/collection/051/115.

122. Meer, *Uncle Tom Mania*, 67, 169–71. See also Roediger, *Wages of Whiteness*, esp. 65–92.

123. *Natal Mercury* (eThekwini, South Africa), November 2, 1865, 2; cf. Thelwell, *Exporting Jim Crow*, 48. Jones, *Captive Stage*, 124–35.

124. Eliza Lynn Linton, "The Girl of the Period," *Saturday Review*, March 14, 1868, 339–40, reprinted in Eliza Lynn Linton, *The Girl of the Period and Other Social Essays* (London: Richard Bentley & Son, 1883), 1:1–9; Herbert van Thal, *Eliza Lynn Linton: The Girl of the Period* (London: George Allen & Unwin, 1979), 1.

125. Linton, *Girl of the Period*, 1–3.

126. On the antitheatricality of Linton's essay, see Michelle Liu Carriger, "'Typical Modern Amazon': Freaks of Fashion, Newspaper Nightmares, and the Girl of the Period," in *Theatricality of the Closet: Fashion, Performance, and Subjectivity between Victorian Britain and Meiji Japan* (Evanston, IL: Northwestern University Press, 2023), 39-76. My thanks to Michelle for sharing this chapter ahead of print.

127. Linton, *Girl of the Period*, 9.

128. Gayle Rubin, "Thinking Sex: Notes for a Radical Theory of the Politics of Sexuality," in *Pleasure and Danger: Exploring Female Sexuality*, ed. Carole S. Vance (London: Routledge & Kegan Paul, 1984), 267–319, at 301.

129. Linton, *Girl of the Period*, 4.

130. Eliza Lynn Linton, "Pinchbeck," in *The Girl of the Period and Other Social Essays*, 1:73.

131. *The Girl of the Period Miscellany*, no. 1–9 (1869).

132. *Indian Daily News* (Kolkata), October 2, 1868, 2. Carson incorporated the song into his repertoire; see *Pioneer* (Prayagraj, India), October 12, 1868, 9; *Indian Daily News* (Kolkata), September 14, 1869, 1; September 27, 1869, 1; *Madras Mail* (Chennai), June 5, 1869, 1–2; April 24, 1871, 1; *Times of India* (Mumbai), November 30, 1869, 1; December 4, 1871, 1; January 1, 1872, 1; January 11, 1884, 4. For an example of a minstrel version of the "girl of the period," see "The Young Girl of the Period," in *"Shoo, Fly, Don't Bodder Me" Songster, Containing the Gems of Popular Melodies* (New York: Fisher and Denison, 1871), 90–91; container 49, file 38, Minstrel Show Collection, Harry Ransom Center, University of Texas at Austin.

133. Marjorie Garber, *Vested Interests: Cross-Dressing and Cultural Anxiety* (London: Routledge, 1992), 277.

134. *Indian Daily News* (Kolkata), September 9, 1871, 3.

135. Jane R. Goodall, *Performance and Evolution in the Age of Darwin: Out of the Natural Order* (London: Routledge, 2002), 125.

136. Goodall, *Performance and Evolution*, 126; Grace Egerton, *Book of Words: Miss Grace Egerton's (Mrs. G. Case,) New Characteristic and Musical Entertainment* (Pontefract, UK: W. E. Hownas, ca. 1861), 4–5, John Johnson Collection, Bodleian Library, University of Oxford.

137. Tracy C. Davis, *Actresses as Working Women: Their Social Identity in Victorian Culture* (London: Routledge, 1991), 1.

138. William Shew, *Grace Egerton, (Mrs. George Case*) (n.d.), WA photos 357, Beinecke Rare Book and Manuscript Library, Yale University Library, https://collections.library.yale.edu/catalog/2015045, accessed March 22, 2023.

139. Helen Callaway, *Gender, Culture and Empire: European Women in Colonial Nigeria* (Urbana: University of Illinois Press, 1987), 42.

140. *Chicago Tribune*, January 1, 1870, 4.

141. *Times of India* (Mumbai), December 16, 1873, 1; December 18, 1873, 2. Mehta, "English Drama on the Bombay Stage," 180; Kumud A. Mehta, "Bombay's Theatre World: 1860–1880," *Journal of the Asiatic Society of Bombay* 43/44 (1968–1969): 251–78, at 262–63.

142. *Times of India* (Mumbai), December 18, 1873, 2.

143. Quoted in Mehta, "English Drama on the Bombay Stage," 180n3; Mehta, "Bombay's Theatre World," 263n75.

144. Kathryn Hansen, "Making Women Visible: Gender and Race Cross-Dressing in the Parsi Theatre," *Theatre Journal* 51, no. 2 (1999): 127–47, quote on 127.

145. Brown, *Babylon Girls*, 57, 98–100.

146. *Times of India* (Mumbai), December 18, 1873, 2.

147. *Pioneer* (Prayagraj, India), January 10, 1874, 7.

148. *Daily Southern Cross* (Auckland, Aoetearoa New Zealand), May 10, 1875, 3.

149. Playbill, Mr. and Mrs. George Case, "Odds and Ends," undated, MSB 940.4(3), in Assorted Playbills Collection, National Library of South Africa. A handwritten note reading "Kimberley" suggests it was from a performance on South Africa's diamond range. This playbill was printed in the offices of the *Northern Argus* in Rockhampton, Australia, indicating that Egerton and Case traveled with preset evening-length shows. Egerton advertised her performance of "Ratae Madam Is My Name" in eThekwini in December 1877 (*Natal Mercury* [eThekwini, South Africa], December 29, 1877, 2).

150. *Times of India* (Mumbai), March 19, 1880, 1; April 7, 1880, 1; May 7, 1881, 1. Minnie Williams also performed "The Parsee Belle" in Carson's minstrel show in Chowringhee in October 1877 (*Indian Daily News* [Kolkata], October 9, 1877, 1).

151. Wacha, *Shells from the Sands*, 351. Child performer "Little Etta" also performed "Ratae Madame, the Parsee Girl of the Period" in Carson's minstrel show in Mumbai in June 1877 (*Times of India* [Mumbai], June 14, 1877, 1).

152. Inderpal Grewal, *Home and Harem: Nation, Gender, Empire, and the Cultures of Travel* (Durham, NC: Duke University Press, 1996), 25.

153. See Gayatri Chakravorty Spivak, "Can the Subaltern Speak?" in *Colonial Discourse and Post-Colonial Theory: A Reader*, ed. Patrick Williams and Laura Chrisman (New York: Columbia University Press, 1996), 66–111, at 93.

154. Hansen, "Making Women Visible," 140.

155. See Kukum Sangari and Sudesh Vaid, "Recasting Women: An Introduction," in *Recasting Women: Essays in Indian Colonial History*, ed. Kumkum Sangari and Sudesh Vaid (New Brunswick, NJ: Rutgers University Press, 1990), 1–26, esp. 9–10. See also Lata Mani, *Contentious Traditions: The Debate on Sati in Colonial India* (Berkeley: University of California Press, 1998).

156. *Times of India* (Mumbai), December 18, 1873, 2.

157. See Nicholson, *Colonial Public*, 223.

158. Hansen, "Making Women Visible," 140–41; Nandi Bhatia, *Performing Women / Performing Womanhood: Theatre, Politics, and Dissent in North India* (Oxford: Oxford University Press, 2010), xi-xiv, 8. See also Gupt's recounting of the controversies surrounding the performance of Anglo-Indian performer Mary Fenton in the Parsi theater (*Parsi Theatre*, 125–29; cf. Hansen, "Making Women Visible," 143–47).

159. Grewal, *Home and Haven*, 54.

160. Reprinted in *Englishwoman's Review of Social and Industrial Questions* 9 (October 1868): 73.

161. "Coming Out in the East," *Punch, or the London Chiavari* 68 (1875): 79.

162. *Times of India* (Mumbai), April 19, 1884, 4. See also Nicholson, *Colonial Public*, 242–48.

163. *Times of India* (Mumbai), April 19, 1884, 5. See also N. S. Ginwalla, *The Parsee Girl of the Period (Re-Produced from the Times of India, 19th April 1884* (Mumbai: Bombay Jam-E-Jamsheed, 1884), 1.

164. See *Times of India* (Mumbai), April 21–May 3, 1884.

165. Doseebai C. Jussawalla, "The Parsee Girl of the Period," *Times of India* (Mumbai), April 22, 1884, 4.

166. *Sydney Morning Herald*, September 22, 1875, 10; September 27, 1875, 8. She remained in Australia for a year ("Favourite Entertainers. No. 3. Miss Marguerite Fish," in *The Playgoer* [London], ed. Fred Dangerfield [March 1902], 1:354).

167. Nan Mullenneaux, "Our Genius, Goodness, and Gumption: Child Actresses and National Identity in Mid-Nineteenth-Century America," *Journal of the History of Childhood and Youth* 5, no. 2 (2012): 283–308; Shauna Vey, *Childhood and Nineteenth-Century American Theatre: The Work of the Marsh Troupe of Juvenile Actors* (Carbondale: Southern Illinois University Press, 2015).

168. Bernstein, *Racial Innocence*, 30–68.

169. Bernstein, *Racial Innocence*, 112–33.

170. Mullenneaux, "Our Genius," 295–96; cf. David Dempsey with Raymond P. Baldwin, *The Triumphs and Trials of Lotta Crabtree* (New York: William Morrow, 1968).

171. J. H. Taylor, *Joe Taylor, Barnstormer: His Travels, Troubles and Triumphs During Fifty Years in Footlight Flashes* (New York: William R. Jenkins, 1913), 67; Dempsey and Baldwin, *Triumphs and Trials*, 188.

172. Mulleneaux, "Our Genius," 294.

173. Thelwell, *Exporting Jim Crow*, 89–90; cf. *Cape Argus* (Cape Town), May 8, 1877, 1; March 23, 1878, 1; *Diamond News* (Kimberley, South Africa), November 29, 1877, 2; *Natal Mercury* (eThekwini, South Africa), February 13, 1878, 1.

174. Bernstein, *Racial Innocence*, 41.

175. *Standard & Mail* (Cape Town), April 17, 1877, 1; *Natal Mercury* (eThekwini, South Africa), February 11, 1878, 2.

176. *Era* (London), September 22, 1878.

177. Stoler, *Carnal Knowledge*, 84.

178. *Era* (London), March 14, 1896.

179. "Favourite Entertainers. No. 3. Miss Marguerite Fish," 356–57. Future quotations from the same.

Epilogue

1. *Amrita Bazar Patrika* (Kolkata), March 31, 1904, 4. Future quotations from the same.

2. I discuss other aspects of *The Cingalee* and its relationship to the repertoires of transoceanic blackface and to Dave Carson specifically in Hoxworth, "Racial Impressions, Capital Characters," and Kellen Hoxworth, "Intertheatrical Things," in *Theatre Things: Material Theories and Histories*, ed. Andrew Friedman and Eero Laine (Ann Arbor: University of Michigan Press, forthcoming).

3. Brooks, *Bodies in Dissent*, 79.

4. Pierre, *Predicament of Blackness*, 2.

5. Roach, *Cities of the Dead*, 2.

6. Thelwell, *Exporting Jim Crow*, 183–212.

7. Thelwell, *Exporting Jim Crow*, 200–201.

8. On *The Kentucky Minstrels*, see Michael Pickering, "The BBC's Kentucky Minstrels, 1933–1950: Blackface Entertainment on British Radio," *Historical Journal of Film, Radio & Television* 16, no. 2 (1996): 161–96; Michael Pickering, "Race, Gender and Broadcast Comedy: The Case of the BBC's *Kentucky Minstrels*," *European Journal of Communication* 9 (1994): 311–33. On *Amos 'n' Andy*, see Melvin Patrick Ely, *The Adventures of Amos 'n' Andy: A Social History of an American Phenomenon* (New York: Free Press, 1991); Michele Hilmes, "Invisible Men: *Amos 'n' Andy* and the Roots of Broadcast Discourse," *Critical Studies in Mass Communication* 10, no. 4 (1993): 301–21.

9. Sarita Malik, *Representing Black Britain: Black and Asian Images on Television* (London: SAGE, 2002), 112–13; Christine Grandy, "'The Show Is Not about Race': Custom, Screen Culture, and the *Black and White Minstrel Show*," *Journal of British Studies* 59 (2020): 857–84; David Hendy, "The Black and White Minstrel Show," https://www.bbc.com/historyofthebbc/100-voices/people-nation-empire/make-yourself-at-home/the-black-and-white-minstrel-show, accessed March 22, 2023.

10. *Australian Women's Weekly* (Sydney), November 3, 1982, 144.

11. Stephen Vagg, "Counterfeit Images: A History of Blackface on Australian Television," *Metro Magazine: Media & Education Magazine* 206 (2020): 92–99, at 94.

12. *Australian Women's Weekly* (Sydney), September 19, 1962, 2; *Canberra (Australia) Times*, May 22, 1963, 16; *Australian Jewish Herald* (Melbourne), October 23, 1964, 4; *Canberra (Australia) Times*, June 22, 1984, 13; *Canberra (Australia) Times*, September 28, 1987, 13.

13. *Australian Jewish News* (Melbourne), March 21, 1980, 25.

14. Percy Tucker, *Just the Ticket! My 50 Years in Show Business* (Johannesburg: Jonathan Ball, 1997), 219–20, 270, 301; Programme, 1970, *African Consolidated Theatres Present Brickhill-Burke's Non-Stop Minstrel Scandals*, Killie Campbell Africana Library, eThekwini, South Africa. On African Consolidated Theatres and its founder, Isadore W. Schlesinger, as a key vector of the transnationalization of South African film and performance culture, see James T. Campbell, "The Americanization of South Africa," in *Race, Nation, & Empire in American History*, ed. James T. Campbell, Matthew Pratt Guterl, and Robert G. Lee (Chapel Hill: University of North Carolina Press, 2007), 130–53, at 140–42.

15. Matthew D. Morrison, "Iggy (Azalea) Pop: Is Cultural Appropriation Inappropriate," *Oxford University Press Blog* (blog), February 26, 2015, https://blog.oup.com/2015/02/iggy-azalea-music-cultural-appropriation.

16. Fletcher, *Story of South African Theatre*, 133.

17. Stephen Gray, "The First Night of Stephen Black's *Love and the Hyphen*," *Quarterly Bulletin of the South African Library* 35, no. 1 (1980): 26–40, quotes on 30, 38.

18. Stephen Gray, "The Comic Theatre of Stephen Black in South Africa," *Kunapipi* 4, no. 1 (1982): 62–74, at 63.

19. Loren Kruger, *A Century of South African Theatre* (London: Methuen Drama, 2020), 39.

20. Manfred Nathan, *South African Literature* (Cape Town: Juta, 1925), 198.

21. Gray, "First Night," 33.

22. *Cape Argus* (Cape Town), September 9, 1908, quoted in Fletcher, *Story of South African Theatre*, 133; cf. Gray, "First Night," 33.

23. Quoted in Stephen Gray, introduction to Stephen Black, *Three Plays*, ed. Stephen Gray (Craighall, South Africa: Donker, 1984), 27. Gray's edited version of the script omits this specific quotation and instead simply states, "*Burlesque of 'The Village Blacksmith' or similar piece*" (Black, *Three Plays*, 80).

24. *Port Elizabeth Telegraph* (Gqeberha, South Africa), October 8, 1862, 3. This blackface version of the song was also a standard of the 1868 South African tour of the Christy's Minstrels troupe featuring Harry Raynor, Charles Steele, and Washington Norton (*Cape Argus* [Cape Town], September 5, 1868, 1).

25. Gray, *Three Plays*, 40n38. For more on Chirgwin, see Pickering, *Blackface Minstrelsy in Britain*, 98–99.

26. In addition to the burlesque of "The Village Blacksmith," Sophie also recites a catalog of minstrelized Shakespeare titles: "*Richard der Tird*, en

I Don't Care if You Like it or Not, Er Dem Lot of How You Do erboat Nutting, and *er Merchant of Wieners*" (Black, *Three Plays*, 256n12).

27. Black again drew from the repertoires of transoceanic blackface in his second play, *Helena's Hope Ltd.* (1910), in which he personally originated the role of the Xhosa character Jeremiah Luke Mbene in blackface. Mbene furnished forth a novel, nationalistic, Xhosa-inflected line of blackface caricature that remained in circulation in South African theaters throughout the early twentieth century and beyond. See Robin K. Crigler, "No Laughing Matter? Humour and the Performance of South Africa," *South African Theatre Journal* 32, no. 2–3 (2018): 155–71, at 158–60.

28. Nicholson, *Colonial Public*, 206, 2.

29. His given name was listed as "David Nunez Cardoza" in his obituary (*Englishman* [Kolkata], February 27, 1896, 6). However, it was spelled "David Nunis Cardozo" in a biographical essay twenty years prior (*Indian Daily News* [Kolkata], October 12, 1877, 3). As a listing of his burial plot names him as "David Nunez Cardoza (*alias* Dave Carson)," I give authority to the spelling in the obituary ("Funeral Plots in Lower Circular Road Cemetery, Calcutta," *Bengal: Past & Present [Journal of the Calcutta Historical Society]* [January–June 1910]: 5:314). Though Cardoza was his given name, I refer to him as "Dave Carson" throughout for clarity and in keeping with his prevailing identification in archival records of his performance career.

30. *Bell's Life in Sydney and Sporting Reviewer*, August 30, 1856, 3.

31. Rice, *Monarchs of Minstrelsy*, 39, 58, 87, 123, 148. Noel Ignatiev, *How the Irish Became White* (1995; repr. London: Routledge, 2009), 49–50.

32. On Jolson's assimilation into whiteness through minstrelsy, see Rogin, *Blackface, White Noise*, 5 and passim.

33. I take "working toward whiteness" from David R. Roediger, *Working Toward Whiteness: How America's Immigrants Became White: The Strange Journey from Ellis Island to the Suburbs* (New York: Basic Books, 2005). Elsewhere, Roediger recounts the assimilation of European immigrants, particularly white ethnics, into the racial formations of the United States through minstrel performance (Roediger, *Wages of Whiteness*, 115–31; see also Rogin, *Blackface, White Noise*).

34. "A Kafir Account of Capetown (Communicated.)," *King William's Town and Kaffrarian Banner* (Qonce, South Africa), September 10, 1863, 3. Future quotations from the same.

35. Christopher Charles [C. C.] Saunders, "Eliza's Cape Town, 1863," *Quarterly Bulletin of the South African Library* 35, no. 2 (1980): 50–58, at 50.

36. *South African Advertiser and Mail* (Cape Town), May 20, 1863; reprinted in "The Royal Wedding of 1963—Cape Town Celebrates," *Quarterly Bulletin of the South African Library* 36, no. 1 (1981): 16–34, at 33. See also *Cape Argus* (Cape Town), May 14, 1863; May 16, 1863; May 21, 1863.

37. On "Jack-in-the Green and Attendants," see *Cape Argus* (Cape Town), May 14, 1863.

38. Cole, "American Ghetto Parties and Ghanaian Concert Parties," 237.

39. Pierre, *Predicament of Blackness*, 3.

40. Magubane, *Bringing the Empire Home*, 154.

41. Robinson, *Black Marxism*, xxxii.

INDEX

Page locators in italics indicate illustrations.